SILK & IRON

ALEXIS CALDER

For my daughter.
Never forget how powerful you are.

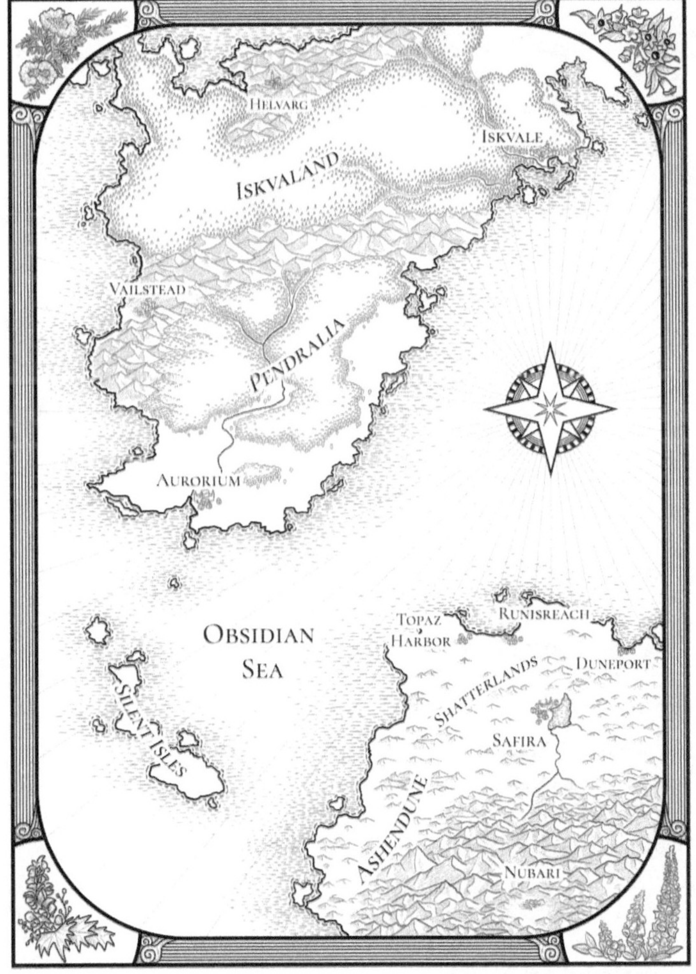

THE PENDRALIAN EMPIRE
HELVARG
ISKVALE
ISKVALAND
VAILSTEAD
PENDRALIA
AURORIUM
OBSIDIAN
SEA
SILENT ISLES
TOPAZ HARBOR
RUNISREACH
DUNEPORT
SHATTERLANDS
SAFIRA
ASHENDUNE
NUBARI

Copyright © 2026 by Alexis Calder

All rights reserved.

No part of this book may be reproduced in any form or by any electronic or mechanical means, including information storage and retrieval systems, without written permission from the author, except for the use of brief quotations in a book review.

Cover Art by Fay Lane
Map by The Illustrated Page Book Design
Editing by Britney Waldrop Edits
Editing by Fae Writer
Proofreading by Arianne from Virtually Ayre

PROLOGUE

BREVAN

SMOKE FILLS THE TWILIGHT SKY, turning the setting sun a violent orange. Screams, sharp and terrified bite into the air, then vanish, overcome by thundering hooves and the yells of the night legion. It's not a fight, it's slaughter. As it has been at every town we visit.

It's colder here as we near the border of Iskvaland. I never thought I'd long for the gloom of Aurorium, but being away from home has a way of making you long for things you took for granted.

My horse's hooves click across the cobblestone street. I move slowly, giving my men time to eliminate any threats. Not that there are any. These people never had a chance.

Women and children are dragged from their homes, forced to their knees in front of the burning buildings. Their tears don't reach my soul anymore. Not that I have anything left of my soul after so many years of service to

Pendralia. Anything I might have once felt was smothered and destroyed. The emperor himself saw to that.

I stop in front of the humble building at the edge of town. It's an old structure made of stones that aren't mined on this continent. Which means, they were imported from somewhere across the Obsidian Sea.

I dismount and nod to the three legionnaires on my right. They draw their swords then charge, slamming into the door until the wood cracks and splinters. They rush inside, each one eager to be the man who retrieves something of value.

I remove my helmet and hand it to one of the men on my left. They'll find what we're looking for. I'm certain it's here. I can feel it. An energy that hums like raw power. While they can't sense it, they usually have no problem finding the secret doors or locked boxes housing the relics.

By the time I approach the building and wait just beyond the steps, I hear the screams of whoever was hiding inside. I wait.

It's not long before the legionnaires exit the home, dragging an old man between them. They toss him to the ground at my feet. He looks up at me, defiance in his eyes.

I stare down at him. He's just like all the others. So much hatred and anger in his expression. It doesn't change anything.

Legionnaires surround him, prepared in case he tries to run. Or worse.

"By order of the emperor, you have been found guilty of using and distributing the magic of the gods. If you renounce your heretic ways and comply, he may have mercy on you." I'm tired of repeating the same phrase, but it's good for the other citizens to hear me. It's a warning.

The man mumbles through gritted teeth and his long white hair rises around his head. I can feel the charge of magic in the air. My jaw clenches. "Wrong choice," I sneer.

In a heartbeat, I pull my sword from its holster at my side then stab him in the chest. Blood oozes from around the blade. I push him away with my boot so I can more easily retrieve my weapon.

The man falls to the ground, still mumbling despite the gushing wound. Wind kicks up around us, sending a spray of pebbles and dust. Another legionnaire approaches, axe in hand. I give him a single nod, and he lops off the man's head. Blood sprays and the head rolls near my feet. His glassy eyes are wide with fear, and I catch the scent of piss. After all that false bravado, he still spent his last moments afraid. What a waste of the god's gift.

I push his head with my boot, so I don't have to see his eyes, then turn to my men. "Find all the relics, then burn the house." I look behind me to where women and children are being loaded into wagons, then turn back to my men. "Burn it all."

ONE

How the fuck did I get talked into this?

I smooth the skirts of my elaborate dress and try to get comfortable. I should be comfortable. I'm on a velvet seat cushion in the most elegant, expensive carriage I've ever seen. But the corset is poking into my ribs, and the piles of fabric are making me sweat. Pulling back the curtains, I peer out the window and my breath hitches. We're nearing the massive black hedges that surround the castle grounds. The stories say they're full of thorns, that the leaves themselves are poisonous.

My heart hammers against my ribs as the carriage rumbles over the cobblestones. This was a terrible idea.

The hedges are getting closer. The leaves are so black they nearly blend together into one dangerous mass. In front of them are several corpses in various stages of decay tied to posts. Rebels and traitors. A warning to anyone considering opposing the empire. Ravens peck at the bodies, their cries sounding excited as they devour the dead.

I slam the curtain closed and lean back against the cushions. My breath is coming too quickly, and I replay everything I learned in my mind, trying to calm myself.

I can do this. I have to do this.

I move the curtain just enough to peek out. We've reached the hedges, and the carriage halts. There are night legionnaires outside the carriage, but none of them turn my direction. They're expecting me, but they're not allowed to look at me.

As we start moving again, I marvel at how thick the hedges are. We're on a smoother road now. No more bumping and rattling. The carriage glides as if we're floating. After so much time spent in the vibrating seat, it's a bit unsettling.

When we've finally passed between the hedges, a lawn appears, dotted with stone sculptures and topiaries made of the same dark leaves.

I close the curtain again and prepare as best I can. I blot my damp face with a handkerchief and smooth my ruffled skirts. I spray myself with the perfume they stowed in the carriage with me.

The carriage comes to a stop, and somehow, I'm going through the motions. It's like I'm watching myself, completely detached from what I'm doing and what comes next.

I drape the black shawl over my head and face the door. The door opens to a tunnel of shadows. I'm vaguely aware of the fact that dozens of night legionnaires have lined up to create that tunnel, their dark magic forming the shadows that conceal me from them and everyone else. It's so thick and murky that I can't even see the castle. The only thing guiding me is the flickering lamplight at the open door they're leading me toward.

I don't feel my legs move, or the ground under my feet. All I know is that I'm walking through those shadows like I'm supposed to and that I make it to the end.

Lanterns guide my way through the halls. There's no welcoming greeting for me. No grand parade, no one.

As the prince's betrothed, I cannot be seen by anybody until he sets eyes on me. It's one of the many rules that the Pendralian courtiers live by. They die by them, too.

The sitting room is beautiful, but modest compared to what I expected of the castle. The floors are gray stone, and tapestries line the walls. A large fire is crackling and burning in the fireplace, filling the room with heat. The only furniture is a red velvet couch. It's a room made for very short-term use.

Anxiety twists in my gut. This isn't exactly the welcome I expected as the princess of Iskvaland.

Footsteps sound. Lots of them. I drape the black scarf over my face, nearly obstructing my view. It's meant to prevent anyone other than my betrothed from seeing me, but it's a welcome barrier that keeps my emotions hidden. At least for now.

"Princess Sabina Volkov, welcome to Aurorium. I am Darius, head priest for the emperor. I'm here to witness your unveiling to your betrothed, Prince Caiden Pendral, crown prince of the Pendralian Empire and heir to the throne."

I incline my head to indicate that I'm listening, but my heart is pounding so hard now that I fear he might hear it in the silence that follows.

The priest steps back, pressing himself against the wall. Details are impossible to make out, but I can tell he's lowered his head so as to not see me. "She is ready, Your Highness."

A million thoughts race through my mind. All the protocols, the suggestions, the rules. So much to learn and never enough time.

His footsteps are quiet, and when he enters, I can only make out his outline. He's tall and broad-shouldered.

"Princess Sabina. I know you have had a long journey, and as soon as we are through with this archaic nonsense, you may retreat to your rooms." His tone is cold, devoid of emotion. Detached.

Fine with me.

He stops in front of me, then reaches for the fabric. Instead of gently folding it, he lifts the whole thing quickly, sending my blonde hair flying in front of my face. I smooth it away from my eyes, then look up at the man I'm to marry.

He's got brown hair that touches his shoulders. His jaw is strong and his lips full. He's got thick brows and brown eyes that almost look amber in this light. He's more handsome than I expected.

"Well, it seems you really do resemble your likeness. That's a pleasant surprise." He takes hold of one of my blonde curls. "It's a pity we could end up with children who have your fair hair. But I suppose that's the price we pay for treaties and the sacrifices we make as royals, isn't it?"

"We could always abstain and produce no children," I offer, mock sweetness in my tone. "Then, you wouldn't have to be disappointed by their hair color."

He releases the strand of my hair. "Women in Pendralia

are to be silent and do as they're told. Are we going to have a problem?"

"Of course not, my prince." I tighten one of my hands into a fist to keep myself from saying what I really want to say.

"Good." He glances over at the priest. "Darius. It is done. I accept the betrothal. She is as expected."

The priest lifts his head, and his eyes find mine. He's just as cold and detached as his prince. I don't know why I expected anything else. It's what I've always been taught about the royals.

"I will make an offering in honor of your betrothal." Darius inclines his head, then leaves the room.

"Brevan," the prince calls.

A night legionnaire steps into the room, eyes downcast. "Yes, Your Highness."

"No need to avert your eyes, Brevan. It's done."

The guard looks up, but he keeps his attention on the prince.

"Escort the princess to her chambers. Her lady's maids should be waiting and will take over from there. But I want you outside her room for now. The last thing I need is a dead Iskvalandian princess on my hands. Nobody in or out of that room without my permission, understand?"

The legionnaire, Brevan, nods. "Yes, Your Highness."

The prince turns and leaves without even a backward glance at me.

"Is he always like that?" I ask Brevan.

"He is a prince. Now, come. I'll show you to your rooms." He steps toward the door, then waits for me to join him.

The halls are dark and full of shadows. Lamplight flickers from sparse lanterns attached to the walls. I'm not sure if it's magic keeping the flames alight or if they use oil to keep them running.

This hall has no other decoration, though we do pass the occasional night legionnaire standing guard. Their eyes follow us, but they retain their stiff postures. The men stationed along our walk wear the typical armor of the Night Legion. The emperor's crest is embossed in the center of the black leather. The armor is stiff and ornamental. Like it would be challenging to move in. I wonder if the night legionnaires who are sent in to raze whole villages wear the same.

"You don't look like a legionnaire," I say to my guide.

"That's because I'm not," he replies.

"So what are you?"

He continues alongside me, not even glancing my way. He leads us up two flights of stairs, then down a long hall.

"You're special, I suppose. Different from the faceless, nameless legionnaires." I tap my finger on my chin, making a show of thinking. "Are you the emperor's assassin?"

No reply.

"No, you can't be. Because you'd be too valuable to be sent to simply babysit me. Are you his cousin? A royal relative too far from the throne to be a threat but too close to be enlisted?"

Nothing. We're still walking. Up more stairs, down another hall.

"A mercenary? Maybe he pays you for your loyalty. Or you're on the run from across the sea. A fugitive from the mines of the Shatterlands."

He continues without any acknowledgement that I'm following alongside him.

"Oh, I know what it is," I say. "You're his lover. Perhaps I won't have to worry about bearing him any children."

He finally glances over at me. "Do you ever shut up?"

"No."

"The prince isn't going to like that."

"Have you ever noticed how nobody ever asks the princess what she likes?" There's something about Brevan that makes me keep talking even when I know I shouldn't.

He stops in front of a large wood door. The hall we're in is well lit, and gorgeous tapestries cover most of the bare stone.

"Does anyone ever ask you what you want?" I chance.

For a second, I think I see the faintest upturn of his lips. "I serve the empire. That's what I want."

"I'm sure your parents are very proud of you," I say in my most princess-like tone.

"They're dead."

"I'm sorry." The concern in my voice is genuine, but I quickly regain control of myself. "I suppose this is the place?" I incline my head toward the door.

"Yes. Your ladies will assist you from here. I will stand guard for now."

"Am I supposed to feel comforted by that?"

"Feel however you like, Your Highness." He leans past me and turns the handle, then pushes the door open.

Before I can come up with a snarky reply, I'm swept into the room in a whirlwind of black silk and dark curls.

The ladies chitter like a group of excited squirrels while they pass me around like their new plaything. They speak in rapid-fire, high-pitched tones that are impossible to keep up with.

"Alright, enough!" someone yells.

They all grow silent, and an older woman pushes through the group. "Give her room. She's had a long journey, and I'm sure she wants to clean up and rest." She drops into a curtsy. "Welcome, Your Highness."

The other ladies are quick to drop into curtsies of their own before backing away. They line up and hastily smooth their skirts and fix smiles on their faces while their keen eyes watch my every move.

"I am Marian, the head lady," the woman says. "I know you weren't allowed ladies from your home, but we will do our best to serve you with loyalty and honor."

The others continue to smile at me, and I remind myself that there is no way any of them would be loyal to me. They are Pendralian. They are loyal to their emperor above all. To them, I'm a lamb sent to the wolves.

"It's lovely to meet you all," I say.

"The bathing chamber is through here." Marian gestures to an arched doorway. "Would you like assistance?"

"No, thank you. I am quite used to bathing alone," I reply.

Marian's smile doesn't falter, but some of the others don't mask their confusion. Perhaps royals in Pendralia don't know how to bathe themselves.

I lift my heavy skirts and walk into the large bathing chamber. The floors are shimmering black tile, the counters black marble streaked with gray. Even the faucets are black. The only splash of color comes from the copper tub set near the back of the room.

"We will prepare your dinner attire, Your Highness. Enjoy your bath." Marian closes the door, and I'm alone again.

I sink to the floor and take a few deep breaths. My hands shake and my head spins. Everything that I'd held in threatens to come out.

I breathe through the anxiety and regret and fear until all that's left is anger. My hands steady, my pulse evens. I lift my head and hold my chin high.

I know why I'm here. I know I made the right choice. And while I almost let fear get to me, it won't win. I knew what coming here meant, and I did it, anyway.

Everyone expects Princess Sabina Volkov to marry the prince. To finalize the treaty and create an alliance between the Pendralian Empire and Iskvaland. An unstoppable force that will dominate the entire world.

The only thing is that I don't plan to follow through with the marriage because I'm not Sabina Volkov.

The princess is dead.

And I am the angel of death who took her place.

Two

THE HEAT IS LONG GONE from the bath, but I linger. I'm not eager to return to the simpering women in the ornate room behind the door.

Someone knocks. "Your Highness? Do you need assistance?"

"I'll be right out." I press my hand against the jagged scar that runs across my abdomen from my belly button to my side. The last thing I want is their coming in here to help me out of the bath. Princesses should not have scars like this.

I step out and wrap myself in one of the black cloths I took from the table near the tub. Of course it's black. They take the royal color to the extreme here.

My hair drips, and I'm leaving wet footprints on the stone. I use another cloth to squeeze out as much water as possible, then cross to the door.

When I open it, Marian waits with an open dressing gown and averted eyes. I turn and slide my arms into it, careful to keep the cloth over my stomach until I can close it around me and tie the belt.

"I dismissed the others for now," Marian says. "If you'd prefer me to call them back, I will."

"No, thank you. I could use the quiet."

She gestures for me to follow her to a stool situated in front of a gray wooden vanity with a large oval mirror. I sit on the gray cushion and find myself in the reflection. It's eerie how much I look like the dead princess. When they came to me asking me to take her place, I thought them insane. I wasn't a spy or an assassin. But I want the emperor dead. I want all of them dead.

"Your hair is so beautiful," Marian says as she begins to brush the wet strands. "It's so rare to see anyone with fair hair around here."

"Because your people used to kill them when they were born." I've spent my life with my head covered in scarves. Aside from my family, my best friend, and my ex, nobody knew what my hair looked like.

A lump forms in my throat. That isn't true. My family is dead and I'll likely never see my best friend again. My ex was the one who asked me to take on this task. It's the only reason he knew to come to me when they attacked the princess's carriage and kidnapped her. They wanted her for ransom to stop the treaty, but they didn't expect her to use the knife she had hidden on herself.

It's not the way I expected to get my revenge, but there is never going to be another opportunity like this. And on my dead family's graves, I'm not going to waste it.

"They don't do that anymore," Marian says.

"Because they learned that most children outgrow it," I say.

"And because it was an outdated and cruel thing to do." She sets the brush down on the vanity. "I'm not sure what you learned about us growing up in Iskvaland, but I am guessing not all of it is true."

"Perhaps," I say.

"We've been taught that the people of Iskvaland have pet reindeer and that all their men are large hairy brutes who drink too much."

I have never been to Iskvaland, so I have no idea what is true. I lived half my childhood at the border, surrounded by people from both Pendralia and Iskvaland. But even there, it was difficult to know which stories were true and which were fabrications. There certainly were enough terrible stories from the people who'd fled from the frozen barrens of Iskvaland. But the people who lived in our village were kind. They weren't like their own stories. "I see your point."

She opens a drawer and pulls out another cloth that's smaller than the ones that were in the bathing chamber. She wraps my hair in it, then twists it until it stays on its own. I clench my jaw.

"It's just to help your hair dry," she says. "Maybe they'll let me show you around the city. You can see how beautiful Aurorium is for yourself."

"I'd like that," I say because what else can I say? That the city is in shambles. That the citizens are starving. That each winter we bury at least one person every morning because they froze to death the night before.

She's silent for a while as she slathers creams on my face

and rubs in strange smelling oils and serums. I have no idea what any of it does, but my skin no longer feels tight from the dry winter, air and it looks brighter somehow. When she reaches for the belt to remove my robe, I stop her. "I'll keep this on."

She holds up a jar of thick cream. "If you want to moisturize later, it's right here." She sets it back down. "They sent up your trunks, but we have a strict dress code here, so they made three dresses in anticipation of your arrival. The royal seamstress will be here tomorrow to get your measurements so she can create your new wardrobe."

"A whole new wardrobe?" So much waste. Three dresses were more than enough.

"I know, I'm sure you'll miss your gowns. All that color." She stares longingly toward the bathing chamber, where I see the blue and yellow gown I'd arrived in discarded on the floor. I probably should have treated that better.

"It's fine. I'll wear whatever His Majesty requests," I say.

"Good. Now, let's finish your hair, and we'll get you dressed."

Somehow, my hair is dry when she removes the cloth. I want to ask if it's magic, but it seems such a frivolous thing to imbue with such a rare gift. Though, the only thing I know about magic is that the emperor is the only one in the empire who can decide who may have it and that he can also take it away. It's one of the things I need to find out while I'm here, but I need to understand the big uses of magic. Like how the emperor is still alive after 500 years.

When Marian finishes plaiting and pinning my hair and

painting makeup on my face, I don't even look like myself. But I'm not myself. I'm a princess.

She calls in help to lace me into the corset and to ensure all the layers of the elaborate black dress are just right. When they finish, I can hardly breathe, but this should be typical for a princess. I should be used to it. I can't let them know that when I put on that dress this morning, it was the first time I'd ever even worn a dress.

"You must be so grateful you're here and that you got to leave Iskvaland," the other lady Marian called in says. "I heard they were going to sell you to an emperor in the Shatterlands until our prince asked them to spare you."

I open my mouth, then close it. How am I even supposed to respond to that?

"Charlotte, is that how you are to address royalty? She is the future empress of the Pendralian Empire. She could have your head for your lack of decorum."

Charlotte's eyes grow wide, and she drops into a low curtsy. "Forgive me, Your Highness. I wasn't thinking."

"It's alright. But I don't wish to speak of my home right now."

"Thank you for your grace, Your Highness," Charlotte says, still in her curtsy.

"Why don't you go and tell them the princess is ready to be escorted to dinner?" Marian suggests.

Charlotte rises and spins, then hurries to the door.

"You'll have to forgive her. All of your ladies are noble daughters, of course, but none of them have ever formally served a royal before. They should be familiar with court etiquette," she glances at them and they straighten, "but I fear they must be out of practice"

I smile at the ladies reassuringly then return my attention to Marian. "What about you?"

"I served our late empress. But I am the only one of her ladies who remains here. The others have all joined the temple of Amate, the goddess of the sun, a tribute to our late empress's piety."

I force a smile, but I'm certain it comes across more like a grimace. There's a lot of secrets buried in this court. Considering Marian is the only one who wasn't sent away, I have to assume she's in the emperor's pocket. I will have to be very careful around her.

A knock sounds on the door, and Marian hurries to open it. Brevan is standing outside. "Good evening, Lady Marian."

"Good evening, Lord Maxwell." Marian inclines her head.

"I am here to escort the princess to dinner," he announces.

I walk to the door, and Brevan offers his elbow. It's a drastic change from our earlier encounter. I don't accept it. Instead, I walk through the door and step into the hall. "Shall we?"

He lowers his arm. "This way."

"Do you join the royals for dinner?" I ask.

"No, of course not," he says.

"What about for balls or parties? Do they have you there as a guest, or do you just stand in the corner and glare at people as they enjoy their lives?"

"I do rather enjoy glaring," he says.

We turn down a few halls and then take a flight of stairs up a level into a grand open space lined with stone columns carved to look like plants. In the flickering lamplight, the vines and leaves almost appear to move. Our footsteps echo in the large empty space.

As we get closer to the columns, I recognize some of the leaves. The different leaves on the columns each belong to a plant that is poisonous.

"What is this place?" I stop and spin in a slow circle, taking in the room.

He points, and I look up at a ceiling made of glass. Stars twinkle above us.

"Used to be a garden for the empress. The emperor had it emptied after she passed."

"Did he love her?" I ask.

"I am certain your marriage will be fruitful and prosperous." He resumes walking.

"I'm not asking about my marriage. I'm asking about the emperor's. I've heard that nobody's seen him since she died. Is it because he's in mourning?"

"This is where I leave you." He stops in front of tall double wooden doors guarded by a pair of night legionnaires.

One of the legionnaires pulls a door open for me, and I walk inside without a backward glance at my escort.

THREE

THE LONG WINDOWLESS room is lined with flickering sconces that cast eerie dancing shadows over the murals on the walls. One entire length is painted like the woods in winter. It's so realistic that the ominous branches seem to reach for me. Wolves twist between the trunks, their paws obscured by painted snow. The other side shows the woods in summer, full of leaves and life. Deer and rabbits stare out at me with vacant eyes. Somehow, the summer side seems more unsettling than the winter.

A table made of dark polished wood sits in the center of the room, lined with red velvet chairs. Candelabras are spaced evenly across it, making the polished surface gleam.

There's one person in the room, and he stands but does not move to greet me. I drop into a curtsy.

"So you do have some sense of manners," the prince drawls.

I rise and find him approaching me now. I wait.

"You couldn't be bothered to greet me properly before," he says.

"You'll have to forgive me, Your Highness. I'd had a long journey and was not myself." The simpering tone I'm using makes my insides crawl.

"You'll have to excuse my father's absence. He is away from court more often than not these days." He offers his hand, palm up. I place mine on top of his, and he leads us to the table.

"Will I get to meet him soon?" I ask.

"I'm not sure. He rarely sees anyone. Though, I thought he would wish to greet the woman he felt was worth a treaty." He yanks out a chair on the right of his, then gestures to it.

"I can tell you don't feel the same," I say as I sit.

"I must admit, you are beautiful." He returns to his seat at the head of the table. "But I can get all the beautiful women I want."

"Is this supposed to impress me? You, bragging about the women you bed?"

"It's supposed to show you that you're only here because my father thinks you useful. If you prove otherwise, I will not hesitate to ensure that you befall one of the many tragedies that are possible in this empire, and I will send your beautiful corpse back to your empire with my condolences and a bouquet of black roses."

"You make it seem as if I am to fear death," I reply as I pick up my wineglass.

"Do you not?"

I take a sip, then set the glass down, staring at him for a long moment before I answer. "I have seen Death. And she is beautiful."

He smirks. "Perhaps you'll enter her embrace soon, another raven in her coven of soul collectors."

I smile at the thought of becoming one of Death's helpers. She can't be everywhere at once, so her most devout followers become ravens after they pass from this world. They collect the souls she can't. "Is that your plan? To kill me to end this alliance?"

"What do you know of our alliance, little raven?"

"Only that I'm to seal it, or rather that our children would," I say.

He takes a sip of his own wine, then leans back in his chair. "My father intends to imbue the Iskvalandian soldiers with magic, then send them with ours to the Shatterlands. The alliance would mean the end of the independent city-states on that gods-forsaken continent."

"Isn't that what you want?" I ask.

His brow furrows just enough for me to know he's thinking about how to answer, but a door opens in the center of the summer mural. Several servants emerge, carrying platters of food.

The scent of delicacies fills the air, and my stomach rumbles. It's been over a day since I last ate, but I am used to being hungry.

The servants wear gray, the same color as the stone on the walls. It has to be intentional, to help them blend in, which brings a fresh wave of rage that heats my face. Some of the people who work here are fourth or fifth generation. It's almost impossible to leave a position at the castle.

They quietly set the platters on the table in front of us, and I watch the prince, forcing myself to mirror his reactions.

He looks bored and anxious at the same time. As if he's both impatient for his food and irritated that he has to wait. Or perhaps it's that he doesn't like the servants being around. A woman in a gray dress serves the prince while another woman does the same for me. I bite back my urge to thank her while roasted potatoes, greens, herbed chicken, and soft white bread are added to my plate.

As soon as the hidden door closes behind the servants, I'm hit with the realization that we're alone. And not yet wed. I may not have been raised noble or royal, but I know that it's unusual.

"Nobody else will join us?" I ask.

"I don't feel like sharing you with the rest of the court just yet." He takes a bite of his food.

"Isn't that going to cause a scandal? The two of us alone?"

"Please. We both know that neither of us is exactly a blushing virgin. I didn't agree to marry you for your piety."

That's news. I lift a brow, curious. "You had a say in this? You aren't just going along with what your father wanted?"

I wonder if the rumors are true. That the emperor is already dead. I can't leave here until I'm certain. And I can't kill the prince without taking down the emperor first. The emperor's reign must end.

"It is what he wanted," he says. "But after I heard about your exploits, I must admit that I was rather intrigued."

Fuck. My pulse races. What exploits? I got about an hour of rapid-fire information about what to expect and how to blend in with the royal family while being shoved into a dead woman's gown. I am making this up as I go and don't know anything about the real princess. We all assumed the prince didn't know anything about her aside from her appearance.

I might be dead sooner than I realized.

"I sent some of my spies to Iskvaland shortly after we were betrothed." He lifts a fork and holds it over his plate. "I know you snuck out of the castle at every chance you got. I know you had a lover you met at the stables. And I know you liked to practice with weapons when your father's soldiers were away. My spies said you were terrible with weapons, but great in bed."

My cheeks heat in indignation for the dead woman. "They watched me have sex?"

"I needed to know what I was getting. Thankfully, they also noted that you were insistent that your lover take his tonic every time you met. So at least I know you aren't carrying another man's bastard."

My chair screeches as I abruptly stand. "You're disgusting."

He stabs a chunk of potato then pops it into his mouth and chews slowly. When he finishes, he smiles, showing straight white teeth. "I'm also your future emperor. Sit back down."

"And I am your future empress. You will show me respect." I glare at him, not caring if it all falls apart right here. I didn't even know the princess. I thought she must be another spoiled royal, but now, I think maybe she and I weren't so different. She must have had a rebellious streak. I wonder if she'd have spied for the rebellion. Or maybe she was hoping to kill the emperor herself and that was why she came. I'll never know. But I feel like I owe her at least a little bit.

"Things don't work like that around here, little raven. The empress is nothing. Your job is to look pretty and carry my children. If you fail at either of those things, I will end you."

"You need this treaty more than my empire does. Our armies outnumber yours. They're stronger, better trained, and not reliant on magic. Your army is fueled by years of nepotism. Your soldiers are wealthy men who serve to gain favor and increase their station.

"Ours are farmers and fathers and hunters who love their country. They fight because they believe in something bigger than themselves. They fight to protect their family and their land. Yours only fight for themselves. Which do you think will win when the time comes? Magic only gets you so far when your legion is full of preening cowards."

I hold my ground. Staring right at the insufferable prince, maintaining whatever sense of composure I can hold on to while I curse myself internally. That was too far. That wasn't the rant of a princess. And I don't know if anything I said about Iskvaland is true. It was all rumors. Stories I heard growing up in the mountains at the border. Propaganda, I was told. Lies. But based on how he is looking at me, I don't think any of it was a lie.

After a long silence, he sets his fork down and stands, then walks toward me slowly. I hold my chin high, my only regret that I couldn't complete the mission. I told them I wasn't the one for this job. I am good at strategy and plans. I'm not cut out for the field. I know speaking to him that way was wrong. I know that isn't how I am supposed to act, but I couldn't stop myself.

The prince stands behind my chair and straightens it, then gestures toward the seat. "Please, sit."

I stay where I am. "I will not marry someone who disrespects me. And I certainly will not marry someone who spies on me. I am not breeding stock. If that is what you are looking for, find someone else."

"I will be more respectful." He inclines his head to the chair.

"And you will not spy on me?" I ask. "How am I to ever bathe again knowing you may have your men watching me?"

"I will not spy on you," he agrees.

"It's a start." I sit, and he pushes me in before returning to his chair.

"Please, eat. I had them prepare something simple because I don't yet know what you like."

"So you can be kind."

"Don't tell anyone," he says.

I pick up my fork and knife and cut off a piece of chicken. "I don't think they'd believe me, anyway, Your Highness."

"You're probably right," he says. "And call me Caiden. You are going to be my wife, after all."

FOUR

THE ROOMS they gave me are something out of a dream. In addition to the bathing chamber and sleeping area, there's a separate sitting room, a writing nook with a desk, and a dining space with a table that seats eight. There's also a small bed tucked away in a tiny room for a servant to sleep near me in case I need anything. Everything is tastefully decorated in black, gray, and cream. It's luxury like I could never imagine and it's more space than the house where I grew up. I didn't know just how different things were between the royals and everyone else.

A log falls in the fireplace, making a series of cracks and pops that sends sparks beyond the grate to the stone floor around the hearth. Marian insisted on building a large fire since I am not allowing her to stay with me.

I pace around the enormous space taking in the floral tapestries that hang on the walls, and pause at a bookshelf near the writing nook. There's only a handful of books there, and they're all about plants. I pick one up and carry it to the large feather bed. It's covered in furs and pillows, and while I hate knowing that my bedding must have cost more than most people will ever see in their whole lives, I can't deny that it's comfortable.

Settling against the pillows, I open the book and begin to read. The plants listed are all native to Pendralia, though someone scribbled notes into the margins next to some entries. After seeing the columns earlier, I know these must have belonged to the empress. I set the book down and look around again. This must have been her room.

Which means, the emperor's room can't be far.

I crawl out of the bed again and slowly move around the room, lifting the tapestries and feeling for any creases or unusual cracks in the stone walls. Didn't emperors and empresses usually have their rooms near each other? Didn't castles have secret passages? Or was that just in the stories?

"Taylan?"

I freeze between the wall and a heavy tapestry of a pair of deer standing between flowering spring trees. I swear I heard someone saying my name. My *real* name.

"Tay? Are you here?"

Nope, not imagining. I shuffle along the wall until I'm uncovered by the tapestry. The room is empty. "Lee? Is that you?"

Lee turns the corner then stops. I instantly glance toward the main door. If anyone sees him in here, he's dead. And there's a good chance I will be as well.

"You can't be here," I hiss. My betrothed literally admitted over dinner that he used to spy on me, and while he says he won't any longer, I don't actually believe him.

"I had to check on you. Fuck. That nightgown is

fancier than anything you've ever worn. You could be royalty. I almost forgot how beautiful you are."

"Don't even think about it," I warn.

"I can't say you look good?" He takes a few steps closer, and I hold up my hand, indicating for him to stop.

"Truly, if they find you here, it's over for both of us. You have to go.".

"Don't worry. We've created a distraction," he says. "I've got at least five minutes."

I press my fingers to my temples. "What did you do?"

"That's what you want to use our five minutes for?"

"I want to know why you're here and what you want." I take a step away from him.

"Did you meet the emperor?" he asks.

"No. Caiden says he rarely meets anyone. I think I have to earn their trust first." Not that I didn't almost blow that tonight, but I am not about to tell Lee that.

"*Caiden*? As in Prince Caiden? Already on a first-name basis?"

"You sent me here as his betrothed."

"I'm just surprised. I thought he'd be the type to insist on titles." Lee shoves his hands into his pockets, then causally walks closer to me. "Find out anything else? Like where the emperor is? Is he even in the castle? Is he away? Is he dead?"

"They told me he's away right now. I don't know if that's a cover or not. I just got here. You're going to have to give me time."

He stops in front of me. "I know. I mostly just wanted to see if you were alright. Make sure they didn't hurt you." He removes his hand from his pockets and reaches for me.

I flinch when he touches me but don't pull away. When he takes my hand, I'm not sure how to react. For so long, this was normal for us. It feels wrong but it's like my body still remembers that it used to be this way. "What are you doing?"

"I just missed you already." He leans closer like he wants to kiss me.

I pull away from his grip and step back. "What exactly is happening here, Lee?"

"What? I can't kiss my girl?"

Everything comes crashing around me. All the things he said and the hurt he caused. The way he turned the rebellion into something darker and deadlier in a matter of days after my mother's death. The way he used my family's deaths as his excuse for so much bloodshed without ever mourning them. "I am not your girl. Haven't been in a long time. What are you doing?"

"I don't know." He runs his hand through his hair. "It's seeing you like this. All dressed like a princess. Probably bedding a prince. It has me all confused and jealous, and I think I made a mistake, Taylan."

"No. You were clear. You made your choice, and it didn't involve me."

"But you agreed to do this. I thought that meant everything was back to the way it was," he says. "That you were over it."

My brows lift and I scoff. "Over it? My whole family is dead, Lee. Gone. Everyone I loved. I'm here for one reason: revenge. I want the emperor and anyone else who had anything to do with their deaths dead. In the most painful and terrible ways possible. I want to watch them all suffer."

"You're not here to kill anyone, Tay. You're just here to get information. You think you're so tough. Think you've had it hard. I have news for you: We've all had it hard. Losing your family doesn't make you special. It just gives you motivation. You're here because of your face. Because you look like a dead woman."

"I know why I'm here. And you're putting it all at risk," I remind him.

"No, you're the one putting it at risk with that revenge talk. You find out where the emperor is. You find out how he's staying alive so long. Then you tell us and let the rest of us do our jobs." He steps closer, and his expression softens. "I know it's been hard on you. I hate that you've had to live like this. I hate that you lost them. I miss them, too. Your brothers were like brothers to me, as well. Remember that. Remember that you're not the only one hurting."

I clench my jaw to keep from pointing out his condescending switch in tactics. At this point, I just want him gone. And then I can figure out where the emperor is, what's keeping him alive, and how to put a blade in his heart myself. I don't care what Lee says. This is all about revenge.

He pulls a red gemstone from his pocket and holds it out. "Take this. As soon as you find what you need, place it on that windowsill. It'll glow in the sun. We'll watch for it."

"Fire ruby?" I ask. The stone will shine like a beacon from my window once I put it there.

"The only one we have. But tell them some story about how it was a gift from your family or something to remind you of home. They're mined in Iskvaland. They should buy it. Tell them you're homesick."

"Got it. But now you need to leave. Before they come in here and find you."

"Be careful, Tay. You know how important you are to me." He smiles the way he used to when he'd say sweet things to me. Back when I believed his kind words and empty promises.

Before I knew who he really was. I won't fall for it again. "Right. Go. I can do this. But it will take time."

He nods, then turns and rushes away, disappearing into a secret passage in the bathroom.

Well, that's going to give me nightmares. No more long baths for me. I wait a moment, letting him get some distance, before I follow him. There is no way I'm not going to find out where that passage leads. Just as I press against the wall, a knock sounds on my door.

I remove my hand and hurry back to my bedroom. "Who is it?"

"Princess, I need to check your room," Brevan calls from outside. "Are you decent?"

I'm in a nearly sheer nightgown, so no. "One minute." I find the robe near the vanity and pull it on as I walk to the door.

I hardly open it a crack before Brevan pushes his way inside. Startled, I scramble away so I'm not knocked over. "Excuse you."

"Emergency, Your Highness." He unsheathes the sword that hangs at his hip and holds it by his side, then storms into the bedroom. He checks under the bed, behind the tapestries, inside the wardrobe. He investigates every crevice and every corner.

My blood runs cold.

He's looking for someone hiding in my room. They know Lee was here. I didn't even make it one night in the castle. They're going to arrest me and hang me. I will haunt Lee for the rest of his life for sneaking in here like this.

I follow Brevan at a distance, expecting him to enter the passageway in the bathing chamber, but he doesn't even pause near the wall. He does another pass of each room, checking every corner a second time, then returns to my bedroom, stopping in front of me. His jaw is clenched, his grip on his weapon tight. He's wound as tight as a spring, and I'm certain he's about to unload all that tension on me.

"Did you find what you were looking for?" I ask.

"There's nobody here," he says.

"Did you expect someone else to be here besides me?" I'm impressed with how condescending I make my tone.

"There was an incident. Rebels tried to scale the north side of the castle. Two made it past the legionnaires and were heading in the direction of your rooms." He peers around again, as if he doesn't believe his own investigation.

"But your men caught them, right?" I ask.

"No. Not all of them. But I will remain with you until they're found," he says.

"That's not necessary."

His eyes narrow. "It's not? Do you have some kind of training I'm unaware of?"

That's when I remember I'm supposed to be afraid of the rebels. I can't afford to keep making these kinds of mistakes. Especially now that I know Lee expects me to fail. I have added proving Lee wrong to my list of reasons for being here. "It's just that my door locks and there's so many legionnaires here and they all have magic. They can't possibly get into my room."

"I'm glad you feel confident in our men," he says. "But the prince has informed me that you have a habit of taking clandestine midnight strolls. I can't risk you doing that."

"That was in my home. Where I was familiar with things. I'm not going to do that here." The real Sabina's habit of sneaking out might end up making things harder for me. Covert exploration of the castle is part of how I plan to figure out the information I need.

"Doesn't matter. His Highness has requested that I stay with you and babysit." He spits the last word out like it's a curse. Like watching me is so far beneath him.

"I won't tell if you don't." I give him my most charming smile.

"I'll be on the window seat, Your Highness. Sleep well."

"You can't be serious," I say, aghast. "I cannot have a man spending the night in my room. What will people say?"

"They'll say the prince has a very loyal lapdog who wasted his night watching over a spoiled princess instead of chasing down rebels like he should."

"Really. You can't be in here," I repeat.

He starts removing his leather armor.

"What are you doing?" I ask.

"I don't usually sleep in my armor." He drops the leather chest plate on the floor. "And since I don't think you're actually going to be attacked, there's not much point in leaving it on."

"Please don't," I say.

"Close the curtains on your bed and go to sleep, Your Highness. I'll be gone in the morning."

"I still don't think this is appropriate." I cross my arms. "I don't know you, and you expect me to feel safe sleeping in the same room as you?"

He uses his toe to push all his armor next to the cushioned window seat with a sigh. I can see the tips of black gift markings on his left forearm where his sleeve is rolled up. It almost looks like a vine. I wonder if they extend onto his arms and chest. He's strong and broad, and without the cover of his armor, the outlines of his muscles are clear, and my mind starts to imagine what he might look like without that shirt on.

Nope. Not doing that. I squeeze my eyes shut for a second, then open them to clear my head.

"Should I call for your ladies? They can join us," he offers in a tone that tells me he knows it's the last thing I want.

"I think I preferred it when you weren't talking to me," I say.

With a smirk, he inclines his head. "Sleep well, Your Highness." He sits on the window seat and removes his boots, then turns so his back is against the wall and his legs stretch out across the cushion. He takes up the whole seat that way. He couldn't lay down even if he wanted to, which means he's either not sleeping or he's sleeping sitting up.

I climb under my blankets and furs with my robe still on, leaving the canopy open so I can watch him. Settling in, propped up against the headboard, I plan to stay awake until the sun rises.

In the firelight, I can tell he's got his eyes closed and his head back. His arms are crossed, and his breathing is steady. Maybe he really is going to sleep.

I fight exhaustion, but it's been a long day and my eyes are heavy.

The next thing I know, cheerful singsong voices call my name, and my ladies are gathering in my room while sunlight pours in from the window. The window seat is empty. The armor and boots are gone.

Five

MARIAN SHOOS the other ladies into the dining room. Their giggles and excited chatter lessen but still carry through the space. I'm glad they're happy, but it's such a stark contrast to the rest of this place.

I wash my face and change into the day dress Marian set aside for me. It's white and gray with a black ribbon around the waist. Thankfully, there's no corset. Apparently, those are reserved for formal occasions. Color, on the other hand, is never permitted.

When I join the ladies in the dining room, I'm surprised to see breakfast arranged on the table. Bread, jam, fruit, roasted tomatoes, mushrooms, and potatoes. There's a wide variety and, again, far more food than necessary.

The women are gathered in the dining chamber, their backs against the walls. All of them silent. Marian must have scolded them while I was dressing in the bathing chamber.

There's enough food for all of us, but the women are

standing there as if they're going to watch me eat. "Join me for breakfast?" I gesture toward the table.

The ladies chirp with excited *Thank-you*s, then sit at the chairs, leaving the head spot, and the chair on the right open. I glance over at Marian, who gives a single nod, then I take the place at the end. Marian sits on my right.

"Please, eat. There's so much food," I say.

"You first," Marian whispers.

I reach for a strawberry and set it on my plate, then add a biscuit and some jam and take a bite before setting it back on my plate. The others begin to serve themselves.

"I know things are different in Iskvaland," Marian says as she reaches for a slice of bread. "You'll learn how it works around here, and it won't feel so different soon. I'm sorry you couldn't bring any of your ladies. It must have been hard to leave them behind."

"It was." I think of my best friend Anya. I left her a letter under her pillow saying goodbye. I knew if I saw her in person, she'd have talked me out of it. She'll never forgive me for agreeing to this. I hope I will see her again someday, but a lot of things will have to go perfectly for that to be a possibility.

"You said everyone here is from a noble house?" I ask.

"Are your ladies not nobles?" a younger woman with auburn hair asks. Then, she covers her mouth with her hand and looks over at Marian with wide eyes.

"Do I need to give you permission to talk?" I ask.

She nods.

"Please, please talk. All of you. You never need my permission."

The ladies freeze, then look around at each other, and I swear I have not heard them this quiet once.

"That's not really how it works around here," Marian says.

"Can it, though? In my rooms at least?" I smile at them. "It would help make me less homesick."

The others look to Marian, seeking her approval. I notice how young they are compared to her. Marian is probably in her late thirties. The others in the room are closer to my age or younger. At twenty-three, I am nearly the same age as the real princess was. She would have been twenty-three at the winter solstice this year.

"In the princess's rooms, we will do as she wishes but know that as she grows more used to our customs, she may change her mind," Marian says.

The others beam, and the woman who spoke to me looks over expectantly. "Can you tell us about your court? What was it like? What is Iskvaland like?"

"What are the men like?" a brunette with tight curls asks. Her cheeks turn bright pink, and the others around the table laugh.

I don't know how Iskvalandian men differ from those in the empire, but I figure they are likely similar in how they behave. I frown, then catch myself. The ladies are watching me expectantly. "They're not much different from here. Though, they dress better."

"Like your dress yesterday. All that color," someone says wistfully.

"I miss color," someone adds.

"Never anything besides black, white, and gray here?" I ask.

"They take their house colors far too seriously," someone says.

I continue to converse with them and ask them their names and questions about their lives. Listening to them talk about what they enjoy and why their families sent them to court helps me understand more about the way things work around here.

There are rules that aren't officially recorded anywhere. About whom to talk to and who to avoid. They have guidance about which dances to sit out and tips on how to get past the legionnaires who guard the doors so you can get some fresh air at the stuffy official events. They even share stories about sneaking into the city, but Marian shuts them down before I get too much information.

"Have any of you ever met the emperor?" I take a bite of my biscuit.

The room goes silent again.

I swallow. "Should I not ask about him?"

"It's just that nobody really does," Antonia, the brunette with the tight curls, says. "At least not publicly."

"My father says he's been away from the empire on a quest for the gods, but we're not supposed to know." Katherine stabs a mushroom with her fork.

"That's ridiculous," Genevieve says. "He was already anointed by the gods; he doesn't need to curry any more favor by going on a quest for them."

"Nobody's seen him in a long while," Marian says. "Sometimes, the crown prince will relay messages from him, but other than that, he sees very few visitors."

"Why?" I ask. "Is he sick?"

All the ladies make the sign of the goddess of health by

tapping two fingers to their chest. I quickly copy the gesture. "I'm sorry. It's just that I was so hoping to meet him. I've heard such wonderful things."

"I understand," Marian says. "But you should know, it's not wise to bring him up. Even in here, it's a risk. While I would like to think that every woman in your service is loyal to you, the first thing we learn in this court is that it's a court of eyes and ears. A court that is always watching. Always listening."

Everyone looks serious, and all thoughts of eating are abandoned.

"Thank you for the warning." I am honestly grateful because I was feeling too comfortable with these women. They seem nice and friendly. But they wouldn't bat an eye at watching their emperor or his Night Legion level a town. They weren't selling the heavy jewels they wore to buy bread to help feed the starving or offering to take in an orphan child. They were not my friends. They never could be.

I catch movement and see Brevan walking toward us. The women gasp and rush to smooth the wrinkled fabric of their dresses, pinch their cheeks, or adjust their hair. All of them watch him with hopeful expressions.

None of them said they were in court to find a husband, but I have a feeling that is their primary objective. But not for Marian. She didn't even flinch when she noticed the legionnaire approach.

"Ladies," Brevan says as he lowers his head in a slight bow. "Your Highness." He drops the bow lower when he turns toward me.

"What a pleasant surprise, Enforcer," Marian says.

Enforcer? Brevan is the emperor's enforcer? He isn't just a legionnaire. He is a hunter. An assassin. He is the one who finds fragments from the ancient temples and other relics that could be used to create magic, then destroys them.

Brevan is the man who ordered them to torch all the buildings in the Point. He burned my home to the ground. They burned with people still inside them until they were nothing more than rubble.

He was responsible for a hundred deaths in one night, but he'd only killed two personally.

Those two were my brothers.

The man who murdered the last of my family slept in my room last night. My hands ball into fists, and bile climbs up my throat. I glare at him with newfound hatred.

His orders and his power come from the emperor, but the stories say he is the one who chooses where to go and who to kill.

I open one hand and wrap my fingers around the knife at my place setting. It would be so easy. He wouldn't suspect a thing. I could probably get to him in time. Just jam the knife into his throat where there's no armor. His pride would probably let me get up close before he even attempted to protect himself.

"...wouldn't you, Your Highness?" Marian is staring at me, then her eyes dart down to where I'm holding the knife.

I release the cutlery—it probably isn't sharp enough anyway—and turn to her with a false smile on my lips.

"Is that a yes?" she prods.

"Um, yes, of course," I say.

"Alright. If you are ready, we can go now," Brevan, the enforcer, says.

Go. Fuck. What did I agree to?

"Are you finished?" Marian asks.

"Yes." I push my chair back and rise. All the ladies do the same. I smile at them. "Thank you for the lovely conversation."

"We'll be here when you return," Marian says. "Now, let me get you a cloak. It's chilly outside."

Outside. I'm going outside. With the man who murdered my brothers.

Six

ONCE WE WALK through the front doors, I look back, taking in the castle from the outside for the first time. Living in the city meant seeing the spires above the ominous black hedges and wondering what the rest of the building looked like.

It is just as dominating and impressive as I always imagined. Sweeping buttresses extend from turrets and arches. Glass windows dot the upper floors, but the lower levels are solid gray stone. Sculptures adorn each ledge and terrace. Closer to the ground, human figures with wings extend out of the stone, like they are flying. Angels weathered over time, making them look beaten and sorrowful instead of proud and inspiring.

The floors above them have more human figures, but without wings. The features are worn and difficult to make out, but I think they're the gods and goddesses. In the center of a row of statues is a huge stained-glass window. I can't make out the scene it depicts, but I am intrigued enough to want to find it when I'm back in the castle.

The other terraces and rooftops are graced with creatures. Each of them different, a varied collection of animal features. Some with wings, some without. Snouts and claws, fangs and tails. Some are more monster than animal, but all are ominous and unsettling.

"This way," Brevan says.

I follow the enforcer toward a waiting carriage, then hesitate. Am I actually getting into a carriage with this man? What if he knows who I really am? What if he recognizes me as one of the people who fled that night?

Guilt squeezes my chest so hard I can't suck in a full breath. I ran that night. I thought that was the best thing I could do. I'm not a fighter, and I didn't want to be a liability to my brothers. When they told me to run, I listened.

I was able to reunite with the few survivors in our meeting place in the catacombs the following day, and I discovered what happened. I spent the next three days in a drunken stupor until my best friend, Anya, found me. We left the rebellion and rented a room. She got a job at a tavern, and I worked at a printer, setting type. Three months later, Lee knocked on my door, begging for my help.

Three months. Or was it four? I'd tried to forget. It was too painful to think about it.

Either way, I should still be mourning their loss. Not playing nice with their killer.

"Princess?" Brevan asks.

I blink a few times and notice he's got his hand out to help me into the carriage. "It's just the two of us?"

"As I said before, the prince extends his apologies for

not being able to attend. He assured me he set aside time for dinner with you tonight, though."

I swallow around the lump in my throat. I can do this. I must do this. I have to play the part.

I let him help me into the carriage, but his touch feels like betrayal against my skin.

He sits across from me, and I pull the curtain aside so I can stare out the window instead of looking at him. My fingers twitch. I'm not a trained killer, and I always struggled with that part of the rebellion. It's why I worked on the inside. Why I helped with strategy and supplies. Why I didn't go out in the field.

Now, I'm holding myself back. I want to lunge at this man and claw and scratch and scream and kick and hurt him as much as he hurt me.

But I know if I kill him, the emperor will put another in his place. A new enforcer who will do the same harm. And I'll be dead. We'll lose our chance to find out where the emperor is and how he stays alive.

I'm the best chance at actual change. If I can keep myself from breaking first.

That is assuming this ride alone with him isn't to quietly dispose of me. Well, if it is, I'll make him work for it.

"It must be difficult to be so far from home," he says.

I turn to look at him. He's wearing his armor again but doesn't have his sword. I still have no idea what we're doing. "Do ladies here often travel alone with men?"

"The prince trusts me. And I can assure you, I want this trip to be quick even more than you do."

"How very reassuring." That doesn't ease my anxiety. I

wish I had a weapon. If I survive this, I wonder if I can find a dagger to hide under my skirts.

The carriage rumbles as we transition from the smooth castle road. We must have passed between the opening of the dark hedges.

The castle is atop a hill overlooking the city, and it'll take a few minutes to reach the luxurious neighborhoods nearest the royal home. I look out the window at the gates that keep people away.

"Many of the emperor's most loyal nobles live here," Brevan says. "This is Duke Glass's residence. He also has a vineyard estate in the country."

"How nice for the duke that he has two homes while so many have none," I snap.

"Doesn't your family have six estates across Iskvaland?"

"It doesn't mean I have to agree with it," I reply.

"How very modern of you." He lifts one of the black velvet curtains to peer outside.

"Have you spent a lot of time in the slums, enforcer?"

He closes the curtain, then turns back in my direction. "I spent all my early years in the legion there."

"And it didn't bother you to see all the suffering?"

"I am not the emperor. I can't change anything about how things work around here." His face is stoic, emotionless as always.

"You have the emperor's ear, don't you? Most people don't have that."

"Is this how you speak to your father?" he asks.

"Yes." I have no idea what the emperor of Iskvaland thinks of the poor in his empire. My guess is he's never once thought about their well-being. But he's not here. I am.

"It's amazing, really. When I visited your father, I didn't hear a single woman's voice. They didn't even allow female servants in rooms where men were meeting. And I was told that you and your mother were in the women's wing, where you spent all your time."

My face heats. The more I learn about what the real Sabina's life was like, the more I want justice for her, as well. "If you're such an expert on my empire, then why are you asking me questions? Go ahead, tell me what it's like to grow up as a woman in Iskvaland. It sounds like you must know more than me... a woman from Iskvaland."

"That tongue of yours is going to get you killed," he warns.

"I've had many compliments on my tongue, Enforcer," I say.

He turns so red that even the tips of his ears are pink. So, his perfect composure can crack. That was far too easy.

"And last I checked, I outrank you as a royal visitor and soon-to-be member of the royal family."

He inclines his head, then speaks through gritted teeth. "Forgive me, Your Highness."

We roll to a stop in front of a street lined with shops. They have glass windows that show displays of their goods and beautifully painted wood signs over their doors. I've never been to this part of the city, and I've never seen shops like this. In the Point, we had shops, but many of them were shoved into spaces between buildings, cloth hung as ceilings and crates lined up as shelves.

Only the butcher, apothecary, and Red's Tavern were permanent in our part of the city. Everything else was sold from carts or temporary stores, or bartered from neighbors.

If you needed something specific, you traveled to one of the other neighborhoods.

The driver opens the carriage door, and Brevan exits, then turns to offer his hand to me. I accept it, head swimming with warnings. I'm pushing it too far. There is no way he's not going to report every single thing I said back to the prince. What kind of princess cares about the common people like this?

He leads us to an unmarked shop. It has no windows or sign.

"What is this place?" I ask.

"I'm not sure. It's not where Jacques usually conducts his business." He knocks on the door.

"Who is Jacques? And what kind of business does he have?" I take a step back, seriously considering returning to the carriage.

He shrugs as if he doesn't know.

"Wonderful. You brought me to a random building for an unknown reason, unarmed." I glance to where his sword usually hangs.

"Trust me, Princess, just because you can't see the weapons, doesn't mean they aren't there."

An opening large enough for a pair of blue eyes to peer through slides open. "Who's there?" The voice is muffled.

"It's Lord Maxwell. I was told you'd be expecting us," Brevan says.

The little window closes, then I hear locks turn and chains rattle. The hair on the back of my neck rises. That's a lot of security for a building on a street lined with upscale shops. Any one of the places surrounding here would fetch a thief a small fortune, and they're protected by easily breakable glass. What could be behind this door?

When it opens, I only see a sitting room. I stay close to Brevan, my hip brushing against him in my attempt to remain near the door. I move quickly, not wanting to be so close to him.

Three couches sit in a horseshoe shape, and a small table is positioned at the center of them. Off to the side is a counter lined with bottles of alcohol and expensive glassware.

A small, hunched old man with circular spectacles and thin white hair smiles at us. Next to him is a large man in simple leather armor. His blue eyes were the ones that looked out at us through the window. His hand rests on a sword at his hip, and he stays focused on Brevan, ignoring me completely. Clearly, I'm not seen as a threat.

"Is this the woman I was told about?" the old man asks. He's got a warm smile, but I don't find it comforting. At least, not right now. I can't figure out what is happening.

"Yes, Prince Caiden sends his regrets that he could not attend himself. There were issues at the port that required his personal attention," Brevan says.

The port? My brow furrows. That's more information than I received earlier.

"It's getting worse, isn't it? Every year, those pirates take more." The old man shakes his head.

"I'm sure His Highness will sort things out," Brevan says.

"Yes, he is his father's son, after all." The old man gestures toward the couches. "Please sit. I'll return in a moment with the items." He shuffles away, and the large man, who I can only guess is security, stands near the door staring at us.

"What is going on?" I whisper to Brevan.

"Have a seat, Your Highness."

"No."

"Please, sit," he says.

"You sit."

"I am not the client, you are," he says.

"The client for what?" My words come out loud enough this time that the guard glances over at me. He lifts an annoyed brow.

"It took me a while to find something that met the prince's specifications, but I think you'll be pleased with what I procured," the old man says as he walks back into the room. He's holding a long flat box and stops when he sees us both standing there. "Is there something wrong?"

"No, of course not," Brevan answers for me.

"I was insisting that the enforcer have a seat first," I say.

"Is that customary in Iskvaland?" the old man asks.

"Well, women don't often share a space with so many men, but it seems that since I've arrived, that's all I do." I cross my arms.

The guard coughs, and the old man's eyes widen.

"She means that she is not used to being escorted by a man. They keep the women very isolated in her empire. But the prince wanted discretion for this visit. I'm sure you understand why he didn't want her ladies to know what she was doing."

"That is customary until the new ladies prove their loyalty. I still remember the scandal over that stolen crown a few years ago. That was some of my best work. It's a shame we never recovered it." The old man sets the box on the table, then removes the lid. "These are by far the most elaborate pieces I've ever procured. And on such short notice, too. They will be expensive, but the prince did say nothing is too good for his future empress."

My jaw opens, and I can't help but stare at the glittering diamonds and jewels laid out in the box. The loose gems are lined up in order of size and color. The others are arranged into necklaces or bracelets or set as earrings or rings.

I've never seen anything like it. I didn't even know gemstones could be so large or so dazzling.

"Will you sit now?" Brevan asks.

"Please, Your Highness." The old man settles on a couch, then gestures to the one next to him.

I walk over to it and take a seat, still stunned by the wealth and beauty of the display. Guilt creeps in as I find myself drawn to the jewels, imagining what it might feel like to touch them. To wear them. I've never seen anything so beautiful.

"His Highness sent me a message last night explaining how it's customary in your empire for a man to gift his wife-to-be jewelry once the betrothal is finalized," the old man says. "He sends his apologies that this wasn't done before and expressed that he wishes you to choose anything you'd like as his gift to you."

"You must have really impressed him last night," Brevan says.

I ignore him and turn my attention to the shopkeeper. "Can you do something simple? Does it have to be so large?"

"You can choose something from this selection, or I can

create a piece based on your specifications. Anything you can imagine," he says.

I point to a blue stone the size of my thumbnail. It's not the smallest stone, but it's large enough that it would make a statement. "I like this one. Can you do something with it for me?"

"Just that stone, Your Highness?" he asks.

"Yes."

"Of course." He inclines his head. "We must save some for the wedding. That's when you must truly shine."

I smile. There is no way I'll still be here by the time the wedding takes place.

"Is there anything else you desire?" he asks. "Can I make you earrings to match?"

"You should," Brevan says. "I think she's trying to be modest. But we both know the prince will be insulted if she doesn't get something larger."

"How about a set then? I'll create something beautiful and one of a kind. Something worthy of our stunning new empress-to-be."

"Thank you," I manage.

"Of course. Please tell the prince I am ever grateful for his patronage." The old man bows.

I stand. "I'd like to return. I'm still recovering from my journey."

The men walk me to the door, then Brevan helps me into the carriage. I feel sick as we ride back to the castle. I knew the wealthy had it better than everyone else, but I'd never seen it up close before. It was like an entirely different world. And none of them ever had to leave their part of the city. They didn't even know what it was like for everyone else. If they saw it, would it change anything? Would they even care? No wonder they allowed the emperor to continue with his raids and destruction. They had everything their hearts could ever desire.

"Did you grow up around here?" I ask Brevan.

"No."

"I thought all the emperor's legionnaires were from the noble families," I reply.

"Most of them are," he agrees.

"So you grew up a commoner?"

"I did, but not in Pendralia," he says.

Fear courses through my veins. Is that how he knows so much about Iskvaland? Is he Iskvalandian? If so, it is a matter of time before I say something that gives me away. I choose my next words very carefully. "Are you from my kingdom?"

"No. But it doesn't matter where I'm from. I was rescued by a Pendralian naval ship after the ship I was on was attacked. From that day on, I was Pendralian."

"I see. How old were you?"

"Eleven," he says.

I turn to the window while I blink away the threatening tears. I know what it's like to lose your family. And the people who saved his life destroyed mine.

Seven

MY ROOMS ARE quiet when I crack open the door, though all the ladies are present. Two of them are reading on the window seat, three are doing embroidery on the couches near the fireplace, and a pair have pulled a second chair to my writing desk and are playing cards. Marian is in the corner speaking to a woman I don't know.

As soon as I widen the gap enough to step inside, the women jump to their feet and drop into low curtsies. It's the most formal greeting I've seen from them, and it makes me take a step back.

"Your Highness." Marian rises from her curtsy, then walks toward me, the other woman following behind her.

The newcomer didn't curtsy, and though all the gowns on my ladies are elegant, she's dripping in pearls and sparkling diamonds. I probably am supposed to bow to her.

"Princess Sabina, this is Duchess Drathmore. She's the late empress's mother."

I incline my head, completely unsure of what I'm supposed to do. In my brief overview about being a royal, I was told to act the part and make sure I curtsy to the emperor. That's about as much as I know, and I'm realizing it is not enough if I want to keep this charade going. "It's lovely to meet you."

"The pleasure is all mine," she says as she moves closer to me. "They were right. You are quite beautiful. You and the prince will have gorgeous children. My daughter would have been pleased. She always wanted to be a grandmother."

The whole conversation is odd considering this woman, the prince's grandmother, doesn't look like she's much older than Marian. The emperor is said to be immortal, but when his wife of over a century died, it gave the rebellion hope. If he couldn't keep his bride alive, surely it means the magic isn't infallible.

But if that is the case, how does this woman appear so young? Was she even older than the emperor? Were all the nobles immortal?

"I'm sorry I wasn't able to meet her. I am terribly sorry for your loss." I do my best to appear sympathetic while contemplating how I could overcome the magic that keeps them alive.

"You honor her by bringing peace to our empire. It was her dream to see a time without war. I hear there's already a truce at the frontline. That for the first time in sixty years, there's no fighting at the border." She smiles.

"That's good news."

"Quite. Now, Marian, who did my grandson hire to dress her for the Darkfall ball?" the duchess asks.

My brow furrows. "Darkfall ball?"

"Every five years when the moons retreat, we hold a

celebration," Marian says. "Did they not have this in Iskvaland?"

Most of the year, both our moons are visible, but for part of the year, we get one or the other. Once every five years, they both vanish from the sky for two weeks. Growing up, it was a time to lock your doors and be inside before sunset. We left offerings of food near our home for any creatures that might pass through the veil. Extra firewood was gathered in advance to keep the fire burning all night.

I can only remember going through it once with both of my parents. Before I moved from our home in the mountains to the city where my life changed forever.

Our first Darkfall after my father's death was spent in a rebellion safehouse. My mother tried to continue some of the traditions from our old life, but there was always so much work to do. Even so, there was joy. It was the first time I saw her smile again. I could almost see my brothers around our modest fire. Felix had just started leading his own missions, Arthur always by his side. My mother was so proud. That was about the time I started helping with maps and documents.

Last Darkfall I spent most of my time with Lee, but I don't want to think about that, either.

I blink away the memories. "It's a little different where I come from."

"That's because the Iskvalandians are superstitious and fearful of the dark," a male voice says. "I hope I'm not interrupting anything."

"What an unexpected surprise." I smile at Caiden as he walks into the room.

The duchess's whole expression softens, and she greets her grandson with a hug. "Don't you look handsome."

"It's nice to see you, Grandmother," he says.

"Your bride is very beautiful." She glances my way. "You're lucky. I've met my share of homely girls from Iskvaland."

It's both an insult against Iskvaland and praise for me. "You're very kind."

She hums, not removing her gaze from me. I think she expected me to react differently.

"What are you doing here?" he asks, ignoring her remarks.

"I arrived back in the city two days ago, and you had yet to call upon me."

I'm grateful her attention is no longer on me.

"I've been busy." Caiden picks a piece of lint from his sleeve.

"Yes, so I hear. Running an empire? Nobody has seen your father in three years," she says. "There are rumors. None of them good. They make you look weak."

"I am not weak. And father is currently overseeing some important operations for us," he says. "Plenty of people have seen him and those who haven't aren't important enough to merit a visit."

The older woman purses her lips. "I remember when there were still manners in this court."

"Do us all a favor, darling grandmother, and tell me why you're really here? Is it to see my father or to spy on my bride-to-be?" He's smirking, as if he's amused by her.

She lifts a finger and wags it at him as if she were scolding a child. "You should have invited me to meet her. I should not have had to make the trip myself, unannounced at that. Like I'm unimportant. I may no longer be the mother of the empress, but I am the grandmother of the future emperor."

He catches her finger, then clasps her hand in his. "I know. And tradition says I was not to show her off until she'd been formally introduced to the court. Which she will be in a few days. Until then, she's not even supposed to have visitors or leave the castle."

"Rules that you've already broken." She rests her hand on her hips. "Jacques was my jeweler first, you know."

"And he's got a big mouth." Caiden tenses his jaw.

"Don't be too hard on him. He only told me."

Caiden looks over at me, then scans the room, as if noticing his audience for the first time. The ladies all gasp and hurriedly drop into curtsies.

"I asked Perla to come." The duchess folds her hands in front of her.

"I already have another seamstress scheduled," he says.

"Cancel. Perla dressed your mother. She should dress the future empress as well." The duchess pats his cheek, and Caiden flinches.

He sighs. "Fine. But you need to leave her be until she's been introduced to the court. There's too much gossip already."

"Alright," the duchess agrees. She turns to me. "It was nice to meet you, darling. I will send an invitation for tea as soon as my grandson removes your restrictions."

"That sounds nice, thank you," I say.

Caiden stares at the ladies until they scurry away before facing me. "Princess, I stopped by to apologize for not taking you myself today and to formally invite you to dinner."

"Of course, Your Highness," I reply.

He nods, then escorts his grandmother from the room.

After a few minutes of staring at the closed door, I let out a breath, and it feels like everyone follows suit. I look around at the ladies, all of their hobbies abandoned. "Were you all putting on a show for the duchess?"

"She's a very traditional woman." Marian smooths the fabric of her skirts.

"And powerful," Charlotte adds. "My mother once told me she had more sway over the emperor than the empress herself."

"You don't want to cross her," Marian warns.

"I heard the empress displeased her mother, and that's why she—"

"Katherine!" Marian cuts in.

Katherine snaps her mouth closed then looks away, her face pink.

"What do you mean? Are you saying the Dutchess had something to do with the empress's death?" I scan the faces around me.

"Of course not." Antonia picks up her abandoned embroidery and drops into a chair. "She's not a royal and with her daughter dead, her only tie to the crown is her grandson. Don't let them get to you."

"Who wants to play cards?" Katherine blurts.

"I'll play." I might not have been out in the field for the rebellion, but my brothers sure learned a lot of information during card games over the years. And whatever these ladies know, I am going to find out.

Katherine, Charlotte, and Antonia join me at the dining table. The others go back to their reading or embroidery, and Marian tells us she has to check about the seamstress.

As we play simple games, the ladies talk. They share gossip about their families and speculate on who is pregnant or who might be the next to be engaged. I listen, hoping to hear something I can use.

"June says her brother is going to visit the temple during Darkfall," Charlotte says.

"Jamison? I thought he wasn't going to be a legionnaire," Antonia says.

"He's not. She said he got a position with someone important enough that they petitioned for him to get magic," Charlotte explains as she plays a card.

I straighten.

"He's not from an important enough family," Antonia says.

"Most of the favored families sent their sons in the last Darkfall," Charlotte says. "There are fewer to go through this time."

"That's true," Katherine draws a card, "I heard there were a few families who were afraid to send their sons after the accident last Darkfall."

"What accident?" I can't help but ask.

"At the temple," Katherine says. "One of the men they sent to meet the gods died. It was like the gods found him so unworthy of magic that they killed him."

"I heard it was because his mother slept with a commoner," Antonia whispers. "She was barely a noble herself. Not enough god's blood in him to withstand the gift."

"What do you mean?" I ask.

"Oh, that's right, you don't have magic in Iskvaland," Charlotte says.

"No, we don't."

"It's the gifting ceremony." Charlotte leans forward and lowers her voice, as if this is a secret. "Once every five years, during Darkfall, the temple doors open and anyone the emperor deems worthy is sent to speak to the gods. They ask for magic and are granted powers."

"Most of the time," Antonia adds. "Or they die."

"That only happened once. Everyone else lived." Katherine takes a card from the pile in the center.

"I thought the emperor gave them their magic," I say.

"The emperor chooses, but the gods have the power." Charlotte kisses her palm and then touches her chest in reverence. The other girls repeat the motion. It's a symbol I've never seen before, but I can guess what it means, and I follow along, not wanting to raise suspicion.

"I thought he gave all the Night Legion their shadow magic." I place a card on the table.

"It's sort of the other way around," Katherine says. "It's the most common gift, and if that's what they end up with, they have to join the legion if they weren't already planning to."

"What if someone doesn't get shadow magic?" I ask.

"Then the emperor finds something else for them to do. But it's very rare," Katherine explains.

"Like the enforcer," Charlotte says. "I'm not sure what he got exactly, but it's not shadow magic."

"Whatever it is, he can use it on me any day." Katherine winks.

Charlotte giggles.

"In front of a princess?" Antonia gasps.

"Really, don't mind me. I grew up with..." I almost mention my brothers. But the princess of Iskvaland is an only child. "What other kinds of magic are there?"

"Well, there's a few people who have elemental magic." Katherine taps on the table as she says each element. "Fire, wind, water, you know. They do special things for the emperor,"

"We're not really permitted to know." Antonia adjusts her chair, pulling herself in closer before playing a card. "Women aren't allowed in the temple."

"That's not true," Charlotte says. "The empress was."

"That's right. She went in. Just before giving birth. I remember hearing the story." Antonia turns to me. "I wonder if they'll send you this Darkfall? You'll probably be with child by the next one. They'll want you to have any extra strength before then."

My mouth goes dry. "What exactly happens in the temple?"

"The gods measure your worthiness and appoint you magic in correlation to it," Antonia explains confidently. "I'm sure you'll get something amazing. With a mother and father from two opposing kingdoms who united all of Iskvaland with their marriage, I'm sure your blood is going to please the gods."

"They've never sent anyone who isn't Pendralian." Charlotte sets her hand on mine. "I don't think you need to worry about it. And I heard they only sent the empress because she was ill."

"That's right," Katherine says. "They thought she might lose the baby, the emperor's heir."

"I forgot about that. I remember hearing the story from my grandmother. She said everyone was so worried." Antonia looks over at me. "She was very old by the time she first fell pregnant. Everyone had started to discuss who would become the next emperor if she never birthed a child."

"Was she trying for immortality like the emperor?" I ask.

"I'm not sure, but I think so since she was empress for so long." Antonia sets down a card. "But I think they must have let her mother gain that gift also. So maybe all the royal family gets immortality?"

"Perhaps that's what the prince has. Maybe he'll live forever like his father." Charlotte shrugs. "Maybe you will, too."

I swallow hard. I'm not sure I want to live forever. Especially if it means living with Caiden as my husband under the emperor's rule.

"Maybe that's the gift he received when his mother went." Antonia shrugs.

"She was pregnant with Caiden in the temple. He's her only pregnancy, her only child," I say to confirm.

The ladies nod.

"It's why people expected something unusual from him." Katherine reaches across the table to pull a card from the pile.

"I've never even heard of him using magic," Charlotte says. "And he never visited the temple, did he?"

"He did," Antonia confirms. "He was a child, though. Probably twenty years ago."

That would have made him very young. Six, maybe. I knew he wasn't much older than me. "What happened?"

She shrugs. "I'm not sure. But Charlotte's right. I don't think anyone has seen him use magic."

"That doesn't mean he isn't hiding something impressive." Antonia plays a card. "He's just not flashy about it."

"That's possible." Katherine glances toward the doorway. "I've never seen the enforcer use his magic, either, but we know it's powerful."

"What exactly does he do?" I move around some of the cards in my hand so I can see them better.

"We know he can use his magic to find the relics of the gods, but there's definitely more to it. I hope there's some shadow magic in there. I was with a legionnaire once who used his shadows in very creative ways..."

"Katherine!" Antonia scolds.

"What?" Katherine smiles at me. "I hope the prince has something useful for you. I hope he's not as formal and cold as he seems."

"This is too far. You can't talk about the future emperor that way!" Antonia's face is red.

"Who else am I going to talk about this with?" I ask her. "You're all loyal to me, aren't you?"

"Well, of course we are," Antonia replies quickly.

I notice the twitch in her eye and wonder who she's reporting to. Is she in the prince's pocket? Or is it just

Marian who is in the emperor's pocket? Or are they in someone else's? The rebels' pocket, even? All I know is that I can't trust her, or any of my ladies.

Eight

Even in the low, flickering light, I can see the injuries. The prince has a purple bruise under his right eye and a large cut down his left cheek. His lips look a little swollen, like he was punched in the jaw.

What could have happened in the last few hours to cause all that? Who was he brawling with? For a brief moment, I wonder if there's someone here who might be on my side.

"You look beautiful. The Pendralian colors really suit you." His gaze drops, taking in the gorgeous steel gray dress that's tied with black silk ribbons.

I hold up the skirts. "It is a beautiful dress, but I do miss my old things. And I miss color."

"My father and his monochromatic obsession." He shakes his head. "Though, it does make quite the statement when we visit other kingdoms. So perhaps I can see why he chose to establish that rule."

Caiden pulls out my chair for me. My stomach churns. I hate being so close to him.

"Thank you," I say as I take a seat.

He pushes my chair in, then makes himself comfortable at the head of the table. There's already wine in the glasses, and as soon as he sips his, I take a large gulp from mine.

"How do you find your ladies?" he asks.

"They're really wonderful," I say. "I enjoy their company."

"Good." He takes another sip of his wine, and I catch a fleeting wince as he sets his cup down. He's got other injuries that I can't see.

I want to ask him about them, but I'm not sure if that's considered impolite. Instead, I focus on my goal. I need to know where the emperor is. Especially if I'm going to have to run from the castle before Darkfall.

"Were you with your father today?" I ask.

"No. But I was attending to some of the matters he should have settled." He gestures to his face. "As you can see, it did not go well."

"What happened?"

"I'd rather not discuss it," he says.

"Why is your father putting you in such dangerous situations?" I ask. "You're his heir. He needs you alive."

"Thank you for your concern for my health," he says.

Now I'm wincing. "I'm sorry. I just don't understand. I know sometimes kings and emperors fight their own wars. Princes, too. But I keep hearing whispers..." I shake my head. "Never mind. It's not my place."

"What whispers?"

I force myself to look hesitant, and he gives an encouraging nod. I sigh, as if reluctant to share. "I've heard rumors that your father is dead. Or dying. That you are secretly already emperor."

His expression darkens.

"It's only that I thought there would be many years of learning before I had to step into the role of empress. If I'm being honest, I need more time. I'm afraid." It takes everything I have to not roll my eyes.

"I can assure you, my father is very much alive. Even if he's making me do his job right now." He sounds frustrated, but honest.

"That's good. That he's alive, I mean." I wish I didn't believe him. If the emperor were dead, I could end this now. Kill the prince. Kill the enforcer. It would mean my own death, but it would be worth it to end their line and cause chaos as the nobles fight over who should rule.

Servants enter through the secret door, and I sit in silence as they add food to my plate. A roast with rich gravy, honey-glazed carrots, and creamy potatoes. My mouth waters at the scents, but I wait for Caiden to eat first.

He takes a few bites, then I pick up my fork and try the food. I close my eyes to collect myself. I didn't know food could taste this good. During our first dinner, I was so stressed, I hardly tasted anything.

"They want to move up the wedding," he says.

I open my eyes and find him staring at me, waiting for my response. "What do you mean?" Traditionally, royal weddings are held in autumn, and we just entered winter. I should have nearly a year to figure out what I need and get out of here.

"The high priest had a vision. Said we must wed at the summer solstice."

"What kind of vision requires that?" I ask.

"He wouldn't elaborate," he says.

I swallow hard. It's less time, but that might not matter, anyway. Not if they intend to send me to the temple on Darkfall.

"I'm not exactly thrilled about it, either," he says. "You're beautiful and smarter than I expected. But let's not pretend either of us wants to wed the other. I know it's our obligation. We both know we have to do this and that we'll need to provide an heir. Once that has occurred, you'll have more freedom around here. More status."

The thought of bedding this man makes my skin crawl. That will absolutely not be happening. But I'm Sabina, not Taylan, so I respond as I think she might. "Of course."

"I need you to learn our customs, to become familiar with my court. I've scheduled your formal introduction for this weekend. My mother's seamstress will be here tomorrow to craft you a new gown. Your ladies can help you prepare. I assume you know how to dance?"

No, there wasn't a lot of dancing in our village or in the city once we joined the rebellion. And certainly nothing that would fit in at court. "I'm afraid the dances I learned might not be the same fashion as here."

"Very well." He takes a deep breath, then blows it out. "I would ask Brevan to teach you, but he's away. I suppose I'll have to do it myself."

"I'm sure one of my ladies can help," I say.

"No, it won't do for them to know you have weaknesses."

I lift a skeptical brow. "Not being able to dance is a weakness?"

"It will make it appear that you were not trained well enough to be my bride. There are many unhappy families in my court. They've been sending their daughters to seduce me for years. Until the treaty, it was assumed I'd marry one of them."

"Like your father did," I say.

He nods. "Yes. My mother was a courtier who caught his eye."

"Is it me you worry for or yourself, Your Highness? I imagine a group of former lovers who were hoping to be your empress are far more of a threat to you than they are to me."

"Not if they think they can bolster their chances by killing you," he says with a shrug.

"And risk losing the treaty? I would think they'd be ostracized from court if they did such a thing."

"If they were caught." There's a hint of a smirk on his lips. Is he actually being playful or did I imagine it?

"I suppose I better learn to dance."

"If not out of concern for yourself, you'll learn to dance so you make me look good," he says. "I can't have a future empress who doesn't improve my status."

I must have been mistaken when I though he was being playful. "So the other women might not be my only threat?"

"This treaty is important, but there are other ways to make it happen."

"I suppose you're lucky my father had a daughter. Where would your treaty be now if I'd been a man?"

"If you'd been a man, I'd be working on a plan to overthrow your kingdom." He grins.

"Why not just do that, then? Why this route? Why now? We've never been allies before. Your people have been at my borders my whole life. If you were going to overthrow us, you'd have done it already."

"You forget, my father has been the one giving the orders. He's cautious, but also shortsighted. We're outnumbered, that's true. I believe that with time and planning, we could defeat Iskvaland. But he doesn't want to wait. He wants the Shatterlands now."

"He's not well, is he?" I ask quietly. "You're already running most of the empire, aren't you?"

He clenches his jaw, and a vein in his temple bulges. I see the wariness on his face now. It is almost hidden by the bruises, but it's there. Dark circles under eyes that have seen too much. I almost didn't see them with the other injuries on his face.

"This treaty is yours. You want Iskvaland's armies," I say. "Your father would never share magic with anyone outside his inner circle, but you found a way. You don't need him, do you? Is it the relics that Brevan's hunting?"

We've been wondering about that for years. Some rebels theorized that the ancient relics of the gods could channel magic or even imbue magic. Nobody ever got to test it out, though. The Night Legion was very good at tracking the relics down. They must do something. Otherwise, why would they destroy whole villages just to claim the forgotten or hidden relics?

"That's enough, Sabina." He rises. "When you finish your meal, the legionnaires waiting at the door will escort you to your room. Marian will stay with you every night.

You are not to leave your chambers unescorted, is that understood?"

I pushed too far. I am supposed to be a princess. His future wife. I'm supposed to submit, but I can't. I glare at him. "Nothing good has ever come from rulers who put ambition before their people."

"Tell your father that. He's the one who came to me on his knees, willing to trade his kingdom for immortality."

I blink, then close my mouth. I should have known. All rulers want nothing more than power, and they don't care who they sacrifice to gain it.

"I will see you tomorrow. Do try to learn your place before then." He walks out of the room without a glance back at me.

I grip my fork so tight my knuckles turn white. I'm furious at the games these monarchs play with the lives of everyone around them. Magic in the Iskvalandian armies will mean more oppression for their people. The right people never seem to gain power.

But at least now I know that the emperor isn't well. If he's not dying, something else is very, very wrong with him. If he's not well, he can't be far from the castle. There's no way they'd want that information out there.

He's in the castle. He has to be. And that means he'll be much easier to kill once I find out where exactly they've hidden him.

NINE

THE DRAWING ROOM is a large space with windows lining an entire wall, filling the space with gray winter light. Gilded mirrors hang on the opposite wall, intensifying the effect. A piano sits in a corner, a large harp next to it. Several string instruments are on the ground nearby, as if abandoned.

The other walls are lined with oil paintings of musicians playing instruments. They're dark and moody, using dark colors that cast shadows on most of the faces. It's at odds with the light in the room. As if two opposing styles were used when decorating.

"Thank you for delivering the princess," Caiden says to the lingering legionnaires who escorted me from my rooms. They bow to their prince, then leave me alone with him.

"Four?" I ask as soon as the door closes. He sent four men to escort me, and two others stayed behind to watch my door. "Is there something you're not telling me?"

"No. I'm simply protecting my investment," he says.

"Brevan is still away?" I ask.

"Yes."

"Why?"

"That is not your concern," he says.

"It is when he was sufficient to guard me by himself and since he left, I now need an entire legion to myself to keep me safe." I set my hands on my hips while I study his reaction.

His expression doesn't change. He's very good at hiding whatever he's feeling. "Six men is hardly a legion, but yes, Brevan is worth at least six by himself. So you do need more if he's not around."

I want him here so I can figure out how to take him down, but I suppose I could settle for him dying by someone else's hand. "I hope wherever he is, he's not in too much danger."

"I wouldn't worry about him," Caiden says. "He's faced death more times than anyone I know, and he always comes out laughing."

"That's an interesting way to describe someone who spends his time wiping out villages and killing innocents." The words are out before I realize what I've said, and I press my lips together to keep myself from saying more.

"You've been asking questions, I see." He makes an amused sound. "Or perhaps you learned more about my court than I realized before they sent you here."

"Of course I learned about your court," I say to cover my slipup.

"Did you also learn that those villages were conspiring against their emperor?" he asks. "Trying to revive ancient blood magic that could destroy all of us?"

"My education must have left that part out." I cross my arms.

"For someone who watched her own father experiment on his people to try to recreate the magic we have here, you sure pass a lot of judgement."

"Maybe I judge that, too," I say.

"You're naive, but you'll learn," he says. "You either show your people who is in charge and protect your power at all costs, or you lose it."

"I think there must be other ways."

"That's because you're a woman. You're meant to be soft. Weak. Loyal and emotional. You're meant to remind me of my humanity, but you would never have the ability to rule. You'd be crushed by a rebellion before your first year on the throne."

Rage burns in my chest, and I'm so hot that my skin feels like it's on fire. Maybe I should just kill him and hope the others can get to the emperor. Rid the world of at least one monster.

"I upset you." He's failing to hide his smirk.

"You underestimate me," I reply.

"You don't have to pretend you're strong. If I wanted a woman who might kill me in my sleep, I'd have found a bride from the Shatterlands."

Now I'm trying to hide my smirk. Because why hadn't I thought of killing him in his sleep? "Is that why you need my father's army? To fight against the women of the Shatterlands?"

"No. I could take them with my men, but I'd rather not risk my legions when I can sacrifice yours."

"What makes you think our armies won't turn against you once you give them magic?" I ask.

He grins, then extends his arm toward me, hand closed into a fist. When he opens his hand, flames rise from his palm, dancing and flickering.

I'm several feet away from him, but the temperature rises. Blue tongues blaze in the center of each flame. My jaw opens, and my eyes widen in surprise.

Shadows fill the room, obscuring all the windows. The only light is from the flames that still burn in his outstretched hand.

My mouth goes dry, and for the first time since I arrived, I'm afraid. I came here knowing I wasn't likely to walk away, but I thought I'd take the prince and the emperor with me.

Suddenly, the flames go out, and we're plunged into darkness. Something tightens around my waist, then around my legs and arms, binding me. I gasp, but my breath is stolen as my mouth is covered by something cold. I fight against the invisible bonds, and I fall to the ground in my struggles.

Light returns from the windows, and Caiden is looking down at me, a malicious grin on his lips. Shadows flow around him and slither across the floor. That's what's holding me in place. I'm bound by dark wisps of shadow. They're getting tighter, constricting me, making it harder to breathe.

"First of all, if they try to defy me, I do hold something dear of theirs. You didn't honestly think you were just here as the assurance of the treaty? You're here because if your father or his armies cross me, I will kill you. You're his only heir. Your people adore you. I did my research, too, Princess."

The pressure around my ribs and stomach is so tight I can't suck in air. Tears stream down my cheeks, and my vision blurs.

"So while we will give your father's armies the same simple shadow magic we give our Night Legion, it isn't true power. They can cast shadows. Obscure the light. It's parlor tricks. Very few in our ranks can wield corporeal shadows. And none of them have more than one kind of magic." He opens his hand, then as he closes it, he twirls his fingers. The binds around me tighten, and I scream against my restraints.

"But what the gods gave me is real. And I can do this to an entire army if I need to." He crouches down in front of me. "Do you understand?"

I'm afraid of him. Real, true fear. Is this why nobody can get to the emperor? I knew they had magic, but I didn't know it was like this. Nobody in the rebellion knows.

He grips my chin and lifts it so I'm looking up at him. "You will know your place, and you will play your role. Do you understand?"

I nod.

"Good girl." He releases my chin, then the shadows ease and I roll to my stomach, resting my forehead against the cool stone floor, gasping for breath.

"Collect yourself so I can show you how to dance properly," he says. "I can't have you embarrassing me."

As I catch my breath, something else rises alongside the fear. Rage. Pure and hot. It doesn't matter if I'm afraid. It just means I have to change my tactics.

He doesn't realize it, but he's told me exactly how to beat him.

I sit up, careful to keep my expression neutral, then extend my hand. With a smile, he helps me up. I smooth my skirts and take my time making sure everything is in its correct place. When I'm finished, I lift my chin and stare at him defiantly.

"Shall we?" He points to the abandoned string instruments; they rise into the air and begin to play. He offers his hand, palm up.

I set my palm in his, my skin prickling with unease at the contact. I want nothing more than to watch him take his last breaths.

He guides me to position, then begins to move his feet to the rhythm of the music. I follow along as best I can, stumbling frequently.

He mutters a few corrections, and I listen and adjust. I learn quickly. I fake a smile. I memorize the steps, following him. Thankfully, it's not a difficult dance and it's not much different than the dancing we did growing up. Ours was with a group in a circle, this is with one other person. The similarities help me get the steps more easily.

When the music stops, I curtsy to him. As soon as I rise, he grabs my chin again. "It's nice to know you can be taught."

I smile. "Give me some time to learn what you like and how things work in your court. I think you'll be surprised by all I can accomplish."

"That's what I want to hear," he says. "I don't think you need another lesson. You'll stay in your rooms until the dinner. I can't have anyone in my court getting a look at you before you're officially introduced."

"Of course, Your Highness."

He hums, then marches to the door and opens it. "Take the princess to her rooms. Nobody in or out without my permission. Understood?"

As I walk between the legionnaires, I can't help but smile to myself. I got under his skin. He wants me to think him powerful because he worries he's not seen that way. There's an insecurity there. A weakness.

And it's my job to exploit it.

TEN

SIX NIGHT LEGIONNAIRES stand outside my room, and Marian never leaves me alone. I need to see where that tunnel leads, and I need to learn more about the emperor, but I'm stuck. I don't even get to leave for meals.

Caiden wasn't kidding when he said he didn't want me to be seen until they introduced me to the court. Frustrated, I pace my rooms while Charlotte and Katherine embroider flowers in front of the fireplace.

I peer out the window and watch the gardeners pruning the topiaries. The sky is gray, and the glass is frosted in places. We'll have snow soon.

I've never been more bored in my life.

After four agonizing days of small talk and rereading all the botany books, there's a knock on my door. I practically jump out of my skin in my hurry to answer.

"I will get it, Your Highness," Marian says.

I sigh, then wait. The other ladies abandoned their embroidery and are staring expectantly at the door. They've been isolated nearly as much as me lately.

"Lord Maxwell, welcome home," Marian says. "I heard you returned to the castle last night."

Brevan steps into the room and finds me immediately. "I was sent to escort the princess to meet with the prince."

I set down the fabric with my terrible attempt at embroidering roses and stand. "I thought I wasn't to leave my room until the dinner."

"Do you need a moment, or are you ready now?" he asks.

I stride toward the door. "I'm ready."

He doesn't even look at me as we walk down the hall. There's an odd stiffness to him. "Were you injured?" I ask.

"No."

"You seem angry."

"I'm not angry."

"Where were you?"

He glances over at me. "I didn't realize you missed my company so much."

"I didn't. I'm bored and perhaps you can entertain me," I say.

"My work for the prince is not your entertainment," he replies.

"I thought you reported to the emperor?"

"I work for the empire," he clarifies.

"How convenient," I say.

He stops walking. "How is that convenient?"

"Because nobody's seen the emperor." I know I'm pressing my luck. The prince warned me, but I have a feeling Brevan doesn't share everything with Caiden. I'm not even sure if the two actually like each other.

"That's not true." He starts walking again.

"Oh, so you visit with him. Is it just you and Caiden, then? Everyone else is restricted?"

"Perhaps everyone else sees him except you. How would you know while locked away in your room?"

He's got me there. But I've heard enough comments under hushed breaths from my ladies to get a sense that even they are worried about the emperor.

"Will he be at this dinner that introduces me to the court?" I ask.

"I don't know."

"Do you know anything?" I ask. "Or do you just blindly follow orders?"

"You really don't know how to shut up, do you?"

I swallow hard, recalling the intensity of those shadows tightening around me.

Brevan's brow furrows slightly. "Are you alright, Your Highness?"

I force a smile. "Fine. I'm fine. Just bored."

"Must be a challenging life," he says. "Sitting around gossiping and choosing which fabric to make your next gown with."

"Did you choose your life, Brevan?" I ask.

"I told you. They found me after the ship I was on was attacked."

"And now, you're here. Following orders. It must be hard polishing your sword and choosing which armor to wear. Making sure your hair looks just messy enough to let us know you don't care how you look."

There's a hint of a smirk. "Maybe I'll stop by and ask you for some beauty tips one day."

"I'm sure my ladies would enjoy that. They—" I stop

walking, realizing we're back in the lower levels of the castle. Probably close to where I first met the prince. "Where exactly are we?"

"I think I'll let the prince explain everything." He guides us through two more turns until we're in front of a large wood door with heavy iron bars on the small window.

"What is this?" I ask.

He pounds on the door, and a pair of eyes peer out, then vanish. There's the sound of keys in locks, then chains rattling. For a moment, I wonder if they've finally brought me to the emperor. What if the prince has him locked up? What if the whole missing emperor mystery was the result of a coup because the prince didn't know how to kill his immortal father?

When the door opens, a man in all black, wearing a hood that covers most of his face, gestures for us to enter.

Or maybe they found out who I really am and they're throwing me in here.

Caiden is standing in a darkened hall, illuminated by a single torch flickering on the stone wall.

"What's going on?" I ask.

"I have a favor to ask of you." His face is devoid of emotion, eyes empty. It's chilling.

He offers his elbow, and I reluctantly take it. My heart hammers against my ribs. As he guides me down the hall, I'm hoping I'm not walking to my own death.

We pass by a large open room lined with torches. Several tables are covered in dark stains. Chains hang on the walls along with a variety of knives, clamps, and other tools. The scents of human excrement and death hang around us.

Caiden doesn't so much as flinch. I hold my breath until we pass the room.

There's a series of cells next. Each one lined with iron bars. Most of the prisoners have a floor covered in hay and trembling people cowering in the back corners. Not one approaches or says anything.

Finally, we stop in front of a cell where the prisoner looks less broken. His clothing isn't as shredded. While bloodstained and dirty, it's not in as bad a state as that of the other prisoners. His fair hair hangs in greasy strands, and he's got the start of a beard. He's been here a while, but not as long as the others.

"Come to gloat?" he asks.

"I think you know my bride-to-be," Caiden says.

The man turns his bright blue eyes on me. He's Iskvalandian. My mind races, and ice runs through my veins. He's going to know. He's going to tell them I'm an impostor.

"Princess, nice to see you again," the man says.

I keep my mouth shut. This is a trap.

"Can you tell me exactly why this man is here?" Caiden gives me a look that's pure warning. There's danger simmering in his expression. "He says he was traveling with you and got separated. But why would he be alone, on horseback, with all the supplies he needed while you were already safely in my castle?"

My heart races and I struggle to come up with a response that won't implicate me. I turn to the man behind bars as if he'll give me an answer. He's watching me, as if waiting for me to take the lead.

"Go ahead, Sabina. You can tell me," Caiden coaxes

with a gentleness I know he's not actually capable of. His brow is slightly furrowed as if he's concerned. The way he changes tactics so quickly is masterful.

I look up at the prince, then back at the man. His face is just as blank as the prince's. But it's not cold. It's just observant. Patient.

"I'm actually not sure who he is." I take a step closer, removing my hand from Caiden's elbow. "You say we've met?"

"I've known you since you were a child, Princess," he says.

"There are a lot of people who have known me since I was a child," I say. "I was surrounded by people constantly. That doesn't mean I know them."

"How very interesting," Caiden says. "One of you is lying. The question is, which one?"

"I'm telling you the truth. I am an ambassador sent with the princess. We were attacked and got separated. I thought she was dead."

I might kill this man myself if he keeps talking. "If that were true, it would mean you failed at your job. And that you continued to travel around Pendralia looking for a dead woman."

"I had to know if you were alive or not," he says. "Just tell him I'm not a spy so I can return to your father. He'll want to know you made it safely."

"I don't remember you," I say, sticking to my story.

"Don't you think my bride would have told me if she'd been attacked?" Caiden places a possessive hand on my lower back, then looks at me.

"I was never attacked. I don't know what he wants with

me," I'm careful to keep my expression neutral. Detached. The same way Caiden looks at most people.

"She's telling the truth," Brevan says.

I start, forgetting he was behind me.

"How very interesting," Caiden lowers his hand from my back and moves closer to the bars. "It seems we have a spy in our midst."

"No! I am not a spy. I came with the princess. I was sent with the treaty. Look in my bags. You'll find it there."

"I didn't see any sort of treaty in your bags," Caiden says. "Though, I did find it odd that Princess Sabina didn't bring it with her as her father promised."

"That's because he had me carry it. It's in my things," he insists. "Go look, you'll find it."

"You didn't see a treaty in those bags, did you?" Caiden asks Brevan.

The enforcer shakes his head. "I did find a relic."

"It was a gift!" The man grabs the bars, each word from his lips coming out with more desperation. "An offering from her father, the king. For you, for your betrothal."

My heart aches. My denial has condemned him, but if not him, it would be me.

"He also seems to believe what he's saying," Brevan says. "One of them is a very good liar."

"Are you calling my bride-to-be a liar?" Caiden asks.

"Of course not, Your Highness."

"Because lying to me would be very, very bad." Caiden glances over at me.

"I wish I could help," I say, looking at Caiden, but aiming my words at the man. Though, I don't think feeling guilty clears my soul in any way. I'm still damning him to save myself.

"I've been between your thighs, and this is what I get from you?" the man says.

I gasp, genuinely surprised. That fades quickly when I realize that if this man is telling the truth, he bedded the princess and can't even tell I'm not her. And he said he'd known her since she was a child? My stomach churns. The more I learn about Sabina, the more anger I feel on her behalf.

Caiden extends his arm, then lifts his hand and dark shadows flow so quickly I almost don't even see them before they slice across the man's neck. His head hits the floor and rolls toward the bars, then his body tips and lands with a thud.

Blood spreads in a dark puddle from the severed neck. I step back before it can get on my shoes.

Caiden glares at me. "Is that true?"

"No, I swear," I say.

He glances at Brevan. The enforcer nods. Caiden seems satisfied with the response, and his shoulders ease a little before he looks at me again. "You can return to your room.

He takes a few steps away, then turns back to me. "Tell me, Sabina, do you still think death is beautiful?"

"When it's needed, yes," I say.

He smiles. "I look forward to introducing you to my court tomorrow. Sleep well, little raven."

ELEVEN

My ladies insist on filling the tub for me. They add rose petals, herbs, and scented oil before adding soap that results in a thick layer of bubbles that float atop the water. Marian practically demands to wash my hair, but I concede since she turns away as I step into the water. Some days are harder than others to hide my scar. At least she agrees easily to let me scrub everything else myself.

As I await the dress I'm to wear, I sit in a soft white dressing gown. It's thicker than usual and so cozy that I wish I could stay wrapped in it all day. We're gathered in the dining chamber, sitting casually around the table. Trays of fruit and cheese and other snacks are artfully arranged for us, but I'm too nervous to eat. The memories of yesterday haunt me, reminding me how quickly I could lose every-thing. I need information, and so far, all I've discovered is that the emperor is alive. Probably.

"Do you think the enforcer will be allowed to dance tonight?" Antonia asks as she bites into a strawberry.

"He never dances. I don't know if he would, even if they let him," Charlotte says.

"He's not technically part of the court," Katherine pops a grape in her mouth. "He's just risen through the ranks. I don't think your father would be happy with that arrangement."

"How do you know?" Antonia asks. "The enforcer might not be from a noble house, but he's the emperor's right hand. Everyone knows that."

"Wait. I thought you said you have to be noble to get a god's gift. He has magic, right?" I ask.

"Well, he clearly has noble blood from wherever he's from," Antonia says with a glance toward the door. "But it's this big mystery."

"I heard he volunteered to go to the temple even though he knew he might die. He was so determined to serve the emperor." Katherine passes me a plate of fruit. "You should at least try to eat."

I accept the plate and make myself eat a berry. The tartness makes me pucker, but I eat another to pacify Katherine who is watching me intently. "What do you all know about the enforcer?"

It would be helpful to learn as much as I could. At least that's what I tell myself. Don't get me wrong, I still want him dead, but there's something intriguing about him. He's not what I expected.

"Not much, really," Antonia says. "He was rescued from a shipwreck and brought here. The emperor raised him alongside the prince. They're practically brothers." She looks over at Katherine. "Which is why any woman would be lucky to finally tie him down."

"I think we all know who you're hoping he decides to court," Katherine teases.

Antonia's cheeks turn pink. "I don't get to choose who I marry, but I wouldn't turn him down."

"Maybe he'll be there dancing tonight." Genevieve spins, then holds out her hand to an imaginary suitor. "Perhaps I'll ask him to dance."

"That is not at all proper," Marian scolds. "In fact, none of this conversation is proper."

"Don't be too hard on them," I say. "It's good distraction. It's not like he's promised to someone." I set my plate down on the table, giving up on eating anything.

"Find another topic. Something more befitting a lady," Marian warns. "I'm going to check on your dress."

We're silent until Marian is gone but conversation returns the second the door closes.

"Does he ever even look at women? I swear he's the most disciplined man I've ever seen," Katherine says.

"I don't think I've ever even seen him with a woman," Charlotte says. "I don't think he knows how to do anything other than work. Maybe when he was younger? He was with the prince all the time."

"Wait, you said he was raised with the prince, right? Why would the emperor do that?" The emperor wasn't known for his kindness.

"I think whatever they saw when they found him must have been terrible," Katherine pushes her plate aside. "He doesn't talk about it, though."

"He doesn't seem to get along with the prince." I remove the cloth that was wrapped around my hair, then run my fingers though my already dry tresses. When I leave here, I need to take one of these with me. "When I see them together, they don't really act like friends. Let alone brothers."

"I hear they used to be close. Something happened." Antonia rises from her chair and takes the cloth from me.

"Thank you," I say as she leaves the room with it.

"Probably a woman," Charlotte says. "Probably chose the prince over him and that's why he doesn't date anymore."

"Then where's this woman the prince stole from his friend?" Katherine asks. "I never see the prince with anyone. I'm not sure he's seeing any women, either."

"That's because he makes them leave before morning." Antonia freezes in the doorway and slaps her hand over her mouth. Then she slowly lowers it. "I am so sorry, Your Highness. I'm sure those were rumors."

"It's fine. I am not delusional enough to think a prince has never had any lovers before he weds."

"I'm sure he'll be faithful to you," she says quickly.

The only thing keeping me from saying something I shouldn't is the fact that I don't intend to marry him at all.

Marian sweeps into the dining room, carrying a dress. "It's here!"

The ladies all rise from their chairs and gasp. I join them, taking in the dress. Black beads cover the white satin bodice in floral patterns. A full white skirt shimmers in the light. The back laces up with a thick ribbon that will criss-cross down my back and continue past my hips, tying into a bow right at my tailbone.

My ladies help me into a corset before lowering the gown over my head. Finally, they tie the laces up the back.

The fabric is soft against my skin, and it fits me like a glove. It's tight around the bodice before flaring out at the waist. The white cap sleeves are embroidered with more floral patterns, similar to the ones in the beading. I wonder if it's an homage to the late empress's love of plants.

The sun dips behind the horizon and lamps glow softly around my rooms while my ladies put the finishing touches on my hair and makeup.

The mood is festive, but I'm at odds with that energy. Tonight is going to be a true test of whether or not I can pass as Princess Sabina.

The ladies here accepted me without question, writing off anything odd as inexperience in their court. The prince and the enforcer just see me as a pawn. I have no idea who will be present at this dinner, but if there's anyone from Iskvaland or from Sabina's past, I could be in trouble. While I know I look similar enough to the princess to fool anyone who's only seen her in paintings, I don't know that I could trick someone who truly knew her.

But then again, the man in the cells said he'd bedded the princess, and he thought I was her.

And to protect my lie, he died.

Marian walks toward me, and I fix a smile on my face, sending the swirling thoughts away.

"You seem nervous," she says.

"I am," I confess.

"It'll be over before you know it. Just smile and bat your lashes, and after tonight, you'll be free to leave your rooms and finally explore your new home." She pats my hand.

That is enough to help me snap out of my worries. I need that freedom.

I'm surprised when a pair of legionnaires I don't know arrive to escort me to the dinner. I wonder if Brevan is off destroying another village.

We walk to a part of the castle I haven't been in yet. So far, I've remained in the north wing, but we cross into the south side of the castle. Immediately, I notice a difference in the décor and overall feel here. More art covers the walls, and sculptures are set into recessed spaces or on pedestals. The stone floors are polished and gleaming. While the rooms I've been in contain luxury, the hallways are lined with only floral tapestries and the floors don't shine.

I slow down as we pass a massive mural showing a battle between two armies, one wearing the emperor's crest. When I notice the dragons, I stop. We all know dragons used to exist, but I heard they'd died out before our empire began.

Night legionnaires drive swords into the bellies of the massive beasts. Archers fire arrows. The emperor's cavalry charge toward the opposing army, facing off against an enemy riding and commanding dragons.

There's no way this is real. It has to be a fantasy. A work of art meant to show the empire's prowess. But the paint is cracking and fading in places. It's been here a long time. Then again, the emperor has been here a long time, too.

"Your Highness," one of the legionnaires says.

I tear my gaze away from the mural and continue on. We pass suits of armor and twisting sculptures of humans contorted into painful positions as they grapple with gods or monsters. More murals of battles line the walls.

When we turn down another hall, I stop again. In front of us is a massive skull. "Is that...?"

"The only known dragon skull," one of the men says. "The emperor found it when he was a child."

Above the skull is a mural of an enormous red dragon. Its jaws are open as if mid-roar. Dangerous pointed teeth glint in the flickering lamplight. Wings fan out from its long scaly body. They stretch so far they don't fit on the canvas, but I can imagine how expansive they would be.

"I see you're admiring my father's favorite painting," Caiden says as he struts toward us.

He's dressed in black and silver. His jacket and trousers are designed to fit him perfectly and for a moment, my heart flutters at the sight of him. Thankfully, I regain sense quickly. Caiden has always been handsome, but tonight, he's every inch the storybook prince that might sweep you off your feet.

When he reaches me, he smirks as if he knows exactly what I was thinking. "Whatever you do, don't ask him about it. He'll spend the next six hours telling you stories about dragons."

The legionnaires on either side of me bow to their prince, and Caiden waves at them dismissively. They rise, then turn to leave.

I return my attention to the painting, wondering if that's what dragons really looked like. "He saw them?"

"He says he did. But there isn't anyone else alive to contradict him." Caiden sounds bored. Like he's heard his father recount tales of his past far too many times.

"Are you calling your father a liar?" My brows rise.

"I'm saying he's a good storyteller." He offers his elbow.

I grip his bicep and take my place beside him like I'm supposed to.

"I assume you'll be on your best behavior tonight."

"I assume you will be as well," I counter.

"I'm not sure if I'm impressed or annoyed that you'd risk anything other than blind obedience after our dance lessons."

"You have made your point more than clear, but I'm still a princess. And while you may threaten me, I know I hold value to you and your empire."

"As long as you know your place, we won't have any problems," he says.

I clench my jaw, swallowing what I really want to say. I've pushed him enough already. I need to be on his good side, earn his trust. "I'll follow your lead."

"That's all I ask."

I bite down on the inside of my cheek and remind myself that the better I play along, the closer I get to putting a knife through this man's chest. Then I smile, knowing that I'm still thinking clearly despite how attractive he is. He's still my enemy, even if he does look incredible tonight.

Caiden guides me down the hall, just beyond the dragon skull. The double doors to a large ballroom are open. Several night legionnaires stand on either side. They bow as we approach and don't rise until we've passed through the doors.

The room is large and ornate. Chandeliers hang from the ceiling, sparkling with light from the flickering flames dotted between the crystals. The walls are painted black, the stone polished and smooth instead of rough like it is in the other wing.

There's already so many people inside the room. It's a sea of black and gray. I'm the only one in white, making me stand out even more than I already did with my fair hair. They part, creating a path down the center for us. As we pass them, they bow or curtsy. I can feel their eyes on me, following me, studying me.

We pass long tables covered in black cloth, already set for dinner. Tall vases filled with black roses and leaves decorate the surfaces. Black plates and goblets are bracketed by shiny silver utensils.

Once we pass those, we stop at a smaller table that faces the others. A large throne lined with black velvet, trimmed in silver, takes up the center. On the right side are two smaller thrones. Each of them a less ornate version of the largest one. The final seat is a well-crafted but simple wooden chair to the left of the large throne.

My pulse races, and my stomach twists into knots. "Is your father joining us?" Based on everything Caiden has said, I wasn't expecting the emperor's attendance.

"He'll give you his approval tonight," he says. "I suppose we'll see if he still wants that alliance with your kingdom, or if he decides to send you back."

"I didn't know that was a possibility." My heart thunders.

"I warned you that you're only safe here as long as we find you useful."

We reach the table, and he pulls my chair out for me, then takes his own seat. Someone behind us rings a bell and then everything moves quickly. People hurry to the tables, and a dozen servants arrive from hidden doors with bottles of wine. Our goblets are silver instead of black, and as soon as the last person is sat, servants quickly pour wine for everyone.

Then all heads turn toward the still-open double doors. A man in long black robes—a priest—slowly ambles in. I recognize him as Darius, the same priest who met me when I arrived. He kisses his palm, then touches his chest before extending his hand, as if blessing everyone in the room. The gathered courtiers repeat the gesture, kissing their palms, then touching their chests, but they don't extend their arms after.

Caiden remains still, so I do the same. Apparently, the royals don't need to show reverence to the gods.

The priest walks up to our table, where he drops into a bow, his attention focused on Caiden. When he rises, he scowls at me before taking the smaller wooden chair next to the throne.

Suddenly, everyone stands, and a tapping sound makes a faint echo around the ballroom. Caiden and the priest stand, so I rise with them. A hunched old man stands in front of one of the double doors. He's clothed in a fine black jacket and trousers, similar to Caiden's. Thinning white hair is combed across a pale scalp. Leaning heavily on a cane, the man takes careful steps toward us. As he passes by, everyone drops to low bows or deep curtseys.

He pauses near a table, then gestures to a woman. She dips lower into a curtsy before rising, then walking over to his side, loops her arm through his. They continue walking and it appears that she's helping stabilize him.

As they get closer, I recognize Lady Drathmore. My brow furrows as an insane thought circles my mind. Could this old man be the emperor? Is this why nobody's seen him?

I dismiss the nonsense idea. It's impossible, isn't it? But what if it's not? What if he's already dying?

When he approaches us, the priest lowers his head. Caiden doesn't, but I intuit that I'm expected to, so I do. This has to be the emperor. My pulse races. What does this mean?

Two servants pull the throne away from the table and Lady Drathmore assists him, then she returns to her seat. The servants push the throne closer to the table, then retreat through the secret doors.

Once he's settled in his chair, he thumps his cane against the stone floor twice. The sound is like a crack, amplified beyond what it should be. It must be a familiar message, though, because after the second crack, they rise from their bows and take their seats again. Caiden sits, so I sit as well.

I force my gaze forward, resisting the urge to study the ancient man in the throne. Has he always looked like this? Were the stories and depictions of him a lie? Or was something wrong with him? My fingers twitch. I want so badly to turn and stare.

The room is deathly silent. The emperor coughs and I risk a glance. He wipes his mouth with a dark handkerchief, but I swear I can see blood on the cloth. I turn back away.

"Welcome, everyone." His voice is weak and raspy.

I fix a smile on my face and turn my attention to him. He glances over at me, then nods once before looking back at his gathered court.

"You are all my most loyal and trusted friends. Since the

loss of my dearest wife, I have not been myself. But with this new alliance comes a brighter future for Pendralia. Our great empire faces new threats and unfamiliar challenges. But with the marriage of my son and the might of the Iskvalandian armies to bolster our own, we will be unstoppable."

Applause and cheers rise from the gathered courtiers. My stomach twists and I swallow down the rising bile. It's a reminder, though. It's why I'm here. This alliance can't happen. And this empire can't continue.

The emperor lifts his goblet. He turns to look at me and raises his cup. "To Princess Sabina Volkov and our newfound alliance with Iskvaland."

"To Princess Sabina Volkov," the courtiers repeat.

I pick up my goblet and smile demurely. In my head, I imagine watching this frail old man collapse to the ground. The courtiers would rush around him, desperate to save their emperor. In the chaos, I might be able to find a weapon and kill Caiden. Brevan would hunt me down and I'd be hanged unless the rebels could get to him first, but either way, the job would be done. And Pendralia would have a chance to rebuild better. My smile widens and the emperor grins back at me. Good thing he can't see what I'm thinking.

"Now, in honor of our future princess, let's feast," the emperor says. Immediately the hidden doors open again, and servants return with steaming bowls of soup, delivering one to each place setting.

Course after course, the servants return to take away plates and replace them with more food. I have to start pacing myself and only taking a few bites of each dish. I'm not the only one. I notice that most plates go back overflowing with food. It's hard to imagine having so much food that you don't eat everything on your plate, but that's what I do now as well. Guilt makes my chest tight.

Between bites, I glance at the emperor. He looks frail up close. His skin is thin and papery, his eyes glassy. Living to be nearly 500 has caught up to him. I thought he'd be frozen in a younger, healthier body. Lady Drathmore looks so much healthier and younger than him, but maybe there's a limit to the magic. Maybe he's not immortal and instead, has reached his peak. Is that why Caiden is marrying now? Aside from the alliance, is he preparing to take over as emperor due to his father's health?

Caiden speaks in hushed tones with his father, the priest sometimes joining in. Despite my attempts to get closer, I can't hear a word the trio says.

Nobody at the long tables seems to care that he's a frail old man. They are engaged in their own conversations, few of them even taking time to glance toward the royals. Have they seen him recently? The citizens haven't seen him since his wife died, but perhaps he's been locked away in here, still engaging with his favorites.

"They will clear the tables after dessert," Caiden says.

I look over at him, surprised that he's turned his attention away from his father. "Thank you for the warning."

"My father likes you," he says.

My brow furrows. "He doesn't know me. He hasn't even spoken to me."

"He heard what you did in the dungeons. How you didn't beg or plead for the duke's life."

My head spins. That was a duke? That man I sentenced to death to protect my own identity was a duke?

I take a drink from my wine goblet to buy myself a moment to steady myself. It is good for me that he is dead. It protected me and has earned the emperor's favor. I should be celebrating.

I set the goblet down. "This is my home now. You will inherit the throne, and I will be by your side."

"That's what I told him," he says. "I told him you were a timid and submissive woman."

"You lied."

"I know."

"But that's what you want. A woman who follows you blindly." I hate that I'm trying to fit the role and play the part. I've found out the emperor is alive, but I don't know if he's mortal. He looks like his immortality might be failing, but I have to be sure.

Caiden smirks, then sets his hand on my leg. "I think it's going to be fun breaking you." His hand moves so he's between my legs, his touch caressing my inner thigh.

I grab his hand and move it to his leg, then drag my fingertips along the top of his thigh to his knee. "I think you'd be disappointed if I gave in." I pat his hand, then pick up my glass and take a long gulp, attempting to mask my sudden mortification. What the fuck was I doing? I didn't want to encourage him.

He opens his mouth to respond, but his father leans over to speak to him. I let out a relieved breath. That could have ended very badly for me.

Dessert is delivered to each guest, and I can't even taste the cake I make myself have two bites of. It's beautiful but is like ash in my mouth.

As soon as the emperor stands, all the plates are whisked

away, and the guests vacate their seats. Everyone moves toward the open area behind all the tables.

Caiden rises and offers his hand. I don't have to look toward the guests to know that all eyes are on me.

He leads us to the back of the room, where everyone gathers around us, watching with rapt attention. They will notice if even a single step is out of place. When Caiden places his hand on my waist and we prepare to start our dance, I glance up at the head table. The emperor and the priest are gone. They aren't in the crowd, and they made no announcement of their departure. I guess my audience with him is complete.

When the music begins, Caiden sweeps me into the dance we practiced together. I follow him but do misstep several times. Caiden doesn't flinch at any of my mistakes and smiles at me as if he is truly enjoying my company. The man is a fabulous actor.

I catch glimpses of my ladies in the crowd, each of them smiling. People's expressions vary from annoyed to contemplative to wistful. I wish I could make notes of each person, as I'm certain their reaction to this would tell me everything I need to know about how they view my presence here.

When the music finally ends, I dip into a curtsy and Caiden bows. The audience claps but it's short-lived, as they all pour into the dance floor with the next song. I use the transition to quickly flee so I can avoid having to dance again.

In the movement, I lose Caiden, but I notice Brevan standing against the wall, watching me. I wonder if he'd take me back to my rooms if I asked.

Antonia and Charlotte find me before I can walk over to him. They squeal in high-pitched tones.

"He looks smitten," Antonia squeals.

"I can't believe how he held you." Charlotte crosses her arms over her chest as if hugging herself. "That hand on your back? That's not proper. I've never seen him break protocol, but he just had to touch you."

"How lucky that your marriage will be to someone who will treat you well!" Antonia sighs.

"Yes, I'm very lucky," I reply.

"And the emperor himself toasted you," she adds. "I heard he hasn't come to any events since the empress died."

"He looks so frail, doesn't he?" Charlotte whispers.

"I know," Antonia says. "I'm worried about him."

"Did he look like that last time you saw him?" I ask.

"No," she says. "I heard stories about how he ages between visits to the temple before, but I didn't realize how bad it gets."

"What do you mean 'between visits to the temple'?" I ask.

"He goes to speak to the gods, and when he returns, he's himself again," Antonia says.

"By 'himself' you mean...?" My heart thunders as I wait to hear what she has to say. This has to be it. This has to be the information I need.

"Well, not old, for starters," Charlotte says. "But maybe he's ready to hand over the empire."

"Charlotte," Antonia hisses. She looks around, then turns her attention back to the other woman. "You can't say things like that. Especially now, with the enforcer so close."

"I'm not interrupting anyone, am I?" A male voice cuts in.

I turn and find Caiden smiling at us.

"If it's not too much trouble, I'd like another dance with my bride-to-be."

"I'm not sure I'm up to that tonight. It's been a lot," I say.

He holds out his hand. "Nonsense."

I accept it, and he leads me to the dance floor again. "I thought you said I only had to do this once?"

"There's been a change of plans." He glances over to where Brevan was, but the enforcer is gone.

In fact, most of the night legionnaires who were stationed around the room are gone.

"What's happening?" I ask.

"Just a few rebels trying to ruin our evening." He leads me out onto the dance floor.

"Again?" I rest my hands on his shoulder and hip, then begin to follow his movements.

His brow furrows. "How did you know?"

"You made another man sleep in my room," I answer.

"Oh, that's right. I did."

"Should we be concerned?" I notice the double doors are now closed.

"No. They can't access this room." His hand moves lower on my back, his fingers brushing against my ass. Whispers follow in our wake.

"So we're locked in and need to distract your court while the night legionnaires take care of the rebels? Is that why you're causing such a scene with your touch?"

He laughs. "You have no business being as smart as you are."

"I don't think it's difficult to figure out what's happening."

"You'd be surprised." He twirls me, and I stumble, but regain my footing enough to complete the spin.

"We did not practice that," I hiss.

"Yet, you did well."

"Shouldn't you be out there helping your men?" If only the rebels could get to him and take him out so I could be done here.

"Every time they break in, there's only a handful of them. Three or four that manage to bypass our defenses. If they do make it past the guards, they always try to get into the library or the vault. It's gotten to the point where we just increase security in those places, and once they reach them, we kill them."

"This happens often?" I knew the rebels occasionally try to get into the castle, but I thought it was for assassination attempts. Then again, I'm not privy to much. Especially since my mother died and Lee took over.

"More often than it used to. But it works out in our favor. There's only so many of them. Eventually, they'll run out of people to send."

"You're using it to kill them off?" I ask.

"See? You are smart." He spins me again, and this time, I'm prepared and keep my balance. "And a fast learner."

The song finishes and he bows to me. I respond with a curtsy, then turn to walk off the floor. He grabs me and pulls me to him, taking us into the next dance.

"This is dance number three," I point out.

"Did I tell you how beautiful you look tonight?" he asks.

"Careful, all these compliments might go to my head," I tease.

"I can tell my betrothed she's beautiful, can't I?"

"You almost killed me, and you threatened me and told me that I needed to fall in line," I remind him.

He toys with the bow at my tailbone, then his hand moves lower than it did before. "And even after I did all that, you still fight me. You're fascinating."

"Fascinating?" I don't hide my skepticism.

"And stunning. Even the hair is growing on me," he says. "Who knew I'd actually want to get to know the woman I'm to marry?"

Twelve

Marian isn't in my room when I return. None of my ladies are. It's a welcome reprieve from all the people I interacted with all night.

After our fourth dance, Caiden introduced me to so many people that I can't remember a single name. It was an endless barrage of shallow compliments and invitations that I smiled through while my betrothed kept me so close I was nearly pressed against him all night.

Being alone, without anyone touching me, is exactly what I need. Even if it is short-lived. I know Marian will return soon enough to help me out of my gown.

I fall to my knees in the middle of my room. Tilting my head back, I close my eyes and breathe. It's the first time I've been alone in days, and the silence is stunning.

Something rumbles, and my eyes snap open. I look around the room, then I hear the sound again. Quickly, I jump to my feet and race to my bathroom. Lee is closing the secret door behind him.

"What are you doing here?" I hiss. "You can't be here.

They were chasing down rebels who broke in tonight. And by the way, they're letting them in so they can kill them off one by one."

"Them, huh? Not *us*? Have you so quickly joined the aristocracy?"

"This isn't a joke, Lee. You can't send anyone else in here."

"Last I checked, the way the rebellion is run isn't your decision," he says. "You made that clear when you told me you were leaving."

"Yet, here I am, deeper than any other member," I point out.

He grins. "Yes, that's true."

"The emperor's alive," I blurt.

"What? You saw him?"

"I did. And he looks terrible. They said he hasn't returned to the temple to replenish his magic in a while. I think maybe that's how he stays immortal. And right now, he might be vulnerable. Can you get someone close enough to him to take him down? Before Darkfall. That's when they give new people magic. That must be when he'll refill whatever magic he uses."

As much as I'd like to be the one who ends the emperor, this opportunity is too good to waste. Someone with more skills should do it so we don't miss out.

"Darkfall. That doesn't give us much time. We were hoping for more." His brows knit and his jaw tenses.

"More time? No. It has to be as soon as possible. We can't wait. And you should know that the prince has magic unlike anything I've ever seen. He can wield shadows that are corporeal and use elemental magic. Fire. Probably other types as well. He's powerful, Lee."

"That's impossible."

"I've seen it." I shudder at the memory of those shadows squeezing me.

"That changes things. It's going to make him harder to kill."

"I can do it."

"That's not why you're here."

"It has to be me. I'm the only one who can get close enough."

Lee takes a step toward me. "How close, Taylan? Are you already in his bed?"

"That's none of your business," I snap.

"It is if I think you might be compromised," he says.

"Are you kidding me right now? You think I would support them?" I move closer to him, my voice getting louder with each word. "After everything they've done to my family? After everything they've done to our city? Our people?"

He grabs my wrist, then presses against my stomach, covering most of my scar with his large hand. "Remember where you came from and the price you've already paid."

I set my hand on top of his. How could I ever forget the night I got that scar?

He releases my wrist then reaches for my face. "I don't know what I'd do if anything happened to you." He leans down. "I can't lose you."

"I'm not yours anymore, Lee."

"But you could be." He tilts my chin up and closes his eyes.

I turn so his lips touch my cheek instead of my mouth before backing away. "I can't."

He sighs as he runs a hand through his hair. "Alright. I get it. You're not ready."

"I'm never going to be ready. You made your choice, and I made mine."

"Right. Old habits die hard, I guess." He turns and starts toward the secret door.

"Lee? Where does that tunnel lead?" I ask.

"The City of the Dead," he says.

A chill runs down my spine. The City of the Dead is a series of crumbling tunnels and chambers filled with the bodies of the deceased. Catacombs from the time before the king. I spent a lot of time down there the first few years we lived in the city. It is one of the only places you can hide from the Night Legion. For some reason, their magic doesn't work there.

"Oh, Lee?"

"Yeah?"

"We really do need to make all this happen before Dark-fall. I don't know how much longer I can fool them." At least, not without compromising myself. The way Caiden spoke to me tonight, the way he touched me...

"Alright. Before Darkfall. Find out where the emperor sleeps. Then, hang your ruby, and I'll come back to relay the final details." He presses his palm to the wall and pushes. The secret panel slides to the side behind the rest of the wall, revealing a dark tunnel.

There's a knock at my door, and my eyes widen. "Hurry. Go." Without looking back, I rush to my bedroom, then open the main door. Caiden is waiting outside. Two legionnaires stand on each side of him. He's holding a black rose in his hand.

"Your Highness," I say, giving a little nod. "It's rather late."

"I know. But I realized I never greeted you properly when you arrived." He hands me the flower.

It's an odd gesture, but I take the flower.

"Walk with me?"

"Now?" It's nearly midnight, but I'm still in my gown.

"I won't keep you too long." He extends his hand.

"Alright. One minute." I rush into my room and set the flower down on the small table in front of the couch, then return to where Caiden is waiting for me.

I walk alongside him, and I notice that none of the legionnaires are following us. "Should I be worried?"

"I'm just taking you for a stroll in the gardens."

"Without anyone to watch over me?" I point out.

"There wasn't anyone there when we had dinner or when we practiced dancing."

"They were right outside the door. And you have warned me about how my life serves only your ambitions."

"'Ambitions' is a strange way to put it," he says.

"How else do you describe your goals of obtaining a disposable army and use them to gain more territory?" I ask.

He makes an amused sound. "You have been listening to me."

"Of course, I'm listening. Even your father said as much at dinner." I'm getting annoyed by how much he underestimates me, but then again, it's better if he does.

He takes us down a narrow staircase that leads to a plain hallway lined with wood doors. One of the doors opens, and a servant steps into the hall. Her eyes widen when she sees us, and she quickly retreats back into the room.

Caiden doesn't seem to notice that the woman was terrified of him.

Of us.

Because the servants don't know that I'm more like them. But am I anymore? I'm wearing a dress that would have fed my family for months, and I've had full meals and warm blankets. I'm playing a role, but it already feels like I'm not the same person I was.

When we reach the end of the hall, Caiden opens a door that leads outside. We're at the back of the castle in an area I haven't seen before. A path extends before us, lined with tiny sparkling lights. On each side are gray stone sculptures of women wearing floral headdresses in sheer flowing dresses. It's exquisite artistry. They look so real, I half expect the sculptures to move. They look out of place compared to the other art I've seen here.

Further along, the statues are replaced by hedges, similar to the ones that enclose the castle. These are only a foot or so taller than me, though. Not as towering and ominous as the ones at the border. I pause and look at the thick glossy leaves. In the faint light, I can tell they're a very dark green. Not completely black as I initially thought.

"This way. I want to show you my mother's garden," Caiden says.

It feels like a different world as we walk between the hedges. I glance over my shoulder and note that we're fairly isolated. You'd have to be at exactly the correct angle to see us.

We reach an iron gate, and Caiden pushes it open.

Behind it is a garden, walled in by more hedges. Rows and rows of flowers fill the space. Stone benches and animal statues are scattered around. It's probably meant to be joyous and serene. But in the dim flickering light, the dark plants and weatherworn creatures look dangerous.

"This was where she spent most of her time," Caiden says. "She loved this garden."

"It's beautiful," I say, because how can I tell him this place is horrifying?

I lean down and inspect the flowers. I think I see roses, marigolds, sage, and lavender. But they're all so dark they appear black. As I lean closer, I grow more sure there's no color in any of them.

"I've never seen flowers like this," I say.

He crouches next to me. "Something about her magic made everything she touched change. All the plants she grew lost their color. I remember her having other people plant them for her, but as soon as she went near them, the color faded into this."

My heart aches for her. I never appreciated color so much until I got here. I can't imagine not having it in my life. A rabbit sculpture stares up at me from between the leaves of a lavender bush. The plant smells like it should, which is strange when the darkness of the leaves and flowers makes it almost appear dead.

"Did she do that with other living things?" I ask. "Animals or people?"

"No. Just plants. Her magic was unique."

"How is it that all the legionnaires end up with the same shadow magic but others get such different kinds?" I ask.

"It's up to the gods. You can request, but ultimately, we don't choose." He stands, then offers his hand to me.

I accept it numbly and let him guide me to standing. "So the gods gave you fire and shadows?"

He smirks. "Among other things."

My brow furrows. "Like what?"

"Maybe I'll show you someday," he says. "Perhaps after you gain your own magic."

"What?" It feels like I've been slapped in the face. "I don't have any magic."

"Not yet. But after you go to the temple at Darkfall, you will." Caiden steps over a vine that's snaked its way across the path and continues deeper into the garden. "Or you'll be dead."

I follow his lead, avoiding the twisting black tendrils that stretch across the walkway. "I don't want magic."

"I didn't ask you if you wanted it."

"Why would I need it?" I press.

"Every empress must enter the temple and be judged by the gods. My mother did."

"I thought your mother only went in because she was desperate. I thought women weren't allowed."

He chuckles. "Who told you that?"

"One of my ladies," I admit.

"Well, nice to know the rumor mill is still going strong. No, my mother went in because she was strong. And she had to prove she was worthy of my father."

"So you want me to prove I'm worthy even though you've told me the whole reason I'm here is because you need me? You obviously don't think I'm worthy of you."

"You're starting to change my mind," he says. "Besides,

there must be at least part of you that's curious. Everyone has imagined what their life might be like with magic. I know you're not exempt."

"Do I want to drain the color from everything I touch?" I shake my head. "No. I don't want that."

"That wasn't all she could do."

"Whatever else she could do, it didn't keep her alive." I feel guilty as soon as the words leave my mouth.

His expression darkens. "This isn't a choice. At Darkfall, you'll go into the temple."

I clench my jaw. I won't be here by Darkfall. "Fine."

"Fine?" The anger on his face dissolves. "Since when do you go along with what I say so easily?"

"Maybe I am a little curious."

He lifts my chin with his index finger. "I like curious women."

My stomach churns, and I fight against the urge to slap his hand away. I'm so focused on keeping my expression neutral that when he lowers his face to mine I back away. "Sorry. I'm not ready for that yet."

"Well, that is disappointing."

"Give me a little more time. It's an adjustment being here and being with you." I swallow hard, hoping I came across as homesick rather than cold.

"I'll escort you back to your room, Princess." His tone is flat, devoid of emotion, but at least not angry.

I'll take what I can get.

We walk to the castle in silence. Each step feels like I'm trudging through mud.

How am I going to do this? How am I going to fake this if he starts expecting me to do more?

Then I remember that he's not worried that I might kill him in his sleep. The absolute perfect time to stab him. If anything, I should encourage him. Taking him into my bed would get me closer but I'm not sure I can bring myself to do it.

When I agreed to this, I made peace with death. I thought I'd get close to a selfish, cold prince who had a whole corral of lovers to distract him from me. I did not account for a prince who might actually fall for me.

THIRTEEN

"Good morning, Princess." Brevan is outside my room when I open the door.

"Good morning," I reply as I turn down the hall.

He walks alongside me. "And where are you heading?"

"I was told I was free to leave my rooms once I met the court," I say. "I met the court last night, so I will go where I please."

He's silent as he continues alongside me. I look over my shoulder and see that two legionnaires still stand in front of my door. I suppose they'll tell Marian where I went when she wakes.

After my walk with Caiden last night, she was waiting in my room. She helped me out of my dress, then slept in the small bed to be near me. I wondered if Caiden made her stay.

After last night, I'm even more eager to find out about the emperor so I can leave. There's a time limit on how long I can delay the prince's advances and I'm not sure exactly what it is. The sooner I finish here, the better.

"I'm just going for a walk around my new home," I tell Brevan. "I don't need an escort."

"There have already been rebels inside this castle twice since you arrived," he says.

"It's not my fault you have terrible security," I tell him. "Besides, they're not after me. They're after something in the library or the vault, correct?"

"How did you know that?"

"Caiden told me."

"You two are getting close."

"Was that judgement in your tone?" I glance over at him.

"Of course not."

"Why does he have you following me around?" I stop at a staircase and contemplate which way to go.

"Library is upstairs," he says.

"What makes you think that's what I'd like to see?" I ask.

"Because that's what the rebels are always after."

I blink a few times and stare at him, hoping he can't hear the pounding of my heart or the rushing sound filling my ears. "What does that have to do with anything?"

"Because you're curious and I'm sure your father wants you to find things out while you're here. You won't discover anything that will be useful to him, but we all expected you to have ulterior motives."

"Is that why I was trapped in my room?" I ask.

"Probably."

"What about the vault?"

He chuckles. "I can show you where it is, but I can't let you inside. Even I don't have the key."

My brow furrows. "What exactly is in the vault?"

"No idea. Probably gold and gems. Why do you ask? You don't strike me as the jewelry type. I had to practically force you to choose something from Jacques."

"You know exactly why I'm curious." There are easier ways to get funding for the rebellion. There must be something of greater value inside. Or at least they must think there is. I wonder if it's something that might help kill the emperor.

"That kind of prying is dangerous," he warns.

"The library is upstairs, you say?" I smile sweetly, taking his warning to heart. I can't keep making stupid mistakes like that. Brevan reads me far too easily. There has to be a way to spend some time around here without him at my heels.

"Yes."

He leads us toward the library, but along the way, we pass an open chamber that catches my eye. Candles burn at an altar in the back of the space. A large mural, spanning several panels, spans all the walls. Each panel shows a different scene, telling a story.

"This was the empress's private temple," he says. "The servants still light the candles for her every day, and they leave offerings on feast days."

"Can I go inside?" I ask.

"Go ahead."

I step into the darkened room, and the temperature drops. Despite the candles and lack of windows, it's much cooler in here. I look at the paintings, recognizing some of the scenes from the stories told on feast days when I was a child.

My parents would host a gathering, and friends and neighbors would come to cook and eat. Sometimes there would be gifts of sweets or wooden toys. The elders would share stories of the gods and heroes, and we'd listen with rapt attention. The best was when they'd use puppets behind a screen and act the stories out with shadows.

When we moved to the city, we stopped celebrating feasts. The people who live in Aurorium have abandoned the gods. Or the gods abandoned them. There were no more feasts, no more stories.

But these vibrant paintings are the stories of my childhood come to life. I move down the wall slowly, taking in the tales of heroes slaying beasts and receiving boons from the gods. Of the gods working together to defeat the monsters they sent to the realm beyond the veil. Of Apophis, the god of chaos, winding around the world with his serpent body in his attempt to destroy everything. And Amate, the goddess of the sun, leading the charge against him to send him to the underworld.

When I reach the center panel on the wall behind the altar, I hesitate. It shows a man and a woman wearing gold crowns, standing back-to-back with their hands clasped. Both of them have winding black gift marks that swirl around their wrists, up their forearms, then vanish under the sleeves of their tunics.

They're dressed in white, and their dark hair is loose and billowing, as if they're standing in the middle of a storm. Darkness and light swirl around them like shadows meeting sunlight.

It's stunning but also sends a chill straight to my bones. There's something so dangerous about the pair. Something familiar. I grasp at the memory, urging the tale to return to my mind.

As the story takes shape, I recall the prophecy about the return of the gods and their full magic to our world. Many people believe it would bring the return of magic to all mortals, while others say it is just for those deemed worthy by the emperor.

We all grew up knowing the prophecy, but it is dismissed as fiction. It is too dangerous to believe a tale that could be interpreted as promising magic to commoners.

The air around me shifts, and I know Brevan is standing next to me. "Is this the prophecy of light?"

"You know the story?" He seems surprised.

"Not well. I wasn't always the best student," I lie, hoping that a princess would have had tutors and classes.

"It was the empress's favorite story. Some hoped she'd be the one to fulfill it since she received a god's gift when she visited the temple, but it could never have been her."

"Isn't it shadows and light? A pair that finds balance?" I ask.

"Yes. That's how I've heard it." He's suddenly very interested in adjusting the leather bracers at his wrist. "But the emperor doesn't have shadow magic."

My brow furrows, and I take a step closer. The shadows that wrap around the pair originate at his feet while the light starts at hers. "Is that why the emperor insists on shadows for all his legionnaires? To try to find the person who might fulfill this prophecy?"

"I'm not sure," he says.

"Do you have shadow magic?" I ask before I can stop myself.

"No."

"But the prince does." I don't like the places my mind takes me as I put the pieces together.

"Yes."

"Is that why he wants me to go to the temple at Darkfall? He's hoping I will get light magic from the gods?"

Brevan's eyes widen. "He wants you to visit the temple?"

I nod.

"I suppose it could be," he says. "He's one of the few who believes in the prophecy."

"And you don't?"

"I've never seen anything that makes me think the gods care at all about what happens in the mortal realm."

"Such blasphemy, and in a temple no less." I gasp over-dramatically. Now I'm the one being disrespectful to the gods.

"They haven't struck me down yet. And trust me, they've had enough reasons to do so."

"I've heard," I say.

He stiffens, then walks out of the temple. When he reaches the hall, he faces me. "When you're ready, I'll show you the library."

I glance at the mural one more time, then turn to leave. If the empress was so interested in this prophecy, what does that tell me? Is there a clue in there about the emperor and his immortality?

"How does it work in the temple for Darkfall? Is the emperor there with you or do you go alone?" I ask.

"We aren't allowed to share what happens in the temple," he says.

"Isn't that convenient," I grumble.

When we reach the library, I stop in the entrance to stare at the rows of shelves lined with books. I don't know why I'm surprised by it after all the other wealth I've seen, but I am.

The room is the size of the ballroom, with windows across the top. Books fill all the space between the floor and the windows. Stone ravens perch atop each like sentinels. It's easily my favorite place in the entire castle.

In the center of the expansive room are a few large circular tables surrounded by chairs and lit by a brass oil lamp. Nearby, a few plush armchairs face a fireplace that's crackling and flickering. Despite the expansive space, it's cozy.

A woman in a silver dress looks up from the thick tomb she's reading. She stands and approaches with a warm smile. "This must be the princess I've heard so much about."

"Juliette, when did you arrive?" Brevan asks.

Juliette is a stunningly beautiful woman with thick brown curls and long dark lashes over deep brown eyes.

She walks over to him and drags her fingers down his chest. "Last night. I'm supposed to stay with you for a while."

I lift my brows in silent question. Maybe she's the distraction I need. What if she's the woman who got between Brevan and the prince? Perhaps she didn't choose Caiden. My chest tightens uncomfortably.

Brevan clears his throat and takes a step back. "In your rooms, you mean."

"Of course. But it's so fun to tease you. One of these days, you're going to meet a woman who gets you to stop being so damn serious about everything." She turns to me. "Wouldn't he be more interesting if he didn't take everything so seriously?"

So, not his lover. I hate the little weight of relief that settles over me. "She's got a point."

Brevan doesn't mask his annoyance. "The two of you should not be allowed to be alone together."

"Oh, I think that sounds like a challenge," she says.

"Or an invitation."

"I'm Juliette." She dips into a curtsy. "It's lovely to meet you, Your Highness."

"Please, call me Sabina," I offer.

"The princess is on a tour of the castle," Brevan says. "We should continue on."

My brow furrows and I glance over at him. "I didn't realize I was on a tour."

"I can take her, Brevan," Juliette cuts in.

"I'm supposed to stay with her." He moves a bit closer to me.

"I think my cousin would be fine with me taking over," she says.

"I disagree," Brevan replies.

"Alright. Tea?" Juliette looks at me. "In my rooms after your tour? Maybe in an hour or so?"

I was hoping to find some books about the temples and Darkfall and magic. Anything that might help me find out about the emperor—but his niece might be an even better source of information. "I'd like that."

Brevan lets out a sigh. "Come along. I'll show you more of the castle, and then you can go for tea."

"It was nice to meet you," I say.

She wiggles her fingers in a playful wave. "See you soon."

Brevan is even grumpier than usual as he leads me around the castle. He shows me another ballroom and a small study that has its own collection of books, and he points out the doors that lead to Caiden's rooms.

"What's the story between you and Juliette?" I ask.

"There's no story," he snaps.

"She's not your ex-lover, is she?"

He gives me a look that could bring a small child to tears. I hold up my hands in mock surrender. "Alright. So not an old girlfriend."

"It's because she's nothing but trouble," he replies.

"You realize that makes me like her more?"

"I was afraid of that," he says.

We travel down a set of stairs we had yet to use, and we end up in a busy kitchen. Servants and cooks hustle around, chopping and stirring and mixing and baking. Several pots hang over a large fire while loaves of bread cook in the oven above it. Someone dices vegetables while someone else is washing dishes in a sink full of suds.

An older woman, wearing a white apron over her gray dress, approaches, a plate of scones in her hands. "This wouldn't happen to be the new princess I keep hearing about?"

Brevan reaches for a scone. "It is."

The woman holds the plate up to me, and I take one of the pastries. It's still warm. "Thanks."

She smiles. "You're prettier than they said."

"She's also already very important to the prince," Brevan says, a hint of warning in his tone.

The woman lowers her head. "Of course, where are my manners? It's lovely to meet you, Your Highness."

"That's really not necessary," I say. "Anyone who brings me fresh scones is a friend. What is your name?"

The woman rises, her cheeks rosy. I never met my grandmother, but I'd like to think she'd be like this. "I'm Elizabeth."

"Nice to meet you, Elizabeth."

"I'm taking her on a tour. She's already been invited to tea with Juliette," Brevan says.

"I'll send up some extra cakes." Elizabeth signals to another servant, who is setting beautiful little sweets onto a tray. Next to it is another tray with a teapot and cup. The servant adds a second cup and more sweets.

"I suppose that means our tour is over," Brevan says.

"As soon as you show me where Juliette's room is," I say, then I turn to Elizabeth. "It was so nice to meet you."

"You as well, dear." The woman smiles at me in a way I haven't been smiled at in years. Like she actually cares about me even though she just met me.

FOURTEEN

"Goodbye, Enforcer," Juliette says as she practically shoves Brevan out of her room. "I've got it from here."

"I'll be right outside, Princess." Brevan looks reluctant as he steps back into the hallway, but Juliette doesn't care as she hurries to close the door.

As soon as we're alone, she spins away from the entry and starts unlacing her dress as she walks. I linger by the door, brow furrowed.

A moment later, the silver fabric is in a puddle around her, and she steps out of the pile in her undergarments. She pulls on her corset strings while walking toward her vanity, tossing it to the floor after it's unlaced. Then she grabs the robe from the wall and tugs it on. "There's another robe in the bathing chamber if you want out of that gown. I swear to the gods my ladies lace me in so tight I can't even walk normally."

"Thankfully, there's no corset for me today," I say.

She lets out a breath. "I think they want to punish me. Corsets every day. Something about trying to make me proper. Tell me, Sabina, how am I supposed to be *proper* when my boobs are spilling out of my dress?"

I cover my mouth to stifle a giggle. She has a point.

She walks over to the small table in front of the windows. The teapot, cups, and plates of sweets I saw in the kitchen are already waiting for us.

I follow her and sit in the chair across from her, and she pours us each a cup of tea. "So, how are you tolerating being in the same room as my cousin?"

"The prince?"

"Yes, that cousin. My most famous cousin, for sure. I do have another, but he's only three. If he were older, I rather think Caiden would have had him killed because of his proximity to the throne. But lucky me, I'm just a woman so I'm not a threat."

"He does seem to hate women," I say.

"They all do. That's why I'm here," she says. "I scared away another suitor. My father is running out of options."

"And how exactly have you managed that?" I ask.

She laughs. "Taking notes to see if they'll send you back to Iskvaland?"

"I don't think that's an option," I admit. "I'm just curious."

"Well, they don't like it when you bed their sisters, I'll tell you that," she says.

I can't mask my surprise.

She takes a sip from her tea, then sets it down. "So here I am. To spend time with my cousin and my uncle and learn some manners. Really, I think it's so when I return, my father can brag that I was with the emperor in order to convince some other idiot into marrying me for the illusion of power."

"I'm sorry," I say.

She shrugs. "You probably know what it's like more than anyone I've ever met."

I'm starting to understand it, even though I'm not actually a princess. "It's not easy, is it?"

"No."

"Can you marry someone who will let you be? Someone who just wants your title?" I ask.

"Is that how he convinced you to stay here?" she asks.

I take a sip of my tea so I don't say something that might get me into trouble.

"They all say that, you know. That you can take lovers. That you can have your own freedom as long as you're discreet. But they don't really mean it. It never worked that way for my mother, at least."

"Is your mother...?" I let the question fade. It's not a polite thing to ask.

"Yes, she's dead. Even her relation to the emperor couldn't save her."

"I'm sorry." I bite down on my cheek to prevent myself from telling her that I also lost my mother. Sabina's mother is still alive. My heart feels heavy when I realize there's a mother who is without a daughter and she may never know. I hadn't considered that part of this before.

Then another thought strikes me. "Wait, if you're the emperor's niece, does that mean your parents are also immortal? Are you immortal?"

She laughs. "I'm not immortal. And my mother was not the emperor's sister. Nobody in my family got immortality," she bites out the last word. "She's his sister's great-granddaughter. Apparently, the emperor had a soft spot for his sister, so he's considered her children and grandchildren to be his kin. Calls us all niece and nephew. Sends us expensive gifts. My father is more than happy to trade my life for luxury."

"That's terrible." I blurt.

She leans forward and pats my hand, then returns to her tea, wrapping her fingers around the cup. "I knew you'd understand. I think we're going to be great friends."

"I think so, too." I smile at her, then take a sip of my tea.

"I hate that our friendship rests on your marriage to Caiden. Between us, I wouldn't want that for anyone I like." She bites into a small cake, then groans in appreciation. "At least there are some perks to our situation." She pushes the plate toward me. "Nobody makes sweets like Elizabeth."

I pick up one of the desserts but hold it for a moment while I consider her words. She's going to be very helpful, even if she might not know about the magic that keeps the emperor alive. "What can you share with me about Caiden?"

She pops the rest of the cake into her mouth, then chews slowly before swallowing. "Aside from the fact that he's even more power-hungry than his father?"

I nod encouragingly.

"He's been spoiled and terrible since we were kids. They used to keep dogs here, you know. But they kept finding them dead. Caiden was testing his magic on them. Torturing them."

My jaw drops, and I set my hand over my heart. "How could someone do such a thing?"

"He's worse than his father. And I suspect that if the emperor wasn't immortal, Caiden would have already found a way to obtain the crown for himself," she says. "Be careful around him."

I want to ask a hundred questions, but I don't want to scare her away or reveal my hand. Yet, there's something about her that makes me open up. "I think I've already pushed him more than I should."

"You're still alive, so you must be doing something right. You aren't his first betrothed."

"Really?"

Her brow furrows. "I thought you'd know. I heard your father required a blood oath saying that they'll honor their agreement with him even if you end up dead... after what happened to the last woman."

My fingers shake, and I quickly set the cake down, then tuck my hands on my lap to prevent her from seeing. If he's got that oath, all his threats about killing me are valid. He really doesn't need me. I am even less protected than I thought. "What happened to her?"

"He found her with another man," she says. "I wasn't here, but I heard he kept her alive for days while he tortured her."

"Was it Brevan?" I ask, remembering the gossip from my ladies.

"Oh, no. It was my brother."

"No." I cover my mouth with my hand, then lower it. "I'm so sorry."

"It was a long time ago. And he did me a favor. Since

I'm a woman, I think they put up with my disobedience. I'm still available for an alliance, but I'm not a threat since I can't inherit the throne myself."

"Was your brother a threat?" I ask.

She chuckles darkly. "You're starting to figure things out, aren't you?"

"Did he even actually sleep with the woman?" I ask.

"I suspect he did. But I'm not sure either of them had much of a say in it. There's a lot of magic in this castle that we're not aware of. Things that happen that shouldn't. Missing memories, people's signatures on documents they never remember signing... Just be cautious."

"It doesn't sound like it matters if I'm careful or not," I point out. "If my father has a blood oath that's good whether I live or die, what protection do I have?"

"I suppose Caiden must find you useful somehow," she says. "Otherwise, he could have just arranged for some kind of accident."

"I guess it's not too late for that." I make myself take a sip of my tea. It's cold so I finish it before setting it back down.

Juliette picks up the teapot and refills my cup.

"Thank you."

She smiles, then refills hers. "True. But I heard the emperor gave you his blessing."

He came to dinner," I say. "He looked...old."

"He is old."

"Really old," I say. "Is that how he always looks?"

"No."

"Is he losing his magic?" I try to sound concerned.

"Yes." She sips her tea.

"Oh, that's terrible." I aim for concern, but it comes out almost sarcastic. I fight against wincing at my mistake.

"Is it?" she asks.

I'm silent while I try to determine her tone. She must have caught my mistake. But she doesn't seem happy about her life here. Is she testing me? Is it possible she'd be on my side? "If Caiden is as bad as you say, I'm not sure I want the emperor going anywhere."

She seems satisfied by my answer and picks up a little flower-shaped cake. "I'm not sure any of us will have a choice."

"What do you mean?"

She chews slowly, then wipes her fingers on her napkin. "His last visit to the temple didn't reverse his aging process like usual. Either the gods are angry at him, or he's reached his limit. If he doesn't regain his youth this Darkfall, I'm not sure he ever will."

"He's been aging for the last five years?" My heart is racing again, but not out of fear. This could be the confirmation I need. "Does that mean he's not immortal anymore?"

She shrugs. "Nobody knows for sure. But I do know he stays very hidden and protected. He's got a lot of enemies, and he certainly isn't giving any of them a chance to test his immortality."

I focus on eating a pastry that's been dipped in chocolate. I know it's sweet and indulgent and beyond anything I'd ever eat as myself, but I can't taste it. My mind is buzzing. The rapid aging has to be why the emperor is in hiding. He's mortal. I was right. Now, I just need to find out where his quarters are and then I could get out of here before Darkfall.

I finish chewing, then swallow. "What is Darkfall like around here?"

"Oh, you're going to love it. The balls, the feasts, the men…Though, I suppose you can't take any lovers. But let me tell you, it's the best two weeks of the whole year. Everyone turns a blind eye during the week of the temple visits. It's like a hedonistic ritual. I was barely past my majority for the last one. My chaperone got drunk and proceeded to spend the whole week in a state of semiconscious undress while she guzzled wine. When it was over, nobody talked about it."

"That sounds intense," I say.

"It is." Her eyes light up as she tells me stories about the things she saw and participated in during last Darkfall.

"What about the men who return from their ceremony? Do they join in the revelry?" I ask.

"Oh, no." She shakes her head. "They're usually too tired. Or too haunted by whatever they went through. I only saw two who were high-ranking enough to stay in the castle. Both looked like ghosts. They retreated to their rooms for two weeks after the celebrations ended and never spoke of it."

"How many usually go for the ceremony?" I ask.

"It varies. Sometimes there's ten or twenty. I've heard that some Darkfalls only have two or three." She picks up the teapot and refills both our cups. "What you really want to watch out for is the absinthe. I swear there's an entire night I can't remember after I tried the stuff."

I listen and laugh as she recalls the funny moments and

happier parts of the celebrations. For those not going to the temple, it sounds like it's a joyous occasion. I understand why everyone is so excited.

We finish the tea and most of the cakes by the time there's a knock.

"Enter," Juliette calls.

Brevan steps inside the room. "Your Highness, the prince has requested your presence."

"Thank you for the tea and the company," I tell Juliette.

"I'm glad you're here," she says. "Maybe being stuck in this castle won't be such a terrible thing for either of us."

Fifteen

THE PRINCE'S quarters are on the upper levels of the castle. A formal sitting room and dining room lead to a sprawling balcony that spans across the two. You can see the entirety of the city below. Cold wind whips around us, and I'm a little dizzy from the height, but I can't take my eyes off the little houses and winding roads far below us.

"It's even more beautiful at night," Caiden says as he approaches. "Sorry for making you wait."

"Your Highness, Princess." Brevan bows, then retreats from the balcony.

I watch from the corner of my eye and notice that he leaves the rooms entirely. Once again, I'm alone with the prince.

Caiden holds up a narrow box. "This arrived, and I had to make sure you received it right away. The council can wait. It's not like anything ever gets done in those meetings."

He opens the lid, revealing a silver chain leading to the

large blue stone I chose. The chain shimmers and the stone sparkles even in the obscured, cloudy light. A pair of earrings with smaller blue stones glitter on either side of the necklace.

"It's beautiful," I say, meaning it. I was glad the jeweler had kept it simple.

Caiden lifts the necklace from its black velvet pillow, then sets the box down on a small table. "May I?"

I turn and lift my hair so he can fasten it around my neck. His fingers brush against my skin, and it sends an uncomfortable crawling sensation down my spine. How can he be so gentle with me while being so horrible to everyone and everything?

"There." He moves so he's facing me. "It's beautiful. And tasteful."

I touch the stone. "Thank you."

"Thank my father," he says. "It was his idea to test you this way."

My brows furrow. "Test?"

"Don't worry, you passed," he says.

"I'm confused." I slide the stone along the chain, anxiously toying with it.

"That's unfortunate," he says. "Here I've been telling him how you're much smarter than I thought you'd be."

I drop my hand to my side. "Was it because I chose something simple? Or was it the specific stone I picked?"

"So you do understand."

"Sort of," I admit.

"It was both," he says. "The fact that you were drawn to the only stone in the selection that belonged to my late mother and the fact that you didn't just ask for everything as some might."

"This was your mother's?" My stomach twists, and bile crawls up my throat. I'm wearing something that belonged to a dead woman. I don't know enough about the late empress to tell if she was anything like her son or husband, but I'm not sure I want to. The few things I have gleaned tell me she was likely just as interested in power as they are. And she stood by doing nothing to rein in her son.

"It's a good color on you," he says.

"Thank you," I reply.

"I have to get back, but I'll see you for dinner tonight."

"Thank you, again," I touch the necklace, "it really is beautiful."

"You're welcome. I'll see you at eight." He turns and walks toward the door.

As soon as he's gone, Brevan comes into the room. "Should we continue our tour?"

"No, I'd like to go back to my rooms. I'm tired," I lie.

"Very well." He's silent on the walk back, though I catch him glancing at the necklace more than once.

It feels like a weight around my neck. Or maybe a collar. Something that marks me as Caiden's belonging. My skin prickles and I clench my hands into fists to prevent myself from tearing it off my throat. With each passing day, the lines blur and I worry I'm becoming more Sabina and less myself.

I need to get out of here.

When I tell Marian I'm not feeling well, she tries to fuss over me. It's a miracle I manage to get her and the other ladies to leave me while I rest.

As soon as they're out of my room, I dart to my bathing chamber and close the door behind me. I pick up one of the glowing lanterns on the counter and hope that it stays lit from magic.

I can't stay in this place much longer. They watch every move I make. I don't know when I'll get this chance again. It takes me a few tries to find the exact place to press on the wall, but my heart leaps when the door slides open and the passageway appears.

There's a tiny, dark stone room that's walled in on three sides. When I take a few steps in, I notice the hole with a ladder that goes straight down. Whoever built this castle had to have put this here intentionally. Was it meant to be a quick emergency escape route, or did it have a more nefarious purpose?

When I reach the bottom of the ladder, I'm in a dark tunnel that extends beyond the arc of light from my lantern. I hope there's more than one route in this passageway. That it will take me somewhere besides the catacombs. If not, maybe I can find another tunnel from the City of the Dead that leads to somewhere else in the castle. There has to be a way to discover where the emperor sleeps.

It's already cold, and I can feel every pebble and stone through the thin slippers they make me wear. The walls are crumbling dirt and rock. Some of them have signs of erosion, leaving a slanted pile on the ground. The whole thing feels incredibly unstable. Nothing like the carefully dug and reinforced City of the Dead.

On my right is an opening that's completely caved in, rocks and dirt blocking the path. I wonder where it leads and if it would be stable enough to use if the rocks were removed.

As I go deeper, I pass two more cave-ins. So far, the route I'm traveling is the only easily accessible option.

The ground grows increasingly rocky the deeper I get but I continue forward, my determination guiding me. If this only leads me to the catacombs, at least I have a way out if I need to escape.

Ahead, there's another tunnel to the right, only this time, it's not caved in. I stop when I reach it and stare at both options. Continue straight ahead or turn down the new path. I don't know which leads to the City of the Dead, but I suspect the turn is toward the castle.

I find several larger stones and put them together until I form an arrow pointing toward the direction I came from. The new tunnel has fewer rocks on the ground, but its ceiling is lower, causing me to have to duck down to continue through it.

Twice, I trip on the skirts of my dress, so I pull them up and wrap the extra fabric around my arm to get it out of the way. I'm certain there's a slope to this path and I'm walking on a gradual decline.

The tunnel widens, and I'm faced with another option. I create a marker for myself and choose the turn on the right again.

Something crawls over the walls, and I hear the scurrying of creatures in their burrows. This tunnel is teeming with life, but I keep my light straight ahead, so I don't have to see the animals that call this place home. It's easier that way.

Ahead, there's glowing light, and I slow as I approach. Are we outside the castle?

I continue cautiously until I reach the opening. I stare in awe at an overgrown garden. Above me is a glass roof and the whole thing is contained by stone walls. While everything is green and flourishing, it's consumed the space. Vines cover the stone walkway and climb up the walls. Plants tangle together, making it difficult to find where one ends and the next begins.

I'm about to step over the greenery, onto the buried stone walkway, when I realize that everything growing in here is poisonous. This garden must have been kept by the empress in secret. But if it was hers, why was everything still green when the outdoor garden was black? Was it someone else's garden or did the empress have power they didn't know about? Whoever was caring for it hadn't been here in a long time. How were all these plants still alive?

The tunnel continues across from me, but without more protection, I can't walk through the overgrowth. Frustrated, I turn around and head back.

While I didn't find a way out of my rooms yet, there are plants in there that might come in handy if I study the books that were left behind on my bookshelf.

I want to find out where the other tunnels lead, but I've been gone a while. Rather than risk anyone finding out that I have a way to leave my rooms, I return to the bathroom and close the secret entrance behind me.

Someone must be watering that garden, which means

the tunnel on the other side must lead somewhere interesting. If this belonged to the empress, she had big secrets and now I've got another mystery to solve. What was the purpose of this garden and did anyone else know it was here?

Sixteen

THE NEXT FEW days blur together. Dinner with the prince, gossip in my rooms with my ladies, Brevan following me like a shadow as I wander the halls hoping for a clue as to where the emperor sleeps.

Each night, I sneak into the passageway and take a different turn, hoping to find something useful. So far, I've come across a dead end and an entry to the catacombs. I marked the catacomb path with stones in case I need to escape quickly, but aside from that and the poisonous plants, there's nothing else of use.

I need to find a way to explore the castle without Brevan at my heels.

It's dreary outside. The rain and fog seem to seep into my room, casting a sense of melancholy that makes all my ladies quiet. I welcome the knock on the door if only to break the boredom.

"Who could that be?" Marian says as she hurries to the door.

I set down my untouched embroidery and turn. Perla, the seamstress Duchess Drathmore sent, walks into the room. Several ladies follow her, each of them carrying bolts of fabric and bundles of ribbon and lace.

My ladies gasp and chatter excitedly, and we all go to welcome the seamstress. At least it's a change and a distraction. While I've been able to wander the castle, none of the other courtiers will speak to me and I'm always accompanied by Brevan. The lack of excitement is getting to me.

"Perla, we weren't expecting you until next week," Marian says.

"This is a special order," Perla says. "Dutchess Drathmore hired me to create a masterpiece for the Darkfall ball. Perhaps a gown to honor Loha. My design will take time, We're already behind as it is."

The ladies gasp and squeal. I smile, and I'm a little disappointed I won't be here to see the finished product. I've always enjoyed the stories surrounding the moon goddess and Darkfall is her time. While she's held captive by the sun during the two-week period of Darkfall, we're to call on her to show our appreciation for her so she'll return when she's liberated.

"Shall we begin, princess?" Perla gestures to a stool that one of her ladies is holding.

"Yes, thank you."

The woman sets down the stool and step on it.

My ladies are touching the fabric samples, holding them up to each other, and layering them with lace or strings of beads. Perla measures me while one of her assistants takes notes and the others show off the samples they brought to my ladies.

Out of the corner of my eye, I notice Katherine is in the nook with my little writing desk. She looks around as if checking that the other ladies are still occupied before quickly opening and peering into the drawers. She moves the books on the shelf, then starts looking around my bed, lifting pillows, then putting them back.

She glances over and catches my eye, her face turning red. Quickly, she returns to the group without looking at me again.

"The prince will be in black and silver, and I think we should have you in silver with black," Perla says. "What do you think, Your Highness?"

I tear my eyes away from Katherine to look at the seamstress. "Yes. That's a good idea."

"Wonderful." She claps her hands, then one of her assistants brings over several bolts of silver fabric. Perla holds them up near my face and makes humming sounds as she compares them.

Once she decides, she sends her assistant away with the correct bolt of fabric.

"Do you make the gowns for my ladies as well?" I ask.

"They will provide their own gowns," Marian says quickly.

"Can you make them?" I ask.

Charlotte and Genevieve look up hopefully.

Perla's mouth forms a surprised O, then she blinks a few times. "I suppose I can. I'd have to hire more assistants, and it would be expensive."

"Shouldn't my betrothed pay for it?" I ask.

Perla smiles. "I suppose you should have your own

accounts if he won't cover the cost. The empress had her own funds."

"Let's do that, then," I say.

The ladies squeal and rush toward me, shouting their thanks.

"I want them to be dressed as beautifully as me," I say. "They should all be in silver. To honor Loha."

"Of course," Perla says.

I step down from the stool, and my ladies swarm around Perla and her assistants. Except Katherine, who is hanging back from the others, her expression blank.

"Katherine, can you please help me change for dinner?" I ask. "I'd like something more formal for tonight."

She curtsies. "Of course, Your Highness."

Marian glances at us, but one of the assistants, brandishing a measuring tape, steals her attention.

"Will you get my black silk dress with the lace, please?" I ask.

Katherine nods, then walks to the wardrobe.

I quickly slip into the bathing chamber, and as soon as Katherine joins me, dress in hand, I close the door behind us.

She hangs the dress on a hook, then faces me. "I know it looks bad, but I promise I have a good reason."

"For going through my room? What were you searching for? Why? Who sent you?"

"I need the fire ruby," she says.

"What?" How does she even know I have that?

She glances around again, as if she thinks there might be someone hiding in the bathing chamber. I can't help but do the same.

"I know who you are," she says.

My pulse kicks up, but I keep my mouth shut and stare at her, waiting for her to say more.

"Someone just told the Night Legion that the rebels are using fire rubies to communicate," she says. "You can't be caught with that on you. I can get it out of your room and out of the castle."

"You work for the rebels," I say.

She nods.

"Then what am I doing here? Why couldn't you just get the information needed?" I ask.

"The only way I was able to get in was as a lady-in-waiting," she says. "I was asked to assist you without letting you know I was here. Obviously, I failed."

"Why did they need me, then?" I cross my arms over my chest.

"I'd have tried. But I can't get as close as you."

With a sigh, I drop my arms to my side. "Maybe. I still can't get a meeting with the emperor or find his quarters."

"You will," she says. "Now, where is the stone?"

"Hidden well. But what am I to do when I need to contact them?" I ask.

"You'll tell me. I have ways of sharing information but right now, I need to get this stone away from you."

"It's in a hidden pocket of the dress I arrived in." I lift my chin toward the wardrobe where the dress is hanging.

"Thank you. I'll make sure it's gone, and as soon as you have what you need, tell me and I'll let them know."

"This whole time you've known the truth?" I ask.

"Sorry. We thought it better if you didn't know, just in case you failed," she says.

"So you could continue in my place." Lee had even less faith in me than I thought.

"That won't be necessary. The prince likes you. You'll find what you need soon, I'm certain of it." She removes the dress from the hook. "Now, let's get you changed for your date with the prince."

SEVENTEEN

"I'll be right outside to escort you to your rooms when you're finished," Brevan says as we stop in front of the double doors that lead to the prince's quarters.

Apparently, Caiden has a free afternoon and thinks we should spend some time together.

My palms are damp with sweat. I can't believe how nervous I am. This won't be like our nightly meals. Dinner is usually short because he's busy, and I tell him I'm tired. Conversations are kept to safe topics. I flirt enough to keep his interest but make sure I'm not over the top. He's been on his best behavior, like he wants to impress me. I have no idea what today will bring.

Caiden himself opens the door. "Come in, Princess."

There's a table in the center of the room that wasn't there last time. A black tablecloth has been draped over it, and there's a chessboard in the center. Caiden gestures toward it. "I thought we could play a game."

"I didn't know you like chess," I say.

"I'm guessing there's a lot you don't know about me," he says as he pulls out my chair.

After he's seated, he gestures to me. "Ladies first."

I'm suddenly grateful for the late nights when my brothers would play chess. I watched more often than I played, but at least I know the rules.

"I haven't played since I was a child," I say as I move a pawn.

"It's been years for me as well. Brevan and I used to unwind with a game from time to time. But I can't recall the last time we did," he says.

We focus on the game, making the first few moves in silence. After a while, I feel like I've reacquainted myself with the board.

"Did you play games with your family?" I ask.

"No. Never. Father was too busy and Mother was... Well, she had her attentions elsewhere," he says.

"Who did you spend time with? Just Brevan?" I ask.

"Sometimes one of my father's councilmen or their children. After Brevan arrived, we kept each other company on occasion, but it wasn't long before both of us were sent to training and no longer had time for games."

"That sounds lonely," I say.

"Can't be much different than your childhood," he points out. "Unless your parents were more involved."

What was Sabina's childhood like? Probably similar to his. "There were a few more children around. Girls," I add because of what Brevan told me, "who I had as playmates."

"Yet, you snuck out alone." He pauses with a pawn between his finger and thumb.

"And that was supposed to be private," I scold.

"I won't tell. I went through my own rebellious phase."

"You did?" I ask. "What was that like?"

"I don't think you're ready for those stories."

There's a knock on the door, and he rises, then answers it. I catch sight of two legionnaires before he steps into the hall. It's not long before he's back in the room, his expression dark. Brevan is by his side. "Warships from Duneport just spotted off the coast. I have to go."

"Would you like me to escort the princess to her rooms before we leave?" Brevan asks.

"No. You'll stay here. Make sure nothing happens to Sabina and that nobody knows why I'm gone. We already have enough unrest. I don't want the nobles finding out that Duneport is getting involved in this."

"I didn't know we were at war with them," I say quietly.

"We aren't, and I'm hoping to keep it that way," Caiden replies. "I need you not to tell your ladies."

"I won't," I promise.

He leaves without a backward glance, all the legionnaires following him.

I'm sitting at the abandoned game while Brevan stands in the doorway.

I gesture toward the chessboard. "Want to take Caiden's place?"

"Wouldn't you rather go back to your ladies?" he asks.

"No."

He enters slowly, then sits at the table. His dark hair is pulled away from his eyes, and he's wearing his black leather armor. I wonder if it's as uncomfortable as the corset I have on under my dress.

I move a piece, then look up at him. "Your turn."

He takes his turn, and I can see just a hint of his gift mark extending beyond his sleeve. I know everyone with a god's gift has a mark, but I've heard they're usually small and kept hidden. I've never seen one in real life. I wonder what Brevan's looks like.

"Giving up already?" He asks.

My cheeks heat. I have no business thinking about his gift marks. "Never." I glance up at him. "Don't rush me."

After I go, he seems to take the game very seriously. He studies the board and is intentional with each action. Every time he leans forward, I try for a glimpse of that mark, but his sleeve covers it.

"You must hate being stuck with me." I set a bishop on the square.

"I go where I'm needed," he says.

"I can't imagine it's a good use of your skills. Making you sit here, where I'm already protected." I glance at him. "I've heard about you. The things you can do."

He lifts his brow. "You have?"

"Of course. The man who burns whole cities to the ground for his emperor."

"We all have our role to play, don't we, Princess?" He moves a knight.

"We do. But we still have choices." I counter his play and he frowns.

"What do you know about choices? You're here to marry a stranger because your kingdom demanded it of you." He's studying the board, his hand moving between pieces while he decides what to do next.

"I know what I'm doing," I reply.

"Do you?" He looks up at me, eyebrow quirked.

"Yes."

"You say you've heard of me, but have you heard about your betrothed? Do you know about him?"

"Of course I have," I say defensively.

He takes his turn, his eyes never leaving mine.

"I wouldn't be here if I didn't think it was worth it," I add.

"Then you understand why I do the things I do." He shrugs. "Your move."

I scrutinize the board and realize he's left his king unguarded. "I don't want you to let me win."

"It's your turn," he repeats.

With a sigh, I move. "Checkmate."

"Well played, Princess."

"You let me win," I accuse.

He stands, then adjusts his armor before gesturing toward the door. "I'll take you to your rooms."

"No. Take me to the library."

He sighs. "Fine."

We walk in silence, but Brevan's words reverberate in my mind. Did I make the wrong choice? Am I going to help anyone? If Katherine was already coming, why am I here? What is the point? So far, I've accomplished nothing.

When we reach the library, I enter the expansive room and expect him to wait outside but he follows me. "Do you think someone is going to harm me in the library?"

"I thought you might need help finding books," he says. "The emperor no longer retains any librarians or priests in here."

While the space is impressive, I notice how cold and

impersonal it is. No fires burn in the hearths today. The only light or warmth comes from the lancet windows above the shelves.

"I'd like to find some books about Darkfall," I tell him.

"I'm not sure there's anything about fashion on the shelves," he says.

"Very funny. I want the history. Why we celebrate it, how it came about, what it means..." What I really want is something about how magic works and if the emperor is truly mortal, but I can't tell him that.

"This way." He walks toward a dark corner of the library, where several shelves are tucked away. The books are dusty and smell moldy. Nobody has touched these tomes in a long time. "Here."

I lean closer to the shelf he indicates and begin to read the spines. Not all of them are labeled, so I get to work pulling the books out and skimming the contents.

While I'm going through them, Brevan gets bored. He sprawls out on a nearby chair, but he continues to scan the room, his head turning slowly as he investigates. Maybe he really is concerned about my safety.

I find four books that seem promising and carry them over to where he's sitting. "I'm ready."

When I return to my rooms, my ladies are huddled together, whispering rapidly. When they see me, they break apart and hurry to their usual positions, picking up their abandoned embroidery or cards.

I set my books down on my bed as I scan the room with a furrowed brow. None of them make eye contact. They're all suddenly focused on whatever is in their hands. "What's going on? Where's Marian?"

Katherine is the first to make eye contact. "She's dead."

I cover my mouth with my hand as I gasp. "What happened?"

"Nobody will tell us." Katherine says. "They just said she had an accident."

I march back to the door and throw it open. Brevan straightens, his hand moving to the hilt of his weapon. Then his expression softens and he drops his arm to his side. "What is it?"

"What happened to Marian?" I demand.

His brow furrows. He doesn't know.

"Find out. Now." I slam the door and return to my room. "We will get to the bottom of this."

None of the ladies are pretending to work on their activities anymore.

"Who's heard anything?" I ask. "Any rumors? Any guesses? I want to know."

They're quiet a long time, then Antonia rises from where she was sitting at the window seat. "I heard it was poison. But I don't know why."

"That's what I heard, too," Charlotte says.

"Do you think she upset the emperor?" Genevieve adds.

"She was sleeping with him," Charlotte says. "Everyone knew that."

"I didn't know that," I say. "Was she with him? When she died?"

"I think so," Charlotte says.

"No, she wasn't. She doesn't go to him during the day. He always calls for her at night," Antonia says.

"Not always," Charlotte returns.

"Are you sure she was still with him?" Genevieve asks. "He's so old now."

There's a knock on the door, and I hurry to open it. Brevan actually looks concerned. "There was an assassination attempt on the emperor. Marian drank the wine meant for him."

"Thank you for checking into that for me." I walk back into the room numbly.

I find my way to a chair and sit. "You were right, it was poison." I wait to feel sad, but it isn't there. I'm shocked. How can she just be gone?

Genevive wipes her eyes, and Charlotte comforts her on the nearby couch. Antonia plops down on a chair. "It's hard to believe she won't walk through that door."

"I know." It doesn't feel real.

I catch sight of Katherine near the window. She's as pale as a ghost. The surprise fades to anger and frustration. Was this planned? And if so, how could they get that close and end up killing his mistress instead?

And then I realize that if someone else is trying to kill the emperor, I'm not alone.

Aside from Katherine, my other ladies are huddled in a group, comforting each other and wiping their tears. I should probably be there with them, but I can use their distraction first.

I head to the window and pause in front of Katherine, leaning close so I can whisper in her ear. "Was it you?"

She shakes her head. "I know as much as you."

"Alright." I pat her on the shoulder and offer a stiff smile. "You should be with the others."

I rub my temples, then sit in the window seat. I'm there

a long time, staring at the clouds and the gardeners trimming the topiaries. The others continue to sniffle and cry but I don't join them. This is their time to grieve and as much as I'm trying to act like I belong, I don't. And I'm not sure I can pretend right now.

Eventually, the ladies find other distractions. They pretend to work on small tasks, but most of them are staring into space. Charlotte and Antonia are huddled together, whispering. Both of them have red faces and puffy eyes. They must have been the closest to Marian.

A knock sounds, then an envelope shoots out from the crack under the door.

Brow furrowed, I hasten to retrieve the letter. Everyone watches me.

"It's addressed to Princess Sabina and her ladies." I open the envelope, then read the card aloud. "Your presence is requested at a ball tonight. Nine o'clock. Grand Ballroom."

"There isn't supposed to be a ball tonight," Antonia says.

"The next one isn't for weeks," Genevieve adds.

"I guess they made a change." I read the note again, making sure I didn't make a mistake.

"Do you think it has something to do with Marian?" Katherine asks.

Yes. I absolutely do. And considering how she died, I can't imagine this will be an uplifting affair. I swallow hard. It's possible this isn't a ball at all. What if it's something nefarious? Someone did just try to kill the emperor.

My ladies watch me with worried expressions. "I'm sure it'll be fine. Maybe the emperor wants to do something to take our mind off it." I force a smile. "You all should go get ready."

"I'll stay and help you," Katherine offers.

"Thank you. The rest of you, I'll see you there," I say.

As soon as the others are gone, I turn to Katherine. "Is there another rebel in the castle? Anyone who might be trying to kill the emperor that you're not telling me about?"

"All I know is that someone takes my messages. But I was told that was their only job."

"We need to know if it was a rebel or if we've got competition," I say. "Can you get a message to your contact now?"

She nods. "I already wrote it. I just need to drop it."

"Go."

I just hope that whoever else is after the emperor is friend and not foe.

Eighteen

"Princess," Brevan greets me. "I'm here to escort you to the ball."

"You left my door," I say, noting the stiff formal uniform he's wearing. It's the first time I've seen him without the leather armor. Well, besides that first night when he removed it to sleep in my room.

"The emperor wanted a formal event tonight." He looks uncomfortable in the starched collar and shiny silver buttons.

I hate how attractive he is in the uniform. I've seen other men in the Night Legion's formal uniform, but none of them wore it the way he does.

"Is Caiden back?" I ask.

"No, he's still away. He might be gone a while."

"Oh."

"Disappointed?" he asks.

"He is my betrothed," I reply.

"That's not an answer." His expression is smug.

"It's not really any of your business, is it?" I snap.

161

"I suppose it's not. Aside from the fact that while he's away, I'm required to be your shadow."

"You left to change," I point out.

"Seven men stood outside your room while I was away," he explains.

"Seven? What exactly are you all worried about happening to me?" I ask.

"It wouldn't be a good look if Iskvaland's princess died on Pendralian soil, would it?"

Anxiety spikes and my stomach twists. She already did, but he doesn't know that. "No. Not at all." The dead princess's face flashes in my memory. Pale skin, lifeless eyes staring at nothing. Blood everywhere. So much blood.

"We should go, they're expecting you." Brevan takes a few slow steps, waiting for me to join him.

I blink away the memory, then catch up to Brevan. "Why are we having this ball?"

"Because the emperor required it."

"Is this something he does often?" I ask.

"No."

"So almost nobody sees him for three years, and suddenly, he reemerges and then decides to throw a ball the night his mistress is poisoned?"

He pauses in front of a staircase, then turns to me. "Yes."

I scoff. "You're not going to give me any information, are you?"

He sighs as he descends the staircase. It's a rare show of frustration that isn't aimed at me. In fact, I'm not sure I ever saw any indication of annoyance aimed toward the emperor before. My insides twist. This can't be good.

I grab his arm and he freezes, his attention going to my hand. I drop it quickly. "You have to tell me something. What am I walking into? She was my lady, Marian. And now she's dead. I don't know how things work around here." I swallow, then blurt out something I know I shouldn't. "I'm scared."

His brow furrows. "I didn't know you were afraid of anything from how you so quickly dismiss your safety."

"I'm more afraid of the emperor than I am the rebels." My eyes widen and I press my lips together to prevent myself from saying more. That was so stupid. Why can't I keep my mouth closed around this man? It's like I just have to hear myself speak around him. Or maybe it's because I want to hear him speak.

I've been here too long. This man killed my brothers. "Forget it. I'm sure everything is fine." I resume my descent, not looking back at the enforcer.

Footsteps follow at a distance, but I continue beyond the stairs, down a hall, and into another. If I make a wrong turn, he'll correct me.

"I don't know why he did this. As far as I know, he's never called for a ball without notice and a reason to celebrate," Brevan suddenly says.

I pause. "So I have a right to be concerned?"

"I have no idea."

I wait until he's alongside me, then allow him to lead us the rest of the way. Thankfully, I manage to stay silent for the duration.

We stop in front of the closed double doors. A pair of legionnaires opens them for us so we can enter.

The ballroom has been transformed. Every surface is

draped with dark green vines. They climb the walls and dangle from the chandeliers. They wind up chair legs and weave around tables laden with delicacies. Even the servants are wearing wreaths of the same vines.

I tiptoe around the plants, afraid to touch anything. They remind me of the vines that overtook the garden I found. And considering Marian was just poisoned, I don't think this is a coincidence.

People in formal dress mill around, conversing and drinking from crystal goblets. None of them demonstrate any signs of concern. In fact, they're laughing and smiling and enjoying themselves.

Charlotte waves to me from across the room. I wave back, then look over at Brevan. Even in a room full of courtiers, he stands out. The uniform fits like it was designed for him. The fabric just tight enough over his shoulders and chest to show his impressive physique. His hair is slicked back in the current style, and while I think he looks better with it loose and messy, there's no denying he pulls this off well. I hate that he's the most handsome man in the room.

"Go on," he says. "I'll be nearby."

I also hate that I feel better knowing he's here.

I join my ladies, complimenting each of them on their gowns. Katherine is missing, though. I scan the crowd for her and hope she's somewhere in the mass of people.

"Princess Sabina," a male voice says.

I turn and face an older man with a gray beard and thinning gray hair. He's dressed in black but has a purple handkerchief stuffed into his breast pocket.

He bows. "It's an honor to meet you. I am Sir Lennox."

He straightens. "I met your father during the Ruby Wars before you were born. He's a fair and powerful man. You must pass along my well wishes when you next visit."

"Of course," I say, inclining my head. "It's lovely to meet you."

He gestures to the women standing next to him. One is probably his age. She has silver hair and an elegant face, though she looks like she's never once smiled in her entire life. The other is younger, probably twelve or thirteen summers. "My wife, Lady Carol, and my daughter, Margaret."

"Nice to meet you both," I say.

The women curtsy.

"It was lovely to make your acquaintance, Princess," he says. His wife and daughter dip into a half curtsy, then the family walks away.

"They've been social climbing for generations," Antonia whispers. "Only earned that title two generations ago, but they're desperate to go higher. He's trying to marry off his daughter to anyone with influence."

"Poor girl," I say.

"Only if she gets a bad match. If he's successful, it'll raise her status and her children's status."

"Is that what you want?" I ask. "To marry the highest-ranking man you can find?"

"Isn't that what you're doing?" she asks.

For a moment, I forgot that I'm seen as nothing more than a princess who will marry a prince. "You're right. I suppose that's the best we can hope for."

"No, the best we can hope for is a man who won't beat us," she says.

I suddenly wonder if that's why the empress had so many books on poisons.

A hush falls over the crowd, and the hairs on my arms stand on edge. I follow the direction of everyone's stares to a raised platform featuring a single black throne.

A dark-haired man dressed in black velvet, trimmed in silver, approaches the stairs that lead to the platform. He's followed by several night legionnaires in their dress uniforms. When he reaches the throne, he stands in front of it, then extends his arms toward the crowd.

Everyone drops into bows or curtsies. I follow their lead as my head swims. This can't be the emperor, can it? He wasn't able to gain back his immortality until Darkfall, right?

"My most faithful and loyal friends," he says with a booming voice.

Everyone stands.

"Tonight, I have called you here to celebrate life. As you know, we lost one of our own today. Lady Marian was a loyal, longtime companion to my late wife. She served her empress and her empire well."

People make the sign of the gods or bow their heads. I lower my own head in respect.

"The culprit was no doubt aiming for me, thinking me weak in my aged form. While we both drank the poison, the gods saw fit to revive my immortality before the poison could harm me. Unfortunately, Marian was not gifted by the gods." He takes a breath and lowers his eyes.

When he looks back up, there's a glimmer of something sinister in his expression. "She will be missed by everyone who loved her, but her death was not in vain. You see, this tells us that we have a traitor in our midst. A spy. An assassin. Maybe more than one. So I called you all here tonight in the hopes that my message will reach our spy. My eyes are everywhere and will find you."

My pulse is so fast it's practically vibrating. He's immortal again. And he knows there's at least one traitor in his court. We lost our chance.

"Tonight, we celebrate the return of my immortality and many more centuries of my rule!" He claps and musicians begin to play. "Dance! Make merry!"

The courtiers around me clap in return, then begin to pair off to dance. I step back so I'm not on the dance floor while I let the news sink in.

We failed. Even if I find out where the emperor sleeps, how are we going to kill him? That was my original task. Find his weakness. If the gods renewed their gift of immortality because someone poisoned him, how are we to overcome that?

"Princess Sabina," a deep male voice says.

I turn to see the emperor himself standing in front of me, his hand outstretched in offer. "My son is not here to accompany you, but perhaps you'd allow me the privilege?"

The ladies behind me gasp, and I think Antonia is swooning so hard she might faint.

I set my hand on top of his. "I'd be honored."

He smiles, then escorts me to the dance floor. I position myself the way I practiced with Caiden and am quickly swept into the dance. The emperor is light on his feet and graceful. Up close, I can see how much he resembles his son. He's got the same brown hair and nearly amber eyes. The same strong chin. The same serious expression. He could almost be Caiden's twin. Especially since he hardly looks any older than him now.

"I'm sorry about Marian," I say softly.

"I am, too. And for you," he says. "I know she'd taken you under her wing."

"Yes, she was very kind. Motherly," I add.

"She liked you very much."

"I liked her, too." I smile.

"It's unfortunate that she met her end in such a gruesome fashion. The poison wasn't quick. Horrible to witness. My doctors couldn't do anything. Not even reduce her pain. We had to sit there and watch her suffer until it finally took her."

My stomach twists, and real tears blur my vision. My throat is so tight I can't speak. Nobody should have to meet their end that way.

"Don't worry, Princess. We've suspected a spy in our midst for a couple of weeks. We thought they were after you, actually."

"Why me?" I ask.

"To prevent the alliance, of course," he says.

I turn away from him, my mind a swirling tangle of thoughts. Of course, they'd suspect that. It's exactly what the rebels did, and he doesn't know they'd already succeeded.

But what if there's others who want the princess dead?

I scan the room and find Brevan watching my every move. The tiniest smirk tugs at his lips when he catches my eye. He knows I was searching for him. I look away, my cheeks heating.

"They still might be after you, but when I showed up as

a weak old man, they must have thought they could get to me." The emperor leads me into a gentle spin.

I thought the same, so I don't doubt him. I swallow hard, unsure of how I should respond to this information.

"But you don't need to worry. Brevan will stay with you until they're caught. And we will catch them. We always do." He returns his hand to my lower back, resuming the dance.

"I'm glad you're alright," I finally say. "And I do feel safer with your enforcer guarding me. But I also wonder if that's a waste of his skills?"

"His relic hunting can wait," he says. "He only returned to Pendralia the day before you arrived. Spent the last two years tracking relics in the mountains near the Iskvalandian border. He even met your father a few times."

"Two years?" I don't mean to blurt it out, but it isn't possible. If he's been away all this time, Brevan couldn't have killed my brothers or started that fire. If the Emperor is telling the truth, that means Lee lied to me. Why would he do that?

"I know that must seem like nothing to you. You've given up your home forever. And I should thank you for that. Your sacrifice—leaving your homeland and your kingdom to wed a stranger—will save so many lives."

I'm still trying to wrap my head around the fact that Brevan hasn't been in Pendralia for two years, but the emperor's words only get worse.

"Save lives? Caiden told me you intend to give the Iskvalandian army magic. That you're going to invade the Shatterlands."

"That's true. But they have wild magic. And they're

cultivating new relics from the stardust they mine. If we don't stop them, they'll be more powerful than the gods themselves."

"Isn't that blasphemy?" I ask.

"Why do you think the gods allow me to live so long? They have tasked me with this righteous purpose."

"I'm lucky I'm here, then. And that I can help in my own way," I say.

"I have a feeling you'll help more than you realize." He spins me again, then pulls me closer. Bile climbs up my throat and I resist the urge to push him away from me.

"I hear you spend a lot of time in the empress's temple."

"I do," I agree.

"Then you are familiar with the prophecy of light."

I nod.

"My wife thought it would be me and her, but alas, she didn't receive light magic when she visited the temple. And the gods never saw fit to grant me shadows. Though, they gave them to my son. It must be him. When you enter the temple, you will ask them to make you a wielder of light. We haven't seen one in three centuries. And the last one was killed before she could find her match."

"What if I don't want magic?" There is no way I will enter that temple.

"You might not yet be married to my son, but you are now a member of my empire. And everyone in my empire does as I command," he says, his tone stern but not angry.

"And if I don't get light?" I ask.

"You will. The gods have told me it is time for the prophecy to be fulfilled."

"I am not worthy of being part of the prophecy," I lower my eyes.

"The gods are the only ones who can determine that."

I face the emperor. "What if I die in the temple?"

"We'll send in someone else until we find the woman who can match my son." He smiles, but the words are clearly a threat.

"Then I better not die." I smile back, knowing the only way to save myself is to make sure he's dead first.

When the music ends, I curtsy, then leave the dance floor to find my ladies. Antonia and Genevieve are dancing with very handsome, well-dressed men. Charlotte and Katherine are watching, occasionally leaning over to whisper something to one another.

I join them, and they throw a barrage of questions at me about my dance with the emperor. I indulge them and tell them how kind and graceful he was.

A handsome, young member of the Night Legion approaches, and he bows when he reaches us. "Lady Katherine, would you honor me with a dance?"

His face is red, and he holds his hand out expectantly. He's nervous.

Katherine bats her lashes and giggles. "I would love to dance with you, but I hurt my ankle in the garden yesterday. Charlotte is perfectly healthy, though."

He moves his hand toward Charlotte. "Lady Charlotte?"

Her cheeks turn deep crimson, and she accepts his hand and the two of them get swept onto the dance floor.

I move closer to Katherine so I can whisper. "Did you leave the message?"

"Yes."

"We have a new problem, though," I say.

"I can see that."

"He said the gods made him immortal to save him after he drank the poison," I say.

She looks over at me, eyes wide. "He didn't even go to the temple?"

I shake my head.

Her face pales. "I didn't know that was possible."

"He also knows there's a spy in his court," I say. "Maybe more than one."

"We're going to have to be more careful," she warns.

"Yes."

"They want you to kill him," she says.

"What?" It's what I want, but Lee warned me against it. "What changed?"

"They don't think they can get close enough. They need you to do it. And fast."

"I don't know how to kill an immortal," I hiss.

"Then we find out."

"Before Darkfall," I say. "Because I am not going into that temple."

"They want you to go through the ceremony? To get magic?" Her eyes widen.

"Yes, but we both know I won't survive," I remind her.

"Alright. There has to be a way. The empress died. That means the emperor can, too. We'll figure it out."

Brevan walks toward us and I elbow Katherine. She presses her lips into a tight line, and I fix what I hope is a pleasant, non-suspicious expression on my face. When he arrives, he bends at the waist in a formal bow. "Princess, may I have this dance?"

Katherine pushes me toward him. "Go."

I take his hand and let him lead me onto the dance floor. Flutters fill my chest, but I tell myself it's nothing. Just proximity to an enemy. The same as Caiden or the Emperor.

But he isn't the same. It doesn't feel the same. And he might not have killed my brothers.

I look up at the enforcer as he leads me in the movements. He isn't as graceful as the emperor or Caiden, but he knows the steps.

He's a head taller than me, and he's broader than I realized. I knew he was tall and well-built but being this close to him highlights the size difference between us.

When he spins me, I falter, but he catches me and resumes the dance flawlessly. "Thanks."

"It's nice to see someone who makes my dancing look good." He chuckles and I can't help but laugh with him.

His hand on my back feels steady and strong. Despite everything I've been through, and his reputation, I know he'd never harm me. Which makes no sense. I have no business feeling anything other than loathing for Brevan.

I've hated him since we met. More so since I found out who he is. Lee told me the enforcer was responsible for my brothers' deaths. That he killed them personally. But if he wasn't in Pendralia, how could he have?

That doesn't make him a saint, though. Even if he isn't the one who killed them, he already has so much innocent blood on his hands. He's just as guilty as the rest of them.

"The emperor told me you were away for two years," I say.

His eyes find mine. "Yes."

"Aren't you bored just standing outside my door after two years of burning down villages?" The question is a reminder to myself about who he really is.

"I know you don't think highly of me, but you really aren't in a place to judge, Princess," he answers.

"I don't kill innocent people for fun," I say.

"Neither do I," he replies.

"But you order your men to kill people. And we both know most of them are innocent," I counter.

"Yes." His jaw tenses and I get the sense that he's holding back. Like he wants to say more.

"Why?"

He lifts a brow. "Why?"

"You could tell him no."

"Like you did when your father demanded you marry a stranger?"

"I don't have your skills. I wouldn't last on my own. I can't fight. Can't defend myself. Can't work as a mercenary or hunt. I wouldn't make it more than a few weeks before I'd be dead. Or worse."

He's silent a while as he moves through the motions of the dance, but he looks like he's far away from here. There's definitely more to him. He's probably got as many secrets as me. I step on his toe, and he winces slightly but doesn't comment.

I crossed a line. Good. I'm not here to make friends. And even if he didn't kill my brothers, he's killed enough people to keep him on my list. He's just as bad as the rest of them.

"You're right." He locks his eyes on mine.

"I am?" I can't mask my surprise.

"I could survive on the run. I wouldn't last as long as you think I would, but I could probably live a decent life long enough to enjoy it." He's studying me, waiting for my reaction.

I don't break his gaze. "Then why don't you? Or do you enjoy killing so much?"

"I don't enjoy it. Sometimes there's more to things than you know, Princess," he says.

"Then tell me."

"No."

I roll my eyes. "You want me to overlook your crimes, but I won't. I know what you do. I know how much blood is on your hands."

"What about your own hands?" he counters.

I mentally scramble, trying to think of what he might mean. Did Sabina have a dark past? Was she killing people? Did she do things I don't know about?

"Your union is going to cause more deaths than I ever could."

"I can't help that," I say.

"Then, you understand my predicament." The music ends and he bows. "Thank you for the dance."

As he walks away, I remain on the dance floor, staring at him. He's nothing like I thought he was, but there's no denying that he's dangerous. Probably more than I thought.

But if he didn't kill my brothers, who did? Who raided us that night? Who burned down the Point? My neighborhood is in ashes and my family gone, but Brevan isn't the culprit. And whoever it is still walks free somewhere. That is wrong. So very, very wrong.

Nineteen

KATHERINE SITS across from me in the library, her finger trailing along the text in the book she's reading. I return my attention to my own research, my eyes blurring from strain. Growing up, we were all taught how to read, but once we learned, there wasn't a lot of options to continue. I read with the rebellion, and while working at the printer, but not this long without a break.

I close my eyes and press my palms against them to try to alleviate some of the strain. When I open them, Katherine is gone from her spot. She's back at the shelf, selecting a new book.

When she returns, she sets it in front of her, then slides another across the table to me. I look at the gold printed title. *Rituals for Darkfall.*

I shove the other book I was reading aside and open the new one. The first chapter is called "Preparing for the ceremony." I begin to read.

"How much longer?" Brevan asks.

I glance over at the enforcer, who is pacing the length of

the library. He's alternated between pacing and sitting in one of the plush chairs for the last several hours.

"I'm rather enjoying myself," I say.

He walks over to me and stares down at the book. "Darkfall? Still? Aren't you tired of that yet?"

"We don't celebrate the same way in Iskvaland, and I want to be prepared," I say.

"Fine." He sits again, stretching his legs out in front of him. He's abandoned his leather armor today, and when he sits, the sleeve of his dark tunic rises above his wrist. More of his gift mark is now visible. The thick swirling lines wrap around his wrist, ending in points at the base of his hand.

He catches me staring and pulls his sleeve down.

"Why do you cover it?" I ask. "Why does everyone in the Night Legion cover theirs?"

Katherine looks up from her book.

"My marks are none of anyone's business," he says.

"Don't you usually just get one? To go with your gift?" Katherine asks.

"There are many different ways they show," he says.

Katherine shrugs and goes back to her book. I stare at Brevan for a heartbeat longer, then return to mine.

The lanterns on the table flicker to life, guided by some kind of magic. It's enough to make me look up at the windows. The sky is steely blue, the color of twilight. We've been here all day.

My stomach grumbles as if the acknowledgment of the time has reminded it that I haven't eaten since breakfast.

With a sigh, I close the book I was reading and add it to the stack. Nothing. No information about how a gift is given or how a gift could be avoided. And absolutely not a single thing about immortality.

"Find anything interesting?" Brevan asks.

"Yes," I lie. "Did you know there used to be a whole weeklong celebration in the city prior to Darkfall? Everyone celebrated together. Nobility, royalty, and commoners."

"I didn't," he says.

"I saw that mentioned in some of the books, too," Katherine says. "The emperor used to give gifts that the citizens could use to sustain themselves through the dark nights. Grain, oil, coin. Things to help them. They used to believe you had to stay in your home for the entire time the moons were gone."

Interesting how they had the same tradition I grew up with but that the beliefs in the city had changed over time. "That would be a nice gesture. We should bring it back. The people could use the gifts."

"If the emperor stopped that tradition, it must have been for a reason," Brevan says. "Traditions change."

"But they can be brought back," I say.

"I suppose so." He shrugs.

"When does Caiden return?" I ask. "I wonder if he could ask his father for us?"

"He had to extend his travels," Brevan says.

I cross my arms. "And nobody thought to tell me this information?"

"I didn't think you'd care," he says.

"Well, I do."

"I'll keep you informed in the future." He inclines his head.

"You should ask the emperor," Katherine says. "You are going to be the princess of Pendralia. You could ask him."

I smile at her. It's a great idea. It gives me a reason to see him. Hopefully, in his private rooms. "Brevan, can you arrange that? Can I request an audience with him?"

"Nobody meets with him," he says.

"Caiden does. But he's not here and I am."

"I'll see what I can do but only if we can be done in here. It smells weird, and the ravens are giving me the creeps."

I look up at the statues above the bookshelves. The stone birds are in various positions. Some are poised to fly away, others have their wings tucked and stare down at us. "I like them."

"Of course you do," he says.

<hr>

As Brevan and I walk back to my rooms, we come across Juliette speaking with one of the legionnaires. He tenses when he sees us coming and backs against the wall. Juliette turns and smiles, then races toward us.

"I missed you at the last-minute ball," I say.

"I had a terrible headache. I'm sorry I couldn't attend." Her face falls, and her tone turns sympathetic, she grabs hold of my hand and gives it a squeeze. "And I'm so sorry about Marian."

"I didn't know her well, but nobody deserves to go like that." I return the squeeze.

"I agree. It's just awful," she says. She drops my hand then bounces up to her toes. "I know what will make you feel better. How about dinner? Tonight?"

"Yes, I'd love that."

"Bring one of your ladies. I'll inform my maid that we need dinner for three"—she looks at Brevan—"or should that be four?"

"I'll wait outside your rooms, no need to make a fuss over me," he says.

"Nonsense. If you're there anyway, you might as well join us." She grabs my hands. "In fact, bring all your ladies. Let's have a proper meal. It'll be fun. I'm sure they could use it after their loss."

"That's very nice of you," I say.

She bobs into a curtsy. "See you at seven, Your Highness."

Juliette welcomes us to her rooms, and we all stop to marvel at the decorations the second we step through the door. I'm surprised that Brevan follows us. I thought for sure he'd insist on staying in the hall despite Juliette's invitation.

My ladies dressed as if they were attending a ball and insisted I do the same. My gray gown with black lace trim matches the décor and doesn't look like too much next to Juliette's white and gray ballgown.

"Sabina." Juliette curtsies, then turns to my ladies. "Ladies. Thank you for joining me tonight. Please come in."

"Thank you for inviting us," I reply as we enter her room.

Brevan bows to Juliette in an unusually formal way, then leaves the group. He's probably checking the rooms for anything suspicious. My ladies follow next, all greeting Juliette like an old friend.

"I'm so glad all of you could come. Usually, my exile to the castle is dreadfully dull. It's nice to have friends to spend time with," Juliette chirps.

I look to see where Brevan has gone and I'm surprised to find him standing in the back of the room, his body tense, as he speaks to another man. He's older, with gray hair that might have once been any color. His bright blue eyes make him stand out, though. Iskvalandian eyes. Like mine.

"Is that another friend?" I ask.

"Oh, yes! Nikolay, come here please, I want to introduce you," Juliette calls.

The man strides over to us, a wide grin on his handsome face. "Well, well, Juliette, you didn't warn me that I'd be surrounded by so much beauty this evening."

The ladies giggle and Charlotte and Genevieve both turn pink. I offer a smile, but I'm not impressed by the flattery. There's something about him that doesn't feel right.

"Princess Sabina, ladies, I'd like you to meet my dear friend, Nikolay. He's a former ambassador from Iskvaland, turned Pendralian. Perhaps you met when you were young, Your Highness?"

My blood runs cold.

"I never had the honor," Nikolay says. "I haven't been back to Iskvaland in more than twenty years."

Tension eases from my shoulders. "What a surprising gift to meet someone from home," I say, then quickly move farther into the room to avoid more conversation with him.

He bows, then rises. "It is an incredible honor to be in your presence, Princess. Though I may be more Pendralian than Iskvalandian now, please consider me your devoted servant."

"That is very kind of you." I incline my head.

A hand brushes against my back like the flutter of a butterfly's wing. So brief I might have imagined it. I don't need to turn to know Brevan is behind me. He must not trust this man, either.

"Everyone, please make your way to the dining chamber for dinner," Juliette announces.

Candles and vases of black roses adorn every surface. Black lace is draped over the tables and furniture. It's stunning and looks nothing like it did last time I was here.

"It's beautiful, Juliette. How did you have the time to do all this?" I ask.

"I have nothing else to do around here," she says.

The dining room table has a cloth covering it made of some kind of shimmery black fabric. Silver plates, goblets, and cutlery wait at each of the place settings.

Two servants stand in the back of the room, wine bottles in hand. It's a much more formal event than I anticipated. Tea with Juliette did not prepare me for this side of her.

Nikolay pulls out the chair at the head of the table. "Your Highness?"

I hesitate, then take the offered seat. Juliette sits next to me, and Katherine sits next to her. Nikolay chooses the seat on my other side.

As everyone settles around the table, I notice Brevan whispering with Charlotte, who is sitting by Katherine. Charlotte gets up, and he takes her seat. He's diagonal from Nikolay.

The servants fill wineglasses, then leave the room. Everyone is silent, and most of my ladies are sipping their wine. I take a drink from my own cup because it gives me something to do.

"When did you return to the city, Nikolay?" Brevan asks, breaking the silence.

"Last night. When I found out Lady Juliette was here, I knew I had to pay her a visit." He takes a sip of his wine, then sets the glass down. "Last I heard, you were still at the border, burning down towns and stealing family heirlooms from old women."

The air is thick with tension. There's history here, and I want nothing more than for them to keep talking.

"Don't worry, the deals you made with the emperor held strong, and we weren't allowed into any of your estates." Brevan glances at me, then returns his gaze to Nikolay.

I don't miss his hint and know Brevan said that entirely for my benefit. He doesn't want me to like Nikolay. But why?

"I have nothing to hide, as you and the emperor well know," he says.

"How's that petition to return to Iskvaland?" Brevan asks. "Has the king reinstated your titles?"

"I have no use for Iskvalandian titles." He looks over at

me. "No offense, Princess." Then he fixes his gaze on Brevan again. "I am Pendralian. You of all people should understand how it works to renounce your homeland."

I lean slightly forward. Does Nikolay know the enforcer's history? I know Brevan doesn't want to share, but I can't help my curiosity.

"Well, as interesting as this is, gentlemen, I'm afraid you're both being rather rude by leaving the rest of us out of the conversation," Juliette says.

Nikolay inclines his head. "Of course, I apologize. Sometimes we men forget how to behave in such exquisite company."

I notice that some of my ladies actually blush from his words.

"Princess, how have you found the transition to Pendralia? I have to say, I didn't miss Iskvaland as much as I thought I would."

"It helps when there are such wonderful people here to occupy my time," I say.

"Will they let you return after the royal wedding?" Charlotte asks.

"Perhaps," he says. "You know, there is one thing I do miss."

"What's that?" Juliette asks.

He looks over at me with a lecherous grin, then says in Iskvalandian, "Taking royal women to bed after they've had too much to drink."

The color drains from my face, and my jaw opens, but before I can respond, Brevan is out of his seat, his chair crashing to the floor behind him. He grabs Nikolay by the collar and pulls him from his seat.

Servants walk in just then, platters of food in their hands. They all freeze, their eyes wide.

"Was that a threat?" Brevan asks with a growl. "The emperor should have taken your head."

"Let him go!" Juliette is tugging on Brevan's tunic, trying to pull him off Nikolay.

I stand, then slam my fists on the table. The plates and silverware rattle, and gasps surround me. "Both of you, stop it now."

Juliette releases Brevan, but the enforcer doesn't loosen his grip on Nikolay's collar.

The older man grasps Brevan's hands. "You heard the" —he switches to Iskvalandian—"spoiled bitch"— then returns to Pendralian—"stop it."

My face heats, and I round the table, fully intending to stop this myself when Brevan punches Nikolay in the face.

The older man cries, then presses his hand over his jaw where the punch landed. "You asshole!" He spits blood on the floor.

"Both of you, out!" Juliette screams. "This is supposed to be a party!"

"Don't let me see you around her again," Brevan growls. "I'm sure the prince would love to hear what you said about his future bride."

Nikolay gives Juliette a glance, then hurries from the room, his hand still covering his face.

"You, too," Juliette says to Brevan.

He inclines his head, then leaves the dining room. I watch him walk out and fight the desire to chase after him.

"Are you alright?" Juliette slides her arm around me. "I'm so sorry. I will never invite him to anything again."

"What did he say?" Genevieve asks.

"He said he likes to sleep with drunk royal women," Antonia says.

The other women gasp.

My brow furrows. "I didn't know you speak Iskvalandian."

"My parents insisted I learn as many languages as possible." She shrugs.

"Well, I'm glad the enforcer punched him." Genevieve takes a sip of her wine, then sets the cup down. "And if he comes anywhere near you, we will be sure to inform the legion so they can remove him."

"I had no idea he was like that," Juliette says. "He was always so kind."

The servants are still standing in the doorway. "Juliette." I tilt my head toward them.

"Oh, gods. I'm sorry you had to see that. I assume you understand that this doesn't leave this room?"

They nod.

"Dinner, anyone?" Juliette says.

The servants hesitantly walk farther into the room, and when nobody stops them, they begin adding food to all the plates before hurrying away.

Conversation slowly returns, starting with safe topics like when the ladies think we'll get snow and what everyone wants to wear to the next ball. Once they're all eating and laughing and more relaxed, I excuse myself for a moment.

When I step outside Juliette's room, I find Brevan waiting in the hall.

"I'm sorry you had to see that." He keeps his gaze forward, looking anywhere except at me.

"Thank you." Those stupid flutters return to my chest.

"You're welcome."

"I should get back," I say.

"Probably," he agrees.

"I'm glad you were there." I sigh, then say something I shouldn't. Again. "I do feel safer when you're around."

He looks at me for the first time since I walked out here. "I'm just doing my job."

"We both know this is so below your skills. You're wasted guarding one woman when you could do so much more."

"You're worth it," he says.

My cheeks heat.

"I mean, there's a lot resting on your upcoming wedding."

"Of course." I turn toward the door, then pause with my hand on the knob. "Do you want me to send some food out for you?"

"No."

Of course not. "Alright. I'll see you when I'm done, I suppose?"

"I'll be right here."

Twenty

"Sorry to interrupt your reading, Princess," Brevan inclines his head, then looks at the other women who are sitting nearby with books of their own, "ladies."

I set down my book and look at the open door. "Forget to knock?"

He closes it, then knocks, then opens it. "Better?"

Charlotte giggles.

He's dressed in a simple tunic and trousers today. The fabric is good quality and they fit well, but he could be a merchant. Why does he look so good in everything? "No armor today?"

"It's being cleaned and repaired. I'll have it back tomorrow," he says.

"The emperor granted your meeting," he says.

"When?"

"Now."

Of course it's right now. I smooth my hair and walk to the door.

"Do you want company?" Katherine asks.

"The emperor said he'd only meet with her," Brevan says.

Katherine's shoulders slump.

"He's not looking for a new mistress yet," Antonia hisses.

"That's not why I offered," Katherine snaps.

I give Antonia a look that makes her return to her embroidery, then follow Brevan into the hall. "Thank you for asking him for me."

He walks alongside me. "I told you I would."

"I do think giving gifts is a good idea. A way for the emperor to get back into his people's good graces." I glance at Brevan.

He looks skeptical. "I don't think he sees himself as having fallen from their graces."

"People are starving. Freezing to death in the winter. Desperate. And they don't see an emperor who cares for them. They can't see the wars or the treaties. All they care about is if they can find their next meal."

"I might not lead with that," he suggests.

We turn down a hall and walk down a flight of steps. I note the large painting of a woman holding a banner with the emperor's crest. Leading the charge in front of the Night Legion against an opposing force, she is meant to be Tela, the goddess of war. And this painting wants you to believe she leads the emperor's armies.

I pay attention to every turn and every step. I have to know how to get back here if I'm to kill him. If I ever figure out how to kill an immortal.

Soon, I recognize our route. We're traveling toward the ballroom. We've reached the massive dragon skull and the mural above it when Brevan stops. He presses a panel next to the skull, and a secret door slides open inside the dragon's jaws.

"We have to walk through its mouth?" I ask.

"Rather dramatic, if you ask me," he says. "I was terrified to visit him in his quarters when I was a child."

"I'm terrified now," I admit.

"Just be the charming woman I know is buried somewhere deep, deep down, and you'll be fine." He throws me a cocky grin.

"Thanks for that." I ball my hands into fists to prevent myself from shoving him into the dragon's fangs.

We enter into a formal sitting room with a door on each of the other three walls. The entrance we just used closes, melting into the wall. I stare at the empty space. It vanished the same way the secret entry in my bathroom did. Creaking sounds and I turn just as one of the other doors opens, and I catch sight of a bed. The emperor strides out, dressed in a uniform that is not much different from the rest of the Night Legion.

"Your Highness." Brevan bows.

I curtsy.

"Please, stand. There's no need for such formality here," the emperor says.

"Thank you for seeing me, Your Highness." I rise.

"You're welcome, Princess. Have a seat." He settles into a large overstuffed black chair, and I take a smaller wooden chair with silver cushions.

"Brevan told me you had something to ask about regarding Darkfall traditions?" He stretches his arms out on the back of the chair as if he's a normal man. It's such a casual move it startles me. Especially considering how young he appears now.

"Yes," I say. "I saw there was a tradition where the emperor would gift the citizens in the poorer neighborhoods grain and oil or other things that would help them get through winter."

"That's true. I did use to do that."

My face heats. I'm not sure I'll ever get used to the fact that he's been emperor longer than anyone can remember. How many generations have lived and died under his reign?

"Well, I thought it would be something we could bring back. A way to build loyalty," I say.

"And why would I be concerned about loyalty?" he asks.

"There have been two rebel attacks here since I've arrived."

He chuckles. "If you can call those attacks, but I do see your point."

I glance around the room, studying it for later. Were there more hidden doors that could be used to enter? Did he have weapons in here in case the rebels ever found a way inside?

"What would you do if I put you in charge of something like that?" he asks.

I return my focus to the emperor and take a breath while I gather my thoughts. This feels like a trap, but I have to answer him. "I would set up several stations around the city to pass out gifts. We'd want them scattered far enough apart that people could only go to one, and we'd need to ensure we have enough of them so that none of them get overrun.

"I would make sure there were more than enough gifts so everyone in line would get some. That would prevent rioting and create trust."

The emperor moves so his elbows are on his knees, and he leans forward. "That is a good plan, but it'll take months to set up something like that."

"I understand," I say.

"But there may be a way to bring a little piece of the tradition back to the people," he says.

"Really?"

"I'll send my legion with bags of grain for each citizen," he says. "They'll deliver them the week before Darkfall. A gift of celebration on behalf of our new princess."

"That's not necessary. It can be from you," I say.

"Nonsense. It was your idea. And why shouldn't the people love their new princess?" He stands. "Now, I have a meeting to prepare for. You can see your way out?"

"Yes." I stand, then curtsy again. "Thank you, Your Majesty."

He nods, then turns and walks back to his bedroom. My stomach twists as I catch sight of the bed again. I was not mistaken. I know exactly where he sleeps. And it's very easy to find thanks to the dragon skull.

I try to linger to take in more details, but Brevan rushes me out. The door closes behind us just as alarm bells sound. Something explodes with a boom, and dust and debris fly across the hall. Panic rises in me, and I look over at Brevan, wide-eyed.

He quickly presses the wall near the skull, but the entry remains sealed. He runs to the ballroom's double door. It's also locked. "Fuck."

Legionnaires sprint past us. Seconds later, there's screaming, and more explosions shake the castle walls. Dust falls from overhead, and I shield my eyes.

"Stay behind me." Brevan isn't in his armor, but he's pulled two daggers from holsters on his thighs.

He backs up so we're moving against the wall. I think he's trying to hide me, but there's not any place to hide. We're in a dead end at the dragon skull. The hallway in front of us leads to the main entrance of the castle and extends beyond to connect to the rest of the castle.

More legionnaires race by. There's the clashing of metal on metal, grunts and cries, then another explosion. I press against the wall and cover my mouth to keep from crying out. My hands shake and my heart races.

I manage to steady myself when I remember that this has happened before. That the rebels are always met with a swift response. That there's usually only a few of them.

That's when a whole mass of people wearing blue and green and red march down the hall, right past our hallway.

Brevan blocks my view, but I can still hear people chanting and shouting and laughing. I can't make out what they're saying, but they're in good spirits. Probably because I watched legionnaires head to attack them but not return.

This isn't a little group.

"Fuck," Brevan says.

I move enough so that I can see around him, and my heart drops into my stomach. Six armed men are heading our way.

Brevan doesn't hesitate to rush toward the group, daggers at his sides. There's something dangerous about the tensing of his muscles and the way he carries himself. How he doesn't even so much as flinch as the men surround him. He radiates power.

"What do we have here, boys? A noble playing warrior?" one of the men sneers.

"And a little treat over there," another says, eyeing me hungrily.

A few others leer at me, their expressions revealing everything they hope to do to me.

"Tell you what, big guy," the first man drawls, "you give us that little morsel and we'll let you go."

A man with a knife in his grip leers at me. "I think that's the Iskvalandian girl."

"Look at that hair," another says. "I wonder if it feels different than ours."

"I wonder if it's that color everywhere." The first man strokes his chin while his gaze travels up and down my body.

Nausea rolls through me. I tighten my hands into fists and glare at the rebels. If they come any closer to me, I will do whatever necessary to defend myself.

For the first time, I understand why the real Sabina took her life. I'd rather die than let these men have me.

"I'm going to give you one chance to turn and run," Brevan threatens.

They laugh and then the first one charges. He swings his sword, and Brevan moves with feline grace, dodging the blow. He twists, effortlessly slicing his blade across the man's throat.

The intruder grips at his neck, his eyes wide with terror. Blood pours from the wound. Gurgling sounds come when he opens and closes his mouth. He falls to his knees, eyes impossibly wide, then he slumps to the ground. A puddle of crimson spreads around him. Mouth hanging open, his lifeless eyes stare at nothing.

The other men charge Brevan as a unit, all five of them swinging swords and throwing punches. It's a tangle of limbs and steel, and I'm getting dizzy just trying to follow the attacks.

One of the men leaves the fray and charges toward me. I scream and throw my arms up in front of my face in a pathetic attempt to defend myself.

Then, in a blinding flash of light, everything goes quiet. It's like I'm floating, like the world has lost all sense of up and down. There's no ground beneath my feet. No fight in front of me, no man charging at me. It's pure empty oblivion.

I think I might be dead.

The light contracts suddenly, and I'm thrown to the ground, landing hard. The man who'd been charging me falls on top of me, blood gushing from his mouth and slit throat. I cry out and scramble away until his body slides to the ground next to me. I'm covered in blood, but I don't think any of it is mine.

Brevan is on his knees, panting, daggers still in his grip. Four bloody bodies surround him.

It's quiet. Too quiet.

I don't hear any more explosions or fighting. Carefully, I stand and walk over to Brevan. Dark purple smudges surround his eyes, like he's been punched, and blood runs from his nose.

I step over one of the bodies, then crouch in front of Brevan. "Are you alright?"

He looks at me and nods, then winces. "I'm fine."

"You're not fine," I snap.

He tries to stand but falls to his hands and knees instead. I drop down next to him. "Let me help you." I tear a piece of fabric from my dress and wipe the blood off his face. His nose continues to bleed, so I tear more fabric and hold it there for a minute.

Brevan drops his daggers, then grips my wrist with a large hand. I pull back and lower my arm.

"I need. To get to my. Quarters," he says through labored breathing.

This is the man who was supposed to be the most dangerous fighter in the emperor's arsenal? I know there were five of them, but he's exhausted. He stumbles as we walk, like he might topple over at any minute. He did something that cost him.

"What's wrong with you?" The words are out before I can stop them.

He wines as he takes a deep breath. "I'll explain, but not here. I need you to help me to my room."

I hate seeing him like this. "I never thought *you'd* need *my* help."

"I did save your life back there," he says.

"I know. Thank you." I stand, then extend my hand.

He takes it, and I'm surprised when he actually needs my help to get up. It's a struggle, and I almost topple over, but I manage to get him to his feet.

We move slowly to the end of the hallway. Bodies are scattered around the entryway. Both rebel and Night Legion. I scan the faces of the fallen rebels, my brow furrowing. I don't recognize a single person. I don't know everyone in the rebellion, but I know a lot of them. It is a fairly small group, too. As far as I know, we couldn't afford to lose twenty men to one attempt on the castle. Where did these people come from?

Lee is lying to me. He lied to me about Brevan murdering my brothers, and he lied about me being the only way to get into the castle. He must have lied about our numbers and the frequency at which they attempted to break into the castle. I certainly was never aware of any missions to get into the library or vault.

I don't know him like I thought I did. I don't think I know the rebellion like I thought I did, either.

Brevan leans on me as we stumble down the halls. He's heavy and navigating with his weight on me isn't easy. I'm still in disbelief that he's so dependent on me. In his state, he wouldn't be able to return to his room on his own.

"What did they do to you?" I ask.

"It's more what I did to them," he says. "This way."

A few legionnaires pass us, and a pair of courtiers, covered in blood, are being guided up the stairs. They're too busy to notice us. A couple of servants scurry by, and they do look at us, but they quickly turn their attention away.

I follow Brevan's directions to the lower levels, where the servants' quarters are. He has a room at the end of the hall. I help him inside and get him seated on the thin mattress.

"What do you need?" I ask.

"There's a bottle in the drawer." He gestures to a nightstand.

I open the drawer and remove a small green bottle, uncork it, and pass it to him. He downs the entire thing in one gulp. Then, he screams and leans down so his face is on his knees. When the scream ends, he remains folded over, panting.

I sit next to him and set my hand on his back. "It's alright, you're going to be fine. Tell me what you need."

My hand is wet and when I pull it away, it's covered in blood. I lift his shirt and find blood smeared across his back. Black gift marks form shapes that are obscured by all the blood on his back. There's slices across the skin. Like someone dragged a very sharp knife from his shoulder, diagonal across his back to his hip. They come from both shoulders, varying in size but all oozing blood. I grab the blanket from his bed and press it against his back.

He hisses. "I'm fine. Leave me."

"You're hurt."

"I can handle it." He tries to sit, but grunts in pain and remains doubled over.

"Let me help," I say. "It's the least I can do."

I rush to a small chest of drawers, where a water pitcher sits next to a ceramic cup and basin. I fill the cup, then set it next to the bed. Next, I find one of his tunics hanging in the wardrobe and bring it over to him. I pour water on the tunic and begin to wash away the blood.

The good news is that the bleeding is easing, as I clean, but not completely. I rush to get another tunic to press against the wounds. I can't cover all of the cuts at once, so blood slides down his back from the uncovered parts. His original tunic is still pushed up around his neck, soaked in blood.

It takes a long time for the blood to stop. Once it does, I clean the cuts as best I can. The wounds remain, though. Angry and swollen. His whole back is covered in his gift mark, but with the injury, it's difficult to make out details. I force myself to look away. It's only on display because he was hurt while saving me. "There. I think it's done bleeding."

"There's ointment in the drawer."

I find the jar of creamy white paste in the nightstand and scoop some out with my fingers. When I slather it over his wounds, he tenses but remains quiet.

"You should take off this shirt," I say. You need a clean one."

"You're just trying to get me out of my clothes again, aren't you?" he says, but the joke falls flat. He's trying to play off his pain, but he's clearly still hurting.

"How did you know?" I tease, hoping to raise his spirits. "Now, hold out your arms. I'll pull it off."

He obliges but hisses out a strained breath as I remove the blood-soaked shirt and toss it on the ground. The dark lines swirl across his chest, down his arms, and around his ribs to his back. I wonder if all the god's gift marks look like that.

"I can take it from here," he says.

I hand him a clean tunic, and he winces as he tugs it on.

"How did you get those cuts on your back?" I ask.

"It happens any time I use certain aspects of my magic," he says.

"That light. That was you. What was that?"

"A defect," he says.

"It didn't look like a defect."

"I asked for shadows, just like everyone else. Instead, I got something else," he says.

"Is that why you're the enforcer? Because of the magic you can do?"

"No. I'm not supposed to use that magic," he explains. "It's because of other things I can do. And, I suppose, because I'm loyal."

"Why didn't you just fight them off?" I ask. "I've heard stories about you. You could have taken them."

"I could have," he agrees.

"So why didn't you?" I ask.

He lifts his hands and looks down at them. They're covered in blood. I get up and cross to the drawers so I can fill the basin with clean water from the pitcher. There's bloody handprints on handle and I leave more of them on the basin as I carry it to him.

"Thank you." He washes his hands, and the water turns deep red.

After I put the bowl back on the drawers, I rinse my hands, then return to his bed and sit. "Can you tell me what that was? What happened? Why does your magic harm you?"

"Because the emperor doesn't want me to use it."

My brow furrows. "I don't understand."

"Before we get our gift, we go through a binding ceremony with the emperor." He touches his chest, and I notice a thick raised scar. "There's a relic right here."

I reach for him without realizing, and just before I graze his skin, I pull my hand back. My cheeks heat.

"You can touch it," he says.

Curiosity beats reason, and I brush my fingertips over the scar. Something hard rests under the skin. Something that shouldn't be there. "Why?"

"The king has a matching relic."

"I don't understand," I say.

"He uses the magic from a relic to create a bond. Part of the relic goes to us, the other goes to him. It gives him power over us. And I suspect we give part of our power to him."

I'm quiet for a moment, then I touch the relic again. I move my fingers around the edges. Whatever it is, it feels sharp. "So he prevents you from using your magic?"

"He made it so there are consequences for using it. So I can if I have to, but for every life I take, their deaths show up on my flesh."

"The cuts on your back."

"Yes."

"Why did you do it tonight then? You didn't answer that."

"Because I saw what those men had planned for you, and I couldn't risk them reaching you," he says.

"You can read minds?" Terror makes my throat tight.

"Not all minds. And not always their exact thoughts. Sometimes it's images of what they're thinking about. Or a feeling about their intentions."

"In the dungeon, you said I was telling the truth."

"Yes," he says.

"You can read my mind?" No wonder he's been following me around. He knows who I am.

"No, not yours. In the cells, I saw an image of that man

stabbing you in the chest. I don't know if you were telling the truth, but I saw what he wanted to do to you."

My blood runs cold. Why would someone who worked for the king of Iskvaland want to kill the princess?

"I suppose you've saved my life twice, then," I say. "Thank you."

"It's my job to protect you." He says the words like they're rehearsed, completely devoid of emotion. But I swear there's more behind them. Or maybe I'm imagining things.

I blink a few times and send that thought away. I'm imagining things. Life and death situations heighten emotions. Make us feel things that aren't real.

"Is everyone bound to the emperor? All the people who go through the gifting ceremony?"

"Yes."

"He must be full of relics," I say. "Oh gods, that's how he's immortal. The relics. The magic he can pull from the people he's bound to."

"We should go." He stands. "Thank you for helping me."

I know too much. He's worried he'll tell me more. My insides buzz, anxious energy overflowing. The mystery is solved. I know where he sleeps, and I know how he stays immortal.

"You should stay." I touch his arm gently. "Catch your breath, take care of yourself. I'll go right to my rooms and shut myself in. I promise."

He considers me, and I wonder if he's trying to read my intentions. In the dungeon he said he couldn't, but I don't know if that can change. Just in case, I imagine myself walking to my rooms and embracing my ladies. I imagine checking on them to see if they're safe, then sitting around a warm fire together.

"I'll be right behind you," he says.

When he opens the door for me, I step into the hall and walk casually. When I hear the click of the door, I look back to confirm that it's closed. Then, I run to find Katherine.

Twenty-One

My room is full of ladies when I arrive. Juliette pulls me into a bone-crushing hug. Charlotte, Antonia, and Genevieve make a fuss over me, insisting I get out of my bloody dress.

As they undress me, I tell them the story, leaving out the part about Brevan using magic, making sure I let them know that I'm uninjured.

"Thank the gods it's not your blood." Genevieve helps me balance while I step out of my dress.

"I'm throwing this dress in the fire." Charlotte picks it up off the ground, balling it up so she can carry it.

"It will smoke too much," Antonia says confidently. "Have someone burn it outside."

Charlotte walks toward the door but I can't see who she passes the bundle of bloody fabric to. I'm just glad it's gone when she returns.

"These rebel attacks keep getting worse." Juliette bites her lip. "We have to do something about it. You're lucky you're alive."

"I was just in the wrong place at the wrong time," I say

Antonia shudders. "Imagine if they got to the emperor."

"He was perfectly safe," I assure her.

A knock sounds on my door. I tighten the robe around my waist before opening the door. I'm surprised that it's not Brevan.

A young legionnaire averts his eyes quickly. "Your Highness, sorry to bother you. We have orders to check on you. To make sure your room is clear."

I step back so he can enter. Five more follow him. They investigate every corner of my room. Under the bed, in the wardrobe, in the bathing chamber, and dining area.

Once they're satisfied, they hurry back to the door. The man who knocked stops in front of it. "The enforcer is off duty the remainder of the evening. We'll be right outside all night. Don't worry. If there's anything suspicious, we'll take care of it. You're safe."

"Thank you." I close the door behind him. Brevan must be more injured than he let on. I can't imagine what it took for him to send others in his place.

I let out a long breath, then rub my eyes. It's been a long day.

"You need to get some rest." Juliette looks concerned.

"I can draw you a bath," Genevieve says.

"That would be great." I'm about to ask them to leave so I can talk to Katherine, when I realize she's not here. "Has anyone seen Katherine?"

"Not since dinner last night," Antonia says.

"What do you mean? Nobody has seen her since the

attack?" My pulse races. I find a simple dress in my wardrobe and pull it on, then rush to the door.

"Where are you going?" Charlotte asks.

"I need to make sure Katherine is safe," I say.

Juliette stands. "We'll come with you."

All of us step into the hallway, and the guards straighten their postures. The young guard who spoke to me earlier addresses me, "Is something wrong, Your Highness?"

"We need to check on one of my ladies," I explain.

He nods. "We'll walk with you."

I know I don't have a choice. We look like a parade as our group travels through the halls. Antonia guides us to Katherine's rooms.

When we arrive, I knock. Then, wait.

Then, I knock again.

And again.

One night legionnaire must read the concern on my face because he opens the door and steps inside, weapon drawn.

I follow and scan the empty room. "Where is she?"

The guards fan out, checking every crevice. They look sympathetic when they tell me they didn't find anything, either.

"Did she say anything to anyone?" I ask my ladies.

They all shake their heads.

"Maybe the attack scared her and she went home," Charlotte says.

"Maybe." I know that's not the case, but I can't say that.

"You should get back to your rooms, Sabina," Juliette says. "You've had a long day."

The sun is already setting, but I feel an odd mix of exhaustion and anxiety-fueled energy. I know what I need to do. "Alright, I am tired. I'm going to rest. The legionnaires can walk me back. You all should rest, too. I'll see you in the morning."

"Are you sure you don't want company?" Charlotte asks.

"I'm going to take a bath and go to sleep, so I won't be good company," I say.

"One of us can stay with you," Genevieve offers.

"No, please rest in your rooms. You'll be more comfortable."

They don't look convinced, but they curtsy and travel down the hall together toward their own rooms.

The guards escort me to my quarters in silence, and I don't look back at them as I close the door behind me.

I know it's a risk, but if something happened to Katherine, I have to inform the rebels. And they need to know about the emperor. I can't wait.

I run water into the bathtub in case anyone is listening and then I pour in scented oil. While it fills, I wash the blood from my face and hands. As soon as the scents of rosemary and lavender fill the room, I turn off the water. If anyone comes into my rooms, they should smell the oils and with any luck, they'll assume I am still in the bath. I'm hoping it buys me enough time.

I grab a lamp, then open the panel to the secret passage and close it behind me. I follow the stones I left myself to get to the catacombs. When I reach the end of my path, I travel slowly, careful to mark my way again. Only this time, I'm using bones.

"Sorry, Mara," I whisper. "I mean no disrespect to the dead."

Hopefully, the goddess understands why I mark each twist and turn. My time spent down here years ago taught me well. It only took getting lost among the bones once for me to carefully mark every path after that.

I end up at a few dead ends, doubling back more than once. Frustrated, I return to my last marker and wonder what I'm doing wrong. I should have found something familiar by now.

Unless these catacombs don't connect to the ones under the city. I thought they all connected, but what if these are royal catacombs?

I turn toward an opening cut into stone where a skeleton lies with its arms folded over its chest. Under its bony hands is a gold crown.

This whole thing could be prevented if the royals gave one damn about their people. Better yet, if they never existed at all. If not for them, I wouldn't be here pretending to be one of them. I'd be with my family, who would still be alive. I'd have friends and a home. The rebellion wouldn't exist. I sure as fuck wouldn't be in a dark catacomb with the bones of the dead while still covered in someone else's blood.

I reach for the skeleton and throw it to the ground, then I start kicking at the bones, sending them flying in every direction.

These royals with their magic. "Magic can't help you when you're dead, can it?"

I pick up the skull and stare at the vacant holes that used to be eyes. "What did you see? What did you do to maintain your life in luxury while your people starved?" There is no way these royals were any better than the ones who came after.

I throw the skull as hard as I can, and it hits the ground, then bounces, then rolls before coming to a stop. The vacant eyes stare at me, as if judging me. "You deserved that."

That's when I hear laughter. Howling, cackling laughter. Coming from the same direction where I threw the skull.

Nobody spends time in the City of the Dead besides rebels and bandits. Right now, I am willing to take my chances with either in order to get this message out.

I walk slowly toward the sound, but the closer I get, the farther away it seems. I take a couple of turns, marking my way, as I follow the sound. Then, it stops. I hear nothing.

Discouraged, I consider turning around. I've been down here so long my bath will be cold. If someone checks on me, they'll know I am gone.

Then, I see it.

A little star carved into the stone. A rebel mark, a way of showing the path through. My heart leaps, and I move faster, looking for the stars as I continue. I think I recognize where I am, but so much of the catacombs looks the same, so it's hard to tell.

Light shines ahead, and I set my lamp down in an alcove, so it'll hopefully be there when I return.

A ladder leads to a grate. I climb, then shove the grate aside and peer out.

I'm in the city. Silk Row, to be exact. Just a few blocks away from the Point.

I'm in an alleyway, and fortunately, nobody else is here except for a skinny cat, who runs as soon as she sees me.

A raven lands on a pile of trash nearby and caws, locking its endless black eyes on me.

I stare back. "I'm not sorry."

The bird cocks its head, as if saying something.

"Whoever those bones belonged to, they deserved it."

The bird flaps its wings, then seems to nod before it flies away silently.

I think I encountered one of Mara's ravens. And she agreed with me.

The interaction sends a rush of confidence through me, and I stand straighter as I walk out of the alley. Drunks are stumbling around, and a few couples in nicer dress walk arm in arm.

By day, Silk Row is lined with tents selling luxuries I could never afford. The kind of stuff I'm surrounded by daily now in the castle. The shops are temporary, though, and by night, the taverns open and welcome in a different kind of guest.

It's been a while since I had to rendezvous with anyone from the rebellion. I spent the last few months avoiding them at all costs, and I am not sure if they still frequent the same places.

Hoping that some of the old members might visit the Screaming Goat, I make my way to the tavern.

It's hazy with smoke inside, and my slippers stick to the floor. I weave through the crowd, and every head turns as I walk by. It's the first time I've been in here with my hair uncovered. I'm the only blonde in the tavern, and all eyes follow me.

This is the opposite of inconspicuous. Even if I found a rebel to pass information along to, everyone would know who they were talking to. I could get us both killed.

So I stride to the bar and pull a gold hairpin from my hair. I hold it up for the bartender to see. He hurries over and glances from me, to the pin, then back to me. "That looks real."

"It is."

"You shouldn't be flashing it around," he warns.

"How about you take it off my hands and get me some ale?"

He takes the pin and examines it, then nods. "You want some dinner, too?"

I shouldn't, but I nod because I know trading a gold pin for a single ale is a terrible trade. Getting food makes me less suspicious.

When I sit at the bar, two men take the stools next to me. I tense but keep my eyes ahead.

"You're a long way from home," the one on my right says. He smells like sweat and liquor.

I look at him, noting the bend in his nose and the scars on his cheeks. This man has seen a lot of fights in his day.

"Need some company tonight?" he asks.

"If she needs company, she'll be gettin' that from me," the other man says.

This man has fewer scars and his nose is straight, so he's either a better fighter, or someone who avoids a brawl.

The bartender sets a mug of ale in front of me. "These two bothering you?"

"No. They're making polite conversation." The last thing I need is to draw even more attention to myself by having these men thrown out.

The bartender doesn't look convinced but leaves to help other customers. I glance at each man, then take a sip of my ale.

"That dress looks expensive," Broken Nose says. "Would look even better on my floor. I pay well."

"I don't need your money," I say. "I'm waiting on a friend."

"Nobody comes dressed like that unless they're selling," the other man—Straight Nose—says.

"Can I get a napkin?" I call to the bartender.

He drops a cloth square at my place. I fold it into a triangle, then set my ale on top of it. If any members of the rebellion are around, they'll recognize the signal.

Someone taps my shoulder, and I turn expectantly, hoping to see a rebel I know. Instead, it's a bald man with a dark beard grinning at me. He's missing a few teeth, and he smells like the pickled fish they keep in a jar behind the bar. I didn't know anyone actually ate those.

"I can buy you a drink." He slurs his words and wobbles a little.

"She's already got a drink," Broken Nose says.

"Two drinks," Straight Nose adds.

"I can buy my own drinks." I take a sip of my ale.

The wobbly man grabs my shoulder and pulls, then grabs a fistful of my hair and leans his face down, inhaling. I shove him, but he still has my hair, so I end up on the ground. I kick him, and he releases my hair.

Before I can fully move away, Broken Nose is on top of him, punching him in the face so hard he spits blood.

I scramble away just as Straight Nose joins the brawl. A few others jump in, either to defend friends or because they enjoy fighting. I scramble back, moving deeper into the tavern as everyone else rushes toward the bar to watch the fight.

As I'm retreating, I bump into someone, and arms wrap around me. My heart thunders, and then I notice the swirling black marks on the forearms, traveling up to where his sleeves are bunches around his elbows. I recognize them immediately. Fuck. Of all the places for him to be tonight, it had to be here.

I spin so I'm facing Brevan, but he's still got his arms around me. "Go figure the one night I take off is the night you sneak out."

"What are you doing here?" I ask. "You should be recovering, not out drinking."

"I didn't know you cared that much." He grins, and I notice how glassy his eyes look. How much he smells like booze. How he is swaying just slightly while he holds me in his arms.

"You're drunk."

"And you're fucking beautiful. Did you know that?" he says.

Flutters return and my stupid heart feels like it's too full. But he's drunk. He doesn't even know what he's saying. "Let go of me."

He releases me instantly. "I have to get you back to the

castle." Then, his eyes narrow as he catches sight of the brawl. "Why do I get the feeling that you caused that fight?"

"It's not my fault they can't keep their hands to themselves or control their actions. This is on them, and I hope they all end up with broken noses. Fighting over a woman that showed no interest in any of them. Serves them right."

"So it *was* you." He glances at the fight again. "And you're right. They need to learn some manners." He pushes up his sleeves, even though they're already up, and walks past me toward the brawl.

I chase after him and grab his shirt, trying to stop him. "Get back here! You can't fight them."

He ignores me, and the fabric I'm holding onto slips through my fingers.

"Brevan! Stop it!" I shout, but it's too late, he's already joined the fight.

He grabs Broken Nose by the collar and lifts him off the ground. "Is this one of 'em?" He shouts in my direction.

Broken Nose starts stammering apologies. "I swear I didn't know she was with you. I wouldn't have even talked to her if I knew."

Brevan drops him.

"Thank you, thank you." The man whimpers.

Then, Brevan punches him in the face. Blood spews from his nose and mouth, and the man screams. Tears stream down his face, and he reaches for his, once again, broken nose.

"Don't ever even so much as look at her again. Do you understand?" Brevan growls.

The man nods as another man charges Brevan. The enforcer blocks him with ease, then punches him in the stomach. When his attacker doubles over, Brevan knees him in the face, and the man falls to his knees—bleeding everywhere, hand on his face, screaming in pain.

Another charges Brevan, a chair in his grip. Brevan sweeps his leg out under the man's foot, and the guy goes down, landing on top of the previous victim. Brevan kicks him in the stomach, then picks up the chair and raises it over his head.

I rush in, moving in front of the enforcer. "Stop! That's enough! Put the chair down."

To my surprise, Brevan listens. He drops it, and it just misses the men on the ground. The other men stop fighting and stare at me. There's so much blood, so many broken noses and already swelling eyes and lips.

"No more!" the bartender yells. "All of you, outside!"

The men grumble and argue, but the bartender comes from behind the counter and faces the fighters. "Go cool off. Come back when you know how to behave in respectable society."

"And if any of you touch her again, I will rip your hearts from your chest," Brevan snarls.

"I've seen him do it," the bartender says.

The men pale, and they practically run over each other in their rush to leave the tavern. The floor is covered in blood, and I even see a tooth. I wrinkle my nose. Gross.

"Sorry about that." The bartender holds up my pin. "You should keep this, Your Highness."

"No, you keep it. Do something good with it," I say, then I pull out another pin and hand it to him. "For the mess."

His whole face lights up. "Thank you."

"She was never here, you got that?" Brevan says. "If anyone asks, you've never seen her."

The bartender nods.

Brevan wipes his hands on his tunic, smearing blood across the dark fabric. At least this time, I know it's not his.

"Come on." When he grabs hold of my upper arm, I don't resist. I'm going to be lucky if I can explain what I was doing and how I got here as it is.

We're progressing down the street, despite the fact that Brevan is weaving slightly. He's still drunk, and he was able to fight that well. I don't think I want to see what he's capable of when he's not worried about me and sober. He easily could have taken those men today, but he risked using his magic because he was worried about me.

"What are you even doing out here?" he asks. "With your hair and those clothes, everyone knows who you are."

It's a much less formal dress than my new normal, but it's still expensive fabric. In this part of town, it might as well be a gown for a empress compared to what everyone else is wearing. It was stupid. "I was trying to find one of my ladies. She's missing."

"You should have asked someone," he says.

"I didn't want to get her in trouble. I don't know what the rules are."

He freezes, and I turn my attention to where he's looking. A large group of men, most of them bloodied from the bar fight, are approaching us slowly, weapons drawn. The man who was sitting next to me—Straight Nose—is at the front of the group.

"This isn't the Flower District," Straight Nose says.

"You want to slum it down here with us, you have to learn some manners."

"We're leaving. No need to do this." I tug on Brevan's arm. "Come on. Let's go."

"Every need," he says. "We'll be heroes. Kill the emperor's enforcer and break in the princess so hard the prince won't want her anymore."

Brevan steps in front of me. "I don't think so."

"It's just you against all of us," Straight Nose says.

I move around Brevan. "You don't know what you're asking for. He's going to kill you all."

Brevan's hands glow white-hot, and I know he's fighting against that strange magic.

"I'll take my chances." The men run toward us, weapons in their hands, ready to strike.

Brevan unleashes his light with a scream. I squint against the intensity, and when everything goes silent, it takes me a few seconds before I adjust to the returned darkness.

All the men are on the ground, their bodies bleeding and twitching. Straight Nose is clinging to his stomach, holding in his intestines. He's moaning and crying.

Brevan walks over to him with deliberate steps, his jaw tight. His glare radiates rage so palpable I can feel it swirling around me. It's familiar. I felt the same way the night I lost my brothers.

For some reason, this is personal for him. I think I mean something to him. Beyond that of a regular charge he's sworn to protect. The thought terrifies me, so I shove it away. It has to be something else. It might not be about me at all.

Brevan grabs the sword the man in front dropped, then stabs it through his neck. He's dead instantly. Glassy, sightless eyes stare up at the stars.

Nearby, a raven calls from a roof. Three more join it, all of them cawing together as if singing a death hymn for the men in the road.

I set my hand gently on Brevan's arm. "We should go." My voice is calm, soothing. It's not a tone I've ever used before, but it feels like it's what he needs now.

He turns, and as we rush away, the ravens descend on the bodies.

Twenty-Two

Brevan lets me tend to his wounds. I go through the same motions I did earlier, this time prepared for his reactions.

"I'm sorry. I shouldn't have snuck out," I say.

"No, you shouldn't have," he says.

His back is worse. The wounds from earlier haven't fully healed, and now, he's got new slashes. They bleed longer this time, soaking through two tunics before I am able to start cleaning them.

"How did you get past the guards at your door?" he asks.

"I'm quick," I say.

He looks at me like he knows I'm lying. He probably does, but he doesn't say anything.

"You should have been resting," I scold.

"I needed fresh air to clear my head."

"Maybe I needed that, too," I reply.

"You said you were looking for a missing lady. Which one?"

"Katherine. Nobody's seen her since before the rebel attack." I grab the ointment from the drawer and gingerly slather it on his back.

He winces but doesn't cry out. When I'm finished, I close the jar and return it to its place.

"I'll ask around. See if anyone knows where she is," he offers.

"Thank you," I say.

"If you promise me you won't do this again, I will keep your secret."

My brow furrows. "Why would you do that?"

"Maybe I think it's worth having a favor owed by the future empress of Pendralia."

"You think I'd ever get to be empress?" I scoff. "The emperor isn't going to hand over his throne."

"Maybe," he says. "But you'll still be the princess, then. And you'll have Caiden's ear. He likes you."

"What happened between you two?" I ask. "I know you grew up together. That you used to be close."

"People change," he says.

"I suppose they do," I say, thinking of Lee. Of myself.

He stands, then pulls a tunic over his head. It's the last one in his wardrobe. The rest were used to clean his injuries. "You'll hide in the stairwell, and I'll relieve the guards at your door. Then, you can get into your room."

It seems too nice. "Why are you really doing this?"

"I told you."

"And I don't believe you," I reply.

"And you were only out searching for your lady?" he asks.

I take a deep breath. "Alright. Thank you. I will owe you a favor."

He nods, then opens the door for us. The walk back to my rooms is quiet. There's something different between us now, but I don't know how to explain it.

I wait on the stairs, and the legionnaires at my door leave without question. When I reach my door, I nod to Brevan. "Good night."

"Good night, Princess."

"You could have been killed," Caiden says. "I can't believe the rebels sent such a large attack while I was away. This is why I have Brevan with you. If it had just been regular legionnaires, you'd be dead. Then, what would we do?"

I take a bite of melon so I don't have to respond. I wonder if Brevan can hear our conversation from the hall.

Caiden knocked on my door an hour after sunrise. He entered quickly, followed by servants carrying trays of breakfast. Is this what it would be like if we really did get married?

Sitting at the dining table in my expansive rooms over breakfast feels too intimate. I adjust myself in my chair, trying to find a way to feel comfortable. It's not working.

"Did they teach you to fight at all in Iskvaland?" he asks.

"No. That was for the men." I hope it's an accurate answer.

"You need to learn to protect yourself. Brevan can't always be with you. He'll have to leave again soon."

"To go where?" I ask.

"To find more relics," he says. "We can't have anyone using them to harm others."

I sip my juice. More relics. For the emperor to bind people to him. I shudder.

"Are you cold?"

"I'm alright. Just a little shiver."

He finishes eating his eggs, then sets his fork down. "It's decided, then."

My brow furrows. "What's decided?"

"You'll train with Brevan. Learn to defend yourself."

"What? I'm not a fighter."

"That's exactly why you need to learn," he says. "My mother knew enough to save herself. She was attacked once, and her legionnaires were outnumbered. She had to fight off one of the attackers herself. I remember her crying for weeks. That first life you take is the hardest."

Learning how to fight would help me when it comes time to assassinate the emperor. I want him dead. I want the prince dead. I want to be the one who does it. But could I? When it comes down to it, could I take a life?

"Sabina?"

"Oh, sorry. What did you say?"

"I said, I want you to start today. I'll tell Brevan." He sets his napkin down on top of his plate, then stands. "You finish your breakfast. When you're done, let Brevan know."

"Alright." I watch him leave, then let out a breath as I slump into my chair. I was so worried he was going to bring up me leaving last night, but it never came up.

Brevan kept his word.

My ladies arrive just after the prince left. "Look who's back," Charlotte calls as she walks into my rooms.

Katherine waves from behind her. "I'm sorry I worried you all. I wasn't feeling well and went to the infirmary. They should have told you."

I let out a breath of relief.

"Are you feeling better now?" Antonia asks.

"Much," Katherine says.

"I'm glad you're alright," I say.

"I see you had a private breakfast with your betrothed," Charlotte says with a hint of innuendo.

"Did you find out where he went?" Antonia asks.

"He wouldn't tell me. Just that whatever issue he was working on is resolved, so I'm not supposed to worry."

"Well, that's a relief at least," she says.

There's a knock on the door. "I'll get it," Antonia chirps.

Juliette storms in before anyone has a chance to say hello. She stops in front of me, hands on her hips. She starts ranting so fast it's hard to make out her words.

"He's marrying me off to some old guy. Apparently, there's someone who doesn't care about my past misdeeds and even thinks it's endearing. Whatever that means. How could anyone be interested in me after the things I've done? How much worse do I have to act to keep them away from me?"

"Slow down. Who is making you marry?" I ask.

"And who's the old guy?" Charlotte asks.

"The emperor. He's making me marry the Earl of Fleur.

He's not even a well-connected noble. He's not important to the empire. He's already loyal. There's no reason to do this other than to get me out of sight and try to tame me. But they're in for a surprise. I will not be tamed."

"Maybe we can talk to him?" I ask.

"Is there someone better you could suggest?" Genevieve asks. "But you have to make it seem like it's his idea. Men love it when they think it's their idea."

We all look at her.

"It's true," she says with a shrug.

"There isn't anyone," Juliette whines. "Unless you know someone who would leave me alone and let me be. I have no desire to tie myself to any man."

"Don't worry, yet. When is this wedding supposed to happen?" I ask.

"After Darkfall." She plops onto the window seat. "He's coming here for the celebrations, and then the emperor says we'll marry before he returns to his estate."

"Alright. We have a little time." I try to sound encouraging.

"How am I going to get him to change his mind?" she laments.

"I'm not sure yet, but in the meantime, do you want to swing a sword around or throw some knives?" I ask.

She looks at me like I'm insane.

"What are you talking about?" Antonia asks.

"The prince wants me to learn to fight," I say. "I could use some company. It might be good for you."

Juliette stretches her legs across the cushion. "I'm not going anywhere. I want to wallow."

"Alright. Anyone else want to join me?" I offer.

"Fighting is the man's job," Antonia says. "I can't afford to risk word getting out about me training to fight. I might frighten off suitors."

"She's got a point," Charlotte says.

"If you require us to go, I'll go. But if we have a choice, I'd rather not," Genevieve says.

"I'll try it," Katherine offers.

"We'll be back soon," I announce. "There's breakfast in the dining chamber if you're hungry."

Brevan is waiting for me in the hallway. He's got dark circles under his eyes, and his cheeks have no color.

"You look terrible. You sure you should be teaching lessons today?" I ask.

Katherine gasps.

"Sorry, that was rude." I glance over at Katherine who is biting down on her lower lip nervously.

"I know you're just trying to get out of this," he says. "It won't work."

"We were attacked. You were injured. I'm concerned about your recovery."

Brevan tenses. "You are too kind, Princess. Are you joining us today, Lady Katherine?"

I'd almost forgotten she was there.

"If that's alright," she says.

"Of course. But we should get started." He gestures toward the hall.

I walk next to him, while Katherine is on my other side. "What is wrong with you?" I whisper.

He keeps his voice quiet. "You can't act like we're friends, Princess. I crossed a line last night, and I apologize."

"You saved my life. Twice," I remind him.

"That's my job."

"I can still be concerned. You were hurt badly," I hiss.

"Don't worry about me."

"You were at my door all night, weren't you?"

"Again, it's my job," he says.

"When do you rest? Heal?" I ask.

"I'm fine, Princess. This way, we'll be using the legionnaire training grounds today." He picks up the pace, and I know he's finished talking to me. I clench my jaw so tight it hurts. Why do I keep letting him get to me?

We follow Brevan to an outdoor training arena. There's a cold gray mist drifting through the air, and the distant trees are devoid of their leaves. We'll have snow soon.

"There are three different training rings out here," Brevan explains. "We have weapons training, combat training, and magic training. We're going to start with some simple combat training since you won't typically have a weapon available."

"Why wouldn't we?" Katherine asks. "If it's dangerous enough that the prince wants her to train, shouldn't she have a knife or something?"

"Let's not get ahead of ourselves. I wouldn't want either of you to accidentally stab yourself," he says.

When we reach the combat training arena, I'm surprised to see a variety of objects. There's a log hanging by strings between two large stone columns. It sways gently as if someone is pushing it. Ladders sit propped against stone walls, and ropes dangle from other walls. I can't even identify half the unusual things they have set up.

"What is all this?" I ask.

"This is how you learn to fight," he says.

"By climbing ladders?" I don't hide my skepticism.

"Yes."

"Can't you just show me how to stab someone?" I ask.

"Not yet," he says. "Besides, I'm more interested in you knowing how to run away."

"That's not what Caiden said. He wants me to be able to defend myself," I argue. Running won't help me kill an emperor.

"Alright, how about I make you a deal?" he says with a grin.

I know this isn't going to work in my favor, but I also have a feeling I'm not getting away from it. "Fine. What's your deal?"

He points to the suspended log. "You walk across that without falling off, and we'll go play with some knives."

"It's a log."

He gestures toward it. "Go ahead."

"You can do it, Sabina," Katherine cheers.

"Right. Yes." I walk over to it and climb the stool that leads to one side. I grab the ropes that keep it suspended and step onto the log. I'm swaying right away, already having to grip the ropes to keep from falling off.

I might have made a mistake.

I wait for the log to slow so it's no longer swinging as intensely and then take a step. I feel better. Like maybe I can actually do this. I let go of one rope and take another small step. I throw one arm out to steady myself. Then, I release the other rope. I'm balancing on the log. Arms out, I move another step. Then, another.

"This isn't so bad." I look over my shoulder and the log swings. Eyes wide, I struggle to maintain my balance, and I lose my footing and slip. I hit the ground hard. Mud splatters on my face. I wipe it from my eyes and mouth, but my hands are even more covered in the stuff. I lift the skirts of my dress to clear the mud from my face.

Brevan is laughing.

Katherine runs over to me. Her slippers sink into mud, making squelching sounds as she nears. She slides and crashes into me, knocking us both flat on our backs. I'm pretty sure there's mud everywhere. And I mean everywhere.

Brevan looks down at us. "Need some help?"

"From you? No, thank you." I try to sit, but I'm sinking and slipping. Katherine is doing the same. Reluctantly, I hold out my hand, and Brevan pulls me out of the mud pit. Then he helps Katherine.

"I'm guessing our lesson is over for today?" Brevan says.

There's no way I could attempt that log again or climb a ladder or anything else for that matter in my mud-caked dress. It drags behind me, even heavier than usual.

"I need pants," I tell Brevan. "I could do it if I had pants. And boots." I lift my foot to show my stupid satin slippers, only to find that I don't have any shoes on at all. They're lost in the mud.

"So you do," he says. "I'll let Caiden know."

"I'm going to take a bath. Do not follow me," I say.

He drops into an exaggerated bow. "As you wish, Your Highness." When he stands, he's wearing the biggest smile I've ever seen on him.

I pick up the skirts of my dress so I don't trip over them and head back to the castle. Katherine follows behind.

"I'm going to take a bath, too," she says. "And I hope you'll understand that I won't be joining you for lessons again."

"I don't blame you," I say.

Twenty-Three

"Nice pants," Brevan says.

They're too big, but I managed to get them to stay up. At least the boots fit. Some of the ladies already had boots for the colder weather and they offered them to me while I waited for some of my own. My feet are the same size as Antonia and Genevieve so when I destroy this pair, at least I have a second one. They're not the same as what a legionnaire would wear, but I'm not going to be wearing a uniform if I need to fight.

"Want to start at the beginning today or are you ready to try the log again?" he asks.

"I understand that there's a process to train a legionnaire, but I'm not going to be fighting a war. Can't we skip this part?"

"No."

I groan. I thought training might be helpful, but at this rate, I won't learn anything of actual use before I need to get out of here.

I should be in the library researching with Katherine.

She promised me she'd get the new information to her contact last night, and I am eager to meet her in the library later to see if we can find anything new.

"Where do we start?" I ask.

"Balance," he says.

"I am not getting on that log again." I cross my arms.

He points to a plank that spans four tree stumps. It's only about a foot off the ground.

"We couldn't have started with that?" I ask.

"Watching you fall in the mud yesterday was worth it," he says.

"I'm glad I could entertain you."

He points to the plank again.

With a sigh, I make my way over to it and climb on top. I take a couple steps and have to throw my arms out to the side to help me maintain my balance. I hate that it's harder than it looks, and I fall quickly. At least this time, I land on my feet and there's no mud.

It takes three tries before I can cross without falling.

"If you were a new recruit, I'd have sent you to the kitchens already," he says.

"Good thing I'm not," I say. "Wait. You do it. If you're so great, show me."

He hops up onto the plank and quickly walks across without so much as a wobble. He's huge, his feet don't even look like they should fit, but he's traveling across the plank as if it's regular solid ground.

"How long did that take you to learn?" I ask.

"I've never fallen," he says.

"Do the log," I say.

"I'm not the one training today."

"You're afraid," I taunt.

"No, we just have a limited amount of time, and this is your training, not mine."

I grin. "That's because you can't do it."

"Fine." He removes the knives he's got strapped to his thighs and sets them on the ground. Then, he climbs up to the end of the log.

He hesitates.

"You really are afraid," I tease.

"I'm just waiting for it to stop swinging."

"Sure," I say mockingly.

"You're the worst," he grumbles as he takes his first step. The log sways, and he throws his arms out to maintain his balance.

I move closer. "That's not what you told me the other night."

He glances at me but doesn't turn his head. "I have no idea what you're talking about."

"Oh yes, you do," I say. "You called me beautiful. I think you even fought someone to defend my honor."

He stills, then looks over at me. "You and I both know that isn't something I would do."

I wait for him to take a couple more steps before I move even closer. "You and I both know you're lying."

He ignores me and takes another step.

"In fact, I'd go so far as to say you were jealous of that man who had his face in my hair." I decide to add a bit of a lie, just to rile him up. "And his hands on my breasts." I put my hands on my chest for emphasis.

He catches my movement out of the corner of his eye, then he turns. The log rocks. He leans with it, trying to stay on, but the log wins, and he ends up on his ass in the mud.

Brevan glares at me. "You cheated."

"You're too easily distracted," I say. "They're just breasts."

"Stop saying that," he says.

"What, breasts? Does that bother you?"

"Seriously, stop it." His face is red. This is getting to him.

I lean down and whisper, "Do my *breasts* bother you?"

He grabs me and pulls me into the mud with him. I gasp, then throw a handful of mud at him. He catches my wrist and I freeze.

The way he's looking at me is different than usual. There's something almost feral about it. Dangerous.

My heart races, and my mouth goes dry. He reaches for me and wipes mud from my cheeks, then uses his thumb to clear the mud from my lips. His hand lingers on my face, cupping my chin.

I am certain he can hear my heartbeat.

He blinks a few times, then shakes his head and pulls away. "I've never been great at the log." He stands, then offers his hand.

I take it and he pulls me up, then helps me out of the mud pit.

Then, he leans closer and lowers his voice. "But I've never given up when I see something I want."

My breath hitches and shivers run down my spine. It takes every bit of my willpower not to pull him back into the mud with me.

He releases my hand and starts walking. "Come on. We have more to do before we finish today."

Well, that's one way to get me to return to reality. "You can't be serious."

"Ladders," he says. "Climb, then over the wall, then back down the other side."

So we're just going to pretend like that never happened. Like he didn't have his hand on my face. Like he didn't look at me like he wanted to devour me whole.

Like I didn't want him to.

Shoving the thought away, I trudge to the ladder. I need to clear my mind. Focus. Anything but the barrage of images of Brevan with his shirt off.

Katherine and Juliette are both reading in the library when I arrive. Brevan is still covered in mud, after insisting on staying outside my room while I bathed, then escorting me here.

"What happened to you?" Juliette asks him.

"Oh, she got you to try the log." Katherine giggles. "I'm glad I was in here instead."

Juliette wrinkles her nose. "You realize there is running water. You can bathe."

"Later," he says.

"You're going to get mud all over the library," she says.

He scans the room, then grunts. "I'll wait in the hall."

As soon as he's gone, I take a seat next to the others. "Anything interesting?"

"Nothing yet," Katherine says. "I can't find anything about how to kill an immortal."

I glare at Katherine, then speak through gritted teeth. "That's not what we're looking for."

"Relax, Sabina," Juliette says with a shrug. "She told me. It's a win-win for me. If he's gone, nobody can force me to marry that fossil."

"What else did she tell you?" I ask.

"That's it. That Caiden wants the throne," she says.

I watch Katherine's reaction out of the corner of my eye. It was a good lie. If Caiden was the one who wanted to attempt a coup, it wasn't nearly as bad as the truth.

"It goes to show you how paranoid he is, doesn't it?" Juliette says. "His own son doesn't know how his immortality even works, and he didn't bother to give him the same gift. Caiden's going to die before he even gets to be emperor at this rate."

"I thought the same thing," I tell her.

She shoves a stack of books toward me. "These are the ones we pulled so far. Let us know if you find anything useful."

I begin skimming the books, hoping to discover anything that might aid me in my task. How do you kill someone who is immortal? Someone the gods themselves protected when another tried to harm him.

We read until our eyes ache. Nothing.

"I don't think we're going to find it here," I say. "He wouldn't want anyone to know."

"He's practically a god," Katherine says. "How do you kill a god?"

I straighten. "You're right. He is like a god." I jump from my seat and head to the shelves.

Scanning the titles, I move from one end to the other.

"I know I saw it in here somewhere," I mumble.

"Saw what?" Katherine asks.

"A whole section about the gods."

"It's over there." Juliette points.

The three of us pull every book about the gods and set them on the table. There are forty books in several towering stacks.

"It's going to take forever to get through these," I mutter.

"And I can't read anymore today," Katherine says, rubbing her eyes.

"We'll divide them," I suggest. "Each of us takes some, and we'll read when we can. If we find anything, we'll share with the others."

We all have a pile of books in our arms when we leave the library. We left behind some volumes on the table, but we'll come back for them later.

Brevan scans the books in my arms. "Need help?"

"No, you're still covered in mud," I say. "And you smell awful."

He ignores the jab and starts walking. "Thinking of joining a temple? Is marrying Caiden that bad?"

"I don't have a lot to do in my room," I say. "At least this will keep me busy."

"Not what I'd choose to read, but I suppose there are some interesting tales in those books," he says.

"And what is it that you'd choose to read?" I ask.

His brow furrows like he's putting a lot of thought into

my question. I notice how tired he still looks. How the deep purple under his eyes hasn't faded at all. Does he ever sleep?

"You know, I can't remember the last time I read a book," he says. "Maybe I'll borrow one of those from you."

When we reach my room, I hesitate at the door. "Maybe you should sleep in the extra bed since that might be the only way you get any rest. After you bathe, of course."

"I don't think that would be a good idea," he says.

"You slept on my window seat the first night I was here. If that didn't cause a scandal, this certainly won't."

"I'm fine outside your door."

"No, you're not," I say. "You haven't slept, and you probably haven't healed yet, and as much as I give you a hard time, I am grateful for your protection. You have to take care of yourself, too."

"I appreciate it. But you managed to get past the other guards."

"I promise I'll stay in my room. It's the least I can do," I say, and I mean it.

He hesitates, then nods. "Alright. I'll take the night off. You'll stay in your room."

"Sleep well."

When I peek outside my room later that night, he's not there. It's a good thing. He needed the rest. But why am I so disappointed?

TWENTY-FOUR

"SABINA!"

I leap up and throw the covers off the bed. Someone is yelling at me from the hallway.

"Sabina, open up!"

"Juliette?"

"Yes, it's me. Tell these assholes to open the door," she shouts.

"Let her in!" I yell just as I reach the door to open it myself.

She flings herself into the room and falls against me. Sobs shake her, and I wrap my arms around her. She's in a robe, and her hair is a frizzy mess.

"It's going to be alright. I've got you." I'm thrust back into memories of doing the same thing for my best friend, Anya. She would scream and thrash in her bed, soaked in sweat, reliving all her worst days. I'd wake her and hold her until she could catch her breath. My chest aches. Who was comforting her now? She was doing better when I left, but there was still the occasional bad night.

"Don't worry, you're safe," I tell Juliette as I smooth her hair. "You're safe."

She takes a few deep breaths, and the crying eases. When she pulls away from me, she wipes her eyes. Her jaw trembles, and her face is blotchy and red. She's been crying a while.

"What happened?" I ask.

"They woke me this morning to prepare me to see the earl. He's here. He rode all day and night to meet me. Sabina, he's not going to let me get out of this. I can't marry him. I just can't." She wipes her nose on her sleeve.

I know nothing about how marriages work for nobles. And she's the emperor's niece, which makes her royalty.

She paces the room, wringing her hands. "I can't go to a temple. Everyone knows I'm not a virgin. They wouldn't take me, even if I wanted to go." She looks over at me. "Which I don't. But I can't marry him."

I saw arranged marriages growing up. People wed for safety and security rather than love quite often. But there was usually some choice. Or at least the illusion of it.

"Is there another man? Someone else you can say you already pledged your heart to?" I ask.

"No."

"What about a temple to Mara? She doesn't require the same things the others do." As much as I don't want to see her go, it feels like a better option.

As much as I don't want to see her go? I'm losing it. I'm sinking too deep into this persona. It won't matter if she leaves. I won't be here, either.

"You think they'd take me?" she asks.

The acolytes of Mara are considered a dangerous and

desperate group. While nobody knows what they do inside their temples, many of their recruits have bloody or scandalous pasts.

"I think they might," I say. "It's not the easiest path, and it could be worse than marriage, but it might be your only other option."

"It would be a life confined to a temple. Never seeing the rest of the continent or doing anything that brings me joy," she says. "Then, a death of working as one of her ravens."

"Have you met him yet?" I ask.

She shakes her head.

"Do you want to meet him first? See if he's a better option than the temple?" I suggest gently.

"He wants to visit the market with me today," she says. "You'll come, right?"

"Of course," I say.

"What about your ladies? Bring them? Maybe one of them will catch his eye instead. They're all from noble houses."

"And they are interested in marriage," I tell her.

She crosses to me and takes my hands in hers. "Please, please bring them. Tell them I don't want him. Tell them they can flirt and bat their lashes all they want."

"I will," I say. "Maybe he's kind. Maybe it won't be so bad."

"Yes. Maybe." She offers a weak smile, then she drops my hands and looks down at herself. "Oh! I can't go out like this." She races to the door and pulls it open. "Ten o'clock?"

"Yes. That sounds perfect," I say.

"I'll meet you at the entry. Don't let me sit in a carriage alone with him," she pleads.

"I won't," I assure her. She waves as she hurries away.

I don't know any of the legionnaires who are standing outside my door. Brevan wasn't joking when he promised me he would be taking the night off. I look at the closest one. He's young. Probably younger than me. He's got hazel eyes and light brown hair. Might have even been blonde when he was young. "Can you get word to my ladies?"

He straightens. "Of course, Your Highness."

"Can you tell them to dress and join me for breakfast?" I ask. "Oh, and can you tell someone we'll need breakfast?"

"Right away," he says.

"Thank you." I close the door and rush to my wardrobe. If I dress quickly, they won't have to make a fuss over getting me ready.

By the time my ladies arrive, I'm in a day dress. I already washed my face and braided my hair. I even put a little rouge on my cheeks so it looks like I spent more time getting ready than I did.

"We're going to the market," I tell them while we eat. "Juliette's betrothed will be attending with us."

"I heard he's very rich," Genevieve says.

"But he has sixteen dogs. And he lets them sleep in his bed," Charlotte wrinkles her nose. "I like dogs, but that's too many."

"At least you can demand your own room in an estate of his size," Genevieve suggests.

The ladies chatter about the earl for a bit, but Antonia doesn't say a word. I catch her eye and whisper, "Everything alright?"

She sighs, then sets her silverware down loudly enough that everyone turns to her. "I can't be the only one who's heard the rumors?"

"What rumors?" Charlotte asks.

"About his previous wives?" she clarifies.

"I didn't even know he'd been married. I suppose it makes sense, he is old," Genevieve says.

"He's had seven wives." Antonia looks at all of us.

My eyes widen. "Seven?"

Antonia nods. "All died mysteriously."

"Why would the emperor agree to let him wed his niece then?" Katherine asks.

"Because he has ties to the mines in the Shatterlands," Antonia says.

"I thought it was illegal to bring in any of the minerals," I say.

"It is. But do you think the emperor or his inner circle follow those rules?" She waves her hand.

"How did they die?" Genevieve asks. "His wives?"

"Two while with child. Rumors were that he beat them." Antonia shudders. "Two while traveling by ship. They just simply didn't arrive back in Pendralia."

"The others?" Charlotte asks.

"One was said to have killed herself," Antonia says. "The last two, nobody knows. He just returned to court in need of another wife."

"We can't let Juliette marry him," I say. "What would prevent a marriage like that from happening?"

"I'm not sure you can stop it. I think her best bet might be to ask to live apart from him. Convince him that she will be his bargaining chip when he needs one. Perhaps her status will appease him enough that he keeps her."

"What if he had an accident?" Charlotte asks.

"Before or after the wedding?" Antonia asks.

Charlotte shrugs. "Either."

"Then I suppose she'd be free," Antonia says.

"You can't talk like that," Genevieve warns. "Women have been hanged for less."

My mind wanders to the garden in the tunnels. All those poisons. Maybe I should show Juliette.

No. What am I thinking? It's getting harder to remind myself I'm not here to make friends. But maybe it wouldn't hurt if I gave her the books the late empress left behind.

"Maybe you can talk to Prince Caiden?" Charlotte asks me. "Maybe you can ask for a favor or convince him to end the engagement?"

"That's a great idea. I'll do that." Caiden seems to like me. It's possible he'd help. Even if this isn't real, I don't want Juliette in danger. It's not right that she can't choose how she lives her own life.

Conversation shifts to the marketplace. The ladies talk about what they want to purchase or eat and the things they want to see.

When Katherine leaves the table, I excuse myself, leaving the others to continue eating.

Katherine stands near the window, a nervous expression on her face.

"What is it?" I whisper.

"My contact didn't show. The note was still there this

morning," she says. "They've never taken this long to pick up a message."

My heart sinks. "So they don't know about the relics or where his room is?"

She shakes her head. "I'm sorry. I'm not sure what to do."

"We keep our eyes peeled at the marketplace," I say. "If we see anyone we recognize, we'll get their attention. One of us can cause a distraction and the other can share the information." It's not the best plan, but it's all we have time for.

"Alright."

The other ladies join us, all smiles and good cheer. I don't blame them. Even though it's dreary outside, it's nice to be leaving the castle.

When we step into the hall, Brevan has returned to my door. The dark circles are gone, and color has returned to his face. I hate how relieved I am to see him looking better.

"And where might you ladies be off to?" he asks.

"The marketplace," Katherine says cheerfully.

"I don't know if that's a good idea."

"I am not a prisoner," I say. "Besides, we're going with Juliette and the earl. He wanted to go there, and she invited us to join them."

"I hate the marketplace," he complains.

I want to tell him that he can stay behind, but he'd never agree. "Well, we both know you'll be following along so maybe try to make the best of it?"

"Like you make the best of training?" he asks. "Don't think we aren't returning to that tomorrow."

"I know. But no training today. Today, we do something fun." I link my arm with Katherine's. "Shall we?"

Twenty-Five

To my surprise, Caiden is waiting at the door with Juliette and the earl. The earl is even older than I thought he'd be. His wrinkled face is dotted with dark spots, and his white hair is combed over a nearly bald head in thin wisps.

With any luck, he'll die shortly after the wedding and Juliette can live the rest of her life as a mourning widow.

I want to tell her that, but she's standing near him, a fake smile plastered on her face.

"I thought I would join you all on your excursion," Caiden says as he walks over to greet me. He kisses my cheek, the touch making my skin crawl. At least it's brief.

"What a pleasant surprise," I say.

"I've ordered two carriages. The ladies can take the larger so they can gossip," Caiden says playfully.

Where is this coming from? It's making me uncomfortable. It's one thing for him to be kind to me in private but showing it in front of others makes it seem more genuine.

"Your Highness," Brevan says. "I think we should

divide the ladies and ensure they have someone who can fight in each carriage."

"Nonsense," Caiden says. "We'll follow right behind them. If something happens, we'll see."

"Of course." Brevan nods.

I give him a cheeky smile. "Enjoy your man carriage."

He shakes his head.

We pile into the larger carriage. It's a tight fit, especially with our full skirts, but we all manage to have a place to sit. The carriage is luxurious, and the benches are about twice as long as they were in the carriage I arrived in.

The ladies share stories about the market. Apparently, in the summer, there are so many flowers that artisans weave them into sculptures. In the deepest part of winter, they turn ice into the shapes of animals or people.

It's not a long journey, and when we arrive, we're escorted out of the carriage by Caiden, Brevan, and the earl. Though, the latter mostly just stands there nodding along as the other two help each woman down the stairs.

The scents of cinnamon and pine are almost over-whelming as soon as I leave the carriage. We're at one end of the marketplace, and people fill the streets. They dart in and out of shops and stop by little tables set up with vendors selling food or goods. It's not unlike the shops on Silk Row, but none of the tables block the permanent structures behind them.

There are people everywhere. All of them dressed in their finest clothes. Some of the women wear bonnets to cover their hair. I don't see a single scarf used for that purpose. Before now, I've only ever seen a bonnet once before, and I thought it looked rather silly. Now, they're on half the women walking down this street.

Some carry parasols while they hold up their heavy skirts to avoid puddles. The men are dressed in suits, similar to how Caiden and the earl are dressed. Brevan stands out in his leather armor. He and Caiden are taller than most of the men, including the earl. The old man is taller than me, but only by an inch or two. When he walks next to the other men, it makes him look shorter than he is.

I'm bombarded by more scents and sounds the closer we get. I smell herbs and spices I can't place mingling with cooking meat and fried dough.

"We should go to the soapery," Charlotte says. "I want to see if they made any more jasmine soap."

"I love the bath salts they sell. The kind with the roses," Genevieve adds.

"Follow your friends, my dear, and show me what you want," the earl says to Juliette. "I'll purchase anything your heart desires."

She smiles, but it looks more like a grimace. The earl either doesn't notice or doesn't care.

We pass stalls selling fruit I didn't even know you could get this time of year. A winery has a table in front of it selling cups of steaming mulled wine.

"That's what I want," the earl says. "Anyone else?"

I decline, as do Brevan and Caiden, but the earl purchases a mug for everyone else.

At first, nobody notices us. They're going about their business, flitting in and out of shops with bags full of their treasures. Until someone stops and gasps, then bows. People begin to stare.

Others bow, too, and some ladies curtsy. I hear whispers in our wake, but nobody stops us, so we continue along.

After purchasing soap, I stroll with the other ladies, going wherever they choose. It's all new to me, and I look the part of a foreigner even though I've spent most of my life living not too far from here.

As we walk, I scan for any familiar faces or rebellion stars on buildings. I know it's not likely, but I don't want to miss someone if they happened to be here.

It's nearing lunchtime, and we've still only visited about half of the offerings. It's much larger than the marketplace on Silk Row.

A pair of legionnaires rushes toward us, shoving past people who don't move out of their way quickly enough, completely focused on reaching us.

I know before they arrive that something is wrong.

Caiden and Brevan step aside, and while I can't hear their whispered conversation, I watch as their faces darken, their expressions turning to scowls, and their eyes dart to our group on occasion.

My pulse races. They found out. They know who I am. I'm so close but not close enough. All this time for nothing.

"Try this," Charlotte says, handing me a date. I take it from her and try not to look like I'm watching the men too intently.

I don't even taste the fruit when I eat it.

Finally, they return to us, and Caiden sets his hand on my upper arm. "I hate to do this, but something's come up and I have to return."

"Alright, do you want me to go with you?" I offer, because I expect it's the polite thing to do.

"No, you stay with Brevan and the ladies. Have fun," he says. "Anything you want you can charge to the emperor's accounts."

"That's very generous," I reply.

"I'll see you at dinner," Caiden says.

I glance over at Brevan, my brow furrowed in silent question. He shakes his head, then turns his attention to the crowd, avoiding looking at me.

I spend the rest of the afternoon terrified about what I might find when we return. Have I left anything in my room that might give me away? Did someone reveal my secret? Has a rebel who knows of our plan been captured and confessed?

My ears buzz, and I do my best to be happy with the others, but the joy is gone. I needed that reminder, though. Even if this isn't about me, I need to refocus. I should be reading the books in my room, not out here shopping like an aristocrat.

Brevan hands me a flatbread filled with some kind of meat. "You need to eat. You look like a ghost."

I take it from him. "What happened back there? Why did he leave?"

"There's always something," he says. "But it's nothing you need to worry about."

I hate that his words actually loosen the knot in my stomach. If it were about me, I think he'd give me a hint. Then again, why should he? He'd be the first to turn on me if the truth came out.

I look over at him, remembering that he could be in my head right now. "Do you listen to people while you're out like this?"

"Only if I have to," he says. "There's so much noise. So many thoughts. If I try to listen, it's overwhelming. It's better to ignore it unless I have a reason."

I take a bite of the food. It's warm and flavorful. I don't recognize any of the spices, but they're delicious. I eat every bite.

"Do you know who I am?" the earl shouts at a vendor. "I could have you killed. Or I could kill you myself and nobody would say anything."

Brevan and I exchange a glance, then we both hurry toward the disturbance.

In the middle of the street, a woman is cowering in front of the earl. She's hugging herself while she bites her lip and tries not to break down completely.

A crowd has gathered to watch, all of them silent, none of them approaching.

"You need to be taught a lesson." The earl slaps the woman across the face twice.

She gasps, then puts her hand to her red cheek.

I push my way through the crowd and dart in front of her just as the earl lowers his hand to slap her again. He hits me instead.

He recoils. "Your Highness, I didn't mean...Where did you come from?"

My cheek burns, but I don't dare show him how badly that slap hurt. I glare at him. "Turn around. Walk away. Now."

Brevan moves in front of me, his back to me, and I can imagine the look of disdain he must be giving the earl.

"Return to your carriage," Brevan says. "Your visit here is complete."

"I was well within my right to retaliate," the earl says. "Just look at what she did to me."

"It was an accident," the woman behind me whimpers.

I peer around Brevan just enough to see that the earl is pointing to his shirt. It's doused in mulled wine.

"I didn't see him," she says. "I didn't mean to bump into him."

"This is because someone bumped into you?" I march toward the earl. "You cowardly, terrible excuse for a human being."

Brevan grabs me and pulls me to his chest. "He's not worth it."

"I will be telling the emperor about your behavior, Princess. Here in Pendralia, women know their place."

I grunt as I try to break out of Brevan's hold. "You piece of dung. You're a worthless waste of air."

The earl smirks, then his eyes go up, probably meeting Brevan's. "You really need to put her in her place. Before she gets herself killed."

"Did you just threaten the princess?" Brevan asks.

He loosens his grip just enough that I can get out, and I charge the earl, knocking him to the ground. I lift my fist, but Brevan has me in his arms again, pulling me off the asshole before I can complete the punch.

"Get him out of here, now," Brevan demands. "In fact, trip is over. Everyone to the carriages." He turns to the crowd, arms still wrapped around me, so I'm pinned against him. "Show's over, everyone return to your business."

Once he lets go of me, I move around him and see that the earl and my ladies are moving quickly, already several shops away as they head toward the carriages. I turn to the woman who is still trembling behind me. "Are you alright?"

She nods, then gingerly touches her cheek. "I'll be fine. Probably won't even leave a mark."

"He had no right." I bite out the words, furious at the earl.

"I offended him," she whispers. "I should have been more careful. I should have seen him, and then I wouldn't have run into him."

"It was an accident," I tell her. "You didn't do anything wrong."

She makes the sign of the gods, then curtsies. "May the gods bless you, Princess. May they keep you just as you are. Our people could use someone who fights for us."

"I will," I assure her. "I always will."

It is a good reminder about what I am doing. Why I am in this dress, why I am in the castle. "Take me back, Brevan."

He nods, then walks alongside me. He's so close our bodies brush against one another. I think he's worried after what just happened. I shove down the flutters in my chest.

He didn't kill my brothers, and I get the sense that he's just as trapped as I am—as we all are. But that doesn't change the fact that he works for the emperor. Even if his loyalty is forced with a relic, he's still loyal. Which means he's my enemy. And you aren't supposed to feel flutters in your chest for your enemy.

Twenty-Six

THE THING I'll miss most when I leave this castle is the bath. Warm water anytime I want it. A deep tub. Creamy, deliciously scented soaps and luxurious oils. It probably would have been better if I never experienced this. Now I'll know what I'm missing.

A knock sounds on the bathroom door, and I'm grateful I decided to actually take a bath instead of making my way to the poison garden. I considered it as a way to help Juliette. Just a few bundles of leaves tucked away in between some pages of a book. She could take it with her when she moves to the earl's estate. He's old. Nobody would suspect her.

The knock sounds again.

"Yes?"

"Sorry to bother you, Your Highness, but the prince has requested your presence. It's rather urgent."

I don't recognize the shaky voice, but the tone is timid. My stomach twists as I imagine all the things that could be wrong.

I rinse the soap and exit the tub. As I dry off, I try to empty my mind. It does me no good to speculate. I'll find out soon enough.

At least I got one last bath.

I cringe. I can't even keep the thoughts away for a few minutes.

After ensuring that my room is empty, I dress and find the towel that Marian used on my hair. I have no idea how the magic works, but it dries my hair so well that you can't even tell I just got out of the bath.

My face is still pink from being outdoors at the market, so I skip adding any makeup and quickly plait my hair into a long braid, then pin it around my head to hold it in place.

I think I look rather young and innocent this way. Hopefully that will aid me in whatever I'm walking into.

Another knock sounds.

"I'm coming," I say.

The door opens, and Juliette barges in, slamming the door behind her. She leans against it, panting and wild-eyed.

I run to her. "What happened? Did the earl hurt you?" I roll up my sleeves then say through gritted teeth, "Where is he?"

"It's not the earl. Well, it's about the earl, but he didn't hurt me." Tears stream down her cheeks, and she's struggling to get her words out around her sobs. "I came because I needed you to hear it from me first. I'm sorry. I'm so sorry. I swear I didn't say a word about you, but I didn't have a choice. He offered me a deal. I didn't have a choice."

"Juliette, what didn't you have a choice about? What are you saying?"

She looks at me, desperation and fear in her eyes. "I had to. I just couldn't marry him."

"What did you do?" I ask. She couldn't just wait for the poison? I should have taken that to her right away.

"I'm sorry. I'm so sorry."

"Juliette, just tell me."

She wipes her face with her sleeve, then hiccups a few times before she can ease her sobs enough to speak.

"What is it?"

"It's Katherine."

"What about her?" My heart pounds.

"I told the emperor that she was looking for ways around his immortality," she says. "I told him she could be a spy."

"What?" I stumble backward, hand on chest. My heart hammers so hard I can hear it in my ears. The whole castle might be able to hear it.

"He told me there was a spy and that if I could help him find them, that he'd let me out of the marriage. That I could never marry. That I could be free." She falls to her knees. "She's going to die because of me. I didn't think. I was just so desperate. I really thought they'd just talk to her. That the prince would help her since it was his plan. But when they found a fire ruby on her, it was all over. I didn't know. I'm so sorry."

"How could you?" I ask. "We trusted you."

"I know. And I didn't tell him your name, but she might. And I wanted you to know that I will take responsibility for this. I will join you both in the afterlife. I can't live with this shame. I am not this person. I was desperate."

"Stop talking. Right now." The harshness of my own

voice startles me. "You will not be taking your own life. You want to fix this? Finish what she started. Help people. In any way you can."

"I can't."

"You can and you will. You understand me? If I don't make it, you find out a way. You tell everyone you can until someone does something about it."

She nods, a flicker of acknowledgment crossing her face. "I didn't say your name. I swear to you, but saying Katherine was bad enough. She was my friend."

"I know." I'm not sure what else to say. I'm too angry to comfort her. What she did is unforgivable, but I can see why she folded.

A harsh knock sounds, and Juliette scrambles away from the door, her eyes wide with fear.

I mouth the word, *Hide.* And she races to my bathing chamber. As soon as she's tucked away from view, I open the door.

Four legionnaires stand there. All of them wear expressions of pure malice. Two reach out and grab me, each one taking an arm.

"What's going on?" I ask as they drag me from my room. I'm stumbling over my own feet to try to keep up with them.

"Where's Brevan?" I look around for him, desperate to see his face. If he were here, I'd know how serious this was. He'd show it in his expression. But he's not here, which is probably even worse.

"Tell me where we're going," I demand.

They're practically carrying me because I can't keep up

with their pace. As we continue down halls and stairs, icy dread begins to claw its way down my spine.

I recognize this route. I know where we're going.

When they stop in front of the wooden door, one of the guards kicks it instead of knocking. Eyes peer at me from behind metal bars. They're cold and detached. Then, they vanish and the door opens.

They push me across the threshold, then shove me so I have to continue forward. The dungeon smells like mold and decay. Worse than the last time. I don't think I want to know why that is.

"Why am I here? What is this about?" At least I have enough wits about me to act confused. My brothers taught me that. If you're ever captured, pretend you don't know why you're there. Never admit guilt before they have proof. Even then, you continue to deny until death.

A lump rises in my throat, making it hard to swallow. They'd be so disappointed in me. When they died, I walked away. And when I came back, it wasn't to help anyone but myself. I wanted revenge.

They shove me into the torture room I walked past last time, and it only takes a second for my eyes to adjust and see why they brought me here. "Katherine?"

They've stripped her down to her underclothes and chained her to a wall. She hangs by her wrists, her legs probably too tired to hold her up. Her head lolls to the side, but she looks up when she sees me. Her hair is matted, and one of her eyes is swollen shut. Blood drips from her temple down the side of her face, and she's got red slashes up and down her bare arms.

I try to run to her, but the guards detain me. I pull and

struggle. "Let me go. Release me right now. You have no business torturing one of my ladies."

The door creaks, and the legionnaires drag me around so we're facing the newcomers. Caiden saunters in, a malicious grin on his face. Brevan is behind him, his expression stony.

"How could you do this to her?" I shout at them. "How could you?"

Caiden stops inches from me and glares down at me. His eyes are dark, emotionless pools. "She is a spy. A traitor. And she was in your rooms. She spent time alone with you. She was researching in the library with you."

"I was. Alone. Sent. Messages," Katherine says, her words stilted and slurred.

"She used a passageway in your bathroom. Tell me how you wouldn't know that?" Caiden says through gritted teeth. "You are a spy. Sent by your father."

"No. I'm not. I came to for the alliance. To be your wife." Saying those words feels like someone punched me in the gut.

"You didn't know about the panel in your room?" Caiden asks. "You never peeked inside the tunnel?"

"No, I didn't know it was there, I swear," I say.

A vein in Brevan's temple twitches, but he doesn't look at me. He's staring ahead, eyes unfocused.

"Please," I say. "Let her go. Have mercy. She's my friend."

"She's not your friend. She was lying to you. To all of us." He marches over to Katherine, then passes her. There's a fire burning in a hearth, iron pokers sit in the embers.

"No!" I lunge, but I only get two steps before I'm hauled back. I kick and scream, and I manage to break free.

I'm captured again, strong arms pinning mine to my sides. I squirm, but he's too strong. I don't need to look to know it's Brevan. "Let me go," I say, quieter this time. Desperate. "Please."

"Stop talking," he says.

Caiden stalks toward Katherine. Silent tears stream down her cheeks.

"I'll ask you one last time—who were your accomplices?"

"Alone. I. Was. Alone."

Caiden grabs one of the hot irons and shoves it into her side. It singes through her underclothes, and the scent of burning flesh fills the room. Katherine screams.

I squeeze my eyes closed for a moment, then make myself open them. I have to be present. I have to figure something out.

I could confess.

I could tell him the truth.

But then there would be two of us being tortured.

Guilt makes my chest tighten. This isn't fair. It could have just as easily been me.

"Hold her." Brevan pushes me toward the legionnaires who carried me in.

The rough gesture startles me, and before I can react, they have an even tighter grip on me.

Brevan pulls a piece of paper out of his pocket. "We found this in the kitchen, stuffed in a crate that was going to the market, remember? She was delivering it to someone. Her contact is outside the castle."

Caiden returns the hot iron to the flames, then grabs a new one and shoves it into her side. I turn away, but her scream is so intense I can almost feel her pain.

"Tell us who you talked to. Who your contact was." The sounds of sizzling flesh and her screaming tells me he burned her again.

Tears stream down my cheeks. How can I let this continue?

"I. Don't. Know." Katherine's voice is stronger than it was. As if she's fighting back.

She's bloody and bruised, but she's not breaking. Her eyes catch mine, and I see strength. Determination. Power.

She glares at Caiden. "I never. Met him. In case. We were. Captured."

"She's telling the truth," Brevan says.

"Were you going to kill my father, or were you just the spy?" Caiden asks.

"If I could. I'd. Kill you. All," she says.

Caiden pulls another hot iron from the fire and presses it against her cheek. She shrieks in pain, and I make myself watch, hands trembling, eyes welling with tears. My throat is tight, my heart breaking.

Caiden tosses the iron on the ground, then he looks over at me. His expression softens. "I'm sorry you had to see that. And I'm sorry you had to breathe the same air as this traitor."

He walks over to me, and I flinch when he gets close. His shoulders slump as if he's hurt by my reaction. I'm still being held, but I know fighting against the legionnaires isn't the right move. If I'm still playing the part, if I'm making use of this chance that Katherine bought me, I must stay still.

Caiden cups my face. "My beautiful bride. What a terrible ordeal this must be for you."

I don't trust myself to speak.

"Don't worry, my little raven, you're safe here. I'm going to make sure she can never hurt you again."

The tears that filled my eyes spill over and stream down my cheeks. He wipes them away with his thumb, then kisses each cheek.

My lower lip trembles, but I maintain as much composure as I can.

Caiden takes a few steps before pausing to look back. "Brevan, carry our guest to the pit." He points to a pair of legionnaires. "And you two, bring my bride-to-be. I want her to see this serpent meet her end. It'll be good for her. After that kind of betrayal, the only thing that helps is to watch your enemy suffer."

Brevan unchains Katherine, then catches her as she collapses forward onto him. He scoops her up gently, carrying her like a bride. He doesn't look at me as he passes me.

The legionnaires holding my arms guide me forward. They move slower this time, though. As if they don't want to make it to the pit in time. I swallow hard, but my mouth is so dry it's difficult. My eyes sting and my throat burns.

A part of me that still wonders if Caiden is playing a game. If he's going to toss me in with Katherine.

We pass the cells, but I don't look. I can't. I can't see any more pain. It's too much.

The air grows warmer with each step until it feels like we're next to a roaring fire. Then, I see the pit.

A yawning hole in the rock that leads down to nothing but darkness. On the walls around us, torches flicker, providing light. But none of it penetrates that inky black pit.

A few legionnaires stand behind me, and one of them moves closer to the pit. He throws a rock down the hole.

It falls.

And falls.

And falls.

I hear the thud when it lands.

He and his companions laugh. I'm grateful that the men holding me aren't as callous.

Brevan stands near the drop, still holding Katherine.

Her head rolls to the side, and she looks at me. She mouths, *I'm sorry.*

Tears begin again. There's so much I want to say. I want to beg for her life, I want to apologize to her, I want to confess and tell them to take me instead. But I can see the injuries. She's already on borrowed time.

Caiden moves next to me. "Are you ready to see Death, my little raven?"

I turn to him and note the intense joy radiating off him. He likes this. He likes to cause hurt. I lift my chin, then nod.

The gesture seems to be enough for him, and he points to Brevan. "Throw her in."

Brevan hesitates.

For a brief, shining moment, I hope. I look at Katherine. Her breaths are ragged, her eyelids heavy.

Then, they close.

And her chest stops rising.

Brevan moves to the hole, then holds her out like an offering. I whisper a silent prayer to Mara right before he drops her.

She falls.

Her hair fans out around her face, her limbs extend. She almost looks like she's floating.

Suddenly, a roar sounds, and a creature leaps to catch Katherine, jaws open wide, horrible sharp teeth each the size of my forearm. Nostrils exuding smoke and eyes slit like a cat's. I see horns and claws, and wings that hang beside a massive serpentine body.

They have a dragon.

Twenty-Seven

Terror has me frozen in place. Bones crunch, then fire roars up from the bottom of the pit, and I jerk back. My captors release me as they scramble away from the hole.

Only Brevan and Caiden remain still.

The scent of brimstone lingers, and I wait, expecting to see more fire, but it's eerily still, too quiet.

Caiden walks toward me, as proud as a new father holding his babe. "Princess, allow me to escort you to your new rooms. I'm sure you're tired, and we can't have you sleeping in a room with a secret passageway out of the castle."

He loops his arm through mine, and I walk alongside him, numb. Katherine is gone.

And a dragon ate her.

The new room is next door to Juliette's. She stops by to check on me, but I don't open the door.

I don't open it for dinner, either.

When the sun sets and the lamps don't automatically light, I sit in the dark, staring at the smoldering embers of the dying fire.

I can't believe she's gone. I can't believe that I stood by and did nothing. It could have been me. It should have been me.

It shouldn't have been anyone.

Because we shouldn't have to live in a world like this. I ball the fabric of my dress up in my fists. My emotions are a tangled mess. Tears stream down my cheeks but I'm not sure if they're from sorrow or rage.

I race to the door and fling it open. Without a backward glance at my room or the enforcer, I start down the hall.

"Princess, where are you going?" he calls.

I don't stop moving.

"You can't be out right now. Return to your room."

I ignore him. My whole body feels wound as tight as a spring. If I don't get out of this place I will lose it completely.

He grabs my shoulder. "Princess."

I shrug him off. "I need some air."

"It's late," he says.

"I don't care. I need out of this castle right now."

He quickly moves in front of me, blocking my path. "Return to your room before you cause a scene."

"I would rather take your sword in my chest than go back to my room right now," I hiss. "I swear to the gods if you don't get out of my way, I will make you move."

His brow furrows slightly, as if there's the smallest flicker of concern.

I shove past him, half expecting him to restrain me, but he follows alongside me instead.

"And where exactly are you going?" he says.

"I don't know. I just know I can't be here." I make my way down the stairs, needing to find a way to get outside the walls. I don't care where I go, I just need to breathe, and I can't do that here.

"You need to go back to your rooms. Now."

I stop and glare at him. "Or what? You'll feed me to a dragon, too?"

Conversation floats toward us. We aren't alone in the hall. Brevan's eyes go wide and he pulls open the nearest door, then shoves me inside.

We're in a dark linen closet. "What are you doing?"

He covers my mouth with his large hand. "For once in your life, shut up."

I grip his wrist and pull his hand from my mouth and just as I'm about to tell him to go fuck himself, I hear the voices again. They're approaching our hiding place.

"What I wouldn't give to see that bitch bloody and screaming," a male voice says.

"She thought she was so much better than us," a second voice says. "Just because her family owned more land than anyone else."

"Well, now there's none of them left to hold that land. I heard the prince himself burned their whole estate to the ground. No survivors," the first man says.

"It's too bad. I was looking forward to her sister joining her at court next year," the first says.

Their conversation fades as they pass us and I sink to

the floor, horrified by their words. Caiden was every bit the monster I thought he was.

Brevan crouches down next to me, his body outlined by the faint light coming in from the crack under the door. "Are you alright?"

"How old was her sister?" My voice is small.

"Don't do that to yourself. You didn't cause this." He extends his hand. "Come on, I'll get you back to your room."

But I did, didn't I? She was assisting me. This was my fault. How many more would die because of me? I was sent here to find answers, to help people. And all I've done is get people killed.

I rise, then tug on the high collar of my dress, suddenly feeling like I'm suffocating. My breathing quickens and my pulse grows rapid. I feel too hot.

Brevan stands, then reaches for me. "Princess? Are you alright?"

"I can't do this anymore. I can't be here. I can't watch more innocent people die." I tear at the dress, pulling on laces and ties frantically. How did I even get this dress on? Why do I even need these stupid fucking dresses in the first place?

"Deep breaths," Brevan says. "I think we should go. You need to lay down, get some rest."

"Don't pretend you care. You do whatever they ask you to. You're just as bad as the rest of them." I shove him in the chest and he stumbles a little.

"You act like you're some noble hero while you blindly follow orders." I shove him again. "You have more blood on your hands than anyone."

I go to shove him again, but he catches my wrists. "Does that make you feel better, princess? To yell at me and act like you're morally superior? We're the same you, and I. Pieces in someone else's game."

I tug my arms away. "I am nothing like you." I shove him again as tears stream down my cheeks. When I push him again, he captures me in his arms, pulling me to his chest.

I scream and struggle, trying to get free.

"Go ahead. Let it out." He releases me. "You want to be angry at someone? Be mad at me." He holds his hands up in front of him.

I narrow my eyes, suspicious.

"Go on." He makes a fist and punches his opposite hand, then opens them both, palms facing me. "As hard as you can. Get it out. Punch me."

I clench my teeth and ball my hands into fists. Then I punch his open palm. It hurts my knuckles, but I ignore the pain, doing it again and again. He barely flinches.

"Keep going," he encourages. "Harder."

I punch him again.

"I said, harder."

I continue until there's nothing left and all the fight is gone. I'm sobbing now, my whole body shaking. Exhausted, I lean my forehead against his chest. He pulls me closer, holding me with one arm while he rubs my back with his other hand.

We stay like that for several minutes until there's no tears left. I lean back enough to wipe my face and he offers a handkerchief.

"Just in case you come across a damsel in distress?" I ask.

"You'd be amazed by how many damsels I come across." He gently wipes my tears, then hands it to me so I can blow my nose.

"I'm sorry," I say. "I shouldn't have said those things to you."

"Never apologize for seeing what's wrong with the world," he says.

"How do you do it?" I ask. "How do you live with yourself?"

"I end up in bars and drink too much and make a fool out of myself in front of beautiful women," he says.

I chuckle. "You're not like them, are you?"

"I am what I have to be," he says.

"So am I," I admit. "I'm just not sure how long I can keep doing it."

He tilts my chin and his thumb brushes across my cheek. "You're stronger than you realize."

Something electric dances over my skin, making my whole body feel alive. I'm overheating now for a completely different reason, and I swear if I stay too close to this man I'm going to cross a line I won't recover from. "We should go." My words come out breathy.

He moves his hand, then clears his throat. Without a word, he reaches for the door and lets us out.

I'm silent on the walk back to my room but once I'm alone, I grab a pillow and press it against my face. I scream. And scream. And scream.

Katherine is dead but all I can think about is how badly

I want the man who is standing outside my room in my bed.

What the fuck is wrong with me?

Twenty-Eight

When my ladies bring breakfast, I make myself eat. I didn't sleep last night. Every time I got close, I saw the dragon and Katherine all over again.

My face is puffy, and I look like I haven't slept in days.

After I finish eating, I open my door and find Brevan waiting there. He tenses when he sees me.

"How did you sleep?" His tone is as it always is. As if I didn't collapse into a crying mess in his arms last night.

"I'm fine, thank you. Can you please ask Juliette if she'll come to my room?"

He nods, and I close the door.

There's a knock less than a minute later, and I let Juliette inside.

She approaches me cautiously. "I heard."

"Did you hear how?" I ask.

"No."

"Torture. Then, fed to a dragon," I say.

She blinks a few times, then walks to the sitting area and collapses into an overstuffed chair.

I take the seat next to hers. I need Juliette in my corner even if I can't trust her. Being obviously angry with her would be suspicious. Afterall, she discovered a spy who was in my service. I can't show how much I miss Katherine. It takes everything I have to hold back the tears and maintain a steady voice. "She was brave. Insisted she was alone. That she knew nothing else."

"She could have turned both of us in," Juliette says. "Did Caiden say anything?"

"No. I suspect he'll pretend like it never happened."

"I killed her." She looks at me. "And I could have killed you, too."

"I think Katherine would forgive you." I don't know if that's true, but it seems like the right thing to say.

She shakes her head. "I should have just married him."

Some of my anger wanes. What would I sacrifice to avoid marrying Caiden? And wasn't I just as guilty as Juliette? I did nothing. Stood by and watched her die while I shared her crime. "Don't do that to yourself. If you married him, you'd be dead, too."

"We don't know that."

"Don't waste her sacrifice." I say it for both of us. I know I'll need to keep reminding myself. That's the only thing I can do to honor Katherine. It's even more important that I succeed.

We fall into a long silence, then after a while, Juliette looks at me with furrowed brows. "Did you say a dragon? Like a real dragon, or was that a metaphor?"

"A real dragon. In a pit in the dungeon. I think they clipped its wings." My heart cracks again. The beast ate my friend, but it's locked away, trapped, and probably starving.

"You're sure?"

I nod.

"I thought they all died centuries ago." Her brow furrows.

"The emperor has been around for centuries," I remind her.

"Do you think the dragon has something to do with his immortality?" she asks.

"No." I'm certain it's the relics, but I'm not going to tell her that.

"You were just—curious, right? Just helping the prince?"

"Of course," I tell her.

"So, no more research?" Her shoulders sag in relief.

"No. But I do think I need those books about the gods. It will be a nice way to redirect my time. The late empress has a beautiful temple. I think she'd want me to be more pious."

"That's nice. She'd have liked you. And she'd have liked to know that her faith will be taught to her grandchildren one day." She smiles at me. "You didn't get much sleep last night, did you?"

"Why do you think I asked you to come over? I need you to make me look like I haven't been crying all night."

"Of course," she says.

Juliette is still a liability. She didn't give them my name, and I suspect it's because she knows how this game is played. That the whole court revolves around your proximity to power. And as the future wife of the prince, I hold more power than most.

But I know I can't trust her. I can't trust anyone.

Even Lee let me down. Lied about my brothers and deprived me of my only way to communicate when he took my ruby. And now, I'm trapped inside the castle without any way to contact him.

I'm going to have to finish this on my own.

First the emperor, then the prince.

Then, maybe I'll even release their dragon.

I spend hours every day in the empress's temple. I eat with my ladies and engage in court gossip, hoping something that can help me is let slip. I avoid Brevan as much as possible, only making polite conversation with him as he leads me to the temple or to dinners with Caiden. My embroidery improves, and I read several of the books about the gods. I even manage to retrieve the books that were left behind in Katherine's room. I am the model of what a princess should be while I quietly research and buy time.

Sometimes, the prince joins me in the temple. He lights a candle and bows his head, then sits silently. He never stays long.

Dinners with him are quiet and reserved. I ask him about his day. He asks me about mine. But he doesn't share details, and my details aren't interesting.

I still can't find a way to kill the emperor. And I'm running out of time. I'm monitored whenever I leave my room, so books are my only option, and I have to be careful with those after everything that happened.

I scour every inch of the walls in my new rooms and

come up wanting. They must have made sure I got a room with no exits. I am trapped.

Will I spend the rest of my life in this role? Living someone else's life? What happens if I have to go through with the gifting ceremony and the wedding? Having children? Becoming empress eventually?

My head hurts. I rub my temples and close my eyes.

"Are you ill, Your Highness?" Antonia asks.

I look up. "It's just a headache."

"Shall I send for tea?" she asks.

"Thank you." I'm holding a book but mostly I stare at the fireplace, watching the dancing flames. It's still too difficult to focus and I worry that I'm letting Katherine, and everyone in the rebellion, down.

Antonia returns a minute later and sits next to me, embroidery hoop in hand. "I requested peppermint. It's soothing."

She pays more attention to me than ever before. Antonia's desperate to fill the role that Marian, then Katherine, held as my closest companion. It didn't work out so well for either of them, but I understand her desire. She's from the least noble house of all my ladies, even though she makes an effort to be the most proper. She's determined to improve her family's station.

"Sorry I'm late," Charlotte announces as she sweeps into the room. "I overslept."

"Busy night?" Genevieve lifts her eyebrows.

Charlotte's cheeks turn pink. "Trouble sleeping, but I'll take a tonic tonight."

"You're alright," I tell her. "You didn't miss anything."

Charlotte is having an affair with a legionnaire. We all

pretend we don't know, but she's terrible at hiding it. I keep wondering if we need to intervene before she's caught by her family or a higher-ranking soldier.

"Does that tonic happen to get delivered by a certain legionnaire?" Genevive teases.

Charlotte scans the room, her eyes as wide as a child who was just caught sneaking sweets before dinner.

"How's your mother, Genevieve?" I ask to change the subject.

"She's better, thank you." Her shoulders ease and she takes a seat at one of the chairs nearby. "All that praying you did for her helped."

I don't believe that, but it seems to comfort her. "I hope she's able to leave her bed soon."

"The doctors say her breathing has improved and she can probably travel again by spring." She picks up a deck of cards and starts shuffling them.

"Good. I look forward to meeting her," I say. Genevieve's mother was a friend to the empress and from a prestigious family. But she is a widow, so she didn't have as much authority as the houses with men at the helm. It is stupid and outdated, especially given all the stories I've heard from Genevieve about her mother. She has survived more than most men.

A knock sounds on the door, and I flinch.

"That'll be the tea." Antonia rushes to answer.

But it's not tea. It's Brevan. He bows. "Your Highness, may I have a word with you?"

I haven't been able to look him in the eye since our moment in the closet. It was too personal. Too vulnerable. I wasn't sure how to act around him anymore, so I'd been avoiding him. I suppose I couldn't get away with it forever.

I set down my book, then walk over to him.

"How can I help you, Enforcer?" I step into the hallway, hoping we're out of earshot of the others.

"Oh, so that's how we're going to play it," he says.

"You dropped a woman into a pit so she could be eaten by a dragon," I say, choosing to dance around the other topic. Being angry at him for Katherine gives me an excuse. Especially around others.

"She was already dead before I dropped her," he says.

I know that's true; I watched her take her last breath. "That was luck."

"No. It was magic." His expression is deadly serious.

"Your magic?" For the first time since that night, I meet his gaze.

He nods.

"Why didn't you tell me that before? How did you—?"

He holds up a hand to stop me. "Another time." His glance behind me lets me know that we have an audience.

"Fine."

"I'm here because we need to resume your training," he says. "It's been too long."

"I don't see the point if I never leave the castle," I reply.

He leans down and lowers his voice. "There will come a time soon when I won't be here to protect you."

"Soon?" My heart falls into my stomach.

"Don't act like you'll miss me, Princess." He scoffs.

"Of course I won't," I lie. "But I can't deny that you are the best fighter we have."

"Say that one more time for me?" he teases.

"Maybe you should get going." I take a step back, afraid I'm letting myself get too close again.

"And maybe you should be ready for training after breakfast tomorrow."

"I go to the temple after breakfast." I cross my arms.

He leans closer to me. "You're going to go train."

"I don't want to."

"You are. And do you know how I know that you are?"

I put my hands on my hips. "How?"

He pulls me away from the door, then his lips brush against my ear. Chills shiver down my neck, into my arms. "You'll train with me tomorrow because I know you were lying in the dungeon."

I swear I can feel the blood drain from my face. "I have no idea what you're talking about."

He straightens, then takes a step away from me. "Training. Tomorrow. Be ready." He bows. "Princess." Then he returns to his position against the wall, his gaze piercing right through me as if I don't exist.

He knows I was lying.

But which lie did he catch?

Twenty-Nine

"It's raining," I say as I step into the hallway.

"So?" Brevan asks.

"You want me outside in the mud?" I groan. "Of course you do. You'd love to see me covered in mud again, wouldn't you?"

"The thought has crossed my mind, but alas, we will be training indoors," he says. "Let's go."

My shoulders slump. The rain was my ticket out of this.

The only thing I can think about as I follow him down the hall is that he knows a secret about me and I'm not sure which one. "Are you ever going to explain what you said to me yesterday?"

"Soon," he says.

"Do you ever get tired of giving cryptic responses?" I ask.

"Do you ever get tired of asking questions?"

"No."

"Then you understand," he says.

I sigh. He's going to drag this out. At least I know that

"""

he won't turn me over to Caiden. If he was planning to, he'd have done it already.

We're silent as we continue through the castle, traveling down stairs and through halls until I'm not sure where we are. All I know is that I'm pretty sure we're not heading in the direction of the dungeons. I could live the rest of my life happily if I never saw that place again.

It feels like a dark cloud falls around me when I realize that that's probably going to be the last place I ever see.

We're in the lower levels and we pass the servants' quarters before turning into a large open room. A bucket of wooden swords sits in a corner. A target with a few knives stuck in it occupies another corner.

At least there aren't any ladders or logs.

Brevan closes the door behind us, then turns to face me. "How many times did you use that tunnel in your bathroom?"

My face heats. "I didn't know there was a tunnel there."

"You're lying." He moves closer to me. "You see, I thought I couldn't sense when you lie. I can't feel your intentions at all. You're the only person I'm closed off from. But you have a tell. You bite down on the inside of your cheek when you lie. Did you know that?"

My lips part. Is that true? "I don't do that."

"You do."

"I'm not doing it now." I put my hands on my hips.

"You're not lying right now," he says.

"How did you even notice that?" It would have to be such a subtle movement since I wasn't even aware I was doing it.

"It's a little flicker of motion on one side of your lips."

"You must spend a lot of time staring at my lips," I accuse.

"I do."

My face heats for an entirely different reason now.

"So what exactly did I lie about?" I ask, crossing my arms. It's a desperate attempt to change the subject of the conversation back to the lying. Letting myself linger on the fact that he has been staring at my lips is too much.

"You lied to Caiden about the tunnel," he says. "It was quite convincing. Fooled him, but your tell got you."

I resist the urge to let out a breath of relief. There are far worse things he could have caught. I must not bite my cheek with each lie.

"Besides, how else did you sneak out that night I found you at the tavern? There are some terrible guards in the Night Legion, but none bad enough to miss a woman leaving her room."

That's how he knows. He's guessing about me having a tell. "I was worried about Katherine."

"She was probably out meeting with her contact," he says.

"I didn't know that then," I say, careful to keep my jaw in place.

"I know."

"She didn't deserve what happened, you know. She didn't deserve that pain."

"The only penalty for treason is death," he says. "She would have died one way or another."

"But the torture."

"She was a spy, Sabina," he says.

I flinch. It's the first time he's ever used my name.

"I'm sorry, Your Highness," he corrects.

"No, no, it's fine. I like how my name sounds when you say it." What the fuck is wrong with me?

"I shouldn't," he says. "It's not how things are done."

"How did you end her life?" I need to focus, not flirt with him. "She was breathing, then she was gone. Like she fell asleep."

He walks over to the target and pulls the knives out, then returns to where I'm standing. He hurls one at the target. It bounces off the center then clanks on the ground. His brow furrows, and he runs his thumb along the edge of a blade. "These are dull."

"Brevan. What did you do?"

He drops his arms to his side. "I don't know if I should answer. Nobody, I mean nobody, knows of this gift. Not Caiden. Not even the emperor."

"You can make people die?" I ask, horrified.

"No, not unless they're already heading there, I can speed it up. Make it peaceful." He's looking down, as if ashamed by his actions.

"That's a beautiful gift." I touch his arm and when he looks at me, I smile. "Really, it is. If something were to happen to me that put me in that situation, I'd like for you to make it peaceful."

"You won't be in that situation because I'm going to help you learn how to stay alive." He grabs a knife by the point, then hands me the hilt.

"I thought we had to do balance first?" I ask.

"You and I both know that's going to end badly."

I don't disagree, so I take the knife.

"Now, when you have a knife like this, you have to

account for the weight. If it's unbalanced, like these dull blades are, you have to adjust for that. Every weapon will feel different. Will throw differently. Unless you carry your own personal daggers on you everywhere you go, you should practice with a variety of knives to get a feel for how they respond."

"Alright." I'm surprised that I want to learn. And not because the skill would help me, but because it seems to matter to Brevan. I don't want to let him down.

"Try it," he says.

"You're kidding, right? Just throw it? That's all the information I get?"

"Try it first, then I'll help you adjust," he says.

I grip the handle, point down, then lift my arm and throw. The blade doesn't even reach the target and I'm standing embarrassingly close.

Brevan laughs.

"Hey." I shove him. "You did that on purpose."

"I didn't expect you to be that bad," he says.

"How about you actually teach?"

He grabs another knife, holds the hilt, then shows me how to line it up with the target and aim. There's a certain way to flick your wrist when you throw that he makes look effortless. It can't be that hard.

My next four throws all land on the ground. I groan. "It looks so easy when you do it."

"You'll get there." Brevan moves behind me, then grips my wrist with his hand. He guides me through the motions, his body pressing into mine as he does.

My pulse races. My face heats. The places where his hands are touching me feel like they're on fire. I don't want him to back away. I want him to get even closer. To move that hand on my stomach up or down. To explore.

He wraps his other arm around my waist, then rests his palm on my stomach. "Keep your core tight. You're twisting at the last minute, which will change your aim."

I clear my throat and step away from him. "I think I've got it. Let me try."

I throw that knife like my life depends on it.

It hits the target.

I jump and cheer. Brevan captures me, his arms around my waist, and he spins me around. Then, he stops, still holding me elevated so my face is level with his. His warm breath caresses my face and sweat shimmers on his brow.

He's breathing far too heavily for the mild exertion. I know he's feeling the same things I'm feeling. What if I just leaned down a little?

He sets me back on the ground then hurries to retrieve all the fallen knives. "That was good. You were nowhere near hitting the center, but you made progress. Let's keep going. When you get a bullseye, we can be done for today."

It takes me twelve tries before I hit the center of the target. When I do, I drop the other knife I'm holding and jump with excitement.

Brevan smiles. "Good work."

"Now, realistically, am I ever going to throw a knife at someone?" I ask.

"Probably not, it would be more likely that you'd need to stab them at a close distance," he says. "But throwing helps gain confidence. Plus, I wanted to see if you'd give up."

"I don't give up easily," I tell him. Then I realize that's

not true. I gave up after my brothers died. And I've been struggling here to complete my mission.

"Good. Because tomorrow you'll be learning how to defend yourself against an attacker," he says.

"After breakfast?" I ask.

"Yes. I'll be outside your room."

"For now," I say.

"As long as I'm in the castle, I'll be here."

I swear I can still feel the heat from where his hands were on my body. I am not supposed to be thinking about him like this. It is dangerous and stupid. And it is a betrayal to everything my family sacrificed.

"Does the emperor know how to fight? Or does he just count on his immortality?" I ask.

"That's a dangerous question considering what you were helping Katherine research," he warns.

"I know. But the emperor isn't the only one, is he? The empress is dead, but she lived longer than a normal mortal. Her mother is still alive and looks far too young. Is Caiden immortal, too?" What if he is? What if he was given the same gift? That would make it even harder to take them down.

"I don't know how any of that works, and I know it's dangerous to ask. I also know your father continues to search for a way to do it himself." His brow furrows. "Is that why you were looking? Did your father ask you to find out?"

I'm careful not to give anything away when I reply. "No, I didn't even know that he wanted to be immortal. But he did speak about how the emperor was, so I think that's why I was so curious."

"You need to let it go. That curiosity is only going to get you killed." He removes a knife from the target and tosses it in the basket on the ground. I walk over to him and help remove the remaining knives.

"Or fed to a dragon?" I ask. "How does he even have a dragon? We've been told they're all gone."

"They are. He's the last one. The only one left."

"And he's kept like that? In a pit with no sunlight or trees or companionship?" I ask. The emperor is a blight on everything he touches.

"Dragons are dangerous. Unpredictable."

"So are emperors and princes." I drop a knife into the basket, then turn to grab another. Our hands meet as we both try to grab the same knife. Instead of pulling away, I close my fingers around his hand.

We're so close again, and this time, I don't want to move away.

"Anyone can be unpredictable when pushed too far," he says.

"Maybe sometimes that's not a bad thing." My words come out breathy.

He leans closer to me, and those flutters return to my stomach.

"Tell me why you really snuck out that night," he says.

"I needed to get away." I glance down, breaking eye contact. "I miss home." I look back up at him, knowing my words are genuine. I don't have to worry about him catching me lying. "I miss my family and friends. I miss everything."

He places his other hand on top of mine. "I understand that. I was new to this court once, too."

"How did you learn to adjust?" I ask.

"I took things one day at a time," he says. "I found small joys. Things that were just for me."

If I rose on my toes, my lips would touch his. I'm considering it. It's insane. It's stupid. I hate how much I'm drawn to him. Like it's natural to be this close to him.

I feel safe when he's around. "Thank you for watching over me."

"Always." His smile is sad. Probably because he knows our time is limited.

It's the reminder I need to remove my hand and take a step back. I'm already in enough trouble after everything with Katherine. I don't need to add kissing the prince's closest companion to my list of misdeeds.

I just need to resist until he leaves. It's easier that way. Especially because after I do what I came for, he'll never look at me with longing or kindness again.

The door bursts open, and a legionnaire races inside. "Sorry to interrupt."

My cheeks heat, and I'm grateful I just stepped away from Brevan.

"What is it?" Brevan pulls the last knife out and drops it in the basket without looking.

"The emperor requests your presence immediately." He opens his mouth to speak again, then closes it when he notices me watching him. He doesn't trust me. "You should come right now."

"Sabi—Your Highness, can you make your way back to your room?"

"Yes. Go!" I give him a little push. "Don't worry about me."

He hurries from the room, and for the first time, I don't have any guards following me or checking on me. Whatever is going on is clearly urgent. I might have some time on my own. Brevan trusts me to return to my room, and I hate that I'm breaking that trust, but I have to get a message to the rebellion. Which means I have to get out of this castle.

Thirty

Nobody says a word when I pass them in the halls. I keep my chin up and walk with purpose. Like I belong.

Legionnaires straighten their posture as I pass, but not a single one stops me.

My heart hammers and my palms are sweaty, but I have to take this chance. I might not get another one.

My old room isn't guarded. The door isn't even locked. I know it's a risk to use the tunnel, but I can't exactly walk out the front door. It's too well guarded and too many people would see me. This is my only chance.

That is, if the tunnel is even open anymore. I know there's a good possibility that it was walled off or the door was sealed. I'm hoping that since they moved me to my new room, they haven't had a chance to do anything with it yet.

I slip through the door and close it behind me. After a quick check to make sure I'm alone, I drag the chair from the desk to the bathing chamber. After I close the door, I wedge the chair under the doorknob, taking a chance that it holds.

"This is so stupid. You're going to get caught," I whisper to myself. My self-scolding doesn't stop me, though. I slide the panel, and like I hoped, it opens just fine.

Whatever dragged Brevan away needs to be something huge and distracting. Something that keeps him, and everyone else, occupied for hours. I need good fortune right now.

Thankfully, the lamps still burn. Whatever magic they used is strong. I grab one and carry it with me into the tunnel. I'm practically running, turning at all my markings and then following the rebel stars.

Finally, I find the ladder that leads to Silk Row. I stop at the base of the ladder and realize that I can't go out there. It's daylight, and my hair is going to give me away.

The dress I'm wearing has several layers, and it isn't easy, but I manage to tear out one of the underlayers so I can wrap it around my head to cover my hair. It's a poor substitute for a scarf, but it'll have to do.

The rungs are cold in my grip, and when I finally emerge into the city, I'm instantly drenched by a deluge of rain. It pelts me like little shards of ice. My dress clings to my skin and my teeth chatter before I've even made it three blocks.

I can't stop, though. I forge on. Thanks to the weather, I'm often alone on the street. A few people pass, their umbrellas shielding them from the storm. They give me looks of disdain, making assumptions about why I'm out here.

I don't care. The more they dismiss me, the less likely they'll be able to figure out who I really am.

The thought makes me slow my steps for a moment.

Who I really am. Who is that anymore? I'm hiding so they don't see Sabina, the Princess of Iskvaland. But I'm not her. I'm a refugee from Vailstad turned rebel, who lived in the Point, the poorest slum in Aurorium. I'm nobody. But I'm pretending to be somebody.

And I can't be seen as either right now.

A few carriages pass by, sending sprays of water up onto the sidewalk. I avoid most of them, but one hits a huge puddle, and I'm splashed with mud and water. It's not like I can get any wetter.

I recognize the leaning structures and charred remains of the Point. Half the street burned down the night my brothers died.

I swallow hard. It's the first time I've been back since that night. I don't even know if anyone still meets in the usual places.

I avoid looking at the blackened, crumbling remains of the apartments and shops. Thankfully, Red's Tavern is still standing.

I duck inside the dark and dingy building. Patrons look over to see who walked in, but they dismiss me instantly. I'm dripping on the floor, and my once-expensive dress now looks like something a peasant would wear. Maybe the rain isn't such a bad thing.

I'm shivering as I approach the bar, but I stop before I reach a stool because the woman who just came out of the kitchen, two plates of food in her hands, is Anya. My best friend. The one I left behind to go on this insane mission.

She freezes, her expression pure shock, when she recognizes me. It only takes her a moment to reset her face and continue toward the table where she drops off the food. She smiles and jokes with the customers, then turns toward the bartender. "Can you grab two more ales for these gentlemen? I'm going to take a quick break."

The bartender goes to work filling the mugs without question.

Anya walks over to me. "Taylan?"

I nod.

"Oh gods, what happened?" she asks.

Several people can see our interaction. "Is there somewhere we can go?"

She takes my hand and leads me to the kitchen. We pass by the warm fires and continue into a large storage room. She closes the door behind us.

"What is this, Taylan? You leave me a note saying you have to do something and that you may never see me again, then you show up like this?"

"I'm sorry," I say.

"No." She holds her hand up in front of me. "Do not lie to me. Do not give me any excuses. You tell me the truth. Exactly what is going on. And then I will help you. Because I'm your best friend. Even if you shouldn't have left without explanation. Without a goodbye." Tears glisten in her eyes.

My vision gets blurry from my own tears because she's not throwing me out. She's not walking away from me. She's mad, but I earned that. I don't deserve the kindness she's promised without even knowing the trouble I'm in.

"Knowing could get you killed," I tell her.

"We both know it's a miracle I'm even alive," she says. "Tell me. Everything. Do not spare me. You owe me that much."

I open the door a crack and peer out to make sure nobody's listening. An older woman stands in the kitchen, stirring a pot over the fire. When she's done, she sits in a chair near the fire and picks up her knitting.

I close the door. "Alright."

Anya takes my hands in hers, then nods encouragingly. "Start at the beginning."

So I do. I tell her about Lee coming to me, about seeing the dead princess. About agreeing to take her place. Then I tell her everything that happened in the castle and how I still can't find a way to kill the emperor. I tell her about the relics, and the gifting ceremony, and Katherine. Everything spills out until I have nothing left.

She's quiet a long while, then she looks at me. "I know how to kill the emperor."

"What?" How could she know that?

"You sure you want to go through with it? I could get you out of here. Get you on a ship. You could just disappear," she offers. "But Lee's right. As much as I hate to admit it. This is probably our best chance to end their rule. It might be another five hundred years before someone gets this close again. They already dismissed the possibility that you are a spy. If they didn't connect you to Katherine, they don't want to see it. They want to see a docile princess."

She's right. And I came here to end them. "I want them gone. I want them dead."

"Alright." She smiles. "I love you, you know that, right? You're the best friend anyone could hope for. Even if you did leave me with nothing but a note and the entire rent to pay on my own."

"I'm sorry. But please, don't say goodbye yet," I say.

"I have to. We both know how dangerous this is going to be. But you'll need to get back into the castle without them knowing to even have a chance at pulling it off."

"I know. But I can't do it if you say goodbye now," I tell her. "I need some hope that I'll see you again."

She pulls me in for a hug. "Good luck, then. And I'll see you again soon."

When she releases me, she says, "You're certain about the relics?"

I nod.

She grins, then she tells me exactly how to kill the emperor.

When I rush out of the tavern, back into the rain, I feel hope. Actual, real, true hope.

I just need to get close enough. I need to bide my time. And when Darkfall comes, I will kill the emperor.

The chair is still shoved under the bathing chamber door. I take a robe off a hook, hang my wet dress in its place, then pull the robe around me. With any luck, the dress will be dry by the time they find it, and they'll think I left it before they made me change rooms.

The room is empty. Quiet. And two day dresses are hanging in the wardrobe. Nobody is going to notice I changed. Not when all my clothes are variations of the same colors.

I use the towel to dry my hair and hope that there won't be anyone in the hall. Just as I'm about to reach the door, the handle turns.

I move fast, so I'm behind the door as it opens, praying they don't press it all the way against the wall.

Holding my breath, I wait.

Brevan steps in, glances around the room, then leaves and closes the door behind him.

He didn't check the passage. My shoulders slump in relief.

I wait until I hear footsteps fade, and then I open the door a crack.

"Hello, Princess," Brevan says. "Enjoy your stroll in the rain?"

Thirty-One

"I ᴋɴᴏᴡ you took the passageway again. Where were you this time?" he asks.

"Tavern," I say.

"Why?"

"I wanted to see an old friend." I'm going to die anyway. I might as well just give parts of the truth.

"How is it that you have friends in Pendralia?" he asks.

"How did you know I'd be in here?" I counter while I scramble to come up with something believable.

"You weren't in your room." He sighs. "I already covered for you once. You owe me the truth."

I swallow hard. He could take me in right now. End everything. But he's not. He's asking for an explanation. It's more grace than I deserve. "She came with me on the journey here, but she didn't return with the others. She didn't want to go back to Iskvaland. In case you forgot, things aren't exactly great for women there."

His eyes narrow as he studies me, as if he's trying to determine whether I'm telling the truth.

"I'm sorry." Guilt settles in my gut like a weight. "I figured it was my last chance to see her. I wanted to say goodbye."

"Is she working at the Screaming Goat?" he asks.

"No, it was a place in the Point." I clench my jaw the second the words leave my mouth. I should not know this much about Aurorium.

"She had a family connection." I add, hoping it helps make it sound better.

I am in so much trouble.

"Red's?" he asks.

I nod.

"That's not a great place for a woman alone," he says.

"Things in Pendralia aren't much better for women than they are in Iskvaland, but at least she can work here. She rented a room. She doesn't have to marry someone she doesn't love."

"Are you still talking about your friend?" he asks.

I stare at my feet, unable to meet his eyes.

"The prince has told me how much he enjoys your company," he says. "How different you make him feel. How much he's come to care for you. It might not be love, but there is worse."

I don't respond.

"Do you feel that toward him?" His tone is vulnerable.

"No." I look up at him. "But I feel it for someone else, even though I know I shouldn't."

It's low. Using the feelings I know he has for me to get out of this. If he hides this, like he hid it before, he'll be keeping things from his own emperor to protect me. This isn't how I should repay someone who's saved my life. Twice.

"You shouldn't say things like that."

"I know."

"You're going to get us both killed."

"I'm sorry."

He runs a hand through his hair and walks away from me. He shakes his head. He's frustrated. I know how he feels.

When he turns back to me, he looks calmer. "Things between Caiden and me are...complicated. Having feelings for his bride is..."

My whole body feels alive at his words. I know it's wrong, but I can't stop myself. "Feelings?"

"But we can't," he says. "You know that."

"I understand." I hate it, but I know how dangerous this is. And it's not just Caiden. It's the betrayal Brevan will feel when he finds out the truth.

"I promise you, I will not use the tunnel again," I say.

"They're destroying it tomorrow." He glances into the bathroom and sees the dress. "I'll make sure the dress is gone before they arrive. But I swear to the gods, Sabina, I can't cover for you again."

"You won't have to," I assure him.

"Go to the library. Stay there. Read something that isn't going to get you in trouble. If anyone asks, you've been there since training. I'll be there soon to escort you to your rooms."

"Thank you," I say. "I owe you."

"Yes, you do. Several favors at this point." He blows out a long breath.

My cheeks heat again because I know what kind of favors I'd like to give him. I curse myself internally. I have got to stop thinking like a lovesick teenager.

"Go on." He lifts his chin toward the door.

I leave without looking back.

<hr>

I'm halfway through a book of fables when Brevan finds me in the library. "Caiden would like you to join him for dinner."

I close the book and carry it with me. It can't hurt for Caiden to see my new reading material.

I turn toward the dining hall.

"No, he wants to have dinner in your room," Brevan says.

"Oh." I turn the other direction, and the two of us finish our walk in silence.

I don't say goodbye when I enter my room. It's best for both of us that way.

Caiden is already waiting for me. The small table in my room is set for royalty. Someone brought in a black tablecloth and crystal candleholders that glitter in the soft light of the candles' flames.

Silver and white plates and crystal goblets wait for us. Between the plates is a platter filled with meat and vegetables and potatoes.

"I heard you had quite the day today," Caiden says.

"I did?" I hedge.

"Yes. Brevan told me it took nearly all morning to get you to hit the center of the target. He's a bit obsessive, that one. Does it really matter where you hit your enemy as long as they go down?"

He picks up a bottle and pours ruby-red wine into each glass. "Please, sit."

I settle in the chair he gestured to, and he sets down the bottle, then pushes my chair in before grabbing the book I placed on the table. "*Fables and Tales of the Shatterlands.* I remember reading this as a child. Some of them frightened me quite a lot when I was small. You might want to be careful with this."

"I won't read it after dark," I say.

He places the book on the small desk, then takes his own seat. "I suppose you should thank my father for summoning Brevan and cutting your training short."

"Yes, I am grateful," I say. "It was bad enough when it wasn't raining."

He sips his wine, then serves food for both of us. It's odd to see him serving me instead of waiting for the servants to take care of everything.

"I wanted to spend some time with you tonight because I have to leave for a few days again."

"Oh no, can't someone else go?" I ask.

"I know, but I'll return in time for the ball," he says.

The ball was quickly approaching, which meant Darkfall was soon. I'd lost so much time already. "Alright, don't be gone too long."

"So eager," he teases. "You know, you really aren't what I expected at all."

"I hope that's a compliment," I say.

"It is."

"Then, thank you, and I feel the same about you," I say.

He grins. "I know."

We make small talk while we eat. About the weather and the lack of snow. About the tales I read in the book. About my favorite holidays in Iskvaland. Thank goodness I heard most of the stories when I was very young.

"I've never heard you speak Iskvalandian," he says suddenly. "Your Pendralian is so perfect. It's hard to believe you weren't born here."

"My father has had us speaking both as long as I can remember. And I had Pendralian nannies and tutors."

"Say something in Iskvalandian," he says.

I tense. This is a test. This isn't random. He knows exactly what he's doing. I force a smile, then in perfect Iskvalandian, I say, "It's raining today and the weather is very gloomy. I miss the snow."

Thankfully, my parents had insisted we learn Iskvalandian when we were young. We were so close to the border that there was ample time to practice. Some of our neighbors didn't even speak Pendralian.

He smirks, then replies, in Iskvalandian, "You're even more beautiful when you speak in your language."

The compliment makes my stomach churn. I switch back to Pendralian. "I feel weird using it around here."

"You can speak to me with it anytime," he says.

When we finish eating, he calls servants to clear away the dinner things. They also build us a roaring fire. He sits on the couch that faces the fireplace, making himself at home.

My chest feels tight. He's showing no indication of leaving my room anytime soon.

He sets a deck of cards on the table in front of the

couch. "How about a round of poker? My father says it's not a game for gentlemen, but I find it relaxing."

I join him on the couch, careful to leave some space between us. "I've never played." *Lie.* I am very good at this game. My brothers taught me far too young and conned me out of quite a lot of pocket money before our mother prohibited gambling in the house.

"I'll teach you." He shuffles, then deals, and goes through the task of teaching me how to play.

It's a simple enough game, and I get the hang of it quickly. After our fourth round, he gathers the cards, shuffles, then sets the deck down without dealing.

Caiden moves closer and wraps his arms around me, his expression hungry. I smell wine on his breath as he moves closer to brush the hair away from my face. When he presses his lips against my neck, my eyes widen. My insides are screaming and my skin crawls. It takes everything I have to maintain calm.

He pulls the collar of my dress aside, then kisses my shoulder before moving to my collarbone, then back up my neck to my chin.

"You're so tense," he says. "I know you've done this before."

I want to slap him. Instead, I shift enough to give me a little space. "It's different with you."

His expression darkens. I offended him.

"You're a prince." I reach for his face. "A future emperor. My future husband. What if you're disappointed by me?"

"I don't think we'll have that problem." He leans closer to me and presses his lips to mine.

I kiss him back, eyes open. It's repulsive and I bristle, my whole body tense. I feel like the walls are closing in on me. Like the ceiling is lowering. Any moment I'm going to be crushed to death. When he sweeps his tongue into my mouth it takes everything I have not to gag. I used to think kissing was the same, that feelings didn't matter. I was wrong.

He slides his hand up my side and cups my breast. The added sensation is too much and I pull away abruptly. Panting and wide-eyed, I must look insane. I touch my lips, trying to make it seem like I'm overwhelmed in a good way.

"See? You have nothing to worry about," he says.

"Except for pregnancy," I say. It's all I have left. The only way to talk him into keeping his trousers on. "If I fall pregnant before we're wed, they'll say I was unfaithful. I'll be hanged. I sat through several lectures about waiting until after our wedding."

"We'll keep our clothes on." He returns his lips to mine, and I try to go along with it.

He must sense my reluctance this time because he pulls away. "They really got in your head, didn't they? I know how much you want this."

"I guess it's just been a while," I say.

He releases me, then walks toward the table. I let out a shaky breath. Hopefully it's over. Instead, he returns with my wineglass. They'd left our glasses and two more full bottles of wine behind after they cleared our dinner away.

"Here. It'll take the edge off." He hands me the glass.

I take a long drink, then attempt to smile. What do I do? Just the feel of him touching me makes me want to peel my own skin from my bones. I take another sip. After what just happened with Katherine, what would happen if I asked him to leave?

He sips his own wine, and an idea occurs to me. I set down my glass, then go retrieve both bottles. With a playful smirk I place them on the table. "I propose a new game."

He lifts a curious brow.

I pick up the deck of cards. "Poker. Only, loser drinks a whole glass."

"I think I'll like this game," he says with a wicked grin.

I fill his glass entirely before topping off mine. Then I deal the cards. I win the first hand. He downs his whole cup, and I refill it. I lose the next hand. I drink my whole glass.

I win the next two, then lose one.

I'm starting to feel the wine, but Caiden is visibly drunk. His words slur slightly. And based on his squinting, I think he's having trouble seeing.

I win the next hand and cheer him on as he downs another glass of wine. At this point, he can't even tell which cards he's playing. I pour more for both of us and call for a toast to his health. He downs it all again without prompting.

He leans on me, his eyes glassy. He's a happy drunk, thankfully. This time when he kisses me, I kiss him back, but I'm not thinking about Caiden. With the wine in my system, I can't get Brevan out of my head.

It's his mouth on mine. It's his tongue teasing mine.

When I pull away from the kiss, Caiden's eyes are heavy.

"Why don't you come to bed?" I ask.

"I thought you'd ask never," he slurs. "You-you're beautiful. Even the hair."

"Thank you." It's not easy helping him to the bed. I'm swaying a little on my feet and things are foggy, but I'm not drunk enough to lose awareness. I know what that's like. I did that nightly for weeks after my brothers died. I don't like to think about the fool I made of myself repeatedly during that time. Or what my brothers would think of me now.

I manage to pull back the blankets and get him on the bed. He giggles as I help him out of his tunic and trousers. I could go the rest of my life with never hearing this man make that sound again.

"You lie down. Be patient. I'll be right back," I tell him.

"I'll be waiting," he says.

I wink at him before I saunter toward the bathing chamber. I close the door behind me then run the faucet as cold as I can get it. I splash the water on my face to help me sober up.

Then, I lean against the wall and I wait.

By the time I leave the bathing chamber, Caiden is sound asleep. I cover him, then I strip off my clothes and slip on his tunic. I lie on top of most of the blankets, covering myself with only the top layer so I'll have some warning if he wakes up wanting to touch me.

The cold water wasn't enough to eliminate the wine's effects, and soon, my eyes are too heavy to keep open.

Someone knocks on the door. I sit up at the same time as Caiden. He groans and rubs his head. He looks over at me, then down at his naked body, then back at me. "Well, good morning, beautiful."

"Good morning," I reply.

"Is that my tunic?" he asks.

I bite my lower lip and shrug.

"Looks good on you."

The knock sounds again. Caiden tugs a blanket free from the bed and wraps it around his waist before going to open the door. I pull a blanket around myself and slide out of the bed.

"Coming," Caiden calls. He pulls it open as wide as it can go and leaves it that way while he stumbles back into the room and starts picking up his abandoned clothes. "Wait there, I'm on my way out."

I take a few steps toward the door and see Brevan standing there. For a second, his face falls, that mask of indifference slipping.

I would give everything I have to not have to see that look on Brevan's face.

He hides it quickly, but I recognize heartbreak.

"I'm sorry, Your Highness. I came to take the princess to training. I can come back later."

"Give me five minutes," I call.

"Could you get me a hangover tonic?" Caiden asks.

"Of course." Brevan leaves the doorway before he's even finished speaking.

Caiden rubs his head again. "How much did we drink last night?"

"Too much," I say.

"What happened?"

I act hurt. "You don't remember? Our first night together and you don't remember?"

His mouth opens, then closes like he's struggling for words. "Of course, I remember. Just maybe not as well as I'd like."

"We did drink a lot," I say playfully. "But what they say about Pendralian men is absolutely true."

"And what do they say about Pendralian men?" he asks.

That they're selfish lovers who don't know how to please a woman. I clear my throat. "That no other men can compare."

He stands a little straighter at the remark.

I turn so my back is to him, then tug off the tunic. I cover my chest with my arm before tossing him the shirt. I quickly step into a day dress and lace up the side before I face him.

Caiden has just finished pulling his tunic and trousers on when a knock sounds again.

"Come in," he calls.

Brevan enters the room. His expression hard and cold. He hands Caiden a small vial of purple liquid, then holds out a second one. "I thought you might want one as well, Princess."

I accept the vial and drink the contents. If he's trying to poison me, I'd deserve it.

"I'm late for a meeting." Caiden kisses my cheek and leaves without another word.

I stand in silence with Brevan for a long while. He won't even meet my eyes. Finally, I can't take it. "It isn't what it looked like."

"He's your betrothed. It's not my business," he says to the ceiling.

"It's important to me that you know I didn't sleep with him."

His gaze finally meets mine. "Why?"

"You know why."

"You were naked. In the same bed."

"He was naked. I was wearing his tunic." I wince. That makes it sound worse. "I wanted him to think we had sex."

Brevan glances at the bottles of wine on the table. "Did he hurt you?"

"No. But he would have taken what he wanted if I didn't come up with another way."

"How drunk was he?" Brevan asks.

"We went through three bottles of wine. He drank most of it."

We're silent for a while, then I add, "I don't want to be alone with him again." I'm surprised by how small my voice is. I clear my throat and pretend to be confident. "But I know I won't have that luxury."

"We should go," he says. "I'm going to teach you how to kill a man today."

Thirty-Two

The wine bottles are gone, and my bed has clean sheets when I return. I'm sweaty and sore and exhausted. Training with Brevan was awkward. Even though I think he believes me, he was distant. But the lesson was good. Better than good. I'm pretty sure I could actually kill someone now.

On the walk back to my room, I let him know I had a headache and requested to skip dinner in favor of sleep. I hope it is enough to keep Caiden from visiting. I am not going to be able to trick him again.

I fill the bathtub, then soak until the water turns cold.

Horses come charging into our village, the cavalry on their backs yell and scream. The men throw torches on houses as they race down the street. Shadows flow in their wake, wrapping around them like snakes.

Legionnaires follow, brandishing swords, axes, and knives. They run into buildings, dragging people out.

There's so much screaming. So much blood. I cower in my brother, Felix's, arms. He's whispering something to me, but I can't make out the words. We're hidden, but we're not safe. Any minute, someone is going to throw a torch on the porch we're under, or they'll see us and drag us out.

I'm searching for any signs of our other brother, Arthur, or our parents. They're out there fighting. I know Felix wishes he was with them, but he promised our mother he would stay with me. At thirteen, he's nearly old enough to join the battle. Instead, he's comforting his eleven-year-old sister.

There's another explosion and I bury my face into his chest. Felix pulls me tighter against him. After the ringing in my ears subsides, I look out again. There are so many boots racing over the snow. Our village is vastly outnumbered.

The streets run red as blood stains the fresh snow. Jana, the woman we buy our bread from, is dragged from her home by her hair. She's in her underclothes, but they bunch up around her as a legionnaire pulls her through the snow, so her breasts are showing.

She claws at his hands, cursing him as he pulls her. When the legionnaire releases her, she grabs hold of his leg and bites him. He swings an axe, and it lodges itself in her skull.

I turn and press my face against my brother's chest. I think I'm crying, but I can't tell anymore. Nothing feels real. This has to be a nightmare.

My brother smooths my hair, then turns my head. "Watch. Watch, little warrior. Don't look away."

I wake with a start, covered in sweat. I look around, getting my bearings. I haven't dreamed about that night in years. I pull my knees to my chest and rest my head against them. I'd forgotten that nickname. They never used it after that night. It was a piece of me that was left with the ruins of our old village.

When we were young, I'd follow my brothers everywhere. I begged to learn to fight like them. Sometimes they'd indulge me and let me spar with them with sticks. They'd call me a little warrior, and I enjoyed the attention they gave me. The training was fun. I didn't understand that it was for a purpose. My father would scoop me up and tell me fighting wasn't my job. That the men would protect me.

But he died the night of that attack. He left three young children and his wife behind.

My mother turned into a fighter after that. Determined to see a better future for her children.

I stayed in the background. Helping, but never picking up arms. What good did it do, anyway? My father was still dead despite his years of training.

Then I gave up on all of them when I turned my back on the rebellion.

Their deaths have to mean something. They can't just be gone and forgotten. I can't let that happen.

I leave my bed and pull a robe over my shoulders. I

know how to kill the emperor. I just need to find the right weapon.

Brevan isn't outside my door when I open it. Instead, there's a yawning legionnaire. His eyes widen when he sees me. "Princess, is everything alright?"

"Yes, I'm fine. I skipped dinner and hoped I could find a snack in the kitchen."

"I don't know," he says. "I was told to make sure you don't leave your room."

"I won't take long. I'll just find some bread or something, then come right back." I smile sweetly.

"Don't believe her," a deep voice says.

I know it's Brevan without seeing him, but I look anyway. "I thought you weren't going to leave my door?"

His hair is tousled, and his tunic is untucked. He's got a sword hanging at his side, which seems out of place given his clothing choices. My eyes widen when I notice his trousers aren't tied at the waist. Fuming, I turn away from him. I don't think I want to know who he was with just now. "I'm going to the kitchen."

"Then I'll go with you," he says.

"Then maybe you should tie up your trousers," I hiss over my shoulder.

"Should I stay or go?" the young legionnaire asks.

"Stay," I shout at the same time that Brevan says, "Go."

"Which one is it?" he asks.

"Your orders come from me. Not from her. Go," Brevan commands.

I'm already several paces away, but Brevan catches me quickly. "You're not jealous, are you?"

"I have no reason to be," I say. "But maybe I'm angry

that you were off with some woman and left an inexperienced legionnaire at my door."

"If it makes you feel better, I wasn't with a woman. I took a nap and forgot to tie my trousers after I put them back on."

The visual of him without his clothes on flashes in my mind, and I scoff, mostly because I'm angry at myself for not pushing him out of my head. "It doesn't matter. You can do whatever you want. I know they're going to send you relic hunting soon, anyway."

"Actually, I'm here a while longer," he says.

That gets me to stop walking. "Why?"

"Caiden left after dinner tonight. The emperor went with him."

"When will they return?" I can't exactly kill the emperor if he's not here.

"They didn't say," he says.

"That's not helpful. That could be tomorrow or weeks from now," I say.

"They're not usually gone more than a couple of days." He stops walking. "Kitchen's this way." Brevan points behind us, to a flight of stairs I'd passed in my hurry to get away from him.

I huff out an annoyed breath, then backtrack. At least I have more time to find the weapon.

The kitchen is lit by a small fire burning in the hearth. It's only unoccupied for a few hours each day, so I'm counting it as good luck that there's nobody else here.

"I knew I should have sent up dinner for you," Brevan says.

"I wasn't hungry at the time. Besides, I'd still be asleep if not for the nightmare." I press my lips together before I say anything else. I don't want him to know what my nightmare was about.

He looks younger tonight. Softer. Maybe it's the dim firelight, or the clothing. Whatever it is, it's a side of him I haven't seen before. "Homesick?"

"Yeah."

"How about a sandwich?" he asks.

"Are you offering to make me food?"

"I know my way around this kitchen pretty well," he says.

"Alright." I sit on one of the stools at the table in the back. It's probably for staff to eat or prep ingredients at, but I prefer it to any of the fine tables I've sat at while here.

Brevan moves around the kitchen, slicing a round loaf of bread, then pulling ingredients from the pantry. He prepares two sandwiches on simple plates and carries them over to the table.

He sits in the stool across from me.

"Thank you," I say.

"You're welcome."

I take a bite of the sandwich. It's sliced vegetables and cheese with some salted meat. "This is delicious."

"I perfected it after long training days when I was younger."

"It was kind of the emperor to take you in. It must have been interesting living in the castle after being somewhere else your whole life," I say.

"It was."

What was Brevan the orphan like? How might his life have been different if he'd remained with his family, whoever they were. "Did you know right away that you wanted to join the Night Legion?"

"Shortly after I arrived. I thought it the best way for a boy with no family to make a place for himself. And to serve the emperor after all he did for me."

"Are you happy with your choice?" I ask.

He finishes a bite of his sandwich. "Most days. But the more I experience, the more I realize that nobody truly gets a choice."

I take a bite of my sandwich and chew slowly while I contemplate his words. I used to think we all made our own choices. That my mother chose to abandon our home and join the rebellion. But she left a town that had nothing left and needed to feed her children. What other options did she have?

When I look back on my own life, I see the path I've taken. So often I chose the route I thought I had to. There were few times I took the route I wanted.

"Maybe nobody gets to choose. There's an illusion of options when we're young, but I don't think it even existed then."

"I learned that younger than most by watching Caiden. If a prince doesn't get that luxury, what chance do any of us have?" he says.

"What happened between you and Caiden?"

He chews, then puts down his sandwich. "After our gifting ceremonies, he was angry at me for the power I had. My magic was so destructive and dangerous. He thought his father had favored me and asked the gods to give me more."

"He was jealous? I've seen his magic." I rub my throat, then drop my hand. "It's plenty strong."

"It is," he agrees.

"But yours was more powerful." The flash of light plays in my mind. "And I haven't seen it at its full strength, have I?"

"No, you haven't," he says.

"So the emperor bound your magic to make his son feel better?" That sounds insane, even for Caiden.

"I think he bound it because he was afraid of it. If I ever turned against him, or lost control, it would be catastrophic," he says.

"You wouldn't, though." I don't know why I'm so certain. This is the same man who has a reputation for destroying whole villages and killing without remorse. But the Brevan I've come to know doesn't resemble the one I was warned about. How is it possible he could be such a monster?

"I might. I used it without considering any consequences twice since meeting you," he says.

"And how often did you use it before me?" I ask, afraid of the answer.

"Since being bound?"

I nod.

"Never."

My hands tremble and I move them to my lap so he can't see. We're walking a dangerous line here and I think we both know that. I need to change the subject.

"Thank you for the sandwich." I climb off the stool. "We should probably get back."

"Of course." He clears the plates and I wait for him near the door.

We take our time, strolling slowly down the dark and abandoned halls. When we pass the temple, I glance inside. Two candles still flicker in the darkness.

"Caiden is hoping I'll help him fulfill the prophecy," I blurt.

"I know. Is that why you're at the empress's temple so often? To ask the gods for—"

"—For them to not give me magic, yes," I say.

His brow furrows. "I've never met anyone who didn't want magic. Man or woman."

"I've seen the destruction and pain it can cause." The memory of my village flashes in my mind. I've always wondered if our fighters would have had a chance if not for the magic of the legion. "It doesn't seem worth it. And it doesn't seem fair."

"Because the emperor limits who gets it?"

I nod.

"Can you imagine more people with my power? If everyone had magic, we'd kill each other off." He stops in front of my door.

"Or maybe we'd find ways to use it for good," I say as I reach for the handle. "Ways to harness it for other things besides harm."

"I forgot people could be like you." He leans against the wall, facing my room.

"What do you mean?"

"You have hope. I forget that is even possible."

I smile. Maybe I will figure out a way to finish what I started here. I step into my room, then glance over my shoulder. "Good night. Thank you again."

Only one dim lamp burns on the small desk, but it's enough light to get back in bed. As soon as I'm under the covers, I catch movement near my window.

I'm not alone.

THIRTY-THREE

Antonia emerges from behind my curtains.

I swallow the scream I was about to release and scramble from my bed. "What are you doing here?"

When she steps out more, I can see the black eye and swollen lip. Blood is smeared across her face.

"What happened?" I lead her to the bathing chamber and turn the water on so it can warm up.

"I told him to stop," she says. "But he didn't like that."

I wet a cloth and begin gently cleaning the blood from her face. "I'm so sorry."

My door bursts open, and Brevan charges in, sword drawn. Antonia and I both scream.

He lowers his sword, then returns it to the sheath at his side. "I'm sorry. I heard...I thought..." He moves closer. "What happened?"

"It's nothing," she says.

"Someone didn't like her saying no," I say.

"Sabina, no, it's fine. It'll heal."

"It's not fine." I place the bloody cloth under the hot water.

"Who?" Brevan asks.

"I can't say. I don't want him to do worse." She doesn't look at Brevan.

"Who?" Brevan asks again.

Antonia's lower lip trembles, but she manages to speak. "Lord Daley."

"Do not leave this room. Either of you." He fixes a terrifying gaze on me. "You understand?"

"We won't," we both say in unison.

He slams the door on his way out.

"What's he going to do?" Antonia asks.

"I don't know if we want to know. Now, let me get you cleaned up. Do you want to take a bath?" If Caiden had his way last night, I know I would have needed to wash myself over and over.

"I'm supposed to take care of you," she says.

"Hush. Tonight, you be the princess and I'll be your lady." I smile gently.

"I'd like a bath," she says. "As hot as possible. I don't even want to feel my skin ever again."

"I understand," I say. "Roses? Lavender?"

"No lavender," she says. "Orange?"

I look at the oils and salts sitting near the tub. There's a pot of salts that has flecks of orange in it. I smell it to check. "We have orange salts."

She nods. "Thank you."

"Do you need help getting out of your clothes?"

She nods, and I notice she's moving slowly. Her face

wasn't the only thing injured. When Brevan comes back, I might have to hunt this man down and kill him myself.

Once she's in the tub, I give her some privacy and close the door. Her cries are soft at first, then grow to louder sobs. I want to make it all go away. To fix it for her. But the only way to fix it is to eliminate the problem. Men like Caiden who think they can have anything they want. An empire that treats women as property and not people.

I'm starting to understand what my mother fought for. And moreover, I understand why she was willing to die for it.

I must be successful. Not for revenge. But for justice for Antonia, for me, for everyone who's been harmed by the way things are.

I collect myself as much as I can, then walk over to my door. Brevan is in the hallway. "You're back."

"I didn't want to intrude. Is there anything you need?" his tone is gentle.

"He hurt her." My eyes burn from holding back tears.

"I know," he says.

And somehow, I know he understands the rage and sorrow behind my words.

"I took care of it."

I don't know what he did, but I trust him. The realization is both oddly calming and terrifying. "Thank you."

He nods. "Good night, Princess."

Antonia shares the bed with me. She wakes from nightmares several times. She's terrified of being touched but doesn't want me to leave her side. I'm careful to give her space and offer soothing words when she wakes. I don't sleep at all.

When morning arrives, she excuses herself to dress in her room, then returns shortly after with all my ladies. Bruises linger but she's wearing a smile. When the others ask her about her injuries, she laughs and tells a story about falling off a horse.

I change the subject to the weather as I invite everyone to the dining chamber. Antonia catches my eye and mouths, *thank you*.

It's snowing. The first snow of the season. The servants bring hot chocolate with our breakfast.

I keep watching Antonia, waiting for her to break, but she doesn't.

She's strong, but she shouldn't have to be.

It's not long after breakfast when a knock sounds. I'm already dressed for training and after a quick goodbye to my ladies, I leave the room. I'm grateful they're all together so Antonia isn't alone.

Brevan is silent on our walk to the training room. We're nearly there when we hear someone running behind us.

"Enforcer!"

There's an out-of-breath legionnaire behind us. We double back to meet him. "I have news." He glances over at me nervously.

"You can speak in front of her," Brevan says. "She is going to be our next empress."

"Of course, it's just...not really something a lady should hear," he says.

"I'll live," I assure him.

He hesitates again, but Brevan gives him a look and he speaks, "We found a body this morning that was mauled by wolves. It took us a while to identify it, but we think it's Lord Daley. Nobody's seen him since last night."

I gasp, then cover my mouth with my hand. The name registers a moment later and I glance over at Brevan.

"Why was he out alone at night?" His tone is cold.

"Nobody knows."

"He was never the brightest," Brevan says dismissively. "Probably took a snack with him when he went for a walk."

I lift my brows. Really? A snack? Nobody is going to believe that.

"That would explain it," the legionnaire says. "We haven't seen any wolf attacks in years."

"Send a unit to investigate the castle grounds. Find out if any new dens have been built close by. See if there were any cubs born. If he got too close to a pup, the mother wouldn't have hesitated. Tell the others to be careful but not to harm the wolves. Those beasts in our woods have protected us from assassins and thieves too many times to harm."

"Thank you, Enforcer. I'll pass it along." He runs off in the same direction he came from.

"What a strange situation. A lord eaten by wolves." I watch Brevan out of the corner of my eye.

"Everyone knows if you go out at night with food in your pockets, you're tempting the wolves. It's his own fault, really. He should have been more careful." He starts walking again.

"Yes, I'm sure he'll be missed. Not by me, but by someone." I brush my fingers against his, careful not to linger. "Thank you."

<hr />

Once we're in the training room and the door is closed, Brevan pulls a bundle of fabric tied with a string from his waistband. "I got these for you."

I accept the package and untie it. I can tell by the shape that it's two knives before I open it, but when I remove the fabric, I gasp. The handles are blue and white with little shards of sea glass embedded in them. The iridescent blue blades shift to purple or teal depending on the way I move them in the light. I've heard the Pendralian steel workers could make magic with their wares, but I'd never seen it before.

"These are gorgeous." I look up at him. "They have to be worth a fortune. I can't possibly accept them."

He's smirking.

"What?"

"I knew you'd say that. Turn them over."

I comply and on the handle is my name engraved in the Iskvalandian spelling. The other handle says, *Princess*.

My vision is blurry, and I blink back tears. "Thank you. This is the most thoughtful gift anyone's ever given me."

"Keep them hidden if you can." He points to the shards of glass. "Those pieces came from relics. It should improve your aim and make them more deadly."

"You're hiding relics," I say.

"Sometimes," he admits.

"Thank you for sharing that with me," I say.

"I hope you never need to use these. Keep them clean, and if you bring them to me each month, I can keep them sharp for you."

"What if you're not here?" I ask.

"Remember the shop where you got your necklace?"

I touch the gem to make sure it's still there. I haven't taken it off, and most of the time, I forget I'm wearing it.

"He can take care of it for you. You can trust him."

"Are you selling relics to him?" I ask.

"No. To him, they're colorful bits of glass I found on my travels."

I hold the knives to my chest. "Thank you, truly."

"You're welcome. Now, let's see what you can do with them."

We spend the next hour practicing with the knives. They're easier to throw than the blades in the basket, but they're sharp. I nick my finger, drawing blood. Brevan makes us go back to the practice knives after that.

When we finish, I wrap my presents back up in the fabric and tie the bundle closed so my ladies won't see what's inside. "How will I carry these? I can't exactly wear a holster."

"Perla is making your ballgown, right?" he asks.

I nod.

"She sewed knife pockets into all the dresses the empress wore. You might want to check yours." He holds open the door for us. "Come on, I'm sure you're eager to get back to your ladies."

His words surprise me. Not because of what he said, but because I find I do want to return to them. Especially

Antonia. I hold the knives close to my chest as we walk down the halls. I'm going to check all my gowns when we return. If anyone tries to harm any of my ladies, I won't hesitate to protect them.

Is that why the empress had knives on her? Or was it for a different reason? Every time I learn something about her, I'm left with more questions. "What was she like, the empress?"

"Strong. But quiet. I never once saw her disagree with the emperor, but Caiden told me she was fierce behind closed doors. I have a feeling she'd have liked you."

A group of legionnaires straighten as soon as they see us. Brevan nods to them and they return the gesture with stiff movements.

I wait until we're out of earshot. "How did she die?"

"Poison," he says.

How was that possible? I found her books. There were poisonous plants that were carved into the columns around her garden space. The one her mourning husband destroyed after her death...And there was the hidden garden.

"You know my old rooms?" I ask.

"Yes, they've sealed the passageway" he says.

"No that's not what I'm asking. Whose rooms were they?"

"They belonged to the empress's favorite lady," he says.

"I thought Marian was her favorite."

"No," he says. "Marian is the only one who agreed to stay after the empress's death. All the others asked to join a temple in her honor."

I wonder if they'd speak to me if I visited them. Maybe

they could answer some of my questions. I'm still thinking about how I can convince them to allow me to visit the sun goddess's temple when we reach my room.

"Same time tomorrow?" I ask.

"I think we'll take the day off tomorrow," he says. "You might be busy."

My heart sinks. "I thought Caiden was still away."

"He is." He leans over me and knocks on the door.

It opens immediately, and my ladies chatter with the same energy they did when I first arrived at the castle. Then I notice that there's a new face among them. I gasp. Shock and excitement explode through me—it feels like I was just dropped into cold water.

"Anya?" I can't believe it. How is she here? How is this real? Am I imagining things?

She smiles wide and tears glisten in her eyes. "Nice to see you again, Princess."

She's dressed like a lady, and I hardly recognize her.

"How are you here?" I look over at Brevan. "Did you do this?"

"I may have talked Caiden into letting you have a lady from home," he says. "Told him you were homesick."

I throw my arms around his shoulders and hug him. He pats me on the back and moves out of the embrace quickly. His face is red. "I'm glad I could be of service, Your Highness."

I realize my mistake and take a step away from him. "Thank you." Then I enter my room and close the door before my ladies can ask any questions.

Anya crosses the room and pulls me in for a hug. I

squeeze her back. I don't deserve this kindness from Brevan. I know he's falling for me, but he's falling for someone who doesn't exist. Anya is a good reminder of who I really am. Of where I came from and why I'm here.

I realize that when I read Sabina on the knife, I read it as *my* name. Not *hers*. I need to get out of here before I lose myself or before I destroy Brevan.

"Thank you for coming," I whisper.

"Of course. I'd have been here sooner if you let me," she says.

"I know."

"Later, I want to know anything new. I want to help," she whispers.

"I don't want to lose you."

"I know what I'm getting into," she replies, then releases me, and quickly steps back.

The other ladies are watching us. Genevieve and Charlotte smile as Anya returns to the group, but Antonia has her arms crossed in front of her chest and she's chewing on her bottom lip. She looks worried. She probably thinks she's lost the place she's been working to gain.

"How about cards?" I ask. "Genevieve, Charlotte, can you teach Anya how to play *Assassin* and then we can all play the next hand? Maybe in the dining chamber? I'll call for more hot chocolate."

"Of course," Genevieve chirps. Charlotte nods, then grabs the cards from the table near the fireplace. Anya happily joins them and they retreat, leaving me with Antonia.

"How are you?" I ask.

She drops her arms and fixes a smile on her lips. "I'm great. Your friend is lovely. She said you've known each other since you were children."

"Teenagers," I clarify.

"That's sweet."

"I'm going to need your help with something," I say in a conspiratorial tone.

She perks up at that, her eyes widening slightly. "Anything."

"Help her fit in? Her family was newly noble. She may need some assistance so she looks like she belongs." I'm not worried about Anya. While I worked behind the scenes, she was in the field. She's lived a thousand lives already, traveled all over the empire. She can blend in anywhere.

I am worried about Antonia. She's chasing power. Making her think she's my confidant may gain me her loyalty. At least for now.

"Of course," she says.

"I couldn't ask for anyone better by my side." I offer my hand, unsure if she wants to be touched. She takes it and I give her a squeeze. "Thank you."

***

We spend the rest of the day sipping hot chocolate and catching Anya up on the court gossip over cards. She gets along with the other ladies, and it's hard to believe she is just a rebellion kid like me.

She stays behind after the others leave, and as soon as the door closes, she passes me a piece of paper.

"From Lee. I sort of visited him after you stopped by."

She winces. "I'm sorry. I was worried about you. He gave me this just in case I saw you again."

I open the note, read it, then crumple it into a ball. Rage burns in my chest.

How could he do this?

THIRTY-FOUR

I READ the note several more times. This has to be a mistake.

Change of plans. Keep them alive.

Something happened. Something changed. "What is he thinking?" I cross the room to the fireplace and toss the paper in.

Anya grabs the poker and stokes the fire until the paper is nothing but ashes.

I stare at the flames as I repeat his note over and over: *Change of plans. Keep them alive.*

She returns the poker to its place. "I asked him that when he gave me the note."

"And? What did he say?" I glance over at her.

"He said there's a plan."

"But he wouldn't tell you?"

Her shoulders slump. "They still don't trust me."

I ball my hands into fists. "After everything you did for them?"

She touches my arm. "It's alright. I left. I'm not part of it anymore. They don't have to trust me."

"But you are. By coming here, you're involved again," I say.

"It's not the same. I'm not here for them. I'm here for you. I might not be the fighter I was, but I've been getting better. I think I could do it again if I had to."

"You don't have to be. I've got this under control." I sigh, then drop onto the couch. "At least I did."

Anya sits next to me.

"Did he say anything else?" I ask.

"Just to tell you *hello* for him." She rolls her eyes. "He's still not over you."

"He's made that clear." *But he's also a liar.*

I look over at Anya. "Did you say anything to him about the emperor?"

"No."

I rub my temples and walk in a slow circle. I wasn't sent here to kill anyone, but then he changed his mind. Now we're back to the original plan? But why? What was I still doing here if there's a new plan?

The only reason I agreed to come here was to see the end of this reign. What happens if I do it anyway? What happens if I disobey? Technically, I left the rebellion. This whole thing is a favor. And I truly thought this would be a one-way trip. But now I don't know what to do. I didn't even get to tell Lee where the king's rooms are. None of this makes any sense.

Anya's watching me with concern etched into her brow. If I try something, and fail, they'll torture her and kill her because of me. It's no longer just my life on the line.

I fucked up. I should never have said anything about her to Brevan. My heart aches, and my chest feels tight. That is the other complication. I am falling for the enforcer, and the thought of betraying him is tearing me apart. It shouldn't. I'd already betrayed him by lying about who I really am. There isn't any future for us. If he found out the truth, he'd kill me. If I continue this farce, I marry his friend.

It's lose-lose.

"Tay?" Anya sets a gentle hand on my shoulder.

"You should call me Sabina," I say. "They can't find out you know the truth. If something happens, you swear to them that you thought I was her. That I fooled you."

"I'm not letting you do this alone." She takes my hand.

"You have to. Swear to me. If there's a way to save yourself, you do it. Please." My tone is pure desperation.

"If something goes wrong, we escape. Together."

"I can't leave while they're alive. I stand out too much. Someone would find me and ship me back to them. Or to Iskvaland. This whole thing was a mistake."

"You still want them dead, don't you?" she asks.

"Of course I do. But it's too risky. If I try, and I fail, they'll come after you."

"You're forgetting I know how to take care of myself."

Her hand is trembling slightly. A physical reminder of what she's been through. She left the rebellion a few days after I did. She was away from the city when the attack on the Point happened. I still don't know the details of her mission, but for one of our best to walk away from the field, I know it must have been awful. I can't ask her to fight again. I can't put her through that.

I set my hand on top of hers. "I'll figure it out. Maybe Lee has something in mind. We'll wait. The emperor and prince aren't here anyway, so we can't do anything right now."

"Alright," she says. "This is your mission now. I'll follow your lead."

"Stay with me tonight?" I'm afraid she'll disappear if she leaves.

I can't sleep. Anya snores softly next to me. I remember what it was like sleeping on a bed in the castle for the first time. So plush and pillowy it was impossible not to sleep. Now, it feels more like it might swallow me whole.

I hate the danger she's in by joining me, but selfishly, I'm happy to see her.

I still can't believe Brevan found her and brought her here. For me. Because I told him I was homesick. My chest feels tight. It's the most thoughtful thing anyone's ever done for me. Better than the knives. I don't deserve his kindness.

The bed shakes a little as I crawl out, but Anya doesn't stir. I tiptoe to the door and open it a crack. Brevan is at his post, so I step into the hall.

"Is something wrong?" He's instantly alert, hand reaching for his sword.

"No, nothing's wrong."

His shoulders visibly relax.

"I don't know how I'll ever thank you enough for what

you did for me." I wrap my arms around myself as the guilt bubbles up. If he knew the truth, he'd hate me.

"I know how hard it is to live somewhere new."

"Where are you from?" I ask, hopeful he'll answer truthfully this time.

"Nowhere."

"Everyone is from somewhere," I say.

"It doesn't matter. I'm here now," he replies.

I nod and stop pushing. I have no right to ask him to divulge his past.

"Is your friend adjusting alright?"

"I think she's thrilled she's not sleeping in a drafty room tonight," I say.

"Especially with the snow. It must remind you both of home."

"It does. I used to love the snow. It was magical at night when the moon would turn it silver." I'd stare out the window for hours when I was young to watch the snowfall. It wasn't the same after we moved to the city.

"Come with me." The smile on his face is playful. It's an expression I haven't seen on him before.

I hesitate, and glance behind me, knowing Anya is alone in my room.

"She'll be safe," he promises. "We've added more security since the last rebel attack."

I'm still a little unsure, but I can't resist his outstretched hand and the excited glint in his eyes. My heart thunders and reason tumbles from my mind. I'm grateful he can't read my thoughts because I'd probably do just about anything to see him happy.

We enter a room near mine. It's another bedroom, but

all the furniture is covered in fabric. The stale air smells of dust.

"Whose room was this?" I ask.

"It used to be mine. I requested to move to more modest accommodations after I joined the legion. It didn't feel right having so much when the others lived in the barracks."

I can almost picture a young Brevan in this room, but the image is difficult to hold on to. I know very little about his childhood. Did he play with toys, or enjoy reading? Did he lounge on his bed, or fight Caiden with wooden swords?

I suspect that the change of rooms was also about that falling out. Giving him more distance from the prince.

Brevan throws open the drapes to reveal long windows. No, not windows, glass doors. He opens them, revealing a small balcony.

Cold winter air blows into the room, chilling me instantly. I should have grabbed a robe.

I pad over to the balcony, not caring that my feet are going to freeze on the cold metal. Soft snowflakes fall onto my shoulders and stick in my lashes. I reach out my hand and watch them land on my fingers. Then I tilt back my head and open my mouth, letting the flakes fall on my tongue. I laugh, reveling in the simplicity of the moment. I forgot what joy felt like.

Brevan chuckles, and to my surprise, he tilts his own head to catch flakes. After he does, he laughs again, then looks over at me. Snowflakes cling to his dark lashes, too, and stick to his hair. He looks like a fairy king who belongs in an enchanted woodland, instead of a brooding legionnaire. If only we'd met under other circumstances...

I turn away from him before I can let my mind finish that thought and lean against the icy railing. My fingers are freezing, but I don't let go. The cold makes me feel more alive.

From here, I can see to the hedges that separate the castle grounds from the city. The expansive yard is covered in a blanket of sparkling white. The topiaries look like ghosts with their dusting of snow.

The moons are waxing crescents, but they give enough light for a sheen of silver to reflect off the fresh snow. "It's beautiful. Thank you for bringing me here."

When I look over, I find him staring at me instead of the landscape. He's got a genuine smile on his lips, and he appears more relaxed and peaceful than I've ever seen.

"You're right. It is magical in the moonlight." His gaze is so intense, I know he's not talking about the snow.

I'm certain my whole face is blushing. Good thing my cheeks were likely already pink from the cold. A shiver rakes my body, and I tighten my arms around myself.

"We should go back inside," he says.

"No, I'm not ready yet."

"Your lips are turning blue."

"It's just the moonlight."

"So fucking stubborn." He moves closer and wraps his arms around me. "I don't have a coat to give you."

I nestle into him, enjoying the warmth and the feel of his embrace. "This is better."

We stand like that for a while, watching the snow fall on the desolate grounds below. I turn, so my chest presses against his. The moonlight makes him look softer. Younger, even. Like the world hasn't chewed him up and spat him out. I wish he could be this relaxed all the time.

I reach up and rest my hand against the side of his face. My thumb brushes against his cheekbone, feeling his dark stubble.

He catches my wrist with his hand. "We can't."

"Why not?" It is cruel to both of us to keep my hand there, to wish for more, but I can't stop myself. "When do we get to make a choice? Just once?"

His hand slides from my wrist, down my arm, to my neck. He tangles his fingers into my hair, then tilts my face toward his. "You are so fucking beautiful. If I were a better man, I'd walk away right now."

"I don't want you to be a better man." Heat flares low in my belly, warming all of me. I've never felt like this about anyone. This man can ruin me, but I don't care. I might want him to ruin me.

He removes his hand abruptly and takes a step back. He's panting and closes his eyes. "You're a princess. You deserve so much better."

"Like Caiden?" I ask.

He opens his eyes. "See what I mean? You're engaged, and here I am fantasizing about all the dirty things I want to do to you."

I step closer to him. "Tell me."

"Sabina." My name is a warning.

I close the distance between us and press my palms to his chest. "Stop making excuses and kiss me."

That was all he needed. He pulls me closer. My breasts press against his chest, the thin fabric of my nightgown doing little to act as a barrier. Then his lips crash into mine.

The kiss is hungry and intense. The pressure is brutal, then becomes enticingly gentle. He slides a hand to the back of my head, his fingers tangling into my hair while he intensifies the kiss. Deeper, harder. It's possessive and violent. Both of us fighting for dominance with our lips.

When he sweeps his tongue into my mouth, I moan, then match his movements. My fingers move down his chest, and I slide them under his tunic, feeling his bare skin and all those taut muscles.

I've never wanted someone more in my life.

An explosion sounds, and we pull apart, breathless. A fire erupts near the castle gates. Another explosion. More fire. Legionnaires flood into the garden, tearing paths through the white expanse of snow.

Neither of us speaks as we run through the room and down the hall. Anya is in the hallway outside my room, her eyes wide. She glances from me to Brevan, then back again. There's only a hint of judgement in her expression. "What was that?"

"Must be rebels. Stay in your room," he orders.

I nod, then shove Anya inside.

"Barricade the door!" Brevan yells.

Anya and I move quickly. We try to lift the sofa, but it's too heavy, so we carry one of the chairs to the door instead. We shove the other one next to it, then we run to the window just as another explosion illuminates the garden. Hundreds of people run toward the castle. Suddenly, another explosion shakes our room.

They must be inside, but more continue flooding the lawn, racing toward the castle. It's a massive group in a coordinated attack. There was so much death last time, but I have a feeling that was just a practice run for tonight.

Thirty-Five

THUMPS SOUND OUTSIDE OUR DOOR, and another explosion makes the walls shake. Anya backs away, eyes wide with fear. Her hands tremble and sweat beads at her brow. I hurry over to her, but I only make her retreat farther.

I keep my distance but try to soothe her. "It's alright. We're safe in here. They can't get to us."

Something slams against our door, and she yelps, then folds in on herself. She's balled up on the ground, a shaking, trembling mass. Her breathing is too fast, and I worry she'll faint.

"Don't worry," I tell her. "We're safe." Tears slide down my cheeks, but I quickly brush them away. I don't want her to see me upset.

It's not the rebels attacking that has me afraid. It's the sight of my best friend as a shell of herself. She used to be fearless, unstoppable. I thought she was getting better, but this must be sending her back to whatever it was she endured.

Another thud against the door sends me looking for the

knives Brevan gave me. I'm not a fighter, but I will protect my friend.

Something cracks inside me. These are rebels. I'm supposed to be on the same side as them. Would I really kill someone if they came through that door? How could I do that? How could I turn my back on my own?

They wouldn't know me. And if I told them, they wouldn't believe me. Or if they did, how would I maintain my cover?

Another pounding on the door and another explosion. I set my jaw and grip my blades tight. Too tight, I realize. I loosen my grasp and hold them the way Brevan showed me.

There's yelling outside the door, but I can't tell who it's coming from. Which side is winning? What if the rebels win and I can leave? Brevan would be heartbroken. But he also might be dead. I don't want that.

The lines are blurring. I can't figure out which side I stand on anymore. The emperor and prince aren't here, so if I want to complete my mission, I'd have to stay. But Lee said to hold off.

My mind is a tangled mess, and my insides feel like they might explode. I want to scream. I want to break something.

The door shatters, and I turn and lift my arms to shield my face. Splintered wood slams against me. Three men peer over the chair that's still in place. I don't recognize any of them.

"Look what we have here, boys," a middle-aged man with a gray beard says.

"It's the princess. Must be our lucky day," a younger man with startlingly blond hair says.

The third is a brunette who might still be a teenager. His face is full and round, not yet outgrown from his childhood. "Let's take her back with us."

I hold my weapons. "Leave us alone."

"Oh, shit, there's another one back there," the blond man says. "Let's keep 'em both."

They climb over the chair and rush toward me. They're making crude comments as they get closer, clearly enjoying my discomfort.

"I don't want to hurt you," I threaten.

"Did you hear that, Charles?" the blond says to the older man. "She doesn't want to hurt us."

"Then put your knives down and come with us. We'll make it easier on you," Charles says.

"I swear to the gods if you get any closer, I will gut you like a fish."

The youngest man speaks in Iskvalandian, "She thinks she's a fighter."

The blonde man responds in rapid Iskvalandian, "She's bluffing."

They're talking about me as if I'm not here. Telling one another that I'm faking my fight. That I'm supposed to be weak. I am not weak.

"Quit doing that," Charles says. "You know I can't understand what you're saying."

"You're from Iskvaland." My brow furrows. I didn't know there were any rebels from Iskvaland. That would explain why I didn't know them. Maybe they were from a different group.

I shout at them in Iskvalandian. "Leave me alone, I

don't want to hurt you." It's my final warning. I don't want to harm them, but I want to live more.

Charles lunges for me, and I crouch low, then sweep my leg out like Brevan showed me. He goes down. I hate that Brevan was right about balance. Then I shove a knife into the old man's throat. Blood trickles down his neck. He claws at it trying to pry out, then blood fills his mouth, pouring out the sides. His arms fall limp, and his eyes go glassy. His chest stops moving.

"You bitch!" The blond man charges me, and I try to yank out the knife, but it's stuck, so I leave it and swipe at him with my other knife.

He dodges it, then shoves me to the ground. I lose my grip, and the knife goes flying. Quickly, I crawl toward it, but he steps on my arm. I scream. He lifts his foot just as he grabs a handful of my hair to yank me to my knees.

I reach for his hand to attempt to get him to let go, but he pulls harder, then grabs my chin with his free hand.

He spits in my face. "You're a traitor to your own people."

The words slam into me. I don't know which people he's talking about. The rebels? Iskvalandians?

Tears stream down my face, but rage burns in my chest. I spit back at him, then I swipe at his face with my fingernails. He releases my hair with a yell, but kicks me in the chest, sending me to my back.

A blade goes flying over my head and impales him in the chest. Anya is standing next to me, a bloody knife in her hand. She's still shaking, but she moves forward, then slices my knife across the man's throat.

She pushes him, and he falls to his knees, then to the

floor. Anya collapses next to him, her chest rising and falling with rapid, jagged breaths. She stares at the dead man, and I know whatever compelled her to get up is gone.

I make it to my knees and stay like that while I survey the destruction.

The younger man is standing by the door, staring at me. Jaw open, eyes wide, he's frozen in place. Wetness appears on the front of his trousers.

I wrinkle my nose in disgust. "You should go before I pull my knife from your friend's chest."

He climbs over the chair and flees into the hallway, but I hear a thud a second later and then Brevan fills my doorway. The young man didn't make it out of here alive, and I can't say I feel sorry for him.

Brevan shoves the chair aside and is on his knees in front of me in a heartbeat. He holds my face, turning it from side to side while examining it, then scans the rest of me. His brows are knitted together in worry. He runs his fingers down my arm, over the scrapes and cuts from the shattering door, then looks at my blood-soaked nightgown. "Whose blood is this?"

"Theirs."

"You're sure?" he asks.

"I'm sure."

He leans his forehead against mine, then wraps his arms around me. "Thank the gods you're alright."

"You're the one who saved me."

"I wasn't here. I should have been, but I wasn't," he says as he leans back so he can look at me.

"If you hadn't taught me how to use those knives, I'd be dead."

He looks at the bodies on the ground. Both with bloody necks. One still has a knife in his chest. "Good throw."

"That was Anya." I pull away from him and look for my friend. She's sitting in the back of the room with her head to her knees.

Without a word, Brevan helps me up and follows me at a distance when I rush over to her. I sit next to her, but don't touch her. "Anya, it's over."

I look up to Brevan for confirmation that I'm telling her the truth. He nods.

"Tell me what you need," I say. "Do you want me to hold you?"

"No."

"You saved my life," I tell her.

"I know. But I took his." She doesn't even look up at me.

I lean my head against the wall. I'd done the same. I killed someone. A rebel. Someone who was supposed to be on the same side as me. The guilt is tearing Anya apart, but I can't find that within me.

Maybe I'm just as much of a monster as those I came here to kill. I look up at Brevan, seeking some kind of reassurance.

Brevan reaches for me, then catches himself and pulls his hand back. "I'll wait in the hall."

I fight my own urge to touch him. "Thank you."

He nods, then leaves.

I sit with Anya in silence for a long while. Finally, she looks up and turns toward me. "How long have you been in love with him?"

"Brevan? No. It's not like that. I'm attracted to him, sure..." I begin.

She gives me a look that only a best friend can give. "You know it's going to end badly."

"I know." I set my hand on top of hers.

After another stretch of silence, she says, "I'm sorry I'm broken."

"You're not broken," I tell her.

"I am. And it almost got us both killed tonight."

"Don't do that to yourself. You defeated your fear tonight. You fought yourself, and you won." I squeeze her hand. "Then you even saved my life. Someone who is broken couldn't do that."

"I shouldn't be like this," she says. "I shouldn't have panicked. I never used to do that. Not before...."

"Shhh. Don't you worry about that." I know she doesn't want to tell me what happened, even if I wished she would share. "You'll be back to the way you were when you're ready. It won't last forever."

She takes a deep breath, then looks around the room. The bodies are still on the ground, crimson puddles surrounding them. "I guess we'll move to my room."

"Yeah. That's a good idea." I stand up. "Brevan?" I call.

"Yes, Princess?"

"Can you please check on my ladies?" I ask. "See if anyone is hurt. Let them know I'll be in Anya's room and to not come to mine."

"Let me escort you to your new room, and then I'll check on them. You shouldn't be in there with the dead."

I step over the bodies on my way out, leading Anya by our clasped hands. I don't even bother to say a prayer for the dead. I don't need Brevan's gift to know their intentions were bad.

They might have been working for the rebellion, but I have to wonder about their motives for choosing that path. Some men just seem to like to fight and would join whichever group allowed them that pleasure. I've seen it in the Night Legion for years. I never thought I'd see it with the rebels.

Thirty-Six

WHEN I OPEN the door to let my ladies in the next morning, Brevan isn't outside. Six legionnaires are standing there, and each of them inclines their head at me as the ladies hurry into Anya's room.

My ladies are dressed in their usual finery, but they all look tired. I'm guessing nobody slept last night. Even though none of them were harmed, I know how frightening it must have been.

Anya's room is smaller than mine, but we all sit around the fireplace together. Genevieve stares into space, a cooling cup of tea between her palms. Antonia and Charlotte both sit with books in their laps, but they rarely turn the pages. Anya sips tea on the couch next to me.

I hate that I can't do anything to break the gloom. At least it has continued to snow, and most of the tracks and blood are buried under the fresh powder.

I check for Brevan several times, but he's still away by lunch. My ladies are more talkative by now, and we even get a lively game of hearts going. None of us brings up last night, though.

Finally, sometime in the late afternoon, there's a knock on my door.

"I'll get it," Charlotte calls.

"No, you sit, I'll get it," I say.

Anya gives me a warning look, but I ignore it. I know what kind of trouble I'm asking for, but I can't stop myself. My heart leaps when I see Brevan at my doorway. "No training today?" I ask playfully.

When his expression remains steely, my smile fades.

"What is it?" I ask.

"The emperor and prince have returned early due to the attack. They have called a meeting of the court. You're all expected to be there tonight."

My heart sinks. "When did they get back?"

"Early this morning."

"A meeting so soon can't be good news," I say.

"It's not," he says.

I reach for him, then catch myself and pull my arm back. "Can you tell me?"

"No." His expression is stone. There's not even a hint of what he knows.

"Alright." I don't press. I think that at this point, if he could say something, he would. Whatever this is, it's out of his hands.

"Please join the court in the throne room at six." His jaw is tight, his movements stiff. "The emperor will host dinner at seven in the ballroom. Formal dress is expected."

"Are you leaving again?" I ask quietly.

"I won't be at your door, but I'm not leaving the castle," he says.

"Will I see you later?"

"I will be in attendance." His tone is so stiff and impersonal.

"I'm sorry. About last night…" I whisper. That's the only thing I can think of. I ruined it. I shouldn't have kissed him. It was too far.

His expression softens and he whispers, "The only thing I would change about last night would be staying by your side. You shouldn't have had to fight those men off yourself."

I bite my lower lip to keep from saying what I really want to say. I want to ask him about the kiss. I want him to clarify that he really doesn't regret that.

"Ladies," he says loudly, then inclines his head to the women in my room. "Princess." He bows. "I will see you all this evening."

I shut the door, then catch Anya's eye. She's practically screaming her warning at me. My cheeks heat. Was I that obvious?

I pass the ladies and close myself into the bathing chamber. Covering my face with a bundle of drying cloths, I scream into them. I'm in so much fucking trouble.

Anya is wrong. I'm not falling for him. I already fell. If I had to choose between Brevan and the rebellion, I'm not sure I could be trusted to make the right decision.

The throne room is right off the main entrance to the castle, not far from the ballroom where I first saw the emperor. The large iron doors are decorated with a dragon on each side. Their tails overlap, crossing over the doors and almost making the shape of a heart. Their wings spread wide as if they're in flight.

It makes me sick to look at it. The dragon in the dungeon is probably as vicious as the stories say, but I'd be furious, too, if someone kept me locked in a dark pit.

They push the doors open, and I enter, followed by my ladies. A few other members of the court come behind us. We're the first to arrive, and the legionnaires guide us to stand in front, facing the throne. The courtiers who arrive after fill in the spaces behind us. Nobody stands closer than our group. I'm not sure if it's because of my stolen status as a royal or if there's a more sinister reason for it.

I stare at the massive black throne atop an oval dais. There are no stairs facing us so they must be in the back. The throne itself is made of black-stained wood sculpted to look like it's part of a tree. There are knots and leaves carved along the surface, which looks like the texture of wood. A black velvet cushion rests on the seat.

There are no other chairs. Not a chair for the priest or Caiden. Just the emperor's lone throne. I wonder if the empress used to have a chair of her own.

Behind the throne is a massive curtain that spans the entire wall. I've never seen so much fabric in one place before. Not knowing whether the room expands beyond it or the curtain blocks doorways and windows makes me uneasy.

The fabric ripples, then parts. Two legionnaires hold

the material to the side so the emperor can walk through. Caiden follows him. Then, after a few seconds, Brevan and the high priest come through the curtain.

The men climb stairs at the back of the dais, and the emperor settles into his throne. Caiden stands at his right, the priest at his left. Brevan stands next to, and slightly behind, Caiden.

A hush falls over the gathered group as the emperor stares out at his inner circle, his most loyal members of the court. At least that's how Genevieve explained it to me.

The priest steps forward. "The gods have spoken through our mighty, wise emperor. I am here to share it with you as it was told to him."

He lifts his hands, palms facing us, then closes his eyes. I almost laugh at how ridiculous he looks. He acts as if he is channeling something, but he already knows what he's going to say.

And I am willing to bet my life that whatever it is, it did not come from the gods.

"Darkfall will bring great sorrow and ruin."

Everyone around us murmurs. Even my ladies gasp and move a little closer together. I watch Brevan. He doesn't flinch. His eyes stare ahead, bored and distant. His jaw is tense, his posture straight. The perfect model legionnaire. Even his leather armor is impeccable. It looks more ceremonial than the armor I usually see him wear.

"To protect the peace and maintain balance, eight will enter the temple by morrow's eve to ask the gods for their gifts."

The murmurs explode into startled whispers. My pulse races. No one had ever gone before Darkfall.

"Hush. The message continues."

The crowd quiets. I hold my breath.

"The gods have selected their eight. You will step forward when you hear your name."

I know where this is going. My ears are ringing. The room suddenly feels too big, and my limbs are numb. I'm not watching anymore, it's like I'm outside my body, hearing this through someone else's ears.

He reads names I don't recognize, and men step forward, masking their excitement with stoic expressions.

Then he looks at me. The emperor looks at me. Caiden and Brevan look at me. I can't breathe.

When they say my name, it's like I'm hearing it from underwater. I can't make my legs move.

This wasn't supposed to happen. I was supposed to be out of here before this.

"Sabina." Caiden is in front of me, and he clasps my hand. "Don't worry. I'll help you as much as I can."

I see myself closing my fingers around his hand. Moving my legs to walk forward to join the seven men who wait for their big moment. Their glances toward me are not kind. If I was left alone with them, they would certainly ensure I never made it to the ceremony.

Somewhere far away, I hear cheers and applause.

"Now we feast!" The emperor's booming voice breaks my trance, and I suck in a breath, then blink a few times.

Caiden has returned to his father, and the men I was standing with have rejoined their friends and family. The mood is jubilant. People laugh and hug, and their conversations are excited and joyous.

My ladies are all standing where they were when I left

them. Charlotte and Genevieve wear nervous smiles. Antonia and Anya don't bother to try.

I walk over to them, and they surround me, whispering words of encouragement.

Anya manages to get next to me, and as we head to the ballroom, Anya and I slow down so the others can get a little distance. She leans close and whispers, "You and me, tonight, we run."

THIRTY-SEVEN

DINNER IS BEING SERVED at three long tables. The emperor sits at one with his priest, several important-looking officials in uniforms, and a few select courtiers.

The second table is where I'm sitting, next to Caiden and more people in uniforms and exquisite, expensive clothing.

The last table is all courtiers, no legionnaires or officials in uniform. They're likely the less important people but have enough status to be at this event.

"I'm glad you returned safely," I say to Caiden.

He leans over and kisses my cheek. "I'm glad you survived the attack. I can't believe they got into your room. Or that you killed two men yourself."

"One myself, the other was Anya. Speaking of, I have to say thank you for allowing her to join me." I offer a warm smile.

"I'm glad you're happy."

Servants come around the table, filling wineglasses. The prince covers his and shakes his head. "None for me."

I sip my wine. "Still hungover from the other night?"

"I want to be completely sober for later," he says.

"I didn't think I'd have company. Won't I need the rest before tomorrow?"

"Don't worry, I won't keep you up too late."

I take a gulp of my wine, already wondering what I'm going to have to do to get him away from me long enough to sneak out with Anya.

It was going to be hard enough already with guards constantly at the door. I'm really hoping there's a secret passageway somewhere in her room.

"You know, my father told me he wasn't going to have you do the gifting ceremony after all while we were away."

"What changed his mind back?" I ask.

"The bodies you left on the floor in your room. He was impressed by your bravery." He smiles as if he knows something I don't.

"I'm not sure how to reply to that. If I could have chosen for them to pass by my room and not break down the door, I'd have taken that option. I was only brave because I had to be."

"But they did break down your door. Almost like the gods themselves sent a test for you."

"Maybe," I reply.

Bowls of soup are set in front of each of us, and we make polite conversation with the people around us as we eat. I'm seated across from the Duke and Duchess of Bogshire. They laugh at every joke the prince makes, even if it's not funny, and compliment him at every possible moment. They've even started doing it to me by the time we reach the main course.

My ladies are at the end of the table. Given the honor of sitting near me, but not close enough that I can speak with them. They're all directly across from men. I wonder if those men are looking for wives.

The only person I don't see is Brevan. I tell myself that it doesn't mean anything. It doesn't mean that the prince knows about our kiss. It doesn't mean that he's gone. He's just busy. I look toward the door more often than I should in the hopes that he'll walk through it.

By the time dessert is served, my face hurts from fake smiling and I am out of safe, mindless conversation topics.

Musicians file in as dinner is cleared away, and people leave the tables to gather in groups to converse or dance. I just want out of this room.

"I have a bit of a headache," I say to Caiden. "I don't think I've quite recovered from last night yet."

"I'm sorry to hear that. Why don't you rest for a while, and I'll send Brevan to come and get you later. We have some things to do to prepare for the ceremony tomorrow."

"Alright." I stand on my toes and kiss his cheek because it feels like what would be expected of me.

He smiles, then waves over two young legionnaires who seem overly eager to attend to the prince. "Please escort my bride to her room. I need you to wait outside the door until the enforcer arrives. Nobody in or out."

I try not to wince when he says *out*.

"See you soon, Princess," Caiden says.

I give him a small curtsy, then walk toward the door. The pair of legionnaires follows close behind. As I'm leaving, I scan the room for Anya. I don't see her anywhere.

Maybe she left already. If we're lucky, we can find a passageway and get out now.

If we're unlucky, we might have to go later tonight after whatever Caiden has planned. Either way, I will not be at the temple tomorrow.

My heart aches at the thought of leaving Brevan behind, but I know I could never have him, anyway. And there's the whole fact that I failed at what I was sent here to do. But I carry information with me that may help someone else complete the mission.

When I arrived here, I was willing to throw my life away for even a chance at making the royals suffer. Now, I see things a little differently. They still need to meet their end, but it needs to be done properly. We'll need two assassins so they can be killed at the same time, leaving no chance for one of them to catch the killer before the deed is completed.

I'll find Lee and let him know. And I'll also demand he tell me who killed my brothers. And then I'll make plans to make their murderer pay.

I don't say a word to the legionnaires when I arrive at Anya's room. The lamps flicker to life as soon as I close the door. I let out a relieved breath. At least in here, I don't have to pretend. "Anya?"

The room is small enough that I should see her immediately, so I walk toward the bathing chamber to check there. The door is open, and the room is empty.

I guess she is still at dinner and I missed her. I take off my slippers and shimmy out of the formal dress. Caiden didn't give me details, so I pull on a more comfortable day dress, then get to work removing all the pins in my hair.

Anya still isn't here when I finish. I hope she gets back before Brevan arrives.

The fire crackles as a log falls, and the flames grow weaker from the change of position. I throw in a new log and stoke the fire, bringing it back to life.

All I can do is wait. So I read.

A knock on the door wakes me. The book is on my chest, open to wherever I was when I dozed off. The fire is nearly spent, and the lamps have dimmed to the nighttime levels.

"Anya?" I call.

She's still not here.

The knock sounds again.

I wanted to talk to her before seeing Caiden, but it looks like that's not going to happen. I open the door and actually feel tension release when I see Brevan. I hadn't realized how worried I was about him.

"You weren't at dinner," I say.

"Caiden sent me to town for some things," he says.

"That's strange. Isn't it? Or do you normally run his errands?"

"It was unusual. And it was a distraction."

"What do you mean?"

He glances down the hall, then gently pushes me into the room. Once the door is closed, his expression changes. I think he's afraid. I've never seen him afraid.

"I can get you out. But we have to go now. I have a few favors I can call in. You can be on a ship out of Pendralia by sunrise. You can't go home, though. But there's a place I know you'll be safe, if you trust me."

"Slow down. What happened, Brevan?"

He grips my elbows. "They took Anya. I didn't know they were going to. I'm so sorry. I'm the one who brought her here. I know what she means to you."

I sway, but Brevan wraps his arms around me to steady me. It takes me a few breaths before the words actually sink in. "They took her? Is she alive?"

"Yes."

"Where is she?"

"I'm not sure. They left the castle with her," he says.

"Why?" This is my fault. I should have sent her away the second I saw her. It wasn't safe for her here.

"They're concerned you won't go along with their plans."

"What are their plans?"

He swallows. "I can still get you out of here."

"You know I can't leave Anya."

"I know. But I had to try." He brushes his fingers over my cheek. "It's selfish and wrong. I want another man's betrothed. But you're not mine."

"I'm not his. My heart already belongs to someone else."

He crushes his lips to mine, and I kiss him back desperately. It's a goodbye, but I can't think about that now. I want to memorize the way his body feels against mine. The way his tongue teases, the way he tastes, the way he kisses me like he would burn the whole world for me.

I wipe my tears away as soon as we pull apart. I don't

want to make this any harder for him than it already is. "What are they going to make me do?"

"I'm to bring you to Caiden. For a binding ceremony."

I gasp. "I'll be bound to him? Not the emperor?"

He nods.

"Does that mean he'll control what I do? Or be able to punish me like the emperor does you?"

"It depends on how strong the binding is and how strong the relic is. The emperor can't override my free will, but as you've seen, he punishes me if I use power he doesn't want me to. I think he could do more, but I've been loyal. Until now."

"Don't do that to yourself." I step back so we're no longer touching. "I'm not what you think I am. You should forget about me. I'm not worth it."

"Yes, you are," he says.

I'm so tempted to tell him everything. It would be easier on him if he could hate me. But then I'd lose Anya. And it's possible he'd be punished as well. I never should have kissed him. "I wish things were different."

"I know."

My heart aches. I can't linger on what could have been anymore. "If I do this, do you really think they'll bring back Anya?"

"Caiden is a lot of things, but he keeps his bargains. Get him to promise not to harm her in any way. Get him to agree to let her stay by your side. Anything you can think of to ensure her safety. He'll keep his word."

I nod. "He's waiting for me, isn't he?"

"Yes."

"We can't have them thinking something is wrong." I make myself stand tall.

"Sabina," Brevan says.

Every time he says my name, *her* name, it makes my heart soar. I can't imagine how it would feel for him to use my real name. But that's something I'll never know.

"We should go," I say.

He nods, then opens the door.

We walk through the halls silently. It's the middle of the night, and a few legionnaires stand at their posts, but nobody else is around. The halls are dark, lit by sparse flickering lanterns. It feels haunted.

"The empress's temple?" We're nearly there, and the door is open. Light pours out from the room. I look at Brevan, my forehead creased in confusion.

"That's where he wanted to do the ceremony. It'll just be the two of you."

I open my mouth to say something, but Caiden steps out of the temple, a wide smile on his face. He's dressed in black from head to toe. A black tunic and trousers that look oddly out of place on him. They're comfortable clothes instead of his formal style.

He extends his arms in what is probably supposed to be a welcoming gesture. "My little raven, I have something very special for you tonight."

Brevan stops, but I continue, careful not to look back at him. I step into the temple, and Caiden closes the door.

Thirty-Eight

"Where is Anya?" I ask.

"She's at our winter estate, along with your other ladies. I have them preparing your room so it will be comfortable for you when you arrive."

"All of them?" I thought the others were safe but he's not just threatening Anya, he's going to hurt the others as well.

He nods. "You are to be my wife before you arrive there. You must have a room that is worthy of your elevated status."

"We're getting married?" I look around as if expecting a priest to materialize. "I thought we had to wait."

"We'll wed after you recover from your gifting ceremony. The gods want us together as soon as possible," he says.

Brevan's goodbye makes more sense now. It wasn't about the power Caiden might wield over me after this ceremony. It was the fact that I would be his wife.

"As your wife, I will keep all my ladies, correct?"

"Of course," he assures me.

"And they will be under my charge. So only I can make requests of them. They can't be dismissed or harmed without my consent."

"As it should be," he says. "With your new role, you'll have new privileges. Including full command over your ladies and your staff."

"You and your legionnaires will protect them, always. Even if anything ever happens to me. They will be cared for?"

His brow furrows. "Where is this coming from?"

His tone is genuine, and I mask my relief. He doesn't know about Brevan. This is about control and power. Not punishment. "I was nearly killed just last night. If something were to happen to me, I don't want my ladies destitute. I want to know they'd be cared for. Treated with kindness and respect."

He closes the distance between us, his expression softening. "That must have been terrifying for you."

"It was."

He pulls me into his embrace, and I tense instantly, then force myself to relax. I slide my arms around his waist, returning the hug while my stomach churns and I fight against rising nausea. I will never get used to this man touching me. Once I find Anya, I am going to have to kill him. I'm not even sure I'll wait until after the emperor is dead.

When he releases me, he gazes on me with what I can only guess is affection. Though, that look doesn't seem natural on him. There's a strange quality to it. Maybe it's because it's the same look you'd give a child. Or a pet. Which is probably how he sees me.

"Now, we should get this done so you can rest for a few hours before you go to the temple." He gestures to the floor where two large cushions have been set in front of the altar. The benches that were there previously are gone.

I sit, and instead of fear, there's rage bubbling in my chest. I refuse to allow this to control me. Brevan still has free will. If this just curbs any magic I might get, so be it. I don't need magic. Of course, there's the possibility that I'll die in the temple and then this whole thing is worthless.

That thought sends a spike of panic through me, and I reach out and touch his arm. "What if I die in the temple tomorrow?"

"You won't. I know we're destined to fulfill the prophecy."

"If I do, you'll take care of my ladies?" I clarify.

"Stop worrying about them. They're alright."

"I'll feel better if I know you'll protect them," I say, hoping to appeal to his ego. "They need good, kind husbands who won't harm them, or they need to be cared for by"—I fake being choked up—"whoever you marry if I..." I turn away as if the thought is too much.

"It's not going to happen." He smooths my hair. "But if it calms you, I will promise to ensure their happiness and safety."

I look back up at him through tears. It's the first time I've ever faked them. I feel manipulative and evil. But I know what he's capable of, and after the situation with the earl, I can't take any chances. "Thank you." I squeeze his hand and he smiles.

"Now, sit comfortably, and rest your arms on your knees, palms up," he instructs.

I follow his orders while cursing him in my mind. He will not break me. He doesn't own me. I am not his. And I will still destroy him.

I will not perish in the temple. I will save my friend, and then I will make sure he gets everything he deserves.

Caiden is chanting something, but I can't make out the words. Instead, I'm repeating my own words in my head, over and over. I send them to any gods who will listen. To any gods who are willing to help us have choices. To rise beyond our lot in life, to give everyone a chance. To make things better.

But I also ask for revenge.

I swear to you, if you give me the strength to live through this, I will not give up. I will not run away. I will end their reign. I will bring Pendralia to its knees.

It's time for this empire to fall.

I feel Caiden take my hand, but I'm not present in this moment with him. I'm elsewhere in my own mind. I'm pure rage. Seething and hot and red and powerful.

When the bite of a blade slicing my flesh stings, I lean into the pain, channeling it into my anger. I wince as something sharp digs into the wound, refusing to cry out.

"Almost done," Caiden says.

I open my eyes, and Caiden is holding my forearm. Blood drips from the slice he cut into my skin. I can see the outline of a small object there, but I don't feel any pain.

Caiden sets my arm down, then cuts his own arm, then slides in a tiny piece of gold under his skin. He grunts and grits his teeth. Sweat beads on his forehead. Once it's in, he blows out a breath. "We have two pieces of the same relic connecting us now. We'll be forever bound in our magic and soon we'll be bound in marriage." He presses his palm against his wound, then leans forward. There's an eager glint in his eyes. "As soon as you gain your power and we fulfill the prophecy, nobody will be able to stop us."

I glare at him defiantly. I have no intention of fulfilling any prophecy with him and I certainly don't plan to wed him. He doesn't seem to care that I'm not playing along.

"Last step." He stands and removes one of the burning candles from the altar and sets it on the floor between us. He picks up an iron bar from nearby and begins to warm it in the flame.

"This is when you choose the god you'll call on in the temple," he says. "It should be Rey, the king of the gods. He's the one who will fulfill the prophecy." The flames lick the iron bar. "When you're ready, close your eyes."

I close my eyes, but I don't invoke Rey. I have no use for kings. Instead, I call to all of them. Any god who will hear me. As the hot iron presses into my skin, I grit my teeth through the pain and I call to Mara. She's the one goddess we all encounter. She's an equalizer. A healer and destroyer. The problem and the solution.

I let out a cry of pain as the heat singes my arm, then it's over. I open my eyes and look at the throbbing burn that sealed the cut. It's angry and red but at least I'm no longer bleeding.

Caiden grunts through his own burn, but I turn my attention away from him and stare at the mural. And I swear I see a raven fly through the paint, then vanish.

Two priestesses in white robes arrive to dress me for the temple. I'm not allowed to see anyone else until after the ceremony. They bathe me, then dress me in a white robe that looks like theirs.

"Is this how men dress for their ceremony?" I run my hands over the thin fabric. I'm going to freeze outside.

They shake their heads.

"Of course not." I let out an annoyed sigh.

They offer sympathetic expressions. One of them holds up my hairbrush.

"You want to do it for me?" I ask.

She inclines her head, then gestures to the stool in front of the vanity. "Alright. Thank you."

Her touch is soothing as she gently works out all the tangles. When she's finished, the other woman takes her place and begins to braid my hair. I wonder if they don't speak by choice or if it's required of their order. Or perhaps it's more sinister and they can't.

I'm not sure I want to know.

When they're finished, they bow to me, and I return the gesture, which seems to surprise them. "Thank you for caring for me," I say.

They smile, but I don't miss the sadness behind it.

"Are you worried for me?" I ask.

They both nod once.

"I am, too," I confess.

The older of the two points to her heart, then presses her hand flat against her chest. Then she does the same to me. I don't recognize the gesture, but I smile and nod, and she returns my expression with a smile of her own.

They walk me through the halls to the large front doors. All the legionnaires we pass are careful not to stare at me. There is nobody else around. I suspect they were kept away from my path to keep me isolated.

I'm led to a carriage, and the priestesses join me, maintaining their silence. Once we begin, they close the shades. The younger one passes me two coins.

They feel heavy in my palms. I stare at the silver coins a long while before I slip them into the pocket of my robes. Then I look back at her. "I won't be needing them but thank you."

She smirks at that. It's a mischievous look that gives me some hope. I think she believes me. Maybe they give everyone who enters the temple for this ceremony a pair of coins in case they need to pay the ferryman.

I will not be dying today.

The carriage slows to a stop after a long, bumpy ride. I peer through the curtains. We're at the top of what we call the Gods' Mountain, though it's really just a rocky hill overlooking the city.

In the distance, about a mile's walk from where we stopped, are the towering white marble pillars of the temple. There are many temples throughout Pendralia, but each of them is designated to a specific god. This temple is different. It's meant to honor all the gods. As far as I know, the only thing it's used for is the gifting ceremony.

The priestesses make the gesture for the gods, then bow their heads. This is where we part ways. I return the gesture. "Thank you."

I have to be the one to open the door. Caiden told me the rules last night. I open the door; I walk the rest of the distance alone. I enter the temple. It must be done of my own free will.

I glare at the angry red welt on my arm. There was nothing free about that, and even this is under duress considering they're holding my best friend hostage.

But as I step out of the carriage and begin my trek to the temple, I realize that during the binding ceremony last night, I didn't ask to get out of this. I asked to survive so I could change things. So I could make them pay. So I could prevent anyone else from the suffering that they've put me and mine through.

There's a lightness in my steps as I charge toward the temple. I'm not afraid. And I will face the gods with my chin held high.

THIRTY-NINE

THE PATH IS BARELY visible under the fresh snow, but thankfully, it's lined with leafless trees. They look almost magical with the thick layer of snow clinging to their bare branches.

My white robes drag, getting heavier with each step. I shiver under the thin fabric. The path is slick, and twice I catch myself before I fall. I slow my ascent, taking careful steps.

They didn't say I had to get there quickly. I know they'll wait to send the next candidate until after I'm finished, but they're just going to have to wait. I'm not leaving here until the gods give me some answers.

I'm sweating by the time I reach the temple steps, and I lower my hood as I stare up at the impressive structure. Snowflakes catch on my eyelashes and coat my cheeks. I welcome their cool kiss on my warm face.

A wide stairway greets me, white marble steps interrupted by four tall white marble columns. The columns surround the structure. Four in the front and back, eight on each side. There isn't even a roof. Instead, they surround another building. Like a cage of marble.

The interior building is a plain, enclosed stone rectangle with no windows. The stone is far less impressive than the marble, but from a distance, like in the city, you don't see that smaller structure. I always thought the whole thing was made of marble.

After catching my breath, I climb the steps. The entry is an arched opening with no door. The stone building is lackluster. Especially compared to the opulence of the exterior facade. I expected decoration. Sculptures or paintings or gilded objects.

Aside from the entry, the only other light comes from a large circular vat of oil that burns brightly in the center of the room. I don't know who keeps the oil topped up. Maybe it's some form of magic.

I leave a trail of water and mud behind me as I walk toward the center of the room. The wet robes are heavy as they drag across the floor. I peel them from me and drop them to the ground. I'm in my undergarments, but there's nobody here to see me and I'm already warmer without them.

Moving in a slow circle, I search for any hints of what to expect or how to do this, but there's nothing. Just me and the burning oil.

"Now what?" My words echo back to me, and I feel stupid for talking to myself.

What if the whole thing is a scam? Growing up, I always heard the emperor was the one who grants people magic or takes it from them. What if coming here is just a test and the emperor grants the power afterward? What if all those relics he has under his skin are the only way he gains magic? Was that what the binding ceremony was really about? What if everyone who comes here already has magic from the relic the king gives them? Maybe nobody talks about it because they don't want to admit that nothing happened.

I trace my fingers lightly over the burn on my arm. If it's the relics, does that mean Caiden has that power, too? Or is this useless unless the emperor intervenes?

My heart races. If it's the relics, the rebellion needs to find as many as possible. What if all that was missing was the part where the relic was inserted under the skin? Was it really that simple? I need to tell Lee. Then again, do I want Lee to have magic?

I cover my face with my hands and let out a frustrated groan. I am just as bad as the royals if I am starting to question who deserves magic and who doesn't.

There's a thundering sound, and I drop my hands from my face just as a door begins to slide over the opening.

There was no door before.

I run toward the entry, but before I reach it, the door seals shut. "Now what?" I look around as if expecting something to happen. Then I wait.

And wait.

"This is it, huh? The whole big mystery is just smoke and mirrors? Does this temple even mean anything? Can the gods even hear me? Hear us? Hear anyone?" I shout at nothing as I walk toward the flames.

"Quiet now, are we?" I continue past the flames, toward the other side of the room. "Is this some kind of joke? Are you getting a good laugh out of this?"

I'm pacing the temple like the caged tiger I saw once at a

summer festival. The creature walked from one side of the cage to the other, flicking its tail like it was anxious. Like it was biding its time, waiting to release all its anger at being locked up. I imagined the lock coming loose and the beast bursting from the cage. It would run faster than anyone could ever imagine, and in a streak of orange and black, it would fly to the woods, where it could roam and hunt and live.

I feel like that tiger.

I push against the door. I feel around for a button or keyhole. I throw myself against the door again. And again.

I scream into the void. It's pure rage, and my throat burns as I let it out. My hands are balled into fists, my body contracted and tense. I scream with every single part of myself. I release the frustration and anger and fear and hate. I continue because once I start, I can't stop.

I scream for my dead parents and brothers.

I scream for the injustice I've faced and for the injustice that continues without anything to check it.

I scream for hope and loss. For joy and fear. For everyone who died when they could have been saved by a crust of bread or some warm blankets.

I scream for myself.

And then I collapse to my knees, sweaty, panting, exhausted. I lean my forehead against the cool stone floor. I want to cry, but there aren't any tears left. My throat is raw from screaming, but I feel a little better. A little lighter.

Nothing changed. The screaming didn't fix anything. But I still want to.

I sit up, still on my knees. My ass rests on my feet, and I

place my palms on my thighs. I feel clearer, calmer than I have in years.

"Do you hear that?" My voice is a whisper, but it carries in the cavernous space. "I want to fix things. I want things to be better. I can't change what happened to my family. Or to me. But if you give a damn about what happens to us humans, tell me what to do. Tell me how I can make it better."

The fire goes out with a sizzle.

I stand but don't move from my place. The air in the room has shifted. It is thicker. Charged. Anxious.

The flames return, roaring to life with even more intensity. But now they're purple. My brow furrows as I study them. Shades of indigo and blue and even lilac appear as the fire shift and flickers. Every shade of purple imaginable.

"It's beautiful," I whisper.

"I've never responded to anyone who called me to this temple," a clear, feminine voice says.

I look up from the flames. and see a woman wearing black trousers and a black coat that hugs her curves. Gorgeous black wings stretch wide behind her. She struts toward me, tucking her wings in as she approaches.

Her black boots leave bloody footprints in her wake, and on each of her hips silver weapons glint in the purple light. An axe on one side, a knife on the other.

I know without a doubt that she's Mara, the goddess of death.

I lower my head, unsure of how I'm supposed to greet her. A curtsy feels wrong, as does getting to my knees, but she's still a goddess. I lower my gaze until her boots are in view, stopped right in front of me.

I lift my head. "I am not sure how I'm supposed to honor you," I admit.

She smirks. "I came to you, which makes you one of mine. And daughters of death do not bow to anyone."

My lips part, and I try to say something, but words fail.

"Now you're quiet? After speaking to me so loudly these last few weeks?"

I had spoken to her a few times, but mostly out of anger. "I didn't mean to offend. And honestly, I wasn't sure you'd even hear me."

"I hear all of you mortals. I usually just ignore it, but you intrigue me. I haven't been interested in anything in the mortal plane for centuries. Last time I got involved..." She shakes her head. "Never mind."

Well, that sounds terrifying.

She reaches toward me. "May I?"

I'm not sure what she's asking, but I nod. She takes my arm, the one Caiden cut open last night. Her touch is like ice.

"This is amusing. They think they can rein in our magic. Always trying to control the gifts we give you to bolster their own power. Tsk-tsk."

I watch as she examines my arm. "I didn't want him to."

"I know."

"I want him dead."

She smiles at that. "I know."

"I want the emperor dead, too."

"Yes." She traces the wound. Her icy fingers are a balm to the angry red flesh. "Do you mind?"

Once again, I agree, though I'm not quite sure what she's asking.

She drags her fingertip over the injury again—only this time I feel a bite of pain and the wound reopens, looking just as it did when it was first cut. I wince.

She holds her hand above the cut, and a small triangle shaped piece of metal floats out of my skin and into her palm. I gasp.

The object is bloody and leaves streaks of crimson against her pale skin. She grabs it with her forefinger and thumb and examines it. Her nose wrinkles. "It isn't even a proper relic. This has no magic." She tosses it into the flames, and for a moment, they turn bright blue before shifting back to purple.

With a flick of her wrist, the wound returns to the way it was. "We can't have him knowing you took it out. It will benefit you to give him the illusion of control."

"I have to go back and play pretend again?"

"Yes, for a little while. It's not yet time for him to die."

My brow furrows, and I feel like she punched me in the gut.

"May I?" she asks again, her hand almost touching my cheek.

I nod.

She strokes my face like a mother might a child. "You must be patient. This is bigger than you. Bigger than this empire. And you will help me. In return, I will give you all the vengeance you wish."

"What is your price?" I ask.

She lowers her hand, and her smile is that of a proud parent. "That you would ask that question is one of the many reasons I chose to answer your call."

"I won't see any more innocent lives lost," I say.

"Death comes for all mortals."

"But it doesn't have to be that way." I think of my family, all gone too soon.

"It must. And it will be. With you or without you. You can leave here a mere mortal and return with a whisper of magic like those ridiculous shadows their Night Legion has. Or you can leave here with true power."

Mara steps back, the leather of her clothing takes on a purple sheen from the flames. While her demeanor has been almost tender, her entire presence radiates a kind of strength that serves as a warning. "Death is not a choice, Taylan. But this is. What do you choose?"

FORTY

Snow swirls in the icy wind, and I wrap my arms around my body to warm myself. I'm standing outside the temple in my underclothes. I remember going inside, but I don't know what happened or how I got out here.

The temple's arched doorway is sealed. Am I done? Was that it? What happened?

I turn in a slow circle, my mind foggy. Why can't I remember? Brow furrowed, I try to mentally retrace my steps. I walked to the temple. I went through the door. Then my memory goes dark. Everything after is missing.

There's a burst of purple flames in my mind, but that doesn't make sense. Fire isn't purple.

Staring at the temple, I will my memory to return. When it doesn't come, I trudge toward the temple and climb the steps. A gust of wind rushes by, nearly knocking me down.

I fight against it, trying to reach the door. The wind intensifies, and I hold my hands up in surrender. "Alright. I get it."

As soon as I take my first step back down, the wind ceases.

They do not want me back inside that temple.

I inspect my arm and legs. I lift my undershirt. There are no lines on me. Unless the god's gift mark is on my back, I don't have one.

That can't be good.

Did they reject me but allow me to live?

I begin to tremble, and my teeth chatter. I don't feel cold, but my body is reacting. As if reminding me that I'm outside in a snowstorm in my underwear.

Still fighting the fog of confusion, I begin the trek back down the hill to where the carriage is supposed to be waiting for me.

I'm about halfway when I glance back at the temple and notice a trail of red footprints behind me. I gasp, then look down and take a step.

My boots leave crimson stains in the snow.

Like blood.

Heart pounding, I make myself walk forward. When I turn around, the red is gone. Nothing but fresh, seemingly pristine, undisturbed snow behind me. There's not even a single footprint showing where I've been.

I move faster now. Seeing things that aren't there is never a good sign.

My skin is blue by the time I spot the carriage. It's a different one than when I arrived, but I can feel the cold biting into me now and I just want out of the wind and snow.

My hair hangs in wet strands, and my fingers are stiff.

At least my feet are dry and warm. The boots held up well to the weather.

The carriage door swings open, and I let out a joyful cry when Brevan steps out.

He hurries toward me with a thick blanket. "Thank the gods you're alive."

"W-what are you d-doing h-here?" I ask while my teeth chatter.

"Caiden sent me. Told me he couldn't bear to find your corpse if they rejected you."

Another carriage rolls up behind us, and Brevan glances at it. "We have to go. The next candidate is ready."

"H-how l-l-long?" I manage.

"You were gone about two hours. The emperor—he somehow knows when each candidate will be finished. But he never knows the outcome." Brevan helps me into the carriage, then closes the door behind us. He pounds on the roof twice, and the carriage lurches forward.

As soon as we're at a steady pace, Brevan moves next to me, then pulls me against him. His warmth seeps through the blanket, and I lean into it, closing my eyes until my teeth stop chattering.

My fingers hurt, but I move them slowly, and eventually, the feeling in my limbs returns. I don't think I have frostbite. Which is very lucky considering that I have no clothes on.

"I don't remember what happened," I say.

"Nobody does." He touches my cheek. "Your face is freezing."

"Why didn't anyone warn me?" I pull the blanket up so it's covering my nose.

"I'm sorry. I should have told you. It just happened so fast."

"If I died, where would my body be? Left in the temple?"

"No. It's only happened once, but the dead man was dropped right at the carriage. It's why Caiden didn't want to come. He said it would break his heart." He clenches his jaw and a vein in his temple bulges.

"But you came." I lower the blanket from my face.

"I knew you'd live."

"How?" I ask.

"Because I couldn't even let myself imagine any other possibility."

My stupid heart flutters, and warmth spreads from low in my belly. How could the gods be so cruel as to put this man in my life and then prevent me from having him?

"I received word today that Anya and all your other ladies arrived safely at the winter estate," he says.

I sigh in relief. "Good. I can't wait to see them."

"Caiden has already arranged for you to join them after your wedding." He turns away from me and looks out the window but doesn't release me from his embrace.

I'm silent the rest of the journey. There's so much I want to say, and yet, none of it matters. If I don't wed Caiden, Anya and all the ladies who had the misfortune of being assigned to me will die. I can't let that happen.

Just as we pass through the gates, I have an over-whelming urge to vomit. My eyes go wide, and I look to Brevan.

He must know what I'm feeling because he pounds on the roof twice. The carriage stops, and he opens the door. I only manage to get my head out of the carriage before I expel the contents of my stomach.

Brevan holds my hair, then rubs my back soothingly while I continue to retch until everything is gone.

Sweating and exhausted, I climb back into the seat and lean my head against the wall as we began moving.

"You'll be sick for a few days," he says.

I glare at him. "Another thing nobody warned me about?"

"Sorry." He winces.

I throw the blanket off myself, suddenly so hot I fear I might pass out. I'm panting and sweating. "What is happening to me?"

"Nobody really knows but most of us react like this after the temple. Some don't vomit, but everyone feels ill. And tired. You're probably going to struggle to keep your eyes open soon." He tucks a loose strand of hair behind my ear. "But don't worry. I won't leave you unguarded."

The carriage rolls to a stop, and I shove the door open, vomiting again right in front of the main doors to the castle.

Caiden is waiting for me, his nose wrinkled in disgust.

Brevan throws the blanket over my shoulders. "She's already ill."

"I see that." Caiden takes a few steps closer, and I wipe my mouth with the back of my hand.

"Can you walk to your room, or should Brevan carry you?" he asks.

I open my mouth to reply, then begin to heave again. There's nothing left, but my body is still trying to expel whatever it thinks might be there.

"I'll carry her," Brevan says.

When I lean back away from the door, Brevan climbs out, then helps me into his arms. He holds me like a child. Or a bride.

My vision is blurry, and I'm struggling to keep my eyes open.

"See her to her room, then find me. I want to know everything she said when you found her." Caiden turns away from us and hurries to the door.

Brevan is silent as he carries me down halls and up stairs. I slip in and out of consciousness to the point where I'm wondering if this is even real.

He gets me into my—Anya's room, then leaves me with a woman I don't know. She says soothing things and has a kind voice, but I can't quite understand her.

All I know is she manages to wash the sick from me and get me into a nightgown.

I have a vague memory of Brevan returning to carry me to my bed. Then everything goes dark.

There's a crackling fire that casts shadows in a darkened room. Furs and blankets are piled on top of me, and I'm so warm and comfortable I almost close my eyes again. But my stomach rumbles, and my mouth is so dry. It feels like I swallowed sand.

When I sit up, my head spins, and I close my eyes for a moment until it stills, then open them again.

"You're awake."

I try to speak, but my voice is so hoarse it comes out as a croak.

"Don't talk yet. I'll get you some water."

I smile as I watch Brevan throw the blankets he was sleeping under aside and walk to the table to pour me a cup of water from the pitcher.

He carries it to me. "Small sips. I know you're thirsty, but trust me, if you drink too much it'll all just come back up."

I revel in the sensation of the cool liquid as it coats my tongue and flows down my parched throat. It's the best water I've ever tasted.

He takes the cup away from me after a few sips, and I frown.

"I'll give you more soon."

I push myself up more on the pillows so I'm sitting completely upright. "Does Caiden know you're in here?"

"Caiden left three days ago," he says.

"Three days? How long have I been here?"

"Six." He tries to smile, but the creases in his brow show his concern. "But you woke a couple times, and we made you drink some broth. Do you remember?"

I shake my head.

"It's like that sometimes. Everyone is a little different, but we all need to recover after the temple." He hands me the cup again.

After a few more small sips, I finally feel like my mouth is no longer made of sand. I pass him the cup back. "Have you been here the whole time?"

"No. I was in the hall while Caiden was here." He rubs the back of his neck. "He checked on you a few times each day, but after he left, I started sleeping in here. I'll leave tonight, though."

I touch his arm. "Don't go."

"Princess—"

Someone knocks on the door, and I fall back against the pillows with a sigh.

Brevan opens the door, then closes it so I can't hear the conversation. When he returns, he's wearing his enforcer expression. The one that tells me the softness and human moments are gone.

"What is it?" I almost don't want to know.

"The emperor was injured," he says.

FORTY-ONE

THE WORDS TAKE a moment to sink in, then thoughts race in my mind. Did someone try to kill him again? Was this Lee's plan? Or exceptionally good luck? I wet my lips to give myself time to steady my emotions. "I didn't know he could be injured."

"Someone must have figured out a way." He sounds surprised, then clears his throat. "He and Caiden are on their way here so he can recover."

My mind is at war between hoping he dies before he arrives and hoping he survives so I can be the one to kill him.

"How is Caiden?" I ask.

"They didn't say anything about him, so I think he's safe," Brevan says.

"Oh, good." My tone is flat.

"I'll call for the ladies to help you wash and dress," Brevan says. "Should I send up some food?"

"Yes, thank you."

"Is there anything else you need, Princess?" He waits in the doorway, one foot already in the hall.

Yes. I want to beg him to stay. To tell him everything I feel. But that will just make things harder. Caiden will be here soon, and I will be his wife. Anything I do with Brevan puts his life in danger. "No."

When he leaves, it's like he takes part of me with him. And I know that's a part he'll always have.

I let the ladies help me to the bathing chamber and fill the tub but send them out so I can wash alone. When the walk from the door to the bathtub leaves me breathless, I reluctantly call them back.

I'm so weak I need their help to finish undressing. The lady with the brown ringlets gasps, then turns away quickly. She must have seen my scar.

"Childhood accident," I say, deciding to say something, but keep it vague.

"Bridget," the other woman scolds.

Bridget turns around. "It's not the scar, I'm sorry. I've just never seen a god's gift mark before."

It's my turn to gasp. "Where?"

"On your back," the other woman says.

"You didn't know?" Bridget asks.

"She's been sleeping since she returned from the temple," the other woman scolds.

"What does it look like?" I wish there was a way to twist enough to see it.

"You want us to look?" Bridget asks, her voice timid.

"It's usually kept private," the other woman explains.

"Please, tell me," I say. "How else am I to know?"

"It's—" Bridget starts.

"It's the twin moons," the other woman says.

"It's beautiful," Bridget adds.

"Do you know anything about the marks? What it might mean?" Aside from having no energy, I feel the same as always. If I had magic, wouldn't I know?

"I don't," Bridget says. "Do you, Clara?"

Clara shakes her head. "They keep all of that very secret. Even my own son didn't let me see his mark or tell me anything about his visit to the temple."

"If it helps, I don't remember what happened," I say. "They told me that's normal."

She chuckles. "That actually does make me feel a bit better. Would you like me to wash your hair?" she asks gently.

I nod, and she begins pouring water over my head. I've never had anyone wash my hair before, but it is so relaxing I almost fall asleep again.

When I'm clean, they assist me into a nightgown and robe before guiding me to the small table near the window. There's soup and bread and apple slices, and even a piece of cake.

"You don't have to stay. I'm sure you'd rather be elsewhere." They've been so kind, and I don't want to be a burden.

"The enforcer asked us to keep watch over you," Clara says.

Knowing they were sent by Brevan makes me like them

even more. "Would you like to join me? There's plenty of food."

Clara waves her hand dismissively. "We already had dinner, Your Highness."

"Would you like to sit, at least? Maybe have some dessert?" The slice is more like a quarter of a cake.

"Are you sure?" Bridget asks. Clara elbows her. "We're not hungry."

"Please. I don't want to eat alone."

They exchange a glance, then finally sit at the table with me.

Bridget looks excited when I shove the cake toward her.

"Thank you for your help," I tell them and push a fork and knife toward them. "They only gave me one of each, but I won't tell if you want to use your hands."

They smile, and Bridget takes the fork and starts eating the cake.

I try the soup. The broth is warm and flavorful, and it soothes my still-dry throat. "Tell me about yourselves."

We make small talk, with me letting them do most of the talking. They seem nice, but our conversation is very surface level, which is fine with me.

The food helps me feel stronger and I force myself to eat most of the soup.

"Would you like anything else, Your Highness?" Clara asks.

"No, thank you. I think I'd like to rest again," I say. "And can you send Brevan—I mean, the enforcer in?"

"Of course," Clara says.

"I hope we see you again soon," Bridget says.

"Thank you for your help, ladies," I say.

They're only gone a few minutes before Brevan enters my room and says, "They could have stayed with you all night."

"I have a mark," I announce before I even have time to process what he just said. "Sorry. That just came out. The ladies were very kind, but I prefer privacy."

He nods. "I thought so, but I wish you would have accepted their assistance. You're likely still recovering."

"I'm fine," I assure him. "You know about the mark, don't you?"

"Well, the woman who dressed you saw it. She told me you had one."

"What does it mean?" I ask.

"It's somehow linked to the gift the gods gave you, though it's not always clear how."

"I don't feel any different." I toy with the belt of my dressing gown. "How do I know if I even got a gift?"

"You did."

"But I haven't done anything. I haven't summoned shadows or lit anything on fire." My shoulders slump. What if something is wrong with me?

"It will show up eventually. Sometimes it takes a while. There's things you can do to test it, to learn how to wield it. But after you rest more. It's too soon."

I ignore his advice. I've been resting for too long. "Did she tell you what my mark was?"

"No."

I rise from the bed, then untie the robe and shrug it off my shoulders. It falls to the floor around my ankles. I'm wearing a nightgown with small straps on each shoulder. "I want to know what it looks like. The ladies who helped me were not very specific."

"I should tell you to put that robe back on." The look in his eyes tells me he won't.

I push one of the nightgown's straps down. "Do you want to see it?"

He runs a hand though his hair. "I should say no."

"But?"

"But I don't want to."

I lower the other strap so only my hand is holding the nightgown over my breasts. Then I turn my back to him and let the fabric drop to my waist.

He's quiet a long moment, and I start to get nervous. "Is something wrong?"

"It's stunning," he says. "The twin moons. One is full, the other a crescent. Below them is a raven, with its wings open."

"A raven? Can you trace it for me? Show me where it is?"

I shiver as he drags his fingertip gently across the left side of my back. "This is the full moon." He moves to the other side. "This is the crescent." Then his hand drops lower. "This is the raven. Here is the head, the beak, one wing, the other wing, and the tail."

"Thank you." I slide the nightgown back over my shoulders, then turn to face him. I know the fabric is thin enough that he can see my nipples through it. "Can I see yours?"

He lifts his tunic over his head and holds it in one hand. Swirls of black cover his chest and arms. I move closer and place my finger on one of the swirls at his shoulder, then trace it down to his forearm. It spirals around his forearm, then ends in points at the base of his hand. Another circle crosses over, just above his wrist. It's different than the other markings. There are leaves on it, like a vine. But only on that one part. The rest of the swirls are undulating lines.

"How did I not notice those leaves before?" I ask.

"They're new. Appeared the night of that rebel attack," he says.

My brow furrows. "You can get new markings?"

"Yes. Usually they're small. I've noticed it tends to happen when I learn to do something new with my magic. But sometimes, I'm not sure what causes it."

"They're really beautiful," I tell him. "I'm glad you're sharing them with me."

"There's more." He turns so his back faces me, and I suck in a breath when I see the mark there. It's the moons. Both of them—one crescent, one full. "Is it the same as mine?"

"They're on opposite sides," he says. "But I think they're a mirror image to yours."

"Does everyone have the moons?" I ask.

"No."

I return my gaze to Brevan's back. Under the moons, he also has an animal. "That's a dragon." Between the blood and my attempt to be respectful, I hadn't seen the details of his markings before.

"Yes."

"This is beautiful." I trace the shape of the creature, following its head, along to the body, through the wings. "It's life."

He turns around, his brow furrowed with a silent question.

"Your dragon. Dragons represent life. At least they used to, before they were gone," I say. "And ravens are death. They're opposites. Like our moons. What does that mean?"

He takes my hands in his. "I'm not sure, but right now, I'm glad Caiden has never seen my mark."

"How is that possible?" I ask.

"Marks are supposed to be private. We avoid looking and keep them covered," he says. "If he knew mine was the opposite of yours..."

"I don't want him to see mine," I say. "I don't want him to see anything."

"I know, Sabina."

"Brevan?" I want to tell him. I want to tell him everything. I want to hear my name on his lips. My *real* name. I want him to know how I feel. I want to know everything about him and experience everything with him.

"Yes?" He looks at me expectantly.

Anya.

If I break, Anya is dead. We're both dead.

"When will Caiden and the emperor return?" I ask instead.

"Probably tomorrow." He releases my hands.

"I should get some rest, then." I pick up the robe from where I abandoned it on the floor earlier and pull it over my shoulders.

"I'll be outside. If you need anything, call for me." He tucks a loose strand of hair behind my ear. "Get some rest, Princess."

I walk him to the door, then lean against it as soon as

it's shut. What am I doing? I'm in so deep at this point I can hardly remember who I am anymore. Everything is wrong. I want to forget for a little while. Without the worry of the rebellion or my dead family, or that I was supposed to kill the emperor and then not to kill him. And that somehow, I have a god's gift mark and magic of some kind that I have yet to figure out.

I am so fucking tired of all of it. Of feeling angry and confused and sad and all the things all the time. I need a few minutes where I can stop thinking and just exist. Without all the life-and-death pressure.

The only good thing in this place is standing behind that door, and I can't even touch him.

A knock startles me, and I step back, then open the door. Brevan fills the doorway. "I know I should walk away."

I grab his tunic and pull him into my room.

FORTY-TWO

HE KICKS the door behind him, and our lips are on each other the second it closes. I'm grateful he's not wearing the armor tonight as I claw at his tunic, desperate to get it off him. He breaks our kiss long enough to pull his tunic over his head and discard it, then he pushes my robe off my shoulders.

We're kissing and moving toward where I think the bed is, but as I struggle with his trousers, my ass bumps into the small table where the remains of my meal are still set out.

I'm panting when I break the kiss. In the dim light I can see the possessive look in his eyes. It should terrify, but it only makes me want him more. Heat simmers low in my belly, and all I want is this man between my thighs.

He reaches around me, then knocks all the plates to the ground. They crash and shatter, but I don't see them fall because he lifts me onto the table and our lips collide again. This time with more urgency.

It's dangerous and reckless, but I can't resist him

anymore. "Don't stop," I breathe, suddenly worried he'll hold himself back.

"I couldn't if I tried," he says against my lips.

His rough hands slide up my inner thigh, and my skin hums in response. I need more of him.

My tongue finds his, our kiss like a dance, a battle where we both fight for dominance. Sometimes I let him best me only to regain control. It's like nothing I've ever experienced. Just his kiss sends so much heat through me that wetness grows between my thighs. I reach for his trousers, and he breaks the kiss to help kick them aside.

I use the moment to appreciate how incredible his body is. I've seen him undressed before, but it was while he was injured. This time, he's on full display for me. He's achingly handsome. With rippling muscles and firm planes, the man is like a work of art. I run my fingers down his chest. "How is it that you're real?"

He sets his palm on the side of my face, his thumb caressing my cheek. "I wonder the same thing about you." His hand slides down to my shoulder, then toys with the strap of my nightgown. It falls to one side, dangerously close to uncovering me. I pull it back up, and his brow furrows.

"I have a scar. Princesses shouldn't have a scar." I feel like an idiot the second the words leave my mouth.

He takes my hand and drags my fingertips over the scars on his chest. There are fewer here than on his back, but each one tells a story of pain. I hate that the emperor hurt him this way.

Wordlessly, I pull my hand away from him and slowly let down the straps of my nightgown. The fabric falls below my breasts, but it's still covering my stomach. I hesitate, then pull it back up and over my head, then toss it to the floor.

His large, rough palm immediately touches the jagged scar that covers my abdomen. The scar stretches from my belly button to my side, a slice across my midsection that should have killed me.

When he looks up at me, his expression is dark. Deadly. "Who did this?"

"It was a long time ago," I say, shoving down the memory that's trying to surface. I can't go back to that night.

"Is he dead?"

I hesitate, and Brevan's eyes flash with a rage unlike any I've seen from him. My moment of reluctance gives me away.

"I'm going to kill him."

"He's probably already dead," I say. "And he's far away from here."

"If I ever find out who he is, I will hunt him down."

I slide my hand around the back of his head and pull him toward me. "I don't want to think about any other man than you." Then I reach down and stroke his cock.

His mouth meets mine in a possessive collision that has me inching closer to the edge of the table so I can press myself against him. I grab his ass and pull him toward me, desperate for any friction between my thighs.

He reaches down and spreads my legs wider before hooking his fingers into the waistband of my panties. I lift my hips so he can remove them more easily. Then he drops to his knees and grips my ass as he begins to lick my slit. I lean back, needing to hold on to the edge of the table for leverage as his tongue makes circles and his teeth scrape. Little shivers of hot and cold ripple through me as he works his magic, pushing me closer and closer to release. I moan as he thrusts his tongue inside me. His thumb rubs on my clit, and I arch my back, my hips beginning to buck as pleasure builds.

His tongue returns to my clit, and he slides two fingers inside me. Pumping and licking and just the perfect amount of grazing of his teeth. It's so much sensation. An orgasm rushes over me like a tidal wave, and for a brief moment, I see nothing but blinding light.

When my senses return, he's standing and looking down at me, a self-satisfied grin on his lips. I hop down from the table.

"Where do you think you're going?" he asks as he helps steady me.

"You don't get to have all the fun," I say, then I kneel in front of him.

He tenses when I wrap my fingers around his thick length, and his breath hitches. I flick my tongue over the tip, licking up the moisture. He groans. I can't help but smile because I'm just getting started.

I close my lips around him and swirl my tongue as I move up and down his shaft. I stroke the lower part of him that doesn't fit into my mouth and grip his ass with my other hand. His breathing is shallow, and little grunts of pleasure escape his lips. Each noise he makes sends tingles straight to my center.

He caresses the side of my face and runs his fingers though my hair as I continue to lick and suck and bob.

When I remove my mouth, so I can trail my tongue along his cock, he pulls away. "If I don't have you right now, I swear to the gods I might die."

Before I can respond, he lifts me from the ground, and I squeal as he carries me to the bed. He drops me on the mattress, then climbs on top of me, his legs going between mine.

I reach for him, pulling him down on top of me. When his lips crash into mine, I feel him at my entrance, and I lift my hips, encouraging him. I gasp as he enters me in a single hard thrust, and then there's something like relief as my body adjusts to him. It feels so right, the two of us like this. Our bodies entwined, moving in unison as we chase bliss. My skin tingles and hums as if the very air around us is charged. Each touch is magnified, every kiss electric. I will never have enough of this man.

I hold on to him, digging my fingers into his back as I gasp. My hips rise and fall, and my back arches as everything reaches a crescendo.

"Let go, let it all go," he says.

I fall apart under him, shockwaves of pleasure shooting through me, making me shake and moan. Brevan groans as he finds his own release, and the whole room flashes with a blinding light. It's over so quickly I'm certain I imagined it.

The two of us lie side by side while we catch our breath. Brevan traces his fingers along my arm, then turns to his side. "I don't know how I'm supposed to stay away from you."

"Then don't." I shift so I'm facing him.

"We have to be careful," he says.

"We will be."

He clasps my hand, then lifts it to his lips and kisses it. When he pulls it away, he freezes, eyes wide. "This wasn't here before."

A dark tendril spirals from my wrist to my elbow. Small leaves appear along it, making it look like a vine. I sit up and examine the new markings. "How?"

Brevan sits, then holds out his arm. The curving lines along his forearm are the same as the marks I now bear. I look up at him. "What does it mean?"

"I'm not sure, but this is going to be impossible to hide from Caiden."

"Don't talk about him right now." I straddle him, then press my lips to his. I can feel the curve of the smile before he kisses me back.

If this is the only night I get with this man, I don't intend to sleep.

FORTY-THREE

"Good morning, Princess," Brevan says with a bow when I step outside my room.

He's in his armor. His hair is pulled back neatly, and he's clean-shaven. I knew he couldn't stay the night, but I was disappointed to wake to a cold bed.

"Good morning, Enforcer," I say.

"The prince and the emperor returned early this morning while you were sleeping," he informs me. "You'll be happy to know that they met with the emperor's personal doctor, who says he will make a full recovery."

"That's excellent news." I force a smile.

"I am to escort you to meet with Duchess Drathmore and her friends. They are working on the Darkfall Ball and would like you to join in as it will be your responsibility next Darkfall. Shall we?"

We make a few turns, then go down a flight of stairs. Then we walk down a hall lined with doors. I think it's another part of the castle I haven't been in before. It might take me years to explore the whole place. Which means, I never will, because there is no way I'll be here that long.

Brevan casually turns the handle to a room, then pulls me in after him. He pushes me up against the closed door, and then his mouth is on mine.

I kiss him back as if he's the air I need to survive. It's dangerous and stupid, but I can't stop kissing him. Knowing that every moment with him might be my last makes me abandon reason. I can't walk away from him.

He breaks our kiss to lift the skirt of my dress until it's around my waist. It stays put with him pressed so close to me. I reach for his trousers, which is not an easy feat through all the fabric, but he grabs my wrists and pins my arms to the door. He gives me a wicked grin, then his lips are on my neck, then my cleavage. My breath hitches, and I let out a moan.

He drops a hand to cover my mouth, using the other to maintain his hold on both my wrists. "Shh."

I clamp my mouth shut and swallow back the sounds that threaten to break free as he continues to kiss me everywhere there's bare skin. He releases my wrists, and his free hand travels below my waist, his fingers expertly teasing and rubbing my clit through the thin fabric of my undergarments. It's taking all my willpower to keep quiet, and when he slips a finger inside me, I clamp my hand over my mouth to keep from crying out.

He deftly removes my undergarments and tosses them aside, and then my leg is around his waist. I throw my arms over his shoulders and kiss him while he thrusts into me. I'm so wet he slides right in. It's hurried and intense, and

I'm already fighting against an orgasm. He continues to thrust while kneading my breasts over my dress. Our kiss is desperate but claiming. Like we both know this could be the last time.

Tenison builds, winding tight in my belly, threatening to explode. I pull away from the kiss and bite down on my lower lip to keep from crying out as the pressure breaks, sending shockwaves of pleasure through me. Brevan thrusts a few more times, and little ripples of ecstasy make me tremble over and over until he gasps and stills as he releases. He withdraws quickly, then uses a handkerchief to clean us up before helping me back into my undergarments.

As we walk down the hall, I'm still flushed and over-heated. Brevan's cheeks are pink, and I think he looks a little more at ease than usual. All that dissolves the second we turn into the sitting room where Lady Drathmore and a group of older women are gathered around piles of fabric and bouquets of every size and color.

With his usual stiffness, Brevan bows to the women. "Lady Drathmore, ladies, Princess Sabina is here to assist as requested."

"Thank you, Enforcer," Lady Drathmore says.

He inclines his head again, then leaves the room. I know he'll be standing in the hall, waiting as usual. I don't want to think about what it will be like when the emperor sends him away. Or worse, when Brevan discovers who I really am. I hope I can leave before he finds out. I don't want to see the look of betrayal on his face.

"Princess, thank you for joining us," Lady Drathmore says. "As you know, the organizing of the Darkfall Ball is the empress's duty, but since we no longer have an empress,"—

she takes a breath and her smile falters for a moment before she fixes it back on her face—"it will be your job. This year, the emperor asked me to take on the honor. Next Darkfall will be yours."

"I appreciate any guidance you can give me." I smile, knowing that none of us will be here by the next Darkfall.

"Good. Now, come and meet everyone. My grandson has kept you so isolated that you have yet to meet most of the important people in the empire." She guides me to the group.

There are eight other women, all nobles, and all important. Lady Drathmore introduces each of them and explains what their husbands do and why they are significant. I try to remember their names and how they're connected to the crown, but the information leaves my mind as soon as they start pressuring me to choose flowers and fabric.

A chef wheels in a cart of hors d'oeuvres for us to sample, and the women gossip while we taste each one. A cart full of cakes and desserts follows. I'm starting to find my way into conversations when Lady Drathmore suddenly rises from her seat. We all turn toward the entry, and I stand when I see Caiden walk in.

"You're back," I say, with as much false joy as I can muster.

He doesn't look amused.

"Care to join us in tasting some cakes, Caiden?" Lady Drathmore asks.

"No, thank you, Grandmother. I'm afraid Sabina and I have urgent business with my father." He turns to me. "Right now."

His expression is deadly, and I can feel the blood

draining from my face. I try to fight against the fear and plant a concerned expression on my face. "This sounds serious. Is something wrong?" I hurry to join him.

"Not here, Sabina," he says. "I'll explain when we get there."

Brevan isn't waiting outside the room.

FORTY-FOUR

As Caiden and I near the hall that leads to the emperor's private chambers, Brevan approaches from the other side. We all turn into the same hallway.

I glance at Brevan but look away quickly. Even just seeing him sends my heart fluttering.

We all stop in front of the skull, and Brevan pushes the secret panel that opens the door. Caiden gestures for Brevan to go. The enforcer steps through the threshold.

"Go on," the prince says.

I follow Brevan and Caiden enters behind me. The emperor stands in the corner, deep in conversation with someone I can't see. There's a thud as the door seals us in and the emperor turns, revealing his guest.

I freeze and I think I forget how to breathe.

A familiar face smiles at me, though I've never seen him look the way he does now. His light brown hair is trimmed and his face clean-shaven, his clothes a fine material in the emperor's preferred colors.

Lee.

"Taylan, it's good to see you again." Lee smiles at me like someone who just learned the most delicious secret.

My blood runs cold, and fear crawls down my spine like a spider. Lee can't be here. He can't be talking to the emperor like they're old friends.

"Who is Taylan?" Brevan asks. "And who are you?"

"You remember Ludis, right, Caiden?" the emperor says. "You two played together when you were young. Before the war."

"Ludis?" Caiden takes a step forward. "I thought you were dead." He looks at his father. "You told me he was dead."

"I was, didn't you hear?" Lee says. "Cast out, my birthright revoked, my name dragged through the mud. All because of one mistake."

"Why are you here, Ludis?" Caiden asks.

How is this happening? I look around at the gathered men and the only other person who seems as confused as I is Brevan. Was this Lee's plan the whole time?

"He came to make a deal on behalf of Iskvaland," the emperor says.

"He can't make a deal," Caiden says. "His father told us he was dead. Besides, they sent Sabina for that."

Lee, or Ludis, laughs.

Brevan's fingers curl around the hilt of his sword. I slip a hand into one of the secret pockets sewn into my dress. I can feel the dagger in there. I'm certain its twin is in my other pocket. It turned out, all my dresses had two side pockets, carefully hidden in the folds. I still wonder why, but right now I'm too grateful to be curious. I remove my hand, hoping I was discreet.

"That's the thing, kings have a way of forgiving you if you're their last surviving heir. So my father isn't going to have much of a choice." Ludis smiles like a lunatic. I've never seen him this unhinged. I saw a darker side of him, a side that scared me, after my mother died. When he took over the rebellion, he became someone else. We'd already broken up before my brothers died, but their death was the final straw.

Brevan moves in front of me protectively. "You're not touching her."

"Oh, I don't want her. Taylan's a decoy. It's actually quite remarkable how much she looks like my sister."

I feel sick. The whole time we were together, he knew. He knew I looked like his sister. I swallow down the rising bile. He's fucking insane.

Brevan looks back at me, confusion and hurt in his expression. "Is that true?"

"Of course it's not true," Caiden says. "She entered the temple; she got a god's gift—a peasant can't do that."

"I don't know how she survived that," Ludis says. "I thought the temple would take her. It would have made this part easier."

Caiden joins Brevan in front of me. "Where's your sister, then?"

"I killed her." There's no remorse in his voice. "Do you have any idea how hard it was, how expensive it was, to whisper the right things in the right ears to get my stubborn father to think it was his idea to send my sister to Pendralia? It took years to make that happen."

"You killed her?" I push past the men and face Ludis. "You killed your own sister? That was always your plan?

What did you even need me for? Why did you send me here?"

He grabs my chin, and Brevan pushes Ludis, then draws his sword and points it at him. "Don't touch her."

Ludis holds his hands up in front of him in mock surrender. "Alright. I get it, she's a good lay."

Brevan's nostrils flare, and I grab his arm. "He's not worth it."

"You're actually fucking her," Ludis says with a laugh. Then he smirks at Caiden. "Wasn't she supposed to marry you? But she's fucking a guard? I suppose you can't teach a peasant taste. I mean, she was with me, but she's slumming it now."

Caiden lunges at him.

"Enough!" the emperor shouts, and a boom like thunder vibrates around the room. There's a strange smell in the air, and the hair on my arms stands on end.

"Nobody is killing anybody, do you hear me?" The emperor stands, then walks to the center of the group. He looks at his son. "Ludis will deliver Iskvaland's army to us." He turns to Brevan. "You will remember where your loyalties lie and get your head back on straight. Seduced by a spy? You're losing your edge, Brevan. If you weren't so useful you'd be thrown in the pit."

Then, the emperor looks at me. "And you. You came here in silk, but you'll leave here in irons. Take her to the dungeon and chain her up."

Neither Brevan nor Caiden moves toward me. I glare at the emperor, daring him to drag me to the dungeon himself.

"I said, take her to the dungeon, now!" the emperor

shouts. Thunder booms again, and I can feel the charge of electricity in the air.

"No," Caiden says. He lifts his chin toward Ludis. "He is just as much a spy as she is."

"She's a peasant," the emperor says. "A whore sent in to seduce you both."

Brevan's knuckles are white around the hilt of his sword, but he remains where he is.

"Fine. I'll take care of her myself." The emperor pulls a dagger from his belt and lunges toward me. I reach for my own weapon but can't find my pocket fast enough in the folds of fabric. Just as I finally free my blade, Caiden shoves me to the ground and Brevan blocks the emperor's strike. The metal of the blades sings when they meet. My knife slides across the floor out of reach.

The emperor's blade falls to the ground. Little sparks dance on his fingertips as he stalks toward Brevan. "How dare you defy me. After everything I've done for you. It's a woman who breaks you. You're no good to me if you're not loyal. You'll join her in the dragon's pit, you ungrateful wretch."

Ludis picks up my blade and examines it. He looks down at me. "This is quality work. relics in the hilt." He readjusts so he's holding it the way Brevan taught me. I recoil, prepared for him to strike, but he smiles instead. "Huh. You figured it out."

I have no idea what his true intentions are anymore, but in that moment, I realize two things: he has no intention to harm me, and he still wants the emperor dead. I lock my eyes on his, "Kill him."

"I knew you were still in there somewhere." Ludis spins

to face the emperor, then shoves my knife into the emperor's throat.

I scramble away, and Brevan leaps back just as the emperor falls to his knees. The emperor claws at the knife, eyes bulging with terror.

Caiden draws a blade and aims it at Ludis's throat. The tip brushes against his skin. Brevan draws his sword and stands on the other side of the Iskvalandian prince. "Give me a reason to end you."

The emperor makes gurgling sounds, blood dripping from his mouth and the wound in his neck. He's struggling, his movements stiff and awkward. His eyes search the room wildly, like he's looking for something or waiting for someone to help him.

I stand and move a little closer to where the others are watching the emperor. "He's dying."

The emperor falls to his knees. His skin is gray, his eyes wild and bulging. I don't think he's going to survive, even if we remove that knife.

"What did you do?" Caiden asks. "Why isn't he healing?"

Ludis laughs, then looks at Caiden. "You wanted this. Don't even pretend like you didn't."

Caiden lowers his weapon. Brevan follows his lead.

Ludis rubs his throat, then turns his attention to me. "You don't happen to have another one of those knives, do you, Tay?"

As insane as he is, I believe that he wants the emperor dead just as much as I do. Numbly, I reach into my other pocket and hand the weapon to Ludis.

"Cheers," he says, holding up the knife like he's making

a toast. Then he thrusts my second knife into the emperor's back.

I hold my breath, and then I see it. The light fading from the emperor's eyes. His jaw goes slack, his breath rattles. Ludis kicks him to the ground. The emperor spasms, then stills.

"Long live the emperor," Ludis says.

"Is he dead?" Caiden asks.

"Yes," I say before Ludis can answer. "The knives had relics in them."

Brevan and Caiden both turn to me with looks of surprise.

Ludis smirks. "That's my girl."

"I am not your girl," I snap. "And you are a liar. You set this whole thing up? Even me? How long were you planning this?"

"He's really dead," Caiden says.

"Yes, he's fucking dead," I say. "And apparently, my ex-boyfriend who asked me to spy for him is a godsdamned exiled prince."

"Ex-boyfriend?" Brevan asks.

"Oh, you have got to be kidding me," Caiden hisses. "My father is dead, and you're worried about a woman?"

I step over the dead emperor and stop right in front of Lee or Ludis or whatever the fuck his name is. "You told me he"—I point at Brevan—"killed my brothers."

"Sorry about that," he says. "Needed someone to blame and he does have a reputation."

My face feels hot. "Who killed them, Lee?"

"They're dead. Does it really matter?" he asks.

"Who. Killed. Them?" I demand.

"Fine. Alright, I killed them. Are you happy? I knew you wouldn't do the job unless it was personal."

Rage seethes and twists, and I feel something dark stirring within me. "You took everything from me!" I let the anger come, let it drive me forward. "How could you do that?"

"What the fuck?" Caiden says from behind me.

"He should be dead!" Ludis says.

I turn, and I'm face-to-face with the emperor. His vacant eyes stare at me, and his body is oddly slack.

"Father?" Caiden says.

The emperor stares straight ahead at nothing, unmoving, unspeaking. Fear grips me. He's supposed to be dead. He looks like he's dead.

Brevan swings his sword, and the emperor's head falls to the ground, but his body remains upright. I shove him hard, and he falls on top of his head.

We're all panting and wide-eyed, each of us looking at the other.

Brevan moves closer to me but won't meet my eye.

"Well, this didn't go the way I expected," Ludis sighs. "I just wanted to regain my father's favor. I had an entire plan. It was going to be so glorious." He throws his hands up, then glances over at me. I hold my ground, glaring at him.

"But you didn't make it easy, did you? I had to constantly adjust. And when you survived the temple—" he scoffs, "Well, I had to adjust again. So here I am." He kicks the dead emperor's leg. "Now, look at this mess."

"You still can." Caiden leans down and grabs a fistful of his father's hair. He hoists the head up, then tosses it to Ludis. Blood splatters from the severed neck.

Ludis catches it but wrinkles his nose in disgust. His black clothing hides most of the blood that now dots it.

"Take him this," Caiden says. "Tell him you killed the immortal emperor. Then get me that army."

"I've got a better idea." Ludis drops the head, and it makes a sickening crack.

"What's that?" Caiden asks.

"I'll get you that army, but you have to do something for me," Ludis says.

"Or I could just kill you now and bargain with your father," Caiden says.

"You're willing to give him immortality?" Ludis lifts a brow. "Because unless you provide that, he's not helping you. I read the treaty."

"I'll be married to his daughter," Caiden says.

"I'm not really Sabina," I say.

"Nobody outside this room knows that," Caiden points out.

I grit my teeth knowing that until I have Anya and the other ladies to safety, I can't argue with him.

"Or, you help put me on the throne and we become the young rulers who change the world. We both know what it would mean if we combined our armies." Ludis grins.

"Your father disowned you. Told the whole world you were dead," Caiden counters.

"But I'm not. And with my *sister's* support, and my mother's support, the nobles will fall into line." Ludis takes a step closer to Caiden. "Think about it. Bonded by blood. A huge, glorious royal wedding that makes everyone celebrate putting decades of war behind us."

My stomach twists. That's the last thing I want.

Caiden smirks. "That could work. I have no interest in attacking Iskvaland if we're on the same side."

"Think of what we can accomplish together," he says. "All those mines in the Shatterlands, ripe for the taking."

"This is what we were trying to stop, Lee. How could you?" I step toward him. Brevan captures me and pulls me back. I glare at him, but he's not even looking at me.

I deserve it. I deserve everything that happens to me after my betrayal. I will hate myself for the rest of my life for what I did to him.

Caiden saunters over to me. "I'll give you a choice, my little raven. You can marry me and spend the rest of your life as Sabina of Iskvaland, or you, and all your ladies, can be a feast the dragon will never forget."

"I hate you," I say.

"Don't worry, I think I'll grow on you over time, just as you've grown on me." He traces my lower lip with his index finger, and I have to resist the urge to bite him. "I'm rather disappointed that you spent all that time with Brevan." His eyes travel upward, and I know he's looking at the enforcer. "But I don't think we need to worry about that again. Because if either of you steps a toe out of line, you will lose the thing you hold most dear."

I tense. They have something on Brevan. It wasn't just the relics. His loyalty was purchased the same way mine was. That's why he never left. Why he's following orders even now.

If I don't play along, Anya is dead. All my ladies are dead.

So what do they have on Brevan? *Who* do they have?

"I need a drink, how about you?" Ludis says to Caiden. "I think we have much to discuss."

"Just as soon as I inform everyone that the rebels assassinated our dear emperor," Caiden says. Then he turns to me. "Get yourself cleaned up. I want you by my side when I make the announcement."

Brevan practically carries me out of the emperor's private rooms. He doesn't release me until we're through the dragon's head and the door is closed.

We're silent on the walk to my room. Anya's room. Anya, whose life is on the line because of me. Because of Brevan.

"Did you know?" I ask. "Did you know they'd use her against me when you brought her here?"

"No." He sounds like he's a million miles away.

I probably shouldn't believe him, but I do. "Who do they have? That's how they get you to do everything, isn't it?"

He keeps his eyes straight ahead and his voice low. "There were two of us rescued that day. Me and my sister. She had an exceptionally rare gift at birth. Everyone wanted it, wanted her. So we ran. And then she ended up a prisoner, anyway."

"So did you," I tell him.

"I guess we all are." He stops in front of the door. "I'll wait here."

"I'm sorry. I know it doesn't change anything, and I know you probably don't believe me, but I never lied about the way I felt about you." My throat tightens and I swallow hard as I fight against the threatening tears.

"It's better this way." His jaw is tight, his posture stiff.

A tear slides down my cheek and I wipe it quickly, not wanting him to see me break. For a very short while, I got a taste of what it was like to be happy. I think Brevan did, too. I stole hope away from both of us.

"If you can save her and leave here, you should," I say. "You deserve better."

His hardened expression cracks, and his brow furrows. "No, I don't. There is no balancing my scales, and you know that. You spent enough time pointing out my history when we first met."

"I was wrong. You're not the villain I thought you were." My voice shakes a little, the tears dangerously close to overtaking me.

"Yes, I am, Princess."

"No. You wouldn't do the things they make you do if you had a choice," I tell him.

"As you pointed out, we all make choices. I am the monster they asked me to be. Just as you are what they asked of you."

"It's not a choice when it comes to saving someone you love," I press.

He sighs, and I see just a touch of softness. Or maybe that's in my imagination. "You should go, Princess. The new emperor will be waiting for you."

His words knock the air from my lungs. *The new emperor.* Because that's what Caiden is. I came here to topple an empire. To end the royal line. Instead, I'm joining them. And helping them build the army I wanted to prevent.

I am the monster I came to destroy.

Brevan stands at attention, his expression impassive. As

if he's guarding a stranger. And I suppose, he is. He doesn't know who I am.

I'm not sure I even know myself, anymore.

The room is too quiet. I was alone in my room often, but knowing there'll be no ladies joining me is a different kind of quiet. It hurts more than I thought it would. I wasn't supposed to befriend them, but I will play the role required to keep them alive. At least until I can figure out something better. I hope.

It doesn't feel real. How did I let everything spiral so far out of control?

I strip off all my clothes, leaving a trail of bloodied fabric on my way to the bathing chamber. I wash the emperor's blood from myself as I stare into the mirror. I hardly recognize myself. What have I become? The emperor is dead. Isn't that what I wanted?

But instead of preventing war, I might have brought it sooner.

I sit on the edge of the bathtub, the events of the last hour playing on a loop in my memory.

My mind catches on the emperor standing after he'd been killed. The vacant eyes, the strange sagging of his body. I see it over and over. He stands up, he moves, he loses his head, but his body remains upright until he's knocked over.

A dark sensation slithers through my veins, like something is awakening. It feels like icy fingers trail over my skin. I look down and see new marks spiraling up my formerly bare arm in dark twisting tendrils.

More leaves appear, but they're different from the other arm. While the previous vines have leaves, they're in a simple shape that isn't identifiable as a specific plant. That's not the case on the new mark. I recognize these. They're from a plant that grew in the mountains near my old village.

We called it Living Death, because if you touched it, that part of your skin would turn black and shrivel and die. But it only affected the place where you'd touched the plant. That little part of you would be dead, while the rest of you lived. It was necrotic.

I suck in a jagged breath as I picture the emperor rising again. Rising. Because it wasn't his last stand. He was dead.

And I'd summoned him.

***

Thank you so much for reading *Silk & Iron*. Want a little more? Grab a spicy deleted scene when you join my newsletter and be the first to find out all the news about the next book!

Get your bonus scene at https://BookHip.com/NWJBVWQ

About the Author

Alexis Calder writes sassy heroines and sexy heroes with a sprinkle of sarcasm. She lives in the Rockies and drinks far too much coffee and just the right amount of wine.

- facebook.com/AuthorAlexisCalder
- instagram.com/authoralexiscalder
- tiktok.com/@authoralexiscalder
- amazon.com/stores/Alexis-Calder/author/B07TP5VCGZ

ALSO BY ALEXIS CALDER

Blood and Salt Series

Kingdom of Blood and Salt

Court of Vice and Death

Crown of Stars and Fate

Queen of Serpents and Shadows

Royal Blood Series

Obsession

Hunger

Rejected Fate Series

Darkest Mate

Forbidden Sin

Feral Queen

Moon Cursed Series

Wolf Marked

Wolf Untamed

Wolf Chosen

Royal Mates Series

Shifter Claimed

Shifter Fated

Shifter Rising

Academy of Elites Series

Academy of Elites: Untamed Magic

Academy of Elites: Broken Magic

Academy of Elites: Fated Magic

Academy of Elites: Unbound Magic

Brimstone Academy Series

Brimstone Academy: Semester One

Brimstone Academy: Semester Two

Romcom books published under Lexi Calder:

In Hate With My Boss

Love to Hate You

www.ingramcontent.com/pod-product-compliance
Lightning Source LLC
Chambersburg PA
CBHW022022300726

48970CB00003B/998